Louise Fuller was once
pink and always wanted
princess! Now she enjoy
aren't pushovers, but strong, believable women
Before writing for Mills & Boon she studied
literature and philosophy at university, and then
worked as a reporter on her local newspaper. She
lives in Tunbridge Wells with her impossibly
handsome husband, Patrick, and their six children.

Millie Adams is the very dramatic pseudonym of
New York Times bestselling author Maisey Yates.
Happiest surrounded by yarn, her family and the
small woodland creatures she calls pets, she lives
in a small house on the edge of the woods, which
allows her to escape in the way she loves best—
in the pages of a book. She loves intense alpha
heroes and the women who dare to go toe-to-toe
with them.

BUSINESS MEETS PLEASURE...

LOUISE FULLER

MILLIE ADAMS

MILLS & BOON

First published in Great Britain 2025
by Mills & Boon, an imprint of HarperCollins*Publishers* Ltd,
1 London Bridge Street, London, SE1 9GF

www.harpercollins.co.uk

HarperCollins*Publishers*, Macken House, 39/40 Mayor Street Upper,
Dublin 1, D01 C9W8, Ireland

Business Meets Pleasure… © 2025 Harlequin Enterprises ULC

Business Between Enemies © 2025 Louise Fuller

Promoted to Boss's Wife © 2025 Millie Adams

ISBN: 978-0-263-34483-7

10/25

MIX
Paper | Supporting
responsible forestry
FSC™ C007454

This book contains FSC™ certified paper
and other controlled sources to ensure responsible forest management.

For more information visit www.harpercollins.co.uk/green.

Printed and Bound in the UK using 100% Renewable Electricity
at CPI Group (UK) Ltd, Croydon, CR0 4YY

BUSINESS BETWEEN ENEMIES

LOUISE FULLER

MILLS & BOON

Welcome to the world, Daphne Louise. xxx

PROLOGUE

Hennessy

THE THUMPING STARTS inside my head. In my dream I'm in the office of my family's publishing company. I know it's Wade and Walters because there are shelves of magazines lining the walls and they are swaying from side to side—gently at first, and then more vigorously, so that the magazines start to fall, smacking against the floor one after the other, louder and louder and louder...

My eyes snap open. The pounding is not inside my head. Someone is banging their fist against the door to my apartment. It's probably Mrs Godfrey, my neighbour, looking for her cat.

Picking up my phone, I sigh. Today is my birthday. I am twenty-five years old. There is one message from my best friend, Antony. None from my mother, Jade, which is unsurprising, as she never remembers my birthday. But nothing from my father, Charlie either, which is odd. Charlie is hardly father of the year, but he is sentimental about birthdays. Then again, it's the weekend.

Still clutching my phone, I roll out of bed. My body is shaking, and my head feels as if it is about to split in two, just as if I'd been drinking. Only, I don't do that anymore; I haven't self-medicated with drink or drugs for nearly three years now. But my birthday always has this effect on me. Justifiably, I think, given that my mother walked out of my life at my third birthday party and never came back.

She lives in Rio now with her latest partner. I haven't met him. I didn't meet the last one either. But then, I haven't seen her in three years—not since Las Vegas.

To say that I thought about her after she first left would be something of an understatement. At first, I was upset. For a time—longer than she deserved—I would imagine her returning to clutch me against her. But, as time passed and she didn't return, I played out different scenes where I rained down fury on her.

Of course, when we finally met nineteen years later, it was nothing like I imagined. She was the angry one. I was stunned, paralysed, wordless. My mind twitches at the memory, and of another, because that was quite an evening. Not only did my mother tell me that I was her worst mistake, but I made a fool of myself with my childhood crush: Renzo Valetti.

Just his name makes my cheeks burn. Growing up, I used to fantasise about him being my boyfriend. Not that he knew, much less reciprocated. What with the age gap, and the fact that he is Antony's brother, he always treated me like some irritating kid. Only, I wasn't a kid that night. I was twenty-two and I wasn't thinking straight. Or maybe I was, because kissing him felt imperative, as necessary as my next breath, and he kissed me in the same way…

The thumping on my door snaps me back to the present and I stand up unsteadily. My blinds are still down, but a few splinters of sunlight push past the edges and I use them to make my way to the door and squint through the peephole.

There's one man, one woman. Both are wearing dark suits, both are strangers, and for perhaps a fraction of a second I think they are one of those singing telegrams. It's the kind of idiot thing Antony would think was cute. But even without my contact lenses I can tell that they're not here to wish me a happy birthday.

I blink as an ID is thrust up to the peephole on the other side of the door. Reading the letters, I swear under my breath: FBI. Now I want to close my eyes like a child and pretend that I haven't seen them, but what then? I'm trapped on the fifty-second floor, and I can't hide for ever, so I take a breath and unlock the door, cracking it open an inch.

The female agent steps forward. 'Ms Wade? I'm Agent Carson; this is Agent Merrick.'

'Is this some kind of a joke? Because it's not fu—'

She cuts me off. 'It's not a joke, Ms Wade. We're looking for your father, Charles Winthrop Wade.'

'I know who my father is,' I snap, tilting my chin. 'And he's not here—'

Agent Carson interrupts. 'Do you know where your father is, Ms Wade?'

'No.' I shake my head. 'What's this about?' I'm trying to think what Charlie could have done that has brought the FBI to my doorstep on a Saturday morning. And yet I don't want to think about it. I don't want to deal with whatever it is, to have to handle another of his messes. Particularly now, when I've only been working at Wade and Walters for three months, and I'm trying my hardest to prove I'm not a chip off the old block, not another 'nepo-baby' cashing in on my name.

'Your father is under investigation for fraud, tax evasion, obstructing justice and failure to present himself into custody at the appointed time.'

'Failure to what?' I can't make sense of her words.

'Your father wasn't considered a flight risk.' Agent Carson raises her voice then and glances over my shoulder, as if Charlie is hiding behind the door and might magically leap forward. 'But it appears he has absconded, Ms Wade.'

'Well, he's not here,' I say again, my hand tightening round my phone. 'And I don't know where he is.'

I make to shut the door, but Agent Merrick pushes his foot into the gap like a detective in an old black-and-white movie. 'I'm sorry, Ms Wade, but we have a warrant to search your apartment.'

He doesn't seem sorry. He sounds bored, or at least he looks it. I can't hear how he sounds over the pounding of my heart.

A warrant… Now I think I'm going to throw up. A warrant is real. I want to howl and smash things. What is Charlie playing at? And why didn't he warn me? But I know how and why, because he has been doing this to me since I was a child. And then, as now, bad things are happening and, I am going to have to face them alone.

As the two agents walk past me, my phone rings shrilly, slicing through my panic. I answer it without even looking at the caller's name.

'Charlie?'

'So, you haven't spoken to him, then?' David's voice is sharp—urgent, almost. David Walters is my father's co-CEO, the logos to his pathos. He is calmness personified, so to hear him sounding so stressed makes the world tilt on its axis.

'No. But the FBI are here,' I say, and I hear him breathe out shakily.

'I see. Well, what's done is done. Clearly, we need to discuss our next steps. I've notified the board and arranged an extraordinary meeting at eight o'clock tomorrow morning. But I'd like to see you before the meeting starts, so if you could get there fifteen minutes earlier? Crisis management cascades down from the top, Hennessy, so you and I need to be on the same page.'

The phone feels slippery in my hand. 'Why me? I'm only the CMO.' And I've only been Chief Marketing Officer for three months.

There is silence, then David clears his throat. 'Not anymore. Your father and I agreed that if anything happened to either one of us, as majority shareholders we would decide our stand-in or successor, and you are Charlie's choice. Which means, as of this moment, you are my co-CEO.'

As David hangs up, I lean back against the door and watch the agents move smoothly and efficiently around the apartment.

This can't be happening. I can't deal with this. I can't be co-CEO. But, apparently, I am.

Happy Birthday, Hennessy.

CHAPTER ONE

Twenty-four hours later

Hennessy

HUGGING CHARLIE'S JACKET around my shivering body, I walk swiftly up the steps to the Wade and Walters offices, a herbal tea and a drip coffee for David heating my hands as James the doorman greets me.

After the FBI left yesterday, it took an hour for me to stop shaking. I rang Charlie, but of course he didn't pick up, so I rang Antony and some of my panic faded, as it always does when I speak to my best friend.

Charlie rang me while I was talking to Antony but typically, despite the enormity of the situation, he didn't bother calling back, just left a message.

As I step into the lift, I replay his words. 'You might have a few visitors, but you don't need to worry. You don't know anything, so you'll be fine. I'm in a tight spot right now, Essie, but this'll all blow over. Just keep your head down and play stupid.'

'Play stupid'—that's one of Charlie's mantras. That and 'don't look back'. But his favourite is 'look after number one'.

And he always does. Blood might be thicker than

water, but whisky tastes better—and children and whisky don't mix well. So, I am tolerated in Charlie's life. Sometimes, in his own way, I think he even loves me, but it's always been on his terms. Primarily because after my grandmother died, no one else wanted me, so it was Charlie or nobody.

I scrabble through my feelings, but I'm not worried about him. I know he'll be fine. Charlie is an eel, slipping his way through the cracks in life. And I'll be fine too because I never let anyone get close enough to catch me. At a distance, people only see the Hennessy Wade they read about online but, if they get close enough, they might see the real me—and I can't bear to see the disappointment in their eyes when they realise I'm not worth keeping.

But now is not the time to slip into that spiral of self-destructive thoughts. This might be the opportunity I've been waiting for to show the world and the board that I'm not just there because I have the right surname. I'm there because I am good at my job, I think as I turn over the chip in my pocket that proves I've been clean for nearly two years and eleven months. But that's the trouble with being a poor little rich girl: everyone thinks your life, my life, is a dream ticket.

It isn't. If someone cuts me, I bleed. But I can hardly blame anyone for thinking there are more worthy cases for their sticking plasters. I have more choices than most people do. But, with parents like mine, it's taken me a long time to work out which are good choices, and which are bad.

Speaking of which…

I glance down my legs to my towering heels. I did think about going home to change, but then I would have been late for David, and I want to show him that he can rely on me. And I can explain why I look like I've come straight from a club. I needed a distraction, so I got all dressed up to go out. But then I changed my mind, came to the office instead and ended up staying.

Reaching into my bag, I pull out my laptop. I know Charlie's disappearance is going to be a headache for the business, but I worked most of the night to come up with a strategy that I think will settle any nervy advertisers and shareholders. And, for the first time since David told me that I was stepping into Charlie's shoes, I feel like a co-CEO.

As the lift doors open on the eightieth floor, Callie, my PA, steps forward, looking flushed and dazed, as if she has been out in the sun too long. Which would make sense if it were sunny outside, but today is a rain-flecked autumn morning.

'He's in his office.' Her voice is high and trembling, and there is no need to ask who *he* is. Unlike Charlie, David is always punctual, always reliable, and I feel a rush of relief at knowing he is here by my side.

My appointment as Chief Marketing Officer ruffled a lot of feathers. And, to be fair, I can understand the doubts. Aside from being Charlie's daughter, my CV is patchy, and Wade and Walters is a one-hundred-and fifty-year-old giant in the realm of lifestyle publishing, now in digital as well as print. Our brands are consumed by millions of people across the globe and our flagship fashion magazine, *FROW*, is arguably the biggest influencer in the world. The board was reluctant to appoint me, but David gave me his backing.

'Good.' I smile at Callie reassuringly. She has my back

too. 'I'll find out if David wants you there to take notes… What is it?'

I break off, frowning, as Callie's face stiffens. 'Oh, I thought you knew. I left messages.' She bites her lip. 'Mr Walters isn't here. He's in hospital. He had a heart attack yesterday.'

It feels as though the planet is spinning too fast. Tears sting the back of my eyes.

'Is he okay?'

Callie nods. 'He's fine. They're sending him home today, but they need to do some tests—maybe an operation.'

I half-turn towards the lift. 'I should go see him.'

'It's only family now. We've sent flowers, of course. I'm sorry, Ms Wade, I did try and let you know…'

And it's my fault that she couldn't. I'm not on social media anymore and I've edited down my address book to a few people I can trust, and obviously Charlie and Jade. But the world I walked away from is still out there, and the temptation to scroll through other people's lives, to be in with the in-crowd is always there, always beckoning. Last night's near miss is proof of that, which is why I switched off my phone in the taxi.

'It's fine, Callie. It's not your fault.' I frown as my brain replays her words. 'So, who's in David's office?'

'Mr Walters' replacement.' A flush of colour seeps over her cheeks. 'Mr Walters has decided to take early retirement, so he chose his successor yesterday and he flew in this morning from Australia.'

'Then I better go and introduce myself.'

Later, I wondered why I didn't put two and two together and make four right there and then, because there's only one man on the planet who has the power to turn a perfectly sensible, thirty-something PA into a quivering wreck. But now, I'm so knocked off-balance by the news about David that I walk briskly into his office…

I stop so suddenly that Callie bumps into me.

My heart feels like a dead weight inside my chest. I stare at the man standing beside the window with his back to me, panic slipping and sliding over my skin like suntan oil.

Only, it's not just panic. Something I can't, won't, name flickers down my spine and over my skin, pulling everything tight so that it's suddenly hard to catch my breath. And I hate that even now he can do this to me. That he can make me shake—and on the inside too—before I even see his face.

My stomach clenches and unclenches, my heart starts to pound, and I can't stop either from happening. This is his doing. Just being near him does crazy things to my body, things I can't control. But I need to control them…

'What's he doing here?' I say hoarsely. I don't know why I ask Callie that question, though, because I know the answer. But I can't accept it until I hear it said out loud.

'Mr Valetti is the new co-CEO,' Callie whispers, although she is so shaken, it is a pantomime whisper that is probably audible in Brooklyn.

No.

The word reverberates so loudly inside my head that I'm surprised Callie can't hear it. Maybe Renzo heard it, though, because he turns then and I say quickly, 'There must be some mistake. You can't be my co-CEO—'

'You stole my line.' The deep, masculine voice slices through me like a blade, cutting me off mid-sentence. But then Renzo is good at that—cutting me off, cutting me down. After all, he's been doing it for years.

My legs feel like blancmange, which is crazy. Given all the shocks of the previous twenty-four hours, his presence should barely register on the Richter scale. But this is by far the greatest shock of all.

It feels personal.

It *is* personal.

A shiver runs over my skin as I remember the taste of his mouth and the feel of that kiss as it curled through me, turning me inside out and upside down, making me open, soft and hollowed out with need.

It was carnal, devastating and possessive. The harsh lights of Vegas faded into nothing, and I forgot everything except him. I was his, and Renzo was claiming me... Until he abruptly broke the kiss to tell me that what just happened would never happen again—before listing the reasons why, as if I was some disappointing employee he was forced to fire.

My body turns to a pillar of stone as Callie retreats silently, and I have to dig my heels into the carpet to stop myself scampering after her. My pulse, my breathing—everything—hits accelerate and for a moment, I wonder if I'm hallucinating.

He is unnecessarily, unfairly, conspicuously beautiful—the kind of beauty that demands a piece of marble—with high, fine-cut cheekbones, a strong jaw and those blue eyes. Not the light-blue, Paul Newman kind, that makes you think of summer, but dark, like the sky in the moments before night falls. Just looking at him makes me press my lips together, and my legs too. Which is not just unfair but completely stupid. Futile, really, given how I react to intimacy. But since when has that ever stopped me where this man is involved?

'Where have you been?' Those blue eyes tear into me

as he speaks, and I can't tell if the tension in my body is panic, fury, warning…or something that I don't want to feel for him, and shouldn't feel, and haven't felt for any other man before or since.

Not that there's been that many. Contrary to what is written about me, I've only been with two men. All the rest, the ones that sell their stories, are liars—and drunk or high, which is why they don't remember what really happened. They don't remember that they passed out.

'And good morning to you too, Renzo.'

'I've been trying to get in touch with you since yester-day.' He stares at me accusingly. 'I rang and texted you.'

Which was more than he had done after we kissed in Vegas. My body tenses as I remember that frantic, po-tent encounter in his car, the way our lips fused and how heat rolled through my body like wildfire.

Blanking my mind forcibly, I shrug. 'My phone isn't on.'

A muscle twitches in his jaw. 'Which in itself is ex-traordinary.'

'Thank you,' I say, deliberately misunderstanding him. 'I know Gen Z is supposed to be addicted to their phones, but you know me—I like to buck a trend.'

'Your likes and dislikes are of no interest to me, Hen-nessy.' His blue eyes are dark and opaque, like uncut sapphire chips. 'Being able to communicate with my business partner is.'

My hackles rise. 'If you're so bothered about commu-nication, perhaps you should polish up your small talk. Any normal person would ask me how I am. I mean, it must be a good five years since we last met.'

It isn't—it's three years and two months—but I don't want him to think that I have any memory of that evening.

Maybe he doesn't remember it, because he doesn't correct me. Instead, he gives me one of those looks that he reserves for me, the kind that could cause structural damage to a building.

My fingers curl into fists. I know it shouldn't hurt me as much as it does, and I should be used to it by now, because he's never approved of me, but something's changed. When I was younger, he treated me like an annoying kid. Now there is something else there—a hard, high barrier, as if he wants to keep me at arm's length. The feeling's mutual, and I almost tell him so, but then I notice something that makes my blood congeal in my veins.

I am standing in the doorway to David Walters' office. Except it isn't David's office anymore. I glance pointedly at the lettering on the door that spells out Renzo's name.

'You didn't wait long.'

'Because this is business, Hennessy. In business, time is money.'

I stare at Renzo in silence. He flew in from Australia overnight. But even on a private jet that flight is brutal. Normally, if I do that trip, I wear my biggest sunnies and a hoodie to conceal the worst of the damage from the paparazzi. But Renzo looks as if he has just stepped off a magazine shoot. His tailored dark suit skims his broad shoulders and emphasises the honed, muscular body beneath. And it isn't fair that, as well as being smart and stratospherically successful, he can look that good with jet lag.

Fair or not, it isn't a wise idea to focus on those sleek, beautiful outer garments because the man beneath is as cold-blooded as he is calculating and opportunistic.

I can completely understand why David chose him as

his successor, and why the board is no doubt delighted that he is their new co-CEO. As a shareholder, Renzo has a vested interest in making the business work, but it is his expertise they covet, and I suppose I can't blame them for that. After all, he is the controlling force behind one of the fastest-growing news media companies in the world and, from what I hear, he stops at nothing to achieve his goals. He is equally ruthless at streamlining businesses, sorting the wheat from the chaff without so much as blinking.

But then I knew that already.

I am suddenly so furious with my father for putting me in this position that it is impossible to speak. How can Charlie do this to me? But I don't need to ask that question because the answer is always the same: that, as much as my father claims to love me, he loves himself more.

But at least he doesn't hate me, which is more than can be said for the man whose authority and self-assurance effortlessly fills his new office, and all without him moving a muscle.

'Businesses are not just about money, Renzo. They're about people.'

'Spoken like a true nepo-baby.' He looks at me in contempt. 'Businesses are about profit, Hennessy, and it is profit that pays people's salaries. Perhaps, now you're working rather than just cashing in your dividends, that will become clearer to you.'

His hard gaze lasers dismissively over my mussed-up hair and bare legs. 'Obviously, I don't count flouncing in late in your boyfriend's jacket as actual employment.'

'It's Charlie's jacket. And I wasn't late. As a matter of fact, I came here yesterday evening, and I spent the night brainstorming for today's meeting.'

'And that's what you wear to "brainstorm" in, is it?'

I want to strangle him. Instead, I meet his gaze. 'No. I was going to Garrison Cutler's birthday party…' I break off, suddenly unsure of where that sentence is leading. I only know where I don't want it to lead, and that's with me revealing anything about my private life to this man.

He shakes his head, his lip curling. 'Fiddling while Rome burns. That sounds more like it.'

'And there it is… Congratulations; you almost managed a whole five minutes before you brought up my entitled life. That must be a record.'

His jaw tenses. 'Only because you choose to surround yourself with leeches and layabouts who have no incentive to hold up a mirror to your flaws.'

Wow…and screw you. The thread of tension that has been tightening inside me for hours now threatens to snap. He is so righteous and hateful. Why isn't someone investigating him for being so utterly, utterly vile?

Bunching my hands into fists, I glare at him. 'I'll be sure to share that flattering assessment with my team later. Unless you'd like to. Or here's a thought, perhaps you could stifle your prejudices and deal with reality for a moment? Which is that I'm your co-CEO, and up until twenty-four hours ago I was the CMO here. My old office is at the end of the corridor—'

'A position you earned purely on merit, I'm sure. Who interviewed you, I wonder?'

I could point out that lots of people aside from me get given a leg up through family connections. Or that I am good at my job. But I didn't have an interview and, given my scrappy academic and employment record, I'm not sure I would have got one, so I ignore the sneer in his voice and smile stiffly.

'Quite frankly, I don't have time right now for your

stone-age opinions on dress code, or my career to date. I need to prepare for the board meeting.'

His eyes are dark and fathomless. It feels as if I'm drowning, and I want to reach out and grip hold of the doorframe to stop from being pulled under. But I can't, because then he will know that he has got under my skin.

He stares down at me. 'And we will. But you and I need to have a little chat first; clarify a few things.'

Does he mean that kiss? My heart is like a living thing inside my rib cage as I remember... Renzo's car. His mouth on mine. My hands on his chest. The heat of him, and my heart plunging wildly as I felt his hunger flexing beneath my fingers.

And now he is here, barely a foot away, staring intently at me as if my skull is made of crystal, and close enough that I can almost feel the warmth radiating from his body. So close that I could reach out and touch him.

As if he can read my mind, he takes a step closer. My skin chills as he stares down at me coldly, and I realise that I am wrong. He doesn't want to talk about that kiss. It's a bad memory to him, a glitch in the well-oiled machine that is his life.

'What things? Clarify what?' I ask.

He makes me wait, but there is a glitter in his eyes that makes my breath catch when he finally answers. 'That, for you, the party's over.'

Renzo

Hennessy's chin jerks up with an almost audible snap and I feel my spine snap to attention. I wonder not for the first time what I am doing.

I was in Australia on business, trying to tempt Noah

Barker into selling me his American news network, when David called. David is a good businessman, which is why I originally bought shares in the company, but I've never liked Charlie Wade.

Naturally, it comes as no surprise to me that Charlie has managed to turn a venerated publishing institution into a telenovela. He represents everything I dislike about heirs to business empires. He is entitled and lazy, has the morals of an alley cat and frankly, if he hadn't practically inherited the position of CEO from his father, I doubt our paths would have crossed. He treats Wade and Walters like a piggy bank and has a plate-spinning approach to business that frankly appals me.

As for his private life…

For starters, it's not private, and it's less a life than a series of inter-connecting, random events. But, like business, life needs structure, forward-planning and discipline. Otherwise, there is chaos, and with chaos comes consequences that are both far-reaching and painful.

Spending seven years without a permanent home taught me that. After our parents' deaths, Antony and I were taken into care. My father's cousin was too frail to take us in, and our more distant family members in Italy were reluctant to disrupt their lives. We were fostered several times, eight in total, and spent time in three different children's homes. Each time we moved, there was nothing I could do. I was powerless.

There were other consequences too. The children's home was warm and clean, the food was adequate, and the staff were mostly kind, but there was an almost total lack of physical affection. Aside from Antony, nobody hugged me, and I knew that when I left there would be nobody to hug him.

I couldn't bear thinking about that, so as soon as I could I got a job and a house, and I got Antony back. I've worked hard ever since to keep the random and the unfiltered at the margins of our lives.

Which is why I didn't encourage Antony's friendship with Hennessy, only Charlie had somehow wrangled her a place at Antony's school. I should have removed him there and then, but it was a good school, and so much of his life had been spent moving between foster families. I just wanted him to have stability.

Of course, Hennessy got them both expelled four years later anyway, I remind myself as her glare envelops me.

'You think my life is a party. You don't know anything about my life.'

Oh, but I do. I know that she was named after her father's favourite drink and that her hair is naturally blonde. I know her taste in men is depressingly predictable and that, like every other poor little rich girl I know, she likes 'bad boys' from the other side of the tracks. Or, as I like to call them, losers.

My shoulder blades pinch together, and I feel a surge of adrenaline as I remember that other toxic, pouting man-child who was with her that night in Vegas. 'I know that Garrison Cutler's father has cut him off. Is that why he's sniffing around you?'

'He's not sniffing around me. We're not even close,' she says in that voice of hers—the maddening, citizen-of-nowhere drawl that manages to suggest both intimacy and contempt.

Not close? So why had she gone to his party? Were they just friends with benefits? That question, or rather the answer to it, rolls around inside my head like a discarded bottle on a bar-room floor, and I swear silently but savagely.

She is staring up at me, or rather glowering at me, and my eyes follow the movement of muscle beneath the skin as her shoulders stiffen. She has a ballerina's poise which is at odds with the pugilistic gleam in her eyes, and I feel the contradiction thrum through me like a physical thing.

'You know, it's not just your small talk that needs some attention—you need to learn how to listen. I said I *was going* to a party, not that I *went*. As I mentioned earlier, I came here and worked most of the night, and then I fell asleep, and when I woke up it was too late to go home and change.'

Her chin is jutting up, lips parted, and a surge of heat swells inside me. It's been three years since we last met but it's as if my body is picking up from where we left off. It takes every ounce of my not inconsiderable will-power to keep from pulling her closer and kissing that curl from her mouth.

It's seeing her again, and up close. She has been off my radar since Vegas, enough that I started to think, to hope, that she and Antony might have fallen out for good. But first Antony and then David called me yesterday, and suddenly here she is: the proverbial bad penny.

Only, she's not just trouble, she is torment and tribulation wrapped up in a body so tempting it makes the Big Apple itself seem small and flavourless. Even more than her father, she is the reason I hesitated over getting more deeply involved with Wade and Walters.

She angles her head so that her sugared-violet gaze is almost level with mine. 'In other words, you got the wrong end of the stick.'

'You should have a change of clothes at the office,' I snap, because inconceivably she is right, and for some reason I find myself both astonished and fascinated by that fact.

'This isn't your father's business anymore, Hennessy. It isn't your business either—it's *our* business—and while you and I are conjoined commercially I expect you to be at work on time and appropriately dressed. And to have your phone switched on. You are the face of the business now. It matters how you behave.'

My words echo round the office, and I feel their hypocrisy. It still rankles that I came so close to losing control of myself that night. And that I've had to break my own rule of keeping Hennessy Wade at arm's length.

When Antony found out that David had asked me to step into his shoes, he was thrilled. And then stunned when I said that I was thinking of refusing. More than stunned. When I said that I had reservations about working with her, there was a look of pain in my brother's eyes that was hard for me to ignore. There was anger and confusion too, because he knows how hard I fought to get custody of him when I was old enough, and how important his happiness is to me, so he couldn't understand why I wouldn't do this for him.

But I can't tell him the truth. I can't tell him that, last time I got close enough to help Hennessy Wade, I lost my way. I lost myself and became a ravenous stranger interested solely in feeding her hunger and mine. It wasn't planned; I wasn't even supposed to be in Vegas, but thanks to a storm my plane got grounded. There was a private party at the bar in the hotel that I was avoiding.

But then I saw Hennessy. Up until that night, she was just Antony's friend: a kid; a teenager; a brat. An irritant, not an incitement to lose my head. But she was all woman that night, and I wanted her as a man, and I felt so many things and not one was irritation. I wanted nothing but to burn in the flame of my need and I wanted her to be mine… Then I came to my senses, and I've been avoiding her ever since.

Until now.

And I hate that, not only do I have to fix Charlie Wade's mess, but my motives for doing so are only partially driven by altruism and finances. My one consolation is that she clearly hates it too.

I watch her irises flare, like petals opening in sunlight. Hennessy is angry with her father and me. And with the board members who have elected me as her co-CEO via a virtual EGM. But then, anger is her default setting, even when she is in the wrong. Even when she is cornered, she comes out fighting.

Except that one time.

'Are you done?'

'Not even close.' I pause. 'Take a seat.'

Her eyes widen. She reminds me of a cornered cat. If she had a tail, it would be twitching, and her back would have arched, but I don't care. What matters is that she understands that she can call herself the Queen of Sheba if she wants, just as long as she understands that I am in charge.

CHAPTER TWO

Renzo

HENNESSY STARES AT me in that haughty way of hers that makes me want to jerk her closer and remind her just who she's dealing with.

Instead, I take a step back to let her pass. 'After you,' I say softly. Her withering gaze holds mine as she stalks past me, only she doesn't take a seat, but walks out of the door. And even though my gut and logic tell me I should stamp out this defiance, I can't help but admire her because she is a thoroughbred. There is a swaggering sensuality to how she moves, to the way she owns the space around her, that mesmerises.

And she knows it.

Gritting my teeth, I follow her into what was Charlie's office, closing the door behind me. 'So, where is he?'

Hennessy is gazing out of the window. In the glitzy hotels and clubs she frequents, her beauty, wealth, name and reputation all give her unwarranted power. She can read a room and know exactly who's in and who's out, who will play and who will pay.

But here she doesn't understand the rules. Doesn't see that she is in over her head. Thanks to the decadent decor of Charlie's office, she doesn't look out of place in that dress and heels, but she *is* out of place, out of her depth, and I intend to make that clear to her.

But first I will put her to work—actual work—and by the time I've finished with her she'll be begging me to buy her out.

'That's what you want to talk about?'

Her gaze moves to track a distant plane cutting through the clouds and she pulls her jacket more tightly around her body. My own gaze instantly zeroes in on the taut curve of her bottom.

'Obviously,' I say impatiently. 'It will be a far better outcome for everyone if Charlie can be persuaded to turn himself in.'

'Far better for you, you mean,' she says without turning, and her voice is laced with a disdain that makes me want to shake her.

'Far better for everyone,' I repeat, 'including Charlie. So, if you know where he is…'

'I don't. But, even if I did, I'm not going to shop my own father.'

'Don't be so childish,' I say, and it's a relief to think of her as a child, to think of her as off-limits. My jaw tightens as I take in her mouthwatering silhouette. Except, she isn't a child. She's a woman; she was a woman when I kissed her. She's also a temptation that I need to resist. Losing control again like that would not just be a mistake, it would be all kinds of stupidity and recklessness and, unlike Charlie and Hennessy Wade, I don't do stupid or reckless.

'You're not the daughter of some crime boss, Hennessy. And Charlie hiding out like this is hardly going to make the judge look at him favourably.'

She shrugs. 'Have you tried calling him? I know he'd love to hear about your plans for *his* business.'

The taunt in her voice sets my teeth on edge.

'Don't get smart with me. This is serious. Once news gets out that your father has done a disappearing act, our shares are going to drop through the floor.'

Now she turns. If there was any justice in the world, the scowl on her face should distort her features, but instead it pulls her mouth into a distracting curl.

'If it's too much of a challenge for you, then sell me your shares and leave. It's not as if anyone asked you to march in here and start throwing your weight around.'

'That is exactly what they asked me to do. As for buying my shares, you don't have the funds to do that.'

And she will have even less once Charlie is caught and fined. Does she not know that? I feel a savage frustration with both her absent father and the entourage of hangers-on that buzz around her like flies on honey. Where are they now?

Hennessy holds my gaze, then twists away to stare back through the window. 'I don't know why you're getting so out of shape. Charlie will turn up. He got spooked, that's all.'

'So, you have spoken to him.'

She hesitates. 'He left a message.'

As she turns slightly, giving me the benefit of her delicate profile, I clench my jaw, my whole body, against a sudden rush of heat. She is exquisite. And it's not just me that thinks so. Three years ago, I watched a crowded dance floor part when she walked to the bar, just as if she had waved a magic wand.

But I'm not falling under her spell again. I walk towards her, pulling out my phone. 'So, call him back.'

'I tried.' She spins to face me. Accustomed to mixing with women who dress with low-key, professional elegance, I'm unprepared for the jolt of unprofessional lust that tears through me as her jacket falls open and I get a glimpse of her dress. Made of a figure-hugging black material, it leaves little to the imagination—which is ironic, as my imagination is feverishly offering up all kinds of tempting suggestions as to what might happen if I strip it from her body, and that jacket too… Although I might just burn that.

'But it goes straight to voicemail.'

I shake my head, unsure as to whether it is that shrug or her father's lack of responsibility that aggravates me the most. But Charlie Wade has never been poor. He doesn't know how vulnerable poverty makes someone. How it can break them.

My family emigrated to the US for a better life but, whatever dreams my parents had, they never came to fruition. Money was stretched tight. There was never anything to spare. Nothing to put aside for a rainy day, let alone a stormy one. When the random, unjust cruelty of illness struck, they had no safety net, nothing to catch them, Antony or me.

Even now, when my success has pushed poverty to the furthest edges of my life, that fact is never far from my thoughts. It's what drives me to keep expanding my business, to keep making money and to have control over as many areas of life as possible.

Not that Hennessy has any more understanding of that than her father. Her life has been one long party. She is as careless as a juggernaut, rolling recklessly through the world, never mind the casualties. When she was younger,

I gave her a pass. I mean, aside from being parentless and constantly between homes, I was a normal teenager.

But Hennessy likes to play with fire. Hell, she likes poking active volcanoes. And, with that blonde hair and taunting smile, she has a cool-girl gravitational pull that is irresistible to more law-abiding mortals like Antony.

Don't get me wrong, Antony isn't blameless, but Hennessy is a poster child for good girls gone bad.

I replay that moment when she so casually derailed my brother's previously spotless academic career. Obviously, Charlie didn't turn up for that meeting with the principal, but frankly it wouldn't have made much difference if he had. Hennessy was as brazenly unrepentant about forging an email from me as she was about being caught drunk and dancing half-naked on my lawn. She hadn't so much as blinked when she was expelled.

The tendons in my hands tighten.

My lawn.

My home.

Even now, the fact she did that, that she brought her brand of chaos into *my* personal space, makes a frisson of anger quiver across my skin. I've worked hard to ensure that my home is a safe space. I have rules, alarms, a state-of-the-art security system—and yet Hennessy just walked right in and turned everything on its head.

'Surely you must have some other way to get in touch?'

There is silence as she stares past me. 'I manage just fine,' she says finally.

I look down at her. She hasn't moved an inch, but something is different. There is tension to her posture that feels off, and yet familiar, and for a moment I can't put my finger on it. Then I remember what it is. I remember the party in Vegas when that piece of crap she was 'seeing' had her cornered and her whole body looked limp, just as if she'd been shot.

There is that same limpness now and, even though she is a menace and a complication I don't need, I hate seeing her look so diminished. Because she is young, beautiful and alone.

As if she can read my mind, Hennessy meets my gaze, her eyes flashing with defiance. 'I can look after myself.'

I wasn't going to bring up what happened that evening in Vegas. Never. But before I can edit my thoughts, I say softly, 'Not always.'

And now we are back there—by a circuitous route, but back there, nonetheless.

Her face stills. 'That was an exception.'

Was it? I think back to the moment when I walked into the foyer and saw her backing into the lift with the aforementioned piece of crap demanding that she give him something from her bag. Drugs, presumably, although she denied it at the time. Either way, it didn't feel exceptional. Nobody even looked up, much less reacted.

Except for me.

I didn't hit him. I'd wanted to, and sometimes I think I should have to make him feel, *really* feel the consequences of his actions. Instead, I 'restrained' him. Okay, I might have jerked his arm up his back a little harder than was necessary—hard enough that he started to gibber—but by then I had clocked the tell-tale white powder around his nostrils.

Hennessy was instantly furious with me, even more so when I frogmarched her away from the club. But then in the car her bravado crumbled, and she started to cry. Without even realising what I was doing, I pulled her onto my lap.

My mind takes a sudden, sharp, sexual detour as my body tenses around the memory of that moment, reliving the feel of her soft mouth fusing with mine. Without even looking at her, I know she is reliving it too. I know, because I can feel the air darkening around us.

For a moment we stand and stare at one another in a pulsing silence that presses in on us. Her eyes are narrowed on my face. Our mouths are close enough that I feel her warm breath as she exhales, and I breathe in her scent, that teasing, light scent of hers, as I inhale.

She swallows and I watch her throat, mesmerised. She keeps looking up at me, just looking and looking, and I feel the pull of her hunger, feel my own need to feed that hunger…

I want her, it is as simple as that, and I step forward so that the toes of my shoes collide with hers…

I hear the lift in the foyer, and then a swell of voices, and I am suddenly, furiously angry with myself, but more so with her. Because this is her fault. She unravels me. And I want to punish her for making me a stranger to myself. For a moment, I consider kissing her then pushing her away just to prove I can. That I am immune.

Only, I'm not sure I can take that risk. I jerk backwards, and her eyes widen as I shake my head. 'Not happening, Hennessy. I'm not that desperate or stupid,' I say, and her face hardens.

She can't be held accountable for the two of us being thrown together. Charlie and I bear the lion's share of responsibility for that but still, I am furious with her for putting me in this situation.

'You're not my type anyway.'

'Knowing your type as I do, I take that as a compliment.'

She doesn't quite roll her eyes but there is a curl to her lip that momentarily interrupts my train of thought.

'You want me to take you seriously? Then be a serious person. Start thinking, Hennessy.' Because she is smart, and it enrages me further that she is so careless with the advantages she has.

'I've done nothing but think,' she snaps. 'And no amount of thinking is going to change what's happened. Like I told the FBI yesterday, if Charlie doesn't want to be found, he won't be.'

My shoulders stiffen. 'They've interviewed you already.'

This shrug is accompanied by another of those maddening couldn't-care-less smiles she has turned into an art form. 'They didn't look like they have much of a life outside work '

'This isn't a time to be making jokes. Your father going AWOL is bad for the business. The shareholders won't like it, I don't like it, and you shouldn't like it either, given that Wade and Walters' profits pay your bills.'

'Thank you for mansplaining that to me. I don't know what I'd do if you weren't here.' Her forehead creases as she pretends to think. 'Oh, yes, I do—I'd have a glass of champagne to celebrate.'

As she squares up to me, I realise that the fabric over her bust is almost transparent in places, and suddenly I'm gritting my teeth so tightly that it takes me a moment to reply.

'Of course you would, because you have absolutely no sense of responsibility. You tell me that people matter more than profit—well, here's some statistics that should interest you.

'Wade and Walters employ over three thousand people in twelve countries on six continents. David Walters was so worried about those people, he had a heart attack when he heard about Charlie's latest exploits. But then, you are your father's daughter, so I suppose champagne is never far from your thoughts.'

Her delicate jaw tilts up a fraction. 'And you're Antony's brother. What a pity you don't have his empathy and decency.'

Tamping down my fury, I take a step forward and, although Hennessy doesn't blink this time, I have the satisfaction of watching her face lose some of its colour.

'The moment Charlie lets you know where he is, you tell me. And if he calls, I want to speak to him. Do you understand?'

'Completely.'

I expect her to move away, but she doesn't. Feeling my body respond to her nearness, my voice is harsh when I speak. 'We both know you're not ready for this. And don't give me that crap about being made CMO—you only got that job on the basis that your surname is over the door.

'So, here's what's going to happen. Obviously, the board is going to have some questions about Charlie's disappearance. You're going to need to answer them as best you can. But aside from that I need you to keep that mouth of yours shut. In fact, it might be best all round if you just keep your mouth shut, period, and leave the running of this business to me. Think of your role as a sleeping partner in our relationship.'

'Is that why you date so many women? You send them all to sleep?'

I sigh. 'Can't you just do what you're told, for once?'

'You sound like Principal Farrow. Is this what happens when you're heading towards forty—you start talking like a teacher?'

'I'm surprised you know what a teacher talks like, given your somewhat par-optimal attendance record. And I'm thirty-four.'

'Really?' She mimes surprise. 'You seem so much older.'

She's goading me, like a cat testing her claws. And there is a part of me that wants to laugh, that is enjoying sparring with her and wants to engage, because she is young and beautiful. And she's watching me with those teasing, violet eyes that unlock parts of my brain that I'd rather stay locked.

Locked. Closed off. It's something I've been accused of on more than one occasion by more than one of the women I've dated, and it's true I don't do emotional intimacy. Physical intimacy, yes, but love lacks boundaries. It's distracting and it encourages complacency.

My parents thought that 'love is all you need'. They were wrong. That's why I've been an orphan since the age of eleven. And why I spent seven years of my life being bounced from one foster home to another. Turns out what is needed is health insurance. You need to be in control of the variables that life throws, and for that people need money, not love.

'It's called maturity, Hennessy. It's what happens when you stop thinking your life is someone else's problem to fix, and you don't think it's sexy or funny to see your name in some gossip column.'

Her mouth pulls into a shape I shouldn't find fascinating but do.

'What's the view like up there on that high horse of yours?' she says softly. 'Must be pretty lonely.'

I meet her gaze. 'Says the woman whose father has left her to face his demons.'

She blinks and there is a fierce light in her eyes then that makes everything inside me tilt sharply sideways. 'Just to clarify, Renzo—as your partner, I won't be sleeping with you, at work or home.'

Pausing, she gives me one of those unravelling little smiles.

'Now, I think it's time we talk about our strategy for the next twenty-four hours. I've come up with some publicity triage for when the story breaks about Charlie disappearing. I can email you my thoughts. Or would you prefer me to print it out for you? I know screen time is hard on the eyes when you reach a certain age.'

'An email will be fine.'

She pulls out her phone, all ice-cream cool. I watch her type something with her small, delicate fingers, somewhat destabilised by the shift in her manner. She is not quite the clueless nepo-baby I've painted in my head. It might be an act, but she is talking like a co-CEO.

As if she can read my thoughts, Hennessy looks up from her phone and I feel like I've been kicked by a horse. 'You know, you got one thing right, Renzo—my name is above the door. So. I don't care that you don't like how I live or what I wear. Or that you live like a robot and dress like a hitman, because you are not my boss, you're my business partner.'

'I give you a week.'

Her gaze locks onto mine and there is the same fire and defiance that I saw that day in the principal's office.

'Is this where you warn me not to try appealing to

your softer side?' she says in that imperious way of hers. 'Because you don't need to. I know you don't have one.'

'You're right. I don't,' I say tersely. 'And Daddy isn't here to protect you now, so don't think your name is going to give you special treatment, because it won't.'

'I hate you,' she says then, and I can hear it in her voice. *Good,* I think. It will ensure she keeps her distance from now on.

I shrug. 'I don't care.'

Her hands curl into fists, and I know she wants to thump me. I have a sudden, sharp memory of that moment in the lift when she was squaring up to another man, also twice her size. But this is different, I tell myself. This is for her own good. And, more importantly, mine.

'A word of warning, Hennessy,' I say then. 'That the business is in profit is largely down to the sustained and focused efforts of David Walters and the rest of the C-suite. Charlie's chaotic input is not missed, and the board is inches away from ousting you, so I suggest you think very carefully about pushing my buttons. In fact, if I were you, I'd work very hard to keep me happy, or you will find yourself looking for a new job and a new source of income.'

She jerks backwards, as if I have slapped her. Her eyes are suddenly bright, but the rule is once bitten, twice shy.

'My father will never let that happen.' Her voice is hoarse with emotions that I don't want to name, much less address.

'Then it's lucky he has no say in it.' I glance at my watch. 'We have two minutes until the meeting starts...'

But she stalks past me, and I am left in Charlie Wade's office, feeling not just out of place but more dissatisfied than I have for years.

Hennessy

I slam into the bathroom. I hate him with every atom of my being. He is rude, arrogant, patronising and utterly lacking in empathy.

But apparently none of that is enough to stop me feeling knocked off-course by his presence, as if he just T-boned my car. And I hate that he has this power over me.

I stalk over to the mirror and stare at my reflection. There is a flush of colour along my cheeks and my pulse is visibly jerking at my throat.

Nobody else has ever had this effect on me. I won't let them. I was thirteen years old when I realised that, if people thought I was a hard-hearted bitch, then they would keep their distance. And if they kept their distance then they wouldn't see how vulnerable, alone and scared I was.

It's not something I talk about, even with Antony. He doesn't talk about his family, either. I think he knows it's a sensitive topic. But he has this photo of his family from when he was little, and they look so happy and normal. I used to envy him, but now it scares me, because Antony is a good person. He got the family he deserves. What if there's something wrong with me? Is that why my father only tolerates me, and my mother abandoned me?

So, I have this persona, and mostly I think it's been a win. There is a downside, of course. I don't have friends. I know people—lots of people—and even more people would like to know me. Except they don't really want to know me. They want to touch the glitter and see if it rubs off. What they don't realise is that I wear glitter because I'm always performing. And it's exhausting. The curtain never falls.

My eyes meet my reflection. Aside from Antony—and,

since I started working at Wade and Walters, David—
nobody looks out for me. Jade is a mother in name only,
and my father lives his life as a single, childless man who
just happens to have a daughter. There was a black time
when I found that hard to accept. In the past drink and
drugs made it easier, and moving on to the next place
and new people. But I'm clean now and I want to stop
moving. Because all that other stuff that looks like living to other people—the parties, the yachts, the champagne and the shopping—is all window-dressing for a
life without meaning. You have to stop and stand still to
find that meaning.

My fingers curl round the chip in my pocket. The
voices in the foyer are getting louder. I feel my throat
tighten. The rest of the board members are arriving. The
meeting is about to begin.

Taking a breath, I find a scrunchie and smooth back
my hair into a ponytail and then add a swipe of lip gloss.
These are my people, not his. Okay, I've only been working here three months, and maybe they had doubts. But
they know me, and they'll have my back...

They don't. It doesn't help that by the time I get into
the board room Renzo is already lounging at the end of
the table like Caesar in the senate house, his dark-blue
eyes shuttered by stupidly long dark lashes, his expression unreadable. For a moment, I gaze at him, wondering how he can convey such authority just by existing.

There is a charged tension in the room that makes my
stomach cramp as I take my seat. But the worst is yet to
come. The first half-hour is a nightmarish inquisition
that Renzo tosses down the table with the same speed
and ferocity as if he is serving aces at Flushing Mead-
ows. Nobody offers to help me out, but I do the best I

can which, somewhat surprisingly, is better than I expect. Still, though, I am glad when it's over.

I have to admit that Renzo is well-informed; he has a clear understanding of the mess my father's absence has created and the possible repercussions we are facing. The entire board seems in thrall to his every word so that, every time he speaks, their heads jerk towards him as though he is the reigning tennis champion about to serve for the match point.

I feel sick to my stomach. Will the board abandon me? I thought they would be on my side, but I'm now experiencing that invisibility I've so often dreamed about, and I don't like it. This is my family's business, and I don't want it to go from shirtsleeves to shirtsleeves in three generations on my watch. The last thing I want is to be the family member who oversees its decline.

I suddenly register that the room is silent and that the board members are turned towards me expectantly. I have no idea how long has passed since I was asked the question they are all obviously waiting for me to answer. Or what that question even was.

'Would you like to add anything, Hennessy?' Renzo says then. His voice is smooth but there is an undercurrent pulsing beneath the smoothness that makes my head feel light. I know that he is flexing his muscles.

I shake my head.

'I've emailed you all with my thoughts but I'm glad we've all been able to come together at this moment of crisis and work as a team,' I say, my smoothness matching Renzo's. It's the kind of bland, ambiguous statement at which Charlie excels, and I can sense my co-CEO is dying to unpick my words. I hold my breath, because there is something terrifying about the dark, splintering gaze and the raw power of the man facing me at the other end of the table, and I remember what he said about pressing buttons.

But either I haven't found his buttons, or I need to press harder, because he merely nods.

'We should expect the share price to wobble a little when the story about Charlie breaks. But, once it becomes clear that we are responding swiftly and efficiently to deal with this situation going forward, I'm confident I can control the narrative and stop this turning into a soap opera.'

I clear my throat. 'I think you mean "we".'

'Excuse me?' His eyes arrow across the polished tabletop, and I force myself to stare back at him, even though I feel as if I have been flattened under a wardrobe.

'*We're* confident *we* can control the narrative,' I say, lifting my chin, trying to ignore the way his dark gaze slams into me with the force of a blow.

'Yes, we are.'

My pulse quickens as he abruptly gets to his feet.

'And, to ensure that happens, Ms Wade and I will be working closely alongside one another.'

He moves towards the door. The meeting is over. I can barely get out of the room quickly enough. I crave distance from Renzo, from his bluntness earlier—that weird moment when we were standing so close and he was looking at me as if he was hungry, fierce, intent, and barely able to contain what he was feeling.

Thankfully a lift is already waiting, and it's empty, so I won't have to hang back and pretend I've left something behind. I step inside, turning towards the panel of buttons. As the doors close, I slump forward, angling my head against the glass exterior wall. Glancing at my phone, I realise it has gone one o'clock. I shut my eyes.

I feel exhausted, as if I've been fighting a bear or some other intensely focused predator, and just about managed to escape. But I'm still here. I've survived and, right now, given everything that's going on, I'll take that.

My eyes snap open as the lift comes to a stop. I step into the huge foyer and then stop mid-stride, swearing under my breath. I was so desperate to leave, I left my bag upstairs. My life is in that bag.

'Is this what you're looking for?'

I turn, my skin freezing. The second lift has reached the foyer. Renzo is holding my bag. Had it been anyone else, I might have made small talk, but nothing between us is small.

'Thank you,' I say. Then because I can't deal with this anymore, with him anymore, I turn and walk swiftly towards the doors.

'Hennessy, wait.' There is a roughness to his voice that pulls at something inside me, but I am already outside.

'There she is!'

'Hennessy!'

I hear my name and look up automatically, then swear as a mass of men hurtle up the steps towards me, cameras and booms thrust forward as if they're jousting knights. Except these aren't knights, they're paparazzi.

'Do you know where Charlie is?'

'Is it true your father has gone on the run?'

'What's going to happen to Wade and Walters?'

There is an explosion of flashes and, before I have time to blink, I'm surrounded by a wall of shouting reporters and photographers. I can't help it. I know I should be able to cope; I know that the more cowed you look, the more they attack, but even now after all these years I find it overwhelming.

'No!'

I cry out as they surge forward, and my bag gets knocked out of my hands. I try to reach down for it but in doing so I trap myself.

Suddenly they are stumbling backwards, parting as if in response to some unseen command, and then I see him—Renzo—shouldering his way towards me. He is the one making them move and, catching sight of his face, it's not hard to see why.

He scoops up my bag with one hand and cups my elbow with the other, and he propels me towards a dark SUV that has magically appeared at the curb.

Yanking open the door, he loosens his grip on my arm, and I clamber inside. He follows me in and, as the car starts moving, I inch away from the window as the mass of photographers and reporters swarm forward.

CHAPTER THREE

Hennessy

'WHAT THE HELL were you thinking?'

Renzo sounds as furious as he looks, and suddenly I am furious too, because I'm so sick of this. Sick of people blaming me for things I cannot control. Sick of him acting all holier-than-thou instead of taking my side for once.

'I'm fine. Thanks for asking.'

I glare at him, channelling my fear into fury and focusing it on him, which is unfair I know, but he represents everything I hate about my life: the judgement; the assumptions made about me for which, I admit, I have been largely to blame. But nobody gives me a chance to change them. Nobody wants me to change.

'Everyone is bending over backwards to try and get control of the narrative here. All you needed to do was keep a low profile and stay out of trouble. But you can't do it, can you? Because you love chaos, you love the attention.' I feel a shiver wash over me as his eyes sharpen on my face. 'I told you to wait.'

'I'm not a dog. Or a child.'

His face is all hard bone and steel. 'Then stop acting like one. Stop blaming others for the consequences of *your* actions. Stop expecting people to step in and save you.'

'I didn't need you to save me,' I say, and he stares at me in obvious disbelief, which is unsurprising, as I don't believe what I just said either. But I'd rather hack off my own limbs than admit that.

He nods slowly, his lip curling. 'Oh, that's right. I forgot—you can take care of yourself.'

Ignoring him, I lean forward and bang on the privacy glass.

'Can you drop me at the corner of Fifth and East 74th? Thanks.'

As I sit back down, Renzo's gaze narrows in on mine in a way that makes my breathing go shallow.

'What are you doing?'

'I'm giving your driver my address.'

His dark-blue eyes get even darker. He is looking at me as if I am an animal in a trap, and it is almost impossible to keep from screaming, because I am trapped. Trapped in this car with a man I should be thanking, but whom I can't, because last time I thanked him for rescuing me we ended up kissing. Shortly before he pushed me away, just as if I were a plague carrier. My lungs tighten as I replay that day—a day I've spent the last three years trying to pretend never happened.

'But you're not going back to your apartment,' he says in that autocratic way that comes as naturally to him as breathing.

There is a buzzing sound inside my head. But I don't care what Renzo says. There are few places on earth where I feel safe enough to sleep, but my apartment is one of them.

Tamping down my panic, I hold his gaze. 'Of course I am,' I snap back. 'Where else am I going to stay?'

Renzo stares back hard at me, a muscle pulsing in his jaw. 'I would have thought that was obvious. You'll stay at my apartment.'

There is a serrated edge to his voice as he makes that earth-shattering statement, and there are no words to describe the way it makes me feel. How it snakes through me, twisting and turning, chafing me inside so that I feel trapped inside my own skin.

'No,' I say vehemently, shaking my head. 'No way. Absolutely not. I'd rather sleep on a park bench.'

'In that outfit?' He raises an eyebrow. 'Don't be ridiculous, Hennessy. Or do you think wearing vintage somehow equips you for sleeping rough?'

'I'm not going to sleep rough. I'm going back to my apartment.'

He holds my gaze steadily. 'If the paparazzi are at the office, then they're probably camped out there too.'

My breath catches. He's right, of course, but I wasn't prepared for them at the office. Now I am, it will be fine.

'What difference does it make if they are? I'll have to face them tomorrow anyway. Look, I know what I'm doing. If you give them what they want, then they get bored quicker.'

'Good idea,' he says in that voice of his, the one that makes me feel like Little Red Riding Hood when she meets the wolf in the woods. 'Maybe you could parade around in your underwear like you did in Paris. The whole world loved that. Only they didn't get bored, did they? They waited for you outside the hotel, and when you drove away one of them was following you so fast, he went into the back of your car. Didn't you have to go to hospital with whiplash?'

I square my shoulders. 'That was four years ago, and I didn't "parade anywhere in my underwear". I was wearing pyjamas and a robe, and I was standing on my balcony.'

'They're not going to get bored, Hennessy. Your father is on the run and, while he is, people are going to be eager for updates.'

'I don't care. I want to go home, and you can't stop me.'

The car slows, and I turn towards the door, but Renzo is too fast, and before I can even grasp the handle, he grabs my arms.

'Let go of me!' I thrash against his grip, but he effortlessly pins me back against the seat.

'I will when you calm down.'

The calmness in his voice aggravates me more. 'How can I be calm when you're restraining me like this?'

'It's for your own good,' he says flatly. 'I'm not about to let you jump out of a moving car. And I can't allow you to go back to the apartment. The press will be waiting, and there are too many of them. And they will want more than you will want to give.'

Tears sting my eyes at the blunt truth of his words, because it's true. They will want more. They always do. I don't want to admit defeat, but right now I don't think I can face dealing with them. In the past, I always moved on when there was any heat, but I can't do that now. I can't walk away from the business. And I don't want to. I want to prove that I'm not just a nepo-baby. So, I need to stay in New York.

'Then drop me at the nearest hotel.'

His nearness is making me feel dizzy and untethered. I try to think of something with lots of weight, such as that poem by Emerson that Antony and I had to learn for English.

Renzo arches one eyebrow 'And what—you'll check in and stay under the radar for the duration?' He stares down at me intently, and I lose myself momentarily in the blueness of his gaze. It's a different kind of drug, but just as dangerous and intoxicating.

'I don't think so.' Now he shakes his head. 'You're acting as if this is some kind of funfair ride, but you can't just hop on and off.'

'Pity. I mean, who doesn't love a merry-go-round?'

He leans in so close that I can see that he is a man at the end of his tether. 'I don't.'

I glower at him. 'Not everyone is as fun-phobic as you. Normal people love funfairs.'

'And shareholders and advertisers hate scandal. So, unless you can find some other appropriate person to babysit you, you'll stay at mine.'

'Why not just go the whole hog and send me to a nunnery?' I practically spit the question at him, but he doesn't reply. He doesn't need to. The hard twist to his mouth makes it clear that the discussion is closed.

I angle my face towards the window and feign interest in the clouds scudding across the bruised-looking sky. I've stayed in so many places around the world, one more won't make any difference. Only, I can't do it cold. I let my arms go limp, and after a moment he releases his grip.

'I still have to go to my apartment,' I say quietly. 'There's things I need.'

I try to keep the urgency out of my voice. I fail. I know because Renzo's eyes lock onto mine and there is a tense, electric moment that swells and fills the car like dry ice at a club.

Renzo

Outside the window, the city seems to twitch like a needle on a lie detector.

'What things?'

I scan Hennessy's face as she gives me one of those none-of-your-business looks she's so good at. Does she mean drugs?

'I need some clothes.'

'Then buy some. We can stop *en route*.'

'No. I want *my* clothes. Besides, how's it going to look if someone snaps me on a shopping spree when Charlie's on the run for tax evasion?'

She has a point, but there is tension in her voice that matches the sudden stiffness in her shoulders. She is holding back, hiding something, distracting me with her reasonableness. Or maybe it's her scent that's distracting me—that light, floral perfume that drifts like woodsmoke through my dreams, teasing my senses so that I wake feeling hard, hungry and reckless. Like a stranger.

'It'll be fine. I can be in and out in five minutes,' she says carelessly, but there is still tension there. 'I can call Sam, the concierge. He's known me for ever, and he's completely Team Hennessy. If you drop me off just up the block, he'll let me in through the trade entrance. I've done it before,' she adds, still doing her careless act.

I make her wait before I reply. My first instinct is to refuse. But I don't trust her not to try and sneak back on her own. Far better that I keep an eye on her.

'Fine. We'll swing by your apartment and pick up your stuff on one condition.' I hold her gaze and she stares back at me warily.

'Which is?'

'That I come in with you.'

Her eyes widen, the pupils flaring. 'You don't need to do that. I can find my own apartment.'

'I'm sure you can, but I have no intention of letting you out of my sight. That's my offer. Take it or leave it'

Her pulse is beating jerkily in her throat. She gives me one of those unblinking stares that takes in everything about me and gives back nothing.

'Whatever.' She slumps back against the leather upholstery, her arms wrapping around her waist. 'Have it your way.'

'That's how I like it,' I say, not just because it's true, but because I like watching that flush of colour seep along her cheekbones.

Ten minutes later, Kenny, my driver, pulls in several hundred metres up the street from her apartment building. 'Here.' I reach into the side of the door and pull out a New York Mets baseball cap. 'Put this on.'

'Wow.' She takes it and glances over Kenny's shoulder at her reflection in the rear-view mirror, miming confusion. 'It's like magic—I hardly recognise myself.'

I sigh. 'Unlike you, I don't make a habit of consorting with criminals, so I don't carry a whole bunch of disguises around with me.'

Something skids across her eyes, and then she tilts up the delicate arc of her chin.

'So, are we good to go?'

I look at her critically. Most people look anonymous in a baseball cap. But Hennessy isn't most people. On the plus side, it's Sunday afternoon so no one's around. I nod and she shoves open the door and moves, *sashays*, down the street like some catwalk model. Swearing under my breath, I stride after her, catching her hand in mine and locking my fingers.

Her eyes turn to mine, the pupils pulsing outwards to swallow her irises. It's like an electric current jerking through my veins.

Outside the office when she was engulfed by the paparazzi, my body was so awash with adrenaline, I barely registered the momentary contact between us as I led her to the car. But this touch is different. It makes the super-sized buildings disappear. Makes my brain blank, and my body feel as if it is loose and shapeless, but also tense, alert and quivering with a longing I have never felt for anyone.

I feel the ripple of her irritation dance over my skin as she attempts to free her hand, but I merely tighten my grip. She rolls her eyes. 'Why are you so untrusting?'

'Would you like the long form answer or just the edited highlights?' I ask, and she stares at me steadily and then pulls the cap lower over her face.

Sam is waiting for us at the back door. He is old enough to be Hennessy's father.

'Hi, Sam, thanks for doing this. You really are a treasure.' Hennessy's face and voice soften as he shuts the door behind us. 'How did Lynette's operation go?

'She's doing well. She was stoked about the flowers you sent her.' Sam lowers his voice. 'There's a whole bunch of photographers and some people from the news stations out the front of the building, so it's lucky I was here. I mean, some of them look like real lowlifes.'

He glances up at me as if to include me in that statement, his eyebrows meeting in the middle, but before I can introduce myself Hennessy says, 'Oh, I forgot—this is Jonas, my security detail.'

She unlocks the door to her apartment, and we step inside.

'Jonas?' I say as I shut the door.

'I thought you wouldn't want me using your real name.' She stares back at me and gives me one of those taunting smiles but there is an edge to her voice as she speaks. 'We don't want your squeaky-clean reputation brought into disrepute.'

I hadn't given much thought to what Hennessy's apartment would look like. Chaos, probably—piles of magazines, discarded clothes, half-drunk martinis everywhere. But the apartment is immaculately, disconcertingly, tidy.

'What's wrong?'

Hennessy is staring at me, her forehead creasing in that way it does when she is confused. I stifle the urge to reach out and smooth her skin.

'Nothing. I was just wondering if you had a bag you need me to get down?' I lie.

'It's fine. I don't need your help.'

She makes as if to close the door to her bedroom.

'What are you doing?'

'Getting changed.'

I shake my head. 'Later. We don't have much time. Just grab your stuff and we can go.'

We have another of those staring competitions but then she gives up and disappears into a walk-in wardrobe, and I watch from the doorway as she pulls clothes off the rails.

'Just be selective. I don't like lots of luggage.'

I would have bet my shirt that Hennessy would be an indecisive packer, but she proceeds to pack her moderate-sized case quickly and efficiently. Then she hesitates and I sense her watching me, although she is not looking in my direction.

'What is it?'

'I'm thinking. Can't you find something to do? You employ thousands of people. Surely there's someone, somewhere on the planet, you can call and persecute for a few minutes?'

'I have no idea where you get this perception of me, but I don't persecute my staff.'

She does that looking thing again. She has so many ways of looking at me and each one makes it impossible for me to turn away. 'So, it's just me, then.'

I watch as she begins to move swiftly through the apartment, lifting cushions and peering under chairs. She is obviously searching for something, and there is tension in her movements now that makes me edgy. 'Okay, we're done here,' I say. 'We need to leave.'

Her head snaps up, her violet eyes wide with panic.

'No, not yet.'

'Look, I told Kenny to circle the block. But those guys outside have a sixth sense for sniffing out a story. And if they spot the car, we're going to have a rerun of what happened outside the office.'

She edges backwards and folds her arms. 'There's something I need and I'm not leaving without it.'

It.

I feel anger and frustration that my body can't contain, and I remember why I don't want her in Antony's life. Why I tipped her off my lap three years ago. She is chaos personified. If I let her lead me, she will take me to the outer edges of the map beyond the realm of control and reason.

I watch her push an armchair away from the wall and

edge back into the bedroom. I don't know what I'm looking for, but I shake out her duvet and check under the
pillows. I'm on the verge of losing my temper when I
notice that the huge floor-to-ceiling mirror is not flush
against the wall, because it is a door. As I push it ajar,
a light flickers on and I glance inside, expecting more
rails of clothes.

But then I realise it's a room without any windows, that
the door is made of steel and there is a radio frequency
ID access control box on the wall...which makes this a
safe room. More accurately, it is the room I expected to
see when I walked into Hennessy's apartment, minus the
half-drunk martinis. But there are clothes everywhere,
and the duvet sprawls haphazardly across the bed.

'Okay, we're good.'

Her voice cuts across my thoughts and I shut the door
quietly and return to the living room just in time to see
Hennessy zip up her bag.

There are no photographers or reporters outside the
back door when Kenny pulls up beside us smoothly. I
should feel relieved as Hennessy slides onto the back
seat, but I can't stop thinking about that messy bed in the
safe room. Because that's the thing about safe rooms—
panic rooms, whatever you want to call them—they're
standard in my world. And these days they're not some
spartan bunker from a dystopian movie. Most, including the ones in my properties, are as stylish as a five-star
hotel. But typically, they are not in frequent use, at least
not as a bedroom. So why did it look as if Hennessy slept
in there? Make that, sleeps there regularly.

That question, or more accurately the possible answers to it, preoccupies me, and Hennessy seems simi-

larly preoccupied by her own thoughts, so the journey to my apartment passes in silence.

There are no paparazzi waiting. But then, my address is off-grid, and I don't court publicity like the Wades do. The penthouse has its own entrance, and I inhale the calmness of the foyer as if it is pure ozone.

As the doors to the lift open, Hennessy hesitates. It is a whisper of a pause, so infinitesimal I doubt anyone else would notice, but it triggers a sudden vivid memory of that lift in Vegas, and I hesitate too. But then, lifting her small, defiant face to mine, she steps inside and the doors close.

My nerve endings stiffen like antennae because we are alone. And will be alone until tomorrow morning. I feel the word pulse inside me like an alarm.

Alone.

Alone.

Alone.

My blood scrapes sluggishly through my veins as her nearness envelops me and I have to stop from flattening myself up against the walls of the lift. Or her body. Annoyingly, either would draw attention to the mess inside my head, so instead I stare fixedly at the doors. As they open, I step aside to let her pass. She has recovered her poise outwardly, but her pulse must have missed the memo, because I can see it beating jerkily against the soft skin of her throat.

As I press my card against the security pad. I feel her watching me. She won't be able to leave without me knowing, and I wonder if she's going to kick up a fuss, but after a moment she follows me into the huge living area. She walks slowly around the room, occasionally pausing, like a deer sensing danger.

'So how does this work, then?'

She turns, her eyes locking onto mine, and I blink. It doesn't matter how many times she looks at me, it always feels like the first time.

'Am I taking the sofa, or are you? Or are we topping and tailing?'

Topping and tailing... My chest tightens. That was something we did in the kid's home when someone had a bad dream. I hadn't so much as forgotten doing that as pushed it aside, like so much of my time spent in care. But now, as I remember the ache of misery and the swamping feeling of powerlessness, I sense Hennessy's gaze on my face, and I shake my head.

'Neither will be necessary. There are three guest bedrooms with *en suite* bathrooms. The kitchen is through there and there's a gym and a pool downstairs.'

Her sugared-almond eyes are steady on my face. 'You know, you're wasted at Wade and Walters. You should be a realtor.' Blowing out a breath, she glances across the living room again and then turns to face me. 'I'm going to get changed.' She holds out her hand for the bag I am holding, but I don't give it to her. 'What are you doing?' She frowns. 'I need my bag.'

'And I need to see inside it before I give it to you.'

Her eyes widen. 'What for?'

'Enough.' I slice the air with my free hand, exasperated by the chaos she has already brought to my life today— all the risks I've had to take, the rules I've had to bend to keep her from causing even more drama. And my reward? Lies, defiance and a *faux* naivety that makes me want to shake her.

'Don't play the innocent with me, Hennessy. I may not run in your circles but that doesn't mean I was born yesterday. I know you hid something in there back at the apartment. Just like you were hiding something from that creep in Vegas.'

'By "something", I take it you mean drugs.' The haughtiness in her voice matches the disdain in her eyes but her hands are clenched by her sides, the knuckles white.

I shrug. 'If that's the case, I'm giving you a chance to tell me so.'

'I don't know about being born yesterday but I think someone must have dropped you on your head when you were born.' She shakes her head. 'I wasn't hiding drugs from Alex. I was hiding his car keys—to stop him from driving, because he was stoned.'

'And you're such a good citizen.'

The sneer in my voice makes the delicate curve of her jaw tighten. 'Not often, no, but on that occasion I was trying to do the right thing. Not that it's any of your business.' She stares at me coolly. 'You know, I thought I was staying here as your guest, but you're acting like I'm under house arrest. News flash—you're not in charge of me.'

'Wrong,' I say flatly. What's more, unlike in Vegas, I'm in charge of myself this time. I'm not going to be swayed by that trembling mouth or the quiver in her voice. 'You're living under my roof, my rules. Last time, I gave you the benefit of the doubt. That's not happening here.'

'There's such a thing as privacy, you know,' she snarls, and I catch a glimpse of her small, white teeth.

I hold her gaze. 'Last chance…'

She grabs for the bag, but I lift it out of reach and, given that she barely reaches my shoulder, she would need a stepladder even to come close.

'You can't do this, Renzo.'

'Oh, but I can, and I will. You might be able to wrap every other man around your little finger, but I see you. I know exactly how low you stoop, so tell me what's in the bag or I'll find out for myself.'

Her face stiffens, as if I've slapped her. Her arm drops, and she steps back unsteadily, but I tell myself that I don't care. That somebody needs to call time on her little antics.

'You're wrong. But nothing I can say will change your mind.'

She reaches into the pocket of her jacket, pulls out something and slams it against my chest. 'But maybe these will. If not, call Carrie—Carrie Kilroy. She's my sponsor. You can get her number from the local AA. They're online.'

AA? I am knocked sideways—stunned, wordless. Questions swirl inside my head but, before I can voice any of them out loud, she turns and walks swiftly out of the room.

Hennessy

I don't know where I'm going. I just know that I'm this close to bursting into tears and I can't let Renzo see me cry. Not after what happened last time. My heart aches as though it is bruised. Because he does remember what happened in Vegas, and he hates me for it. But he was wrong then too.

Breathing raggedly, I move swiftly through the apartment, past doors and up a flight of stairs until I am outside on the roof terrace and there is nothing between me and the sky. For a moment, I breathe in deeply, seeking calm, trying to fill my lungs with air and push back against the pain beneath my ribs as I pace back and forth. When finally my legs slow, the lights of the city are brighter than the sun.

I need to leave, that much is clear. Whatever predators await me at my apartment, anything has to be better than staying here and fielding this barrage of accusations and prejudice from Renzo.

To my relief, the hallway is empty, and I jab the lift button. It takes three more jabs before I remember that it is locked, and Renzo has the key card. But the stupid thing is that, even if I could leave, I wouldn't. Everything that matters to me is in that bag, and besides, I have nowhere to go. Only 'inappropriate' people want me in their lives, and I can't be around those people. I don't want them in my life. I never did, but nobody ever asked me what I wanted.

I turn and let my body slide down the wall. Sucking in a breath, I press my head against my knees and push back against the lump building in my throat. Tears burn the back of my eyes.

I hate Renzo. I hate that he thinks so little of me and I don't know what I'm going to do. Because, honestly, who am I trying to kid? I can't run Wade and Walters. I'm only just managing my own life. I can't be responsible for three thousand other people's lives as well.

'*Hennessy?*'

I freeze. Between the triangle of my elbow and thigh, I can see a pair of hand-made leather brogues. Renzo is standing beside me. My stomach rolls. I may be many things, but I'm not a coward, so I lift my head. He's lost the jacket and tie and undone the top button of his shirt and he's holding my bag in one hand. In the other is a cuddly, brown bear: Albert.

'I'm guessing that is what you were hiding.'

I thought he would laugh at me, scorn me—a grown woman with a cuddly toy. Nobody knows about Albert. I am surrounded by—I correct myself: used to be surrounded by—people who pounce on any weakness and exploit it for their own ends. But Renzo's face is expressionless, which is maybe why I am able to nod.

'Why didn't you tell me you were doing AA?'

He drops the bear into my lap and my hands tighten around Albert's familiar body. 'I didn't think you'd listen or believe me. You have a habit of not believing me.'

Something flickers in his eyes. 'Does Antony know?'

I nod. 'But you wouldn't listen to him either.'

He stares at me. 'Because he has a blind spot where you're concerned.'

'We're friends.'

His gaze narrows and I know that he wants more than anything for that not to be true. But it is true, and he hates me for it. And for getting Antony expelled. But most of all he hates me for kissing him. I push the kiss away. I can't have that in my head right now.

'So, you've been going to meetings?'

My pulse jolts sideways as he sits down on the floor next to me. Even though there are several layers of clothing between my skin and his, I can feel the heat of him. It is almost impossible for me to stay sitting because he is so close. At least his voice is not soft. I find kindness hard.

'There's always a meeting somewhere. I just go wherever I am. But Carrie's been with me since the start.'

'She seems very committed.'

The walls of the hallway seem to shudder. 'You spoke to her?' I thought he'd changed his mind because of the sobriety chips I'd slammed against his chest.

'I did what you said—I called the number on the website. It took a little time, but they got through to her, and she called me back.'

I stare at him, torn between disbelief and astonishment. But then, is it so surprising? Renzo is like the Terminator. He probably doesn't sleep, eat or give up. He is legendary for both his thoroughness and his persistence.

'What did she say?' Something between pride and panic shoots through me. How much did Carrie tell him? She is my sponsor, so it should be confidential.

'Not much.' He smiles then, a little slant of a smile that makes my centre of gravity tilt sharply. 'She's very much Team Hennessy, but she confirmed your story.'

It's not a story, it's my life. 'Story' makes it sound like a fairy tale, which is pretty much what most people think my life is like. Of course, they mean the sanitised, animated versions with fairy godmothers, handsome princes and happy-ever-afters. But I don't have a mother, or not one that acknowledges me, and instead of princes in my life there are frogs. Except frogs are cute and they're fit for purpose. As for happy-ever-afters…

'Did you try rehab?'

Renzo's voice snaps me back into my body. I screw up my face. 'For a nanosecond. But how long do you think that would have stayed off the front pages?' I ask.

'Fair point.' His gaze is calm and my pulse flickers as it lingers on my face.

'And those places are filled with people like me. I wanted to be around people who were different—get a different back story, a different perspective.'

'Walk a mile in another man's shoes.' That slanting smile comes again.

There is a micropause. For a moment I am mesmerised

by the clean curve of his mouth and then I glance down at my heels. 'Not these ones.'

His eyes follow mine, linger a moment, and his gaze vibrates through my skin.

There is a beat of silence and abruptly he gets to his feet and holds out his hand. I hesitate, then hand him Albert. He tucks him into the bag, reaches down and pulls me to my feet. Maybe it's the heels, or perhaps it's because I haven't eaten since yesterday morning, but I lose my balance.

Who am I kidding? It is him.

Renzo's hand tightens around mine as he steadies me. My fingers twitch against his skin, and I feel his pulse lighting up the veins in my arm. I stare up at him mutely, drinking him in, as something dark moves in his gaze.

The air flutters and ripples outwards. There is sudden stillness in the room, like a held breath, and I know that he is aching the way I ache.

Our breaths hitch as one and we crack at the same time.

CHAPTER FOUR

Hennessy

I REACH UP to touch his face, but he is already fitting his lips to mine. He drops the bag and one hand closes around my waist, the other flattening against the wall so that there is nothing but Renzo's hot mouth and his hard body. And he is hard. I can feel him pushing through the fabric of his trousers, and I feel his hunger. It matches mine.

And that is new. Exhilarating. He pulls me forward, spinning us both round so that I grab his arm to stay upright, my fingers biting into the muscle. Now I am pulling him, taking him with me, which is crazy, because I don't know where I'm going. But it doesn't matter because Renzo is coming with me.

We move backwards, his knee nudging me through the foyer as we kiss fiercely, open-mouthed, unfettered by the past, common sense or the narrow confines of what qualifies as a good idea. This is not a good idea on any level. And yet it feels not just good but essential. It feels necessary and I hurtle into it like a satellite falling to earth, burning up in the atmosphere, because I want this. I want him.

My body is twitching with a need I've never felt, and I moan as he licks inside my mouth. His hands are moving over my body, his fingers shaking, and that makes me shake. I tense as he pulls back a fraction, panic rearing up inside me at the thought that he will stop it. But he pushes open a door and my heart pounds in anticipation as I realise we're in a bedroom. His? I don't know. What's more, I don't care.

I pull his shirt free from the waistband of his trousers and begin unbuttoning it as he jerks my jacket from my shoulders.

'I'll do it,' he says impatiently. He steps back and yanks his shirt over his head.

Oh, wow. I've never seen so much of him naked, and my mind feels as if it is exploding as I stare at his smooth chest and flat, contoured stomach. And then he steps forward and kisses me deeply, his hands skimming my waist, my hips and my belly, and I feel my breath ripple through my body in tandem with my hunger.

'My dress.' My voice is shaking with his nearness and my need to be nearer. 'I want to take it off.' His mouth jerks back from mine and we reach for the shoulder straps at the same time. As it slips over my body, I sway forward, shivering as I feel the cool air on my skin and the heat of his gaze.

Because he is staring at me, staring intently, hungrily, his throat jerking as if he is struggling to breathe past something. My muscles, my nerve endings, every bone in my body, tense and reach towards him. No one has ever looked at me like this. No one has ever made me feel so helpless and hungry at the same time.

'Come here,' he murmurs, and I move without hesitation. Our mouths meet again, and we kiss greedily. He cups his palm over the lace of my bra, his thumb finding my already taut nipple. I arch into him as his other hand slides over my hip beneath my panties, and then his fingers move inside me. My belly clenches and unclenches as he strokes my clit with slow, concentric circles.

'Yes...'

The word rasps from my lips as I squirm against him. I am pulsating beneath his fingers and, swallowing a moan, I press my hand against the hard press of his erection.

'Hennessy...' My name stretches out in his mouth, the last syllable elongating between his lips, his breath hot against my cheek. The sound of his voice, the hoarseness, makes everything inside me soften and I tug at his trousers, freeing him.

My breath catches, and his does too as I wrap my hand around the hard, smooth length of him. He grabs my arm to steady himself and I love that I can make him lose his sense of gravity. He reaches round to unhook my bra, peeling the fabric from my body, and as it floats to the floor I watch the flecks of gold and green in the blue of his irises explode like fireworks. He is at the edge of his self-control, and I like that too. I want to break down his barriers. I want him to shake with desperation. I want him feverish and burning with desire.

I drop to my knees and take him in my mouth as deeply as I can go, which is no more than halfway, clasping his right leg for balance and tilting up my chin so that I can watch his face and see the tension there as I swirl my tongue over the head, grazing it lightly with my teeth.

His hand tangles through my hair, pulling it free, and as it tumbles down my back I lose myself in the taste of him and the way his muscles tremble with the effort of holding back. But I don't want to hold back. I want to chase this restless, stabbing pulse between my thighs. I press the flat of my hand there, trying to catch it, my fingers sliding back and forth. I feel his gaze tense and narrow, feel him swell and harden in my mouth…

'No, not like that.'

His voice is raw-edged, and it scrapes at my senses as he tugs me up, kissing me on my mouth, my throat and collar bone, then sucking my nipples into his mouth. It feels so good that I never want it to stop.

But now he half-nudges, half-tips me onto the bed. I clutch blindly at his arms and pull him closer, grinding against his erection and whimpering at this new hollowed-out, swollen feeling of need that is swallowing me whole.

'I want you inside me,' I say. His blue eyes lock with mine and I see his pupils fatten and splay out. My pulse flickers madly.

'I'll get a condom.'

'It's fine. I'm on the pill. Unless you'd prefer…'

'No.'

The word is out of his mouth as he shunts down beside me and I feel a flicker of nerves. He tugs me on top of him. Maybe it's the position, or the fact that I can see the hunger swimming in his blue gaze, but suddenly everything accelerates into a blur, and I guide him in.

He is big and I suck in a breath. He stills beneath me. 'Okay?'

I nod and he reaches up to caress my breasts. I groan. He does too, the sound vibrating in the space between our bodies. I push against him, and I feel it then—a fluttering pleasure low in my pelvis, warm and liquid, like simmering water. I want to cry with relief, and also laugh, but mostly I want to press against him and pin down that hazy, indescribable ripple of heat. What I want is more of him—more flesh, more skin, more of his searching fingers. Pleasure drifts up inside me like woodsmoke. My nipples are aching, and I am slick and hot between my thighs in a way that I have never been before.

'Renzo...'

His name burns in my mouth and his eyes find mine. I see fire and hunger in the black of his pupils and my head swims as he stares up at me.

'*Ti voglio,*' he says hoarsely, and I feel it deep inside my core. *I want you.*

His words, his need, are like fire in my belly, and I arch against him, the scrape of my pelvic bone against the zip of his trousers unravelling me. I clench around him as he flexes against me. I am pure sensation and heat swells inside me, doubles and then and bursts.

The noise that breaks from my mouth is like the cry of an animal. I don't know myself. I am melting, my blood is dancing, and then Renzo is gripping my hip. His entire body shudders, arching up, dragging me with him as he kisses my face, my throat, my mouth.

For a moment, we lie like that, fused, a mess of twitching skin and hearts thundering, our breath merging and oscillating in the silence of the bedroom as the aftershocks of our orgasms slowly subside. His hand moves over my back, the tips of his fingers caressing and imprinting into my skin like a maker's mark.

Because he did this. He made me into something, someone, new. I wasn't a virgin, but what just happened with Renzo feels more transformative than that awkward first encounter. I feel different, heavy and stretched out in a good way, and my body is tingling.

But then that was my first ever orgasm with a man. On my own, I can sometimes get there, but I've always faked it with a partner. Thanks to porn, I know what is expected, and to be honest my hook-ups are so wasted they neither notice or care that I don't undress and that I can apparently reach a climax simply by touching them. But I would rather people bought into that version of me than know that I am a failure in bed as well as in life.

I know I should move; get up and leave before we spoil it by speaking. But I need a moment to get my bearings, and the pulsing warmth of Renzo's body is irresistible. Just one more minute, I tell myself, and then I'll get up. Only, I might just shut my eyes for a second, because I suddenly feel incredibly sleepy. The stress of the last thirty-six hours, and a languor I've never felt after any intimate encounter, is setting in.

But I won't sleep. I never do…

I wake up to the soft patter of raindrops and a pale, grey light, and my first thought is astonishment that it is morning. And then I feel Renzo's arm on my hip, and I remember yesterday. What we did. What I did. What I felt.

My pulse twitches. We forgot to draw the curtains last night and the sky today is a sludgy grey, but there is enough sunlight for me to see the tiny little red marks on my breast and collar bone where Renzo's stubble scraped against my skin. I place my fingertips against them and press, watching them disappear, only to return seconds later.

I don't know how I feel, what to feel. But then it's hard to describe something without a name. And what do I call us after what happened last night? We're not a couple. We're not strangers hooking up on an app for casual sex. We're not friends with benefits.

We're not friends. We don't even like one another. We are yin and yang, chalk and cheese, oil and water. Only there must be something intensely right between us for sex to feel like that. But I know why it feels that way, why it feels so intense and transcendental. It's because, three years and two weeks after we kissed in Vegas, we finally did the deed. For all that time, both of us have been fighting this inexplicable attraction between us, that sense of something simmering beneath a still surface. Denial is a powerful aphrodisiac. Take it away, and what's left? Just two colleagues, business partners with a common goal.

Business partners…? Remembering the fluttering pleasure spilling over my skin, Renzo's cheek hot against mine and our staggered breaths, I press my thighs together. I can't believe he gave me my first orgasm, or that this was our first and last time together. It feels brutal, wrong, and I didn't anticipate that. But then I didn't anticipate anything, because that would have required me to think, and yesterday I was unthinking. I just *was*.

But now I ask myself the question I should have asked at some point between when I lost myself in the hunger in his eyes and waking up in his bed: what happens next? Because we are business partners, and we are going to be working together closely. Or maybe we won't. Maybe Renzo will chuck the whole thing. He is bound to regret what we did. Either way, I can't change what happened, and I don't want to. But I also don't want to have it centre stage inside my head.

Rolling onto my side, I gaze out of the windows. The light outside is growing brighter. It's a new dawn, it's a new day and, in the words of that song, I'm feeling good. Calmer; in control, for once. Trying to deal with Charlie's mess will be a challenge. But with Renzo in my head and that shimmering, gravitational energy pulling us ever closer, it felt as if I was trying to orbit two separate planets. That's not going to be a problem anymore. We worked it out of our system. I worked him out of my system.

Sliding out of bed, I tiptoe across the carpet, pick up my clothes, let myself out of the room and make my way to the guest suites, collecting my bag *en route*. I choose a bedroom at random, shower and get dressed. Then I smooth my hair into a ponytail and apply my patented 'five-minute no make-up make-up'.

It's then, staring at my reflection that I remember the key card for the lift and, clutching my shoes, I tiptoe back down the hallway to Renzo's room. I really don't want to do this, but the alternative is to wake him, so I take a deep breath and press down quietly on the door handle. Averting my eyes from the sleeping figure in the bed, I walk softly across the room. Fortunately, Renzo is lying on his back, still half-dressed, and I reach carefully into his trouser pocket.

My body stills as he shifts in his sleep, and I stare down at his face. In the dim light, his features look starkly beautiful. My earlier calm dissipates, and I almost feel a sudden panic that we are done. Because it doesn't feel done when I look at him. It feels as if we have only just got started. Then he shifts again, turning his face into the crook of his arm, and I force myself to move.

I let myself back out into the hall, take the key card I retrieved from his trouser pocket and press it against the panel by the lift.

Thank goodness… The doors open, I press the button to the foyer and then gently put the card on the console table. The doors close but it is only when they open again on the ground floor that I let out the breath I am holding, and I walk over to the concierge.

'Good morning, Ms Wade. Can I help you with anything today?'

'Actually, you can.' I smile. 'Could you get Mr Valetti's driver—Kenny, I think he's called—could you call him and ask him to bring the car round?'

Renzo

I wake up to the urgent pulsing alarm of my phone. Before I even open my eyes, I know I am alone in bed. The woman who undid my trousers and ripped up my rule book is gone, presumably to one of the guest rooms. I never thought anything was missing from my life before but now it feels as if something crucial has been stolen from me.

My body tenses instantly, and I roll over and switch off the alarm. Frowning across the room, I feel weirdly disorientated, as if I've woken in a strange place—which makes no sense, given that I've lived here for over five years. But then, nothing makes sense this morning, particularly what happened with Hennessy yesterday.

Covering my eyes with my arm, I swear under my breath. I hadn't planned on taking her to bed. Although, truthfully, I'm not surprised that we had sex. It's been there, circling us ever since she walked into David's office in that stupid, barely there dress. Scratch that—it's been there since we kissed in Vegas, it's just I hadn't needed to face that fact until she sashayed back into my life yesterday.

My jaw tightens. I wanted to get into work early this morning, but it's obvious I need to have a conversation with Hennessy before we go into the office.

Throwing back the sheet, I stalk to the bathroom and

into the shower. I switch on the TV as I shave, brush my teeth and dress. The news of Charlie's disappearance is already the top story on every channel, and I frown. I should be at work. That I'm not is Hennessy's fault. And mine, but mostly hers. It must be. I've had sex with women before and never been late for work the following morning. But Hennessy has taken my life and shaken it like a snow globe.

As I stride towards the guest bedrooms, I feel another ripple of fury, because I can't hear any tell-tale signs of activity, so clearly she is still asleep. I tap on each door in turn, checking the room when there is no reply. When I reach the third bedroom and get the same response I open the door, expecting to see a figure curled beneath the bedding, but the bed is empty. So is the bathroom. For a moment, my brain can't compute what I'm seeing. The floor sways as if I'm standing on the deck of a boat, but then I spot her bag and that steadies me. I know how important that is to her, and that she wouldn't leave it behind.

So where is she? I stalk back through the hall into the foyer. And that's when I see it—the security card sitting on the side of the console, which is where I usually leave it. But I didn't last night. It was in my trouser pocket. Now all that's there is those sobriety chips she thrust against my chest last night. Pulling out my phone, I text Kenny to bring the car round, then walk back into the living area to pick up my laptop.

My phone buzzes: it's Kenny. I stare at the message in disbelief, my eyes narrowing, and I know my mouth has dropped open. Hennessy has hijacked my car. Swearing under my breath, I get another car sent to my apartment and spend the journey silently imagining all the ways I intend to make her pay for her behaviour. Except, that won't do. She distracts me enough when she's here; I don't need her distracting me when she isn't.

I tap on the privacy glass behind the driver's head. 'You can drop me here. I'll walk the rest of the way.'

It feels good, striding down the street, and I'm in the process of congratulating myself for successfully neutralising Hennessy's pernicious effect on my composure when it suddenly starts raining on a biblical scale. By the time I reach the office, I am not just damp but soaked to the skin. My mood is not improved by the crowd of reporters and photographers swarming around the entrance to the Wade and Walters building and during the ride up to the eightieth floor, my thoughts return to my errant co-CEO.

Still fuming, I walk into her office but, like her bedroom, it is empty.

'Where is Ms Wade?' I snap at Gerry, my PA, as she scurries after me.

'She went down to the archives.' She hesitates. 'Would you like me to find you a fresh shirt?'

I glance down to where my shirt is plastered to my torso. But I'm already late enough. That fact swirls inside my head like a swarm of angry bees. I can't remember the last time I was late for anything. Now, not only am I late, but I also look as if I've been spat out of a storm drain.

'No, it's fine. But can you get me a coffee? And pass me those newspapers.' I snatch them from her hand and stalk back out of my office. Today of all days, I needed my mind to be razor-sharp and focused. It is unconscionable to have got so distracted from my true purpose.

I still can't believe what happened with Hennessy, that I let it happen. The irony is I pushed back so hard about the bag because I wanted to prove I was in control. *Good job, Valetti.* But I was so certain she was hiding some-thing. And she was, only it wasn't drugs.

I remember Hennessy's face as I handed her that scruffy brown bear. There was softness, vulnerability, there. And that was my undoing. Only why? I can't re-member ever getting that worked up about any woman. But what happened in Vegas was like an *amuse-bouche.*

I would have stopped it if she'd wanted that, but it would have been hard. She was so sweet, hot and slick, and I woke multiple times in the night, my body hard and aching for round two…and rounds three and four. But she'd looked so young and untroubled in sleep, I couldn't bear to wake her. Now, though, in the cooler light of day, I am glad that I didn't. More than once would be harder to write off as the mistake it is. Although, it didn't feel like a mistake at the time. It felt like poetry.

I make my way downstairs to the archives. It's an of-fice within the office, a glass-sided box in the centre of the legal department. I can't see Hennessy. But the aster-oid belt of young men orbiting the archive room confirms her presence. My jaw tightens. Even down here, in what is essentially the museum of the office, she somehow manages to disrupt the routine running of the business.

As I arrive, her admirers hurriedly melt away and I see her. She is sitting at a desk, flicking through a past edition of *FROW,* looking surprisingly classy in a wrap skirt, fitted white shirt and dark heels. Her hair is in a ponytail that makes me want to reach out and tug at the end like a schoolboy.

Tug her towards me… My fingers close around the chips in my pocket, and I swear under my breath. 'Good morning,' I say tersely.

Her gaze slants up to meet mine, and I feel it fizz on

my tongue as if I'm biting down on a blueberry. 'There you are. I was just finishing up.'

'Good, then you can explain why you're skulking down here instead of upstairs firefighting. Because, in case you haven't noticed, the building is metaphorically burning.' I drop the newspapers onto the table beside her. To a letter, their lead stories are Charlie's crimes and abscondment. 'I've had five calls already this morning.'

'I'm not skulking,' she says calmly and, instead of picking up the papers, she picks up her laptop and slams it shut. 'And that's old news. To you and me, anyway.'

Which is true but does nothing to improve my temper.

'You're sitting in the archives. There's nothing but old news down here.'

She does one of those maddening, provocative shrugs and her ponytail does a little shimmer. 'I was actually doing some research.'

'You're co-CEO, Hennessy. Your job is to lead,' I snap. 'To lead, you need to be visible.'

Her eyes widen. 'Please don't raise your voice at me. And, as for being visible, I've been in the building since seven o'clock this morning.' *Unlike you.* She leaves the end of that sentence unfinished, but the shape of her mouth says it for her.

'What happened to being on time and appropriately dressed?' She lets her gaze float down over my damp shirt.

'I'm late because you took my limo. And I'm soaked to the skin because I had to walk some of the way.' Untrue, but the truth would reveal how deeply she got under my skin.

She bites her lip, and I know she wants to laugh. Which does nothing to defuse my temper.

'You told me to keep a low profile, so I borrowed your car.'

'And you didn't think to tell me?'

'What can I say? You slipped my mind.'

Slipped her mind? *I* slipped *her* mind? I feel a stab of disbelief and outrage, then she tilts up her chin and I have a sudden flashback to when she took me in her mouth. 'Anyway, I thought you might be having a lie-in.'

It's oblique but it's the first time she's referred to what happened yesterday at my apartment, and I feel it like a punch to the gut. Because that is why I feel so tense this morning: Hennessy and her 'take it or leave it' manner. As if I'm some bellboy she tipped for bringing up her luggage who now has the temerity to want another tip.

'Next time, wake me up.'

'But there's not going to be a next time, is there?' She smiles, a sweet smile that knocks me sideways. 'Yes, Gerry?'

I stare at her blankly and then realise that my PA is hovering behind me.

'Sorry to bother you, Mr Valetti, but I have—'

'It can wait. I need to discuss something with Ms Wade,' I say sharply. 'In private,' I add.

As the door closes behind me, Hennessy stands up, her eyes flaring. After seeing her smile at Gerry, her scowl feels unduly harsh. 'You are such a hypocrite. I thought it matters how we behave.'

'It does.'

'Clearly not or you wouldn't be taking your frustrations out on Gerry.'

'I'm entitled to feel frustrated. You took my car.'

'And I explained why, and I'd rather you didn't discuss what happens in my private life at work. Charlie absconding is scandal enough. We don't need any more gossip to power up the rumour mill.'

It feels as if my brain's being pummelled. Apparently, Hennessy Wade is giving me a dressing down about causing scandal. The world has gone mad.

'Rest assured, I won't be discussing it with anyone.'

'Good. Because there is nothing to discuss. Things got a bit out of control, that's all.'

She says this in such a blasé way that I want to reach over and remind her of what 'that's all' feels like. Instead, I say coolly, 'It won't happen again.'

She shrugs. 'Why would it? We both got what we wanted and, now it's done, we can focus on the job in hand.'

I know what I'd like her to take in hand and it's not the job. My body tenses as I remember Hennessy unzipping my trousers and the clumsy, inexpert urgency of her fingers.

'You're right. We did. So, let's just forget about it.'

She frowns. 'Forget what?'

There is a knock at the door. It's Gerry again. 'I'm sorry, but I need you both upstairs. The FBI are here to talk to the CFO, and they want to talk to both of you too.'

As Hennessy moves to follow Gerry, I step in front of her and block her exit. 'Just so we're clear, there are to be no more stunts like this morning. If you need a car, ask me.'

The morning passes in a fever dream. The FBI agents are thorough and professional, but it still blows my mind that my ordered life is now subject to investigation by federal law enforcement officers. Hennessy is interviewed separately, which I don't like, and she emerges looking pale but defiant ten minutes after my interview ends.

Some of the more sensitive advertisers have already pulled their accounts in response to Charlie's fugitive status, so we draft a statement to reassure the ones that remain. And then I spend hours trying to sweet-talk the ones who have left into returning. But it's hard to downplay a story that is front and centre on all of the news outlets. And to add colour to the story they are deep-diving into his scandalous past, which means multiple pictures of Hennessy in her 'wild child' era, and lots of quotes from anonymous but extremely forthcoming 'sources close to the family'.

Despite being in the same building, and often the same room, she and I hardly spend any time together on our own, which is a relief—but oddly disappointing, and also thought-provoking. Her position was hardly meritocratically earned, so I expected her input to be negligible at best. But she is focused, well-informed and she has a good way with people. They like her. Or maybe they just get lost in that magnetic Bermuda triangle of legs, hair and light curves.

Finally, the staff start to leave, and by six-thirty only Hennessy and I remain. In fact, I'm the one who goes to find her. She is typing something into her laptop, but it is the pen between her teeth that pulls my gaze across the room, as if my eyes are on strings. Rogue strands of blonde hair have escaped her ponytail, and she looks tired. But then, it's been a long day, for her particularly.

'You worked hard today,' I say, and she looks up and meets my gaze.

'Careful, Renzo, that sounds almost like a compliment.'

'It's an observation. I saw a different side of you.'

'I saw a different side of you too.' Her eyes flicker over my face, and her attention feels precious, like a hummingbird's wings brushing against a flower. 'You were less robotic. More human.' She pauses and muses for a second. 'Or maybe I mean humane.'

'I'm not a monster, Hennessy. Even if I do dress like a hit man.'

My body tenses as her pupils do that flaring thing and then she glances back at the screen.

'What are you working on?' I ask.

She opens her mouth, then stops. 'It's just an idea. It can wait. Right now, I need to book a flight for tomorrow.'

My pulse stumbles. 'A flight to where?'

'I'm going to Milan.' She frowns. 'It's fashion week, or did you forget?'

'No, I didn't forget. I'm flying out tomorrow.'

'You are?' She looks stunned. 'You're going to fashion week? But this is my gig. You're just a back-up singer.'

'I'm co-CEO of the lifestyle media company that produces the biggest fashion magazine in the world. That is the reason I'm going, but there's every reason for you to stay and keep your head down.'

My tone is definitive, non-negotiable. End of discussion, I think, but Hennessy scowls up at me, her glinting violet gaze snuffing out our brief harmony of moments earlier.

'Of course I'm going. I always go.'

Not happening. It's hard enough keeping her out of trouble here in New York—but chaperoning her in Italy surrounded by twenty-four-hour party people?

'This isn't a mini-break, Hennessy, it's work. I need people with me who know how to behave.'

'I know how to behave, Renzo.'

'Do you also know that the Italians invented the paparazzi?'

She lifts her chin. 'Actually, it was one Italian: Fellini. He named the photographer in *La Dolce Vita* "Paparazzo" because he wanted him to be like a buzzing mosquito.'

'I know the reference, but there are a lot of fountains in Milan, and I know how you love to strip off around water.'

Our eyes collide, full of hostility, but something else too—something that is more confusing. I choose to ignore it.

'Are you still going on about that? I was fifteen. Didn't you do stupid things when you were fifteen? Didn't your circuits ever malfunction?'

I stare down at her. No, they didn't, because that wasn't an option for me. I was working two jobs, after school and at the weekend, putting money aside to prove that I could look after Antony on my own. But that isn't a part of my life I'm about to share with Hennessy.

'Almost certainly. But I didn't end up getting my name in the paper, or myself and my so-called best friend expelled from school.'

'He is my best friend. That's why I did it,' she snaps.

'What's that supposed to mean?'

But her face is already shuttering. 'Nothing.'

'In that case, any chance you had of going to Milan is now less than zero, because you're not leaving this office until you tell me what you meant.'

'You're such a monumental jerk, Renzo.'

I turn and flick the door to her office shut with my fingertips. 'Have it your way.'

She is quivering with fury. 'You know, for someone so smart and omniscient, you can be really dumb.'

'And you're too stubborn for your own good. But, if this is how you want to spend the evening, I'm happy to trade insults all night.'

'Why don't you just ask Antony?'

'I'm asking you.'

'Perhaps you should wonder why you have to.' She glares at me. 'Maybe it might be a starting-off point for some kind of self-reflection.'

I hold her gaze. 'If you're trying to imply that I don't talk to my brother—'

'Oh, you talk. You just don't listen.'

'So, I'm to blame for Antony's expulsion?' That I'm even having this conversation is symptomatic of the chaos Hennessy has already brought into my life. 'Unlike you, I prefer facts to fiction. And the facts are that you hated school and—'

'I didn't hate school. Antony did.' Her jaw is taut. 'Or rather, he hated being a full-time boarder. So, I faked an email from you. I knew you'd tell the school, and when Antony said it was his idea, they'd have no option but to exclude both of us—happy now?'

'Not really.'

'Well, Antony was. He liked being at home at the weekend. Or perhaps you didn't notice. Too busy conquering the world.'

'Everything I did, I did for my brother.'

'Bullshit. You did it for yourself because you have to be in charge of everything. Because you're essentially a tyrant. Any bit of the world you happen to be in becomes your personal fiefdom.'

She suddenly runs out of steam. 'Right, I've told you

what you wanted to know, so now can we agree what time we're leaving for Milan?'

'I don't make business decisions on the basis of some tit-for-tat arrangement.'

'But you said—'

'I said that you wouldn't go if you didn't tell me, not that you would if you did.' Catching sight of her mutinous expression, I sigh. 'It's been a hell of a day, and I think the week isn't going to get any easier, so could you just go with me on this?'

'No, I can't. This is my family's business.'

'You've been working here for three months.'

'And you've been working here a day,' she counters swiftly. 'Besides, I've been coming into this office since I was a child. I watched Charlie work—and I know you don't like how he worked, or like him, but he makes things happen.'

'Yes, he has a real talent for that. Unfortunately, they just don't happen to be the right type of things, unless you think that having FBI agents crawling all over your office is some kind of business opportunity.'

I can see her bristling beneath that airbrushed complexion of hers. 'I watched David work too. I saw the way he treats people, how he showed everyone respect. They loved working for him. He was the sweetest man… *is* the sweetest man.'

There is something precarious in her expression now that blindsides me, so for a moment I lose the thread of my thoughts. That never happens, so my tone is rougher than I intend it to be when I finally reply. 'And now he's a very sick one.'

'Because of Charlie. And you can keep blaming him, blaming me, for that. But it doesn't change the facts.

You might be some business titan, but I know Wade and Walters and I know fashion. And if I don't show, then it sends out the wrong message, like I'm hiding. Like we've got something to hide. How's that going to inspire confidence?'

There is a long, pulsing silence.

'Fine. You can come to Milan. But I'm warning you, Hennessy—you mess me around and I will go straight to the board—'

'I understand.' She cuts me off and stares at me, her gaze cool and assessing. 'As long as you understand this is fashion week, not an undertaker's convention. So that tie has to go. Maybe the shirt too.'

CHAPTER FIVE

Hennessy

WE ARRIVE IN Milan at eight p.m. Of course, in my head it's two o'clock in the afternoon, so it's weird walking off Renzo's private jet into darkness.

We are staying at his apartment on the via Torino. The location is unsurprising, given that it's the most expensive residential street in Italy. Helpfully, it's also within walking distance of the city's famous cathedral, the Duomo, and the *quadrilatero della moda*, Milan's fashion district. All the famous fashion houses are there and many of the shows are held at locations just a stone's throw away.

I glance out of the window of the limousine that picked us up from the private airfield. There are people shopping and catching up after work. Mopeds weave erratically between the buses and cars. It all looks very humdrum, but I wonder who is hiding in the shadows. 'Do you think anyone knows we're here?'

Renzo hesitates, then nods. 'Yes. These days, the paparazzi use flight-tracking apps to find out where the rich and famous are, and even I can't do much about that.'

I appreciate his honesty. Any honesty, really. But, coming from Renzo, it feels like a big deal because telling someone the truth requires an element of trust. But, then again, what do I know? With a father like mine, trust has never been a big part of my life.

'You don't need to worry. I take my privacy seriously, and if anyone decides to test just how seriously, I have ways and means of making their lives very unpleasant.' His blue gaze meets mine and for a moment his heartbeat envelops me. 'And, as my guest, you are under my protection.'

A flicker of warmth dances over my skin and my stomach turns over in a fierce, uncontrollable response to his words. Which is stupid, really, because I know they are just words. Renzo would personally serve me up on a platter to a pride of lions. But then, nobody has ever offered to protect me before. On the contrary, I have spent most of my life feeling like prey surrounded by predators.

My body tenses as I remember the evening that plays out in my nightmares so often. I was nine years old when I woke up to find a man in my bedroom, a stranger, staring down at me. Even now, it has the power to still my breathing. Nothing happened, or that's what Charlie said at the time, and I believed him at first. But then it crept back in. Not what happened, but what might have happened. Every time I got into bed and closed my eyes, he was there, sitting on my bed, staring at me in the darkness. I started having night terrors and Charlie had to install a panic room in our house.

It helped. It still does, but for some reason Renzo's words wrap around me like a protective charm. Maybe because he made my body work like it should, instead of freezing like an actor forgetting her lines. Because that's what has happened in the past. But not anymore. Now I am healed, whole. I have faced my demons. Because that's the trouble with a faceless man—he could be anyone.

Or maybe not *anyone*, I think, glancing over at Renzo.

He is impossible—arrogant, autocratic, overwhelmingly so at times—but he doesn't scare me. There is a straightforwardness to him that is as rare as it is steadying. Maybe that's why the one-time sex worked with him.

And yet, the strange thing is, with other men I'm in control. I select them. I wait until they pass out and then, when they wake, I let them think we had sex.

But I didn't choose Renzo. With him, it was more like a current sweeping me out to sea. And even though it was pulling me further and further away from the shoreline, I felt safe, supported.

On arrival, we are greeted by his housekeeper, Simonetta. She speaks fluent English, so there is no reason for me to flex my Italian. She is a small, dark-haired and elegant woman who stirs up memories of my grandmother for no reason that I can think of, other than that she is quietly spoken and smiles a lot.

I still think about my grandmother. It was only a year of my life. A year of calm bookended by Jade walking out on me and Charlie reluctantly taking me on. We lived in New York, near Central Park. She used to take me to the Plaza for afternoon tea, and every night she would read me a story before bedtime. She was strict, but also kind, and I was happy. Nobody shouted. Nobody smashed things or stormed out in the middle of the night.

She took me to buy my uniform for nursery school. I was so excited I wanted to sleep in my navy tunic, but I never started school. My grandmother died in August and that year of my life turned out to have been the eye of the storm.

'We'll do the full tour tomorrow, Simonetta.' Renzo's voice cuts through my thoughts and I turn to where he is waiting impatiently for me to join him at the bottom of the curving marble staircase. 'I'll show Ms Wade to her room.'

The house is beautiful in the way that all grand Italian houses are. The rooms are well-proportioned with high ceilings and large windows that offer tempting glimpses of the city. As for the interior, it is the same blend of the discreet, neutral aesthetic and comfortable functionality that I have come to think of as Renzo's signature style.

'There's a sitting room through here.' He gestures towards an open door as we reach the first-floor landing. 'Although, I doubt you'll have time to use it. We have a show every day, and meetings, and there are events in the evenings, so we probably won't be back until midnight.' He does one of those stares, this one tinged with bafflement, as if he can't quite understand what I am doing there. 'I take it you've brought something "appropriate" for evening events?'

Boy, does he love that word. I sigh. 'I've been coming to fashion week since I was a child.'

I speak lightly but my body tenses involuntarily. I hated it then. I hadn't worked out how to block out the curious gazes that followed my father as we walked into any room, or how to front up to the strangers yelling my name with their flashing cameras.

'But, as I said in New York, this time you'll be working.'

He turns and continues walking, and I stick out my tongue at his back, then almost trip over as abruptly he spins round to face me.

'I'm down there, and you're this way,' he says, and the distance in his voice scrapes over my skin so that I can almost feel it tingling.

The cagey conversation we had back at the office has led to a kind of cool-edged truce, but we still haven't talked about what happened in New York. Which is fine by me. I don't need to hear Renzo say it was a mistake. That I was a mistake. My mother's already done that. It didn't feel good then and I doubt it will feel good now.

Besides, if Renzo and I talk about it more, there's a risk I might let something slip. Such as how, for me, those frenetic minutes in his bedroom were not just a sublime cohesion of breath and body but a transformative act. That before then my body was an uncooperative, damaged tool.

On the plus side, he has stopped making jibes about my sobriety. In fact, he must have told the stewards that it was a dry flight, because they didn't offer alcohol. I muse on that for a moment, but mostly I remember how I looked up to find him watching me in that assessing way he has, as if I am a puzzle he is trying to solve. Only, there is no puzzle. My life can be summed up in three sentences. My mother hates me, and my father tolerates my presence out of curiosity and a sliver of guilt. I have one friend and a job I got entirely thanks to my surname. And, for a time, I drank too much, and took drugs occasionally.

But I'm trying to live up to the legacy of my name. Trying to make something of myself and my life. Not that Renzo will ever acknowledge that. Even though he knows I'm sober now, our highly charged sexual encounter in his apartment seems only to have confirmed his deepest suspicions—that I bring out the worst in him, in everyone.

'This is you.'

He pushes open a door and I follow his broad back, my gaze hovering on the muscles of his shoulders, remembering how I fell asleep against his chest. It feels like a dream now, or a snatched memory, like a photograph.

'Oh, wow…' I stop, my eyes widening. It's a beautiful room, square and spacious, with a Murano glass chandelier, a beautiful, gilded bed and a pale-green and pink colour scheme that makes me think of pistachio and raspberry *gelato*. 'It's lovely,' I say truthfully.

He is doing that staring thing again, as if I'm speaking in code.

'We should eat.' He frowns, then tilts his wrist to look at his watch. 'I can get Simonetta to book us a table. There's a couple of decent *trattorias* nearby. They always fit me in at short notice.'

My heartbeat jabs the skin of my throat. I didn't eat on the plane, and I know I should eat now, but even before I stopped drinking, I avoided eating out. There's something exposing about sitting opposite someone in a restaurant. Bars, clubs, anything with low lights and loud music, I can handle. If there's a DJ, even better. It's hard for people to start a conversation, much less sustain it, when I'm dancing; and if I'm dancing, I'm already moving. And if I'm moving, then nobody can get close enough to notice that I'm fighting stage fright.

But a meal is different. I'm trapped at a table. There's nowhere to hide. And, frankly, it's awkward enough being a reluctant guest in yet another of Renzo's homes. I don't want to have to eat with him alone in a performative way.

'I'm not hungry,' I lie. 'I might just turn in. Like you say, we've got a busy day tomorrow.'

His gaze keeps me pinned to the floor and then finally he nods. 'Breakfast is at seven-thirty. Don't be…' He checks himself. I know he was about to say, 'Don't be late', but instead he says quietly, 'Don't stay up too late. Sleep well.'

'You too,' I mumble, but he is already walking away.

I watch the door close behind him and wait for a minute to pass. I prefer to sleep in a panic room, but if that's not an option then I lock the door, and if there's no lock then I wedge a chair under the handle. But tonight, I hesitate, even though there is a heavy, old-fashioned key, because I don't feel like I do when I'm in a strange house. Maybe it's because of what Renzo said earlier about being under his protection, but I feel safe in a way that I wouldn't normally. But out of habit I still turn the key.

I let out a long breath. After hours of being in close proximity to Renzo, I am finally alone. Except I'm not. I'm never really alone. I'm not crazy, but there's a whole bunch of uninvited guests inside my head: teachers telling me that I could do better; Charlie's friends with their inappropriate remarks. And, of course, Jade, the one woman on earth who should love me unconditionally but who resents my very existence. Her voice is the most strident, the most critical of all. I can feel it corroding me, undermining me.

Normally, I play music on my headphones to an ear-damaging volume but, thanks to Renzo hassling me, I left them at my apartment. Instead, I take a shower, turn the water on full and let it pound my body until I can't think straight. I didn't lie to Renzo. I was planning to turn in, and I do get into bed and turn out the lights. But then the sheets seem to caress my skin and I remember Renzo's hands moving hungrily over me and the hum of pleasure spilling over my limbs and I have to switch on the light to banish him from my bed. Then I am so wide awake it might as well be dawn.

A cup of herbal tea would help. A tisane. Surely Simonetta will have just such a thing, and I'm sure she won't mind me helping myself. There is a dressing gown folded neatly on the sofa, and I shrug it over the shorts and camisole I wear to bed. It takes a few deep breaths for me to snatch up the courage to brave Renzo's house in the dark but as I open my bedroom door, hugging my laptop to my chest, I realise two things. One, the house isn't dark—there are multiple table lamps, each offering a rich halo of light in every direction—and two, nobody is up. I'm an expert at listening to houses breathe. And this one is sleeping.

It takes me five minutes to find the kitchen. The lights come on as I walk in, which removes the need to look for any switches, but finding the tisanes proves a little harder. As I gaze at the food in the huge walk-in larder, my stomach rumbles. But tea is one thing; cooking myself a late-night snack might wake someone up.

Finally, I discover the teas in a drawer. As predicted, there are multiple options, including what looks like home-made chamomile tea. Having made myself a cup, I sit down at the large, pine table that dominates the room and flip open my laptop. The lights have dimmed overhead, and instead they have lit up under the cupboards, bathing me in a warm, comforting glow as I gaze at the proposal I was working on back in New York. The one I didn't show to Renzo.

It's a good idea—essential, I would say. The September issue is safe, but how many more will there be if we lose any more advertisers? We need to make *FROW* the story, not Charlie, or me. But I don't want to think about that now. Instead, I move the cursor up to the tabs at the top of the page and click first one, then another. My stomach cramps, not from hunger this time, but shame. I know I shouldn't look, shouldn't care after everything he's done and everything he hasn't done, but Charlie's still my father.

Is it him? Heart pounding, I lean into the screen. It could be. Then again…

'I thought you said you were turning in.'

The deep, familiar voice makes me scramble back from the screen so fast, I almost fall off my seat. Renzo is standing in the doorway, his blue gaze sweeping over the scene, the shadowed curve of his jawline stark against the smooth gold of his skin. He looks calm, curious and serious.

My palms itch. *Oh, brilliant.* He's not wearing a shirt. He walks towards me slowly and I feel every footstep loud in my blood as I try not to stare at his torso. He looks engineered, architectural. Tempting.

'I did. But then I thought I'd go through the schedule for tomorrow, get it firm in my head, and I wanted a tisane, so I came downstairs. That's not a problem, is it? I'm not confined to quarters, am I?' I ask to provoke him, although I'm not quite sure why I feel the need to do so.

That's a lie. I do know why. It's because it is late and it's just the two of us standing semi-naked in a softly lit room and it's giving me flashbacks to what happened by the lift in New York, so I need to make things a little confrontational between us.

'You need to call it a night.' He doesn't rise to the bait, but his gaze dips to where the dressing gown has fallen open and there is a rough edge to his voice that feels like a caress.

I nod, mainly to distract him from what's on my screen. 'I was just finishing up.'

Renzo

She's lying. I know because I was watching her from the doorway and she wasn't just staring at the screen, she was poring over it as if it was a crime scene. I tilt my head pointedly, and she shuts her laptop, but not quickly enough.

'You shouldn't look at that stuff.'

Her hair is loose, and she glances down, letting it fall in front of her face.

'I don't. I don't usually.' She hesitates and her throat works through a swallow. For a second, she veers towards anger or defiance, and then abruptly she says, 'Someone's posted a picture of Charlie in Switzerland. I was just trying to see if they were right.' She hesitates then flips open the laptop, leans back and crosses her arms tightly, as if she is trying to stop something from bursting from her chest. 'Do you think it's him?'

It's an amateur snap, probably from a phone, and the man in the photo is turning away, either intentionally or by accident, so it's only a part of his profile. But it's enough to make out the shape of the head and the blond hair. It looks like Charlie. And yet...

I lean in closer, and as I do so my eyes drift from the screen to the neckline of her dressing gown. Whatever she is wearing underneath, it is cream-coloured and edged with lace, and my brain starts suggesting in far too much detail what it would look like if Hennessy took off that robe...

Blanking my mind to the unsettling array of images unspooling inside my head, I straighten up. 'I'm not sure. It could be. But it could also be Michael, the sandwich guy.'

She nods slowly, and her shoulders dip a little, either

with relief or despair. It's hard to read her expression. She is wearing that mask, the one she presents to the world, to me, whenever anyone gets close to the tripwire of her family and her feelings. Because I am starting to understand that Hennessy Wade is not just one person. She's not just the spoiled heiress who selfishly pursues her own agenda and the hell with the consequences. Which is why I suddenly decide to cross the line.

'Are you worried about him?'

Her eyes meet mine. I see her confusion, and I'm confused too by my previous resistance to the idea that she might be worried about Charlie. But then, she seemed so blasé about his disappearance.

'He's never been gone this long before without contacting me.'

Now I'm more confused. I thought she and Charlie were thick as thieves. Are his absences a regular thing?

'Those photos of you outside the office look pretty intense,' I say, pointing to a drone-shot of the paparazzi crowding around Hennessy, my body tensing at the memory of how I found her, pinned against the glass. 'I'm sure when he sees them, he'll get in touch.'

Am I sure of that? Losing my parents so close together and so young upended my world, but it also made me aware of how fragile life is, how vulnerable humans are. That's why I've built this life. Why I have so many checks and measures in place to protect Antony. I know he thinks I am over-protective, but I can't lose him as well. I will do anything to keep him safe.

So where is Charlie Wade? I can't understand why he isn't here with Hennessy, or why he hasn't texted or called. Could something have happened to him? I'm not even his father but my brain is hard-wired to feel that I need to take care of Antony.

'Sorry.'

A low rumbling dams the current of my thoughts mid-flow, and I glance down to where Hennessy is clutching her stomach. 'Are you hungry?' I frown as, in answer to that question, her stomach rumbles again. 'Why didn't you say? Simonetta would have made you something.'

'It's fine. I can wait until breakfast. I don't need you dragging her out of bed now.'

'I wasn't going to.' I shake my head. 'I'm not an ogre, Hennessy. Do you eat eggs?'

Her violet gaze flickers over my face.

'It's a simple enough question.'

As she nods, I reach for a pan.

'What are you making?'

'*Uova strapazzate*: scrambled eggs.'

She surprises me by getting to her feet and coming to stand next to me. I feel something pinch under my ribs. Antony used to watch me cook when he was younger, and it reminds me that he and Hennessy are the same age.

She's young. Too young to be juggling a global business and a father on the run. Although, I'm beginning to wonder what kind of father Charlie is. The Hennessy I knew was a wild child. I thought Charlie just couldn't cope with her. Now I'm wondering if it wasn't so much that he couldn't cope as that he wasn't there.

I crack the eggs in the pan, add a sliver of butter and stir with a wooden spoon until they are almost but not quite set. Taking them off the heat, I add a teaspoon of ricotta cheese, a grind of pepper and then I push them onto a plate.

'Here.' I hand the plate to Hennessy.

She eats with obvious relish, and I wonder when she

last ate or if she has simply been existing on adrenaline and herbal tea.

'Thank you.' She clears her throat. 'For making this for me. It's delicious.'

'My mother used to cook it this way. '

'Was she a good cook?'

'Yes, she was. She was a homemaker. Very traditional.' I see a flicker of curiosity in Hennessy's eyes, and something else, something almost like envy. But then it is gone, and I know I imagined it. Hennessy is an heiress who grew up as part of the bohemian, nomadic jet set who criss-cross the globe in yachts and private jets. My family lived in a tiny apartment in a small town near Naples, and then a different tiny apartment in Brooklyn. Money was always tight. In Brooklyn, we often slept in our coats in the winter rather than switch on the heating.

We are opposites, and not just in upbringing. Our characters are diametrically opposed. That I allowed myself to momentarily forget that is proof that both of us need to get some sleep.

'Right. We should call it a night,' I say firmly, getting to my feet. Reaching down, I pick up her laptop. 'Come on.'

We don't speak as we walk up the stairs, but as we reach the top, she turns to me. 'You don't need to escort me. I know the way.'

I wait, and after a moment she sighs and turns, and I follow her slowly. I don't have a foot fetish but following a woman with bare feet to her bedroom, following Hennessy, is painfully erotic. It is only by sheer effort of will that I am able to force my gaze up to a point above her shoulder.

She stops in front of her door. 'This is me,' she says

softly, and for a moment we just stand there in silence that is full of 'what if?'s and 'why not?'s, and a shivering current of tension that makes my brain momentarily lose functionality.

'I'm going to keep hold of this until tomorrow,' I say after I manage to get my thoughts back on track, holding up her laptop. 'There's going to be a lot of people claiming to have seen Charlie and it'll drive you crazy, trying to validate all of them. He'll turn himself in when he gets tired of running.'

I expect Hennessy to argue, but it has been a long day, and instead she nods. Suddenly I am alone in the hallway, staring at her shut door, left with nothing but her teasing scent and a laptop that doesn't belong to me.

The next few days are intense, which is unsurprising. More surprising is Hennessy. It's not often that I'm wrong about people but she was right: she does know how to behave. In fact, she is a model of grace and decorum, and my remarks about the riskiness of bringing her seem over the top now—fussy, almost. And it turns out that she can speak six languages, including Italian.

'Why didn't you tell me you're multilingual?' I ask as she returns to my side after a conversation with a clearly enraptured Italian designer.

'It didn't come up.' Her mouth twitches. 'Are you worried you said something snippy about me to Simonetta? You didn't, or not when I was there, anyway.'

'You might find this hard to believe but I haven't said anything snippy about you to anyone in any language. I've had some snippy thoughts, but nothing I care to share.'

Her eyes meet mine. 'Nobody could accuse you of

over-sharing. Extreme bossiness and a misplaced certainty of your own rightness, maybe, but not over-sharing.'

The room is crowded with people, I know that for a fact but for some reason I can't see or hear them. It's just me and Hennessy, alone.

'The bossiness I think you're stuck with, but I can correct my misplaced sense of rightness.' I pause. I should be immune to her beauty, but her mouth is such a distracting shape. 'Because I was wrong. You were right—you do know fashion. And your language skills make having you here a bonus.'

Her eyes meet mine and she gives me a small, curving smile that leaves me wanting more before turning to greet someone in flawless French.

For the next four days we are like athletes competing in timed heats. One meeting follows another, each with a different couture house. And then there are the shows. Unlike Hennessy, this is new to me and, truthfully, I thought I would be bored. I took the decision years ago to relegate clothing low down on my list of priorities. But this is true fashion. It is a magical blend of art, performance and beauty. And nobody conjures that magic up better than Hennessy. Even in a room chock-full of models and beautiful people, she is luminous.

And the couture crowd have a different view of Charlie's fugitive status. Heads turn as we take our seats in the front row next to *FROW*'s editor, but Hennessy has that quintessential coupling of perfect bone structure and scandal, so they love her.

It helps that she has inherited a wardrobe of heirloom couture pieces and styles them with accessories that make the fashion set implode with joy and envy. Helps too that her EQ matches her IQ. Watching her mesmerise our fellow diners over lunch, I realise that she has an entire skill set that I don't share and might possibly have under-valued.

I'm not charming, but Hennessy turns heads and softens hearts. Catching sight of one of the younger ad executives giving her a second glance, I feel oddly jealous. We are not a couple, or anything like one, and I have never felt possessive about any woman—the opposite, in fact. I like having sex, I like women's bodies, but I can always walk away. I have always walked away. But, as I watch Hennessy smile that megawatt smile that she has never once bestowed on me, I feel myself wanting to walk over, grab her hand and keep walking until we are some place where it is just the two of us.

Fortunately, I am not stupid or reckless enough to act on that impulse. Once was enough. It will have to be. Hennessy might look intoxicating in that dress of dark-blue silk, empire line with an over-sized pleated cuff— and that I can reel all that off in my head is destabilizing enough—but, where she's concerned, I need to stay sober.

'That went well.'

We are in the car on the way back to the house after a dinner with the head of JVHM, the luxury goods conglomerate. Hennessy is effervescent, excited, and I am too. Because she's right—the dinner did go well. The whole week has.

'It did.'

'I'm glad you agree.' She bites her lip. 'So, I was thinking we might talk about the party?'

'What party?'

She frowns and the sparkle in her eyes flickers like a

faulty fluorescent strip-light. 'I sent you my proposal.' Now her smile twists. 'But I guess you didn't read it.'

I read the tagline to her email, but there was no point in reading on. I already knew it was a no-go.

'A party is the last thing we need to be attaching ourselves to right now. We are trying to contain the fallout from Charlie's disappearance—.'

'I haven't just tried.' She cuts across me. 'I've succeeded. Or aren't you going to acknowledge how positive Monsieur Pinault sounded tonight?'

'He enjoyed your company, Hennessy. Most people do. But any financial commitments we secure will be based on hard, economic facts, not because you batted your eyelashes at them.'

'That's not fair.' It isn't but, no matter that she is sober now, Hennessy is still too like her father for me to trust her judgement in this instance.

'So basically, all that stuff you said earlier was lies. You think my input is worthless.'

I think back to her effortlessly switching between languages. 'Not worthless, no.' I soften my voice. 'You've worked hard all week, but Charlie's partying brand is not good for our optics. Surely you can see that it won't play well with advertisers and shareholders?'

'I disagree.' Her eyes are dark like plums. 'In New York, you said to me that the building was on fire. Well, if you want people to stop staring at a burning building, Renzo, you need to set off some fireworks.'

I stare at her in confusion and admiration because, once again, I know with a sharp, unsettling certainty that she is right. Sinking back in my seat, I take a breath and meet her gaze. 'What kind of fireworks are we talking about here?'

CHAPTER SIX

Hennessy

'*EXCUSE ME, HENNESSY*, the people from Eos just called—they're running five minutes late. Shall I bring them up when they get here?'

I glance up from where I am working my way through the guest list.

'Yes please, Cassie.'

It's already been a long day.

We started at six this morning. It is now ten o'clock, and I doubt we will wrap up before midnight, but I feel energized and excited. This is my project. It's not my trade, but I doubt many professional party planners have been to as many parties as I have. I know what works and what doesn't. And I want people to see that, just because I share his name, I'm not Charlie's daughter. I'm not going to take the money and run. Wade and Walters is my family. This is my business.

And Renzo's. I glance over to where he is sitting on a ridiculously beautiful eighteenth-century *chaise longue*, typing on his laptop whilst talking on his phone in rapid Italian. To keep things under wraps, we are meeting people at the house, and so far, it's working well. Even more impressively, we are working well together, which is a sentence I couldn't have imagined saying last week. Because most people, men particularly, only value my legs, my hair or my smile. Either that or they want to exploit my connections. It's as if I'm just a collection of body parts or a selection of headlines rather than a person. But Renzo is treating me like an equal.

As if he can feel himself being scrutinised, he looks up from his laptop, his incisive dark-blue gaze bumping into mine, and we stare at one another in silence until I can't bear it any longer. I glance back down at my list, but I can still hear his voice. He has a faint Neapolitan accent which gets more pronounced when he is emphasising something. It makes him sound as if he's guillotining the words, as if he's impatient.

I like it a lot. My pulse twitches as I remember that day in the apartment and the sudden splaying of his pupils as he closed the distance between my mouth and his. He was impatient then. Urgent. I was too. And I don't even have to close my eyes to imagine how it felt. It's imprinted into my skin so close to the surface that I feel as if he is touching me now, gripping my hair as he comes uncontrollably inside me and I come apart around him…

'Is that okay with you, Hennessy?'

My face jerks up and I know my cheeks are red because I can feel the heat of them.

'Sorry? I was thinking about the after-party gift bags,' I lie.

'What about them?'

His gaze is sharp, and I have that sensation again that he can see inside my head.

'I was veering towards ethical gifts, but now I think it's not necessary. There's something crass about giving wealthy people free gifts, however ethical, don't you think?'

He doesn't answer, just keeps staring at me, almost as if he is confused. Or intrigued. Or more likely because I've got something on my face. I glance at my half-eaten pastry, then reach up and rub my hand across my mouth. 'Do I have crumbs on my lips?'

Renzo shakes his head. 'No, your lips look...' He hesitates and clears his throat and his eyes drift to my mouth. He stares as if hypnotised and then abruptly glances away. 'They look perfectly normal.'

I run my forefinger slowly over my lips. I have forgotten about the crumbs. Everything in my schedule—the meetings, the calls I need to make—has fallen out of my head. All that matters is that he keeps looking at me like that. As if he sees me, the real me. As if he's claiming me.

Which is ridiculous on so many levels. For starters, he made it quite clear that he sees what happened in New York the same way I do—as unfinished business that got finished. And just because he knows that I'm sober doesn't mean he knows me. If he did, he certainly wouldn't claim me any time soon. Renzo Valetti has a type. He likes those put-together women with classical profiles who meet their personal trainer before work and are a consultant on a not-for-profit in addition to their day job—which is always something intimidatingly senior for their age. They don't have a back story filled with hangovers and hangers-on. And their fathers aren't on the run from the FBI. They're in control of their lives.

Getting to my feet, I walk over to the large gilt-framed mirror that almost stretches the length of the wall. I glance at my face. There are no crumbs on my mouth or anywhere else. So why was he looking at me like that?

'Is my word not good enough?'

I feel as if someone is drawing a comb over my skin as Renzo gets to his feet and walks towards me. Our eyes meet in the mirror as he comes to a standstill behind my right shoulder, and my stomach flutters as though actual butterflies are beating their wings inside me.

We're too close. He's too close for us to be having this conversation, any conversation. I can feel the heat of his body and I know, if I breathe in too deeply, I will smell that scent he wears. The one that acts like catnip on my senses.

I deal with it the way I deal with anything that gets under my skin by treating it like a joke. 'I don't know. After that mix up with your car, I thought you might think it funny if I looked like a dork. What? You're Italian, and you definitely give off a "revenge is a dish best served cold" kind of vibe.'

His mouth pulls up at the corner into a shape that suddenly makes my skin feel feverishly warm.

'I wouldn't lie to you, Hennessy,' he says. 'And I'm not sure you're genetically capable of looking like a dork.'

He moves then, stepping backwards, maybe a foot at most, but my throat tightens with relief. Or regret. Or maybe both. I turn my attention back to my reflection and mess around with my hair to give myself time to get my breathing under control.

'What were you asking me?' I say finally, and oh-so-casually.

'So far, it's just trade press on the guest list. We could open that out to journalists from other organisations. I just wanted to check if you were okay with that. Obviously, my security team would be there to supervise. But after what happened in New York I thought you might feel uncomfortable. I didn't want to assume.'

He's worried about me? That is surprising enough. Nobody has ever bothered to ask how I feel about anything. Not even the people who, theoretically, should care the most. Jade walked out of my life without even saying goodbye. And Charlie never discusses anything with me—not when he moved me out of school, or to an entirely different country with no warning, or even when he hooks up with yet another random woman. Something warm is curling around my body and there is a lump in my throat.

'No, that's fine. I can deal with them. I've been dealing with them all my life.'

'I know that. But what happened outside the office… that shouldn't have happened.' He frowns, and it ought to make his features harsh but there is gruffness to his voice that softens his stubborn, uncompromising face. 'And I want you to know it won't happen again. We might not always see eye to eye, but I will protect you, Hennessy.'

Silence swells between us and I don't understand what it is I'm feeling. Just that his eyes, or maybe his words, are keeping me tethered to him. And he feels it too. The tension between us is not just palpable but sinuous. I can feel it weaving over my skin like warm silk.

'Mr Valetti, Ms Wade…'

We swing round as one, and Renzo takes a step backwards, as if we are performing an elaborate dance. Cassie is there with two women, one tall and dark-haired, the other shorter with plaits.

'Ciao.' The taller woman steps forward and holds out her hand. 'I'm Emilia Blasi; we spoke on the phone.'

'And I'm Oshana Gardner. It's a pleasure to meet you both.'

I smile. 'I've just realised why you're called "Eos"—it's an abbreviation of your first names. I thought it was something to do with Eos, the Greek goddess.'

'Correct on both accounts. Most people get one or the other. But it's quite rare for someone to get both.'

I laugh. 'When your father christens you after his favourite drink, it makes you hyper-sensitive to names.' I take a breath. 'I thought I'd get Charlie out of the way so that he doesn't loom large over what I hope is going to be a very productive and satisfying conversation.'

There is a small, stunned pause but then Renzo steps forward and holds out his hand. 'I think what my co-CEO is trying to say is that we don't choose our relations. So I hope you will judge us—' my heart beats in my throat as he glances over at me '—judge both of us as you find us.'

Everyone laughs then.

'Absolutely.' Oshana is smiling. 'My family would wipe your father off the front page in a nanosecond.'

'Ditto.' Emilia nods. 'My brother is…'

I nod too, smiling, but I never find out what her brother is because I'm not listening anymore. My blood is humming in my ears and my head is spinning. Renzo had my back. *Has* my back.

'So, you might be wondering why I chose Eos,' I say as we take our seats. 'Part of the reason is that you're local. The second is that you are professional party-planners who understand that parties are given, not planned.'

Oshana nods. 'That's very much our philosophy. We want your guests to feel welcome, to feel loved, as if they're visiting family.'

'I want that too. Wade and Walters has been a family-run business for one hundred and fifty years. I think we're still a family now. But the world is changing, and I want our business to change too. Fashion, publishing—both bring a lot of collateral damage to people and the planet, so I want this party to be clean and green and ethical.'

'By "clean", are we talking about a sober party?'

'We are.' Renzo's voice is scratchy with an emotion I don't recognise. 'And by "green", we mean throwing a really great party minimising waste as far as possible, and paying event staff a living wage.'

'The theme is "aurora",' I add. 'For that reason, it will start pre-dawn. We want it to be an awakening.'

Emilia opens her laptop. 'Have you any ideas about decor, food, music...?'

Renzo shakes his head, his mouth curving infinitesimally at the corners, and I know that smile will shimmer inside me for a long time—maybe for ever. 'I'm just the backing singer. Hennessy has all the ideas.'

The meeting goes incredibly well. Emilia and Oshana work intuitively from my suggestions. Through a combination of willpower and connections, Renzo obtains a special licence for the party. Everything is coming together.

The next day passes in a blur.

We go to the closing show of the week, and it is by far my favourite. The clothes are beautiful and ethereally romantic, future heirlooms for those lucky enough to end up owning anything from the collection. But my mind is elsewhere, ticking off lists and double-checking all the various moving parts.

Finally at ten o'clock we are alone, sitting in the elegant dining room and eating some incredible *pasta olio e aglio.* Or, rather, Renzo is eating, forking up his spaghetti with impressive speed and accuracy. I am pushing mine around my plate. We've had a few of these meals now, but none alone without Simonetta discreetly gliding in and out of the room, so this is making me edgy. Maybe it is having the same effect on Renzo because when he looks up from his plate his eyes roam across the room away from me.

But I don't mind because it's giving me a chance to study his face. Unlike most people, he is better looking up close. Everything about him is so definite and flawless. If I could draw him, it would only take three or four lines to capture his essence. He is a sketch by Leonardo da Vinci. A Michelangelo sculpture.

'I don't want to add to my reputation as a tyrant, but I think it would be a good idea for you to eat something.' He picks up his water glass and takes a sip. We are both drinking water and I wonder if that is for my benefit.

'I want to. Only I don't know if I can. I feel so wired.' The words slip out before I have a chance to edit them, and his eyes stop roaming to find my face.

I said 'wired', but I mean terrified. I haven't been to anything like a party for over three years. I stay away for obvious reasons, but I know the party is the best way to distract everyone from Charlie. My fingers tighten around my glass as I picture the guests milling in the stunning space we've created. The pulsing baseline of the playlist. The crush of people on the dance floor. It's a true magnet for me, both pulling and repelling, because, even though I know there will be no alcohol or substances, there will be triggers everywhere, like IED devices just waiting to be stepped on.

'Trust the process. Everything's in place.' He hesitates. 'What are you worried about?'

'I don't know. Nothing. Everything.'

'We have a great venue, great food, great mocktails and DJs who are going to play us into the new dawn.'

I nod.

'So, what is it? Are you worried people are going to bail?'

'No one will bail.' I can't keep the bitterness or the panic from my voice. 'Having me at a party is like the circus coming to town. Everyone loves the circus.'

He leans back a fraction. 'I thought they love merry-go-rounds.'

I shrug, then push my hands under the table to hide their trembling. 'They do. But they also slow down to look at the crash on the other side of the carriageway.'

'You're not a car crash.'

I waggle my fork at him. 'Ignore me. I always get like this when I've got to go out and mingle. And I haven't done it in a while, so…'

He is silent, meditative, as though he was looking at a picture of a duck but now sees a rabbit.

'You don't like partying.'

I curl some spaghetti around my fork and force myself to take a bite. 'Not really.'

'So why go to so many parties?'

'Well, when I was a kid, it was just what happened. My opinion wasn't required. The nearest Charlie got to that was when he asked me if I wanted to go to school and get bullied or go to a party. When you're seven, that isn't a hard choice.'

His eyebrows dip into a V above his nose. 'Perhaps

a better one would have been for Charlie to talk to the school about the bullying.'

'Probably.' I make myself eat another mouthful. That would be the normal response of a parent. But Charlie is allergic to schools. He hates any reminder that he is old enough to be a father. It's one of his contradictions, that he can be so sentimental about birthdays but hate any other reminder of the ageing process.

Renzo is staring past me in silence. There is a stillness to him that almost makes him look like a photograph, and I remember that photo Antony had by his bed at school: the one of his family. He had others of Renzo and him, but just that one photo of his family, and I know why he chose to put that one in a frame. His parents gaze down at their children with such open love and adoration. Neither of my parents has ever looked at me like that. Probably because they don't like what is reflected back at them.

'What about when you were older?'

'By then I was drinking, and alcohol is good at dulling things so that they're bearable. Only then I stopped drinking, and the people in my life don't do things sober. So, I don't go out much. Garrison's birthday was a knee-jerk reflex. But I couldn't even get out of the taxi.'

My body tenses at the memory. Or maybe that's down to Renzo, because now it's my turn to be scrutinised. Studied. I feel a featherlight, silvery shiver dance over my skin as he shifts back in his seat, stretches his arm along the back of the neighbouring chair and tilts up his chin a fraction, just as if he is posing for a photographic shoot. Or beginning an inquisition.

'And yet you've arranged this party.'

'I told you. If the building is on fire…'

'Set off fireworks.' He nods. 'I know.'

Another silence.

'And I wasn't a cheerleader back in New York, but I think you were right. This is going to send out all the right signals. We're in the front row because we matter. You matter,' he adds, and I feel it again, that searing, expansive ripple of heat I want to pretend isn't happening. Because we are past this. Aren't we?

For a moment I hold my breath and then he takes another bite of spaghetti. 'You know I still don't understand how you used to get into those places—hotel bars, nightclubs—there are laws.'

I shrug. 'Private parties have different rules. And Charlie was, is, so brazen. He doesn't think the rules apply to him. If he gets into trouble, he just leaves the country.'

There is a brief silence before he says quietly, 'But you didn't. You knew what Charlie had done before everyone, even David. You could have upped and left, but you stayed.'

'I'm not my father, Renzo.'

'No,' he said finally. 'You're not, you're…'

The sentence teeters mid-air. I feel the thread between us pull tight like the string of a crossbow and I know that I'm magnifying this shimmering, unyielding tension between us. That it's just tiredness, adrenaline and this weird situation with both of us living under the same roof. That if I pulled on the thread, it would break…break the spell. But I can't stop myself from wondering what would happen if I reached out and touched his face.

My heart stops as his eyes abruptly meet mine. 'Go up to bed, Hennessy. I'll deal with this,' he says and there is a trace of impatience in his voice.

As I make my way upstairs, I'm relieved that I didn't

make a fool of myself ahead of such a big day. Except, oddly, it doesn't feel like relief as much as regret.

Renzo

It's the morning of the party. To be accurate, it is five forty-five in the morning. In less than forty minutes the guests will start arriving, refreshed after their first night of sleep since fashion week started, and in about an hour and a half the sun will rise over the city.

Everything is ready to go. I am ready, wearing a surprisingly conservative but beautifully cut suit and a shirt that Hennessy gave me. They were hanging in my wardrobe. A note was pinned to the sleeve of the shirt:

So you don't look too dorky. No tie required.
H
X

I can't remember the last time a woman gave me a present. Maybe that's why I don't throw the note away but fold it up and put it in my pocket, where it joins the sobriety chips I've been carrying around with me for reasons that are less clear to me.

But there is no time to think about that now. I glance at my watch. I am waiting for Hennessy to join me, and she's not late, so I don't know why I feel on edge.

My mouth twists. That's a lie: I do know why. It's because I know she's nervous. Even before we spoke last night, I could tell she was anxious. I thought she was worried about making everything happen, but she has no doubts, no fears, about the party failing.

Incredibly, I am still coming to terms with the fact—

and it is a fact—Hennessy dislikes parties. And yet here she is, hosting one for the fashion elite.

When she suggested coming out here to Milan for fashion week, I assumed her motivation for doing so was driven by self-interest. I thought she wanted an excuse to let her hair down. But she has worked as hard as, if not harder than, anyone this week. And now, despite her anxiety, she is hosting this party—not because she doesn't care about the business, but because she does.

Replaying my conversation with her from last night, I feel a twinge of remorse. I thought she and her father were partners in crime but now it seems more as if she was just dragged reluctantly in his wake.

There is a click of heels. I turn and my brain blanks for perhaps a tenth of a second. I know I'm staring. I also know I am in trouble. Big trouble.

'Hi,' she says softly.

Hennessy is standing five feet away. I try to speak but instead I just nod because her beauty makes words irrelevant. It makes the world and everything in it colourless and indistinct. Her make-up is kind of natural, but also a little bit smudged and smoky round the eye, and there is a sheen of lip gloss on her mouth. As for her hair... For days now, it's been tamed into a variety of complex updos. But this morning that signature mane of hers is loose and rippling down her back to her waist in a boho tangle.

And then there is the dress. Hennessy has worn any number of beautiful, vintage outfits over the last few days, all of them gifted to her by her late grandmother. But this dress... Our eyes meet and the usual current of electricity snakes through me as she bites the edge of her lip.

Stop staring, I tell myself, because it's getting weird now, and I walk towards her slowly. 'You look beautiful.'

'You look pretty good yourself.'

Her eyes flicker over me, and I know it's shallow and unprofessional, but I like how she looks at me.

'Thank you for this. I do have suits but…'

She bites her lip. 'Those are different. There's nothing inherently wrong with them but this is much more you.' She circles me slowly. 'It fits beautifully.'

It does so, yes, I look good. But someone could set me on fire tonight and I'm pretty sure nobody would notice. Not if Hennessy is in the building.

The dress is made of some kind of buff-coloured organza. It is close enough to her skin colour that it looks transparent, but it's not. It is flouncy, and yet not frilly. It is delicate and subtle, but also sexy as hell. In short, it is the perfect dress for the enigma and temptation that is Hennessy Wade.

. 'Is that one of your grandmother's?'

She glances down at herself and nods. 'It's always been my favourite dress of hers, only I was always too skinny to fit into it, but I suppose I've been eating better.' She gives me a faint smile. 'Not this week, just generally.'

'How are the nerves?'

'Not so bad. I'll be fine once it starts.'

'You're fine now.' *More than fine,* I think. I feel dizzy, unbalanced. She unbalances me. 'Don't doubt yourself today of all days, Hennessy. And don't assume that other people will doubt you either. You've had a rough time. But I think they'll be wanting this—you—to succeed. And you deserve to.'

Her eyes jerk up to meet mine, and I can see that she

is confused or shocked by my words, but I am telling the truth. I hold out my hand. 'Let's get this party started.'

Almost from the moment we walk into the huge, disused wool factory I know the party is going to be something people talk about for a very long time. The space has been transformed into something that is nothing short of miraculous. Every piece of decor is made up of upcycled material from the ateliers in the city and other Milanese businesses. Emilia and Oshana have been here all night. They look exhausted but the effect is startlingly beautiful.

There is no time for me to do more than tilt my head towards Hennessy in silent, private acknowledgement of her vision. The guests are arriving. The sun is starting to filter through the windows, creating a chiaroscuro effect that is more beautiful than any artificial lighting. Hennessy is standing beside me as we greet people. It feels almost as if we are a couple, and this is our wedding. We talk and mingle, and I find that I know where she is in the room without even having to look for her. It's an odd sensation but easily explained. After all, we have spent days in each other's company now.

Finally, it's time for the DJ's set.

The music is like a solid wall of sound. But all I can hear is my heartbeat. Hennessy is dancing with Cassie. They are dancing like women dance when they feel safe, their arms reaching for the stripes of sunlight cutting across the room, heads tilted back as if they are laughing, their bodies twisting like double helixes.

Our guests are all beautiful people. But Hennessy makes every other person here look ordinary.

I'm not the only one to think so. She draws the eye like the *aurora borealis*. Just then, she catches sight of me, and suddenly she is here. Her flushed cheeks and tousled hair remind me of that night in New York, and I have to blank my mind to an image of her fingers biting into my shoulder.

'Are you having fun?'

Her eyes soften. 'I am. Are you?'

'Of course. It's a great party,' I say softly.

For the last hour or so we have barely been in the same part of the room, but somehow, we have moved closer together like planets passing in orbit.

'My feet,' she moans. 'Would you mind?' She takes my arm, and I feel that current jolt through my jacket and shirt as she bends over to massage her toes.

'It must be nearly time for the finale.' There is to be a display of giant bubbles. It is Hennessy's idea. They'll have the wow factor of fireworks but without the environmental damage.

'It is. This is the closing song,' she says, and seconds later the music fades out and people start to move past us to the deck that's been built next to the factory.

'Have you seen this?' Two middle-aged men are walking past us, one showing the other his phone.

'Take a look at this. Miss Illegally Blonde's dad is with some woman in Rio!'

I am on the verge of turning and snatching away the phone, only I catch sight of Hennessy's face. It is a perfect blank. But I have a momentary glimpse of the shock and hurt in her eyes. Then she turns, and there is a gap in the room where she should be. Somewhere behind me, I am conscious of a hum of conversation. I can feel the sidelong gazes pressing into my back and then I reach into my pocket and bring out my own phone.

Hennessy

The bathroom is empty because the party is over. I wish it had never started.

In the mirror, my face looks small and stupefied. But then, I am stupid, beyond stupid, for thinking I could change who I am when I know that I can never change. Like Sisyphus pushing his boulder, my efforts simply take me back to where I started. My fingers tremble against the screen of my phone. Sober or not, my past always sucks me back in.

I cower back against the hand dryer as the door to the bathroom bangs open and Renzo strides into the room. I know from the expression on his face that he heard what those men said, and suddenly I am fighting panic and misery. Because if he heard then other people will have too, and all I have done by hosting this party is make everything worse.

'What are you doing? You can't come in here,' I say, spinning back to the mirror and swiping my face.

'Hennessy...' He hesitates. 'You need to come with me.'

'I can't. I can't go out there now.'

The door swings open again, and a couple of waitresses tumble into the room, giggling.

'Could you give us a moment?' Renzo snaps without turning round. His voice is a volatile combustion engine of anger and impatience. 'We're having a private conversation.'

'We just need the—'

'I said, we're having a private conversation,' he repeats, spinning round, his shoulders swelling outwards. 'Don't make me have to call security.'

They reverse back through the door but, as he turns to face me, his anger makes something snap inside me.

'What are you doing? Isn't it bad enough that this is going to be the story now? But I guess that's what you wanted to happen, isn't it? Now you can tell everyone I messed up and then you can buy me out.'

My breath catches in my throat as he grabs my hand and holds it tight. 'You didn't mess up. It was perfect, all of it.'

I want to believe him, but then I see my reflection—the smudges of mascara, the wildness in my eyes. No wonder Renzo abruptly lets go of my hand. He is looking at me as if he's seeing me for the first time.

'That photo. Do you know who the woman is?'

Renzo's question makes me feel both exposed and unseen, and his words scrape against a wound that always feels fresh. Of course I know. And soon the whole world will know. And that neither of the people in the photo thought to tell me that they were meeting up is a reminder that I am, and have only ever been, a nuisance and an intruder.

'Yes, I do. It's Jade—my mother.'

I half-expect him to turn and walk away without looking back. It's what Charlie would do. What he's always done. But instead, he steps closer. 'We need to go.'

I shake my head. 'I can't go out there like this.'

'We're not going outside. We're getting out of here. There's a helicopter waiting for us on the roof. We're going to Amalfi.'

CHAPTER SEVEN

Hennessy

THE FLIGHT TO Amalfi takes no time at all, or at least it feels that way. But then, I am so stunned by the way the party ended that my brain is numb and incapable of forming even simple thoughts. I am unbearably conscious of my own cowardice. Of how I left the party, fleeing like Cinderella when she hears the clock chime midnight.

Only, that's where the similarity between us ends, because Cinderella is good and wronged but, as far as the world is concerned, I'm just wrong. And, judging by the hard, flat, unapproachable expression on his face, Renzo thinks so too. That sweet truce we brokered over the last few days is over. Whatever he said in the bathroom was just a white lie to get me out of the building. He hasn't said a word since we got into the helicopter—or at least not to me. But then, what is there to say except I told you so? So perhaps I should be relieved.

But all I feel is despair. This was my chance to prove I could step up and be the person I wanted to be, but it was all for nothing, because the party will be just a footnote to yet another Wade scandal.

My eyes ache with the dryness of unshed tears. I cannot believe that Jade met up with Charlie. Their marriage was inflammatory, destructive, toxic. They made each other and everyone around them unhappy. But now she is playing Bonnie to his Clyde. I feel as if I am three years old again and I can't blow out the candles on my birthday cake because I am trying not to cry. She didn't say goodbye that day. Didn't explain or apologise. She just upped and left, and I didn't see or speak to her again for nineteen years.

And yet she is in touch with Charlie. Has always been in touch. My fingers bite into the soft, leather arm rests. In the past, I've sometimes caught him talking on the phone, and he had this voice that he doesn't use with anyone else. It's furtive and teasing, combative, conspiratorial. Intimate. Charlie never said anything, and I didn't ask. Didn't care, or maybe I just didn't want to know. But I know now that he was talking to her—to my mother. And now she's wearing a stupid wig and meeting up with him. She can do that for Charlie, but she doesn't even remember my birthday.

As the helicopter touches down, Renzo offers me his hand, but it is a gesture based on courtesy, not empathy.

'I'm going to make some calls. You should get some rest,' he says in a voice that could anneal steel as we walk towards a beautiful, sun-washed villa. But we are moving so fast there is no time to do much more than fleetingly admire the pale-yellow stucco walls.

'*Buongiorno*, Paola,' he says to a tall, grey-haired woman, as we sweep inside. 'Hennessy, this is my housekeeper, Paola. She will show you to your room. I'm afraid there wasn't time to get your things before we left, but they'll be brought down later today, so if you need anything in the interim just let her know.'

He peels away from us, his long strides echoing through the house, and I have a flashback to my childhood and all those other times when I was handed over to some random woman.

'Would you like to follow me, *signorina*? I've put you in the blue room. It has a beautiful view of the sea and the gardens.'

I nod numbly and follow her up the stairs. The room is charming, but not blue. Instead, it is a pale peach that shimmers in the mid-morning sunshine. There is a tray with a small teapot on a table by the bed.

'I made you some chamomile tea. Would you like me to close the shutters?'

'No.' The thought of being locked in the darkness with my self-loathing makes my voice sharp and vehement and I shake my head. 'Sorry, no. That won't be necessary.'

She nods then turns, and moments later I hear the soft click of the door. My heart is beating in a crazy, syncopated rhythm, and I want to cry, but I know if I do then I won't be able to stop. Instead, I pour myself a cup of tea and make myself breathe in every time I take a sip.

Then quite suddenly I feel exhausted, and I sit down on the bed and curl onto my side. My stomach is a hollow ache. Since I can remember, I've felt alone. I have no place in my mother's life, and a grudging one in my father's. But for a short while today I felt accepted, wanted, for who I really am. Renzo was right: people weren't there waiting for me to mess up, they were there to support me.

He was there, supporting me. Even when we got separated, I could feel his gaze tracking me around the room, making sure I was okay. But now, I know he wishes he'd never met me. And I have never felt more alone.

I don't remember falling asleep, but I wake suddenly with a jolt and scramble to my feet, my heart pounding. I didn't lock the door. But the room is empty, and

I make myself move. Moving helps stem the panic, and the square of calming blue sky beckons me, so I walk to the window and rest my head against the glass.

The sea is a perfect strip of shimmering blue, but it is the garden that pulls my gaze down. It's not just the verdancy of it. There is a paved area with a table and seating, and beyond that the garden has been created with the lightest of touches. There is no rigid structure of formality to it, which surprises me, because in my experience Renzo likes to stamp his authority on every living thing.

My body tenses as something moves at the margins of my vision and I inch backwards, pressing my body against the window frame as Renzo appears on the terrace below, almost as if I can conjure him up by the power of thought. He has a phone tucked under his chin and he is talking, pausing occasionally as he paces back and forth across the terrace. I watch, my stomach lurching as he yanks out a chair from the table and sits down to write in a notebook, striking out words with a pen. Even from this distance, I can read his frustration, and I have to press my hand against the wall to stop from remembering the way he squeezed it, that moment of heat and strength.

The skin on my face feels so tight it makes me feel trapped inside my own body. I glance back out of the window. Renzo has disappeared and suddenly I am walking towards the door. I might not be able to shed my skin, but I can get out of this room.

Renzo

'Thanks for sorting this, Ben. I appreciate it. I'll be in touch.'

I hang up on what is my tenth call of the day, lean forward against the table and press my hands into the warm wood, trying to ease the ache in my shoulders. Having spent most of the morning in my study, I am now back outside on the terrace.

It is past lunchtime, but I can't think about food. I feel unpleasantly alert, and my muscles are taut, as if I'm a sprinter waiting for the starter pistol to fire. But it has already been fired.

My eyes flick to the open screen of my laptop. Predictably, the photo of Hennessy's parents together has caused the Internet to break. On the plus side, thanks to the volume of fake news stories and conspiracy theories which dominate social media, there are quite a few people claiming that the picture was AI-generated. Or that it is someone else entirely.

None of which is reassuring to either the shareholders or the advertisers. I breathe in deeply and rub my hand over my face. This is not how I work: firefighting; publicity triage. My business interests are scandal-free models of steady, exponential growth—with one exception.

My ribs stretch around the tension in my chest. I should never have bought shares in Wade and Walters, let alone agreed to be co-CEO. I am pathologically risk-averse. And the Wades are pyromaniacs, arsonists, fire-starters.

All of them: Charlie, Jade... Hennessy? Did she know about her mother meeting up with Charlie? It hurts more than it should to think that she has been lying to me. But then I remember her face. She looked winded, as if everything good had been punched out of her. I know how that feels.

My gaze drifts towards the distant sea. I lived here in Praiano until I was six years old. We were poor. Even as a child I knew that. We lived in a tiny first-floor apartment. It overlooked the main square, so it was noisy even at night, but in my memory at least the sun seemed to shine every day, and I didn't know fear.

That's why I bought a house here. Why I brought Hennessy here. Seeing her panic, her fear, my first thought was to take her somewhere safe. Only, it wasn't a thought. It was something elemental and instinctive. More of an impulse.

Because that is what I am now—that is what I am with her—I am impulsive, reckless. I don't just watch buildings burn, I run into them.

And I should be scared—more scared. Scared of the pain that comes from letting the random and unplanned into my life. I know what happens when you just let things unfold without forethought. I lived through it as a child in care. I fought against it as an adult. That I stopped fighting both angers and confounds me.

'Scusi, Signor Valetti…'

It is Paola, bringing out a fresh pot of coffee. 'Thanks, Paola. Could you bring out some tea for Ms Wade? The herbal stuff. I'm going to go and wake her.'

Paola frowns. 'But she is not sleeping now, *signor*. She has gone to the beach.'

It takes me four minutes to get to the stretch of sand that belongs to the villa. At first, I can't see her. For some reason, I think she might be swimming, so I scan the sea, but then I see her on the beach, and I feel something snake across my skin like electricity. She is walking at the shoreline. Her feet are bare, and the water is curling over them, tugging at the hem of her dress. She is staring out to sea. Her profile is a clean gold line against the dark blue of the waves and she has never looked more beautiful. Or more alone.

The waves are light but vigorous so that she doesn't hear me until I am quite close. She spins round to face me. Her eyes are all irises in the sunlight and there are smudges of mascara beneath the lashes. She looks tired and pale, less substantial but still defiant, and I feel relief that this latest ambush hasn't broken her.

'Paola said you were here. Did you get some rest?'

She nods. 'Did you make your calls?'

The pragmatism of this exchange both reassures and grates on me. I want that softness back in her eyes, but the barriers are back, the trust is gone. She is a fortress.

'I have something I need you to read.'

Her mouth curves stiffly into a smile that looks as if it is made of glass. 'Let me guess. It's something your lawyer helped you compose.'

I nod slowly. 'I know it feels cold-blooded but it's best to take the emotion out of it.'

'Is that how they told you to spin this? As if you're doing me a favour? Just so we're clear, I don't care how you spin it; I'm not signing anything.'

'There isn't anything to sign.'

She stares at me, blinking.

'That's not just cold-blooded, it's illegal. You can't sell shares without a stock transfer form—'

'Hennessy.'

I cut across her, but her voice rises and there is a slight tremor to her hands. 'This is you all over. You're so convinced you're right; you don't even do me the courtesy of asking me the question. You just assume I knew about Jade and Charlie. That I was in on it too.'

Her accusation stings, because I did make that assumption in Milan, and in that moment, I tried to imagine a life without her. I expected relief. What I felt was a bone-crunching misery.

'It doesn't matter what I think.'

'Oh, please.' The laugh that accompanies those words is a brittle, humourless sound that jars with the soft, rhythmic cadence of the waves. 'It only matters what you think. Well, it's not happening. Those shares are mine.'

She is finding it difficult to speak and seeing her struggle wrenches at something inside me. 'They might have been given to me, but I've earned them now, and I'm not selling them to you, and you can't make me—'

'You're right. I can't. But, even if I could, I wouldn't. Listen to me, Hennessy, I'm not trying to force you to sell your shares. This is a letter for the FBI. They called you.'

'How do you know?'

'Because I took your phone.'

Her eyes widen.

'From your bag in the helicopter. I didn't want you sitting in your room, doom-scrolling through photo after photo on your own. When they called, I said you were resting and that you would call back. They made a few threatening noises, but I got my lawyers onto them, and they backed off. While you were sleeping, we drafted this letter.'

She watches me warily as I hold out the laptop. After a moment, she takes it, and I watch her eyes as they scan the document. 'This is the latest draft but it's not definitive. If you don't like the wording, we can change it. All that matters is that we make it clear that you aren't obstructing justice. I saw how shocked you were to find out that Jade is in touch with Charlie,' I add, because it matters to me that she knows that.

Her hands tighten around my laptop, the knuckles whitening in the sunlight.

'When did you last speak to your mother?' I say, gentling my voice. 'You don't need to know the exact day.'

There is a pause, and if I didn't know better, I might think she is scanning her memories, only for some reason I know that this memory is one she wants to shake off.

'But I do know.'

She gives me a small, twisted smile. 'It was that day in Vegas. You know, when…' She hesitates. 'Sorry, to bring it up, but that was the last time I saw or spoke to her.'

I don't know what shocks me more—the fact that she hasn't had contact with her mother for over three years or the careless tone of her voice. It's the same one she used when she was getting expelled. It's designed to provoke, to distract, I realise suddenly. In the past, I got provoked and distracted, but now I focus on her face, and I see that she is close to tears.

'But that would be three years ago.' I choose my words carefully, because there is tension to her now, almost a hostility, that feels deep rooted, as if I have stumbled across an archaeological dig.

'What?' She glances away, shrugs. 'It's only three years. That's short compared to the last time.'

'How long was that?'

She turns then, and her smile twists a little tighter. 'Nineteen.'

My heart jolts. That can't be right. 'But you used to spend weekends with her. I remember Antony telling me—'

'I lied to him.' The violet of her irises is lost in the sunlight, but her jaw and hands are clenched tight. 'I didn't want him to know that she didn't want me.'

I'm still trying to get my brain to restart. 'So where did you go?'

'Sometimes I went home. Sometimes, I'd book into a hotel.'

'You weren't old enough.'

She looks at me pityingly. 'It's not that hard. I'd pretend to be Charlie's PA. Book a room for the two of us, and then turn up and say he was delayed. It wasn't hard to convince people. He's not exactly reliable.'

I remember a day when she had been left sitting at school and I had taken her home. The memory is like a punch to the throat.

'So, you were three when she left?'

'I was exactly three. It was my birthday—another memorable day. She left at some point between pass-the-parcel and me blowing out the candles. And she never came back. My dad dumped me on his mother and then she died a year later, and Charlie had to take me.'

Had to—not wanted to or chose to.

'And you didn't see Jade again until Vegas?'

'It was supposed to be our big reunion. She contacted me out of the blue. Said she wanted to get to know me.'

After nineteen years? My head is spinning.

'That must have been nerve-wracking.'

She nods slowly. 'I was terrified, but I was still drinking then, so that helped. I went to her hotel and at first it was fine. Then she started talking about my birthday and what kind of party I wanted, just as if she had forgotten leaving me on my birthday. And then I realised that she had.'

There is a shake to her voice now, and I want to reach out and take her hands in mine and steady her, but I don't want to do anything that might stop her talking.

'Because it didn't matter. This huge moment in my childhood meant nothing to her.'

'Or maybe she felt so guilty she buried the memory. I mean, she reached out to you.' I don't believe that, but I will say and do anything to take the ache from her voice.

Something flares in her eyes. She shakes her head, and it is the saddest thing I have ever seen. 'I was going to inherit some money from my maternal grandmother on my birthday. That's why she reached out. She got cut out of the will when she married Charlie, so she thought I owed her.'

Now I reach out and lightly touch the back of her hand and she lets out a shaky breath. 'I refused to give her anything. And then she screamed at me. She said I was spoiled and ungrateful. That I ruined her life. That I was the biggest mistake she'd ever made, and then...'

My ribs are squeezing my lungs so tightly that breathing is hard, painful. *And then I bumped into you and gave you a piece of my mind.* A savage deconstruction of her personality largely driven by anger at my own lack of control.

She is crying, and I take the laptop from her fingers and toss it onto the sand and pull her against me. We've only been this close twice, and on both occasions it has led to some kind of physical intimacy. But this is different. There are no sexual undertones, and it feels all the more dangerous for that. But I want, I need, to comfort her.

'You didn't ruin anything. You were a baby. Your parents were both adults. That makes them responsible.' I lift her face and smooth my thumbs over her cheeks.

'She never wanted me.'

'That doesn't make you a mistake, Hennessy. It makes

you unplanned. Penicillin was unplanned. Columbus dis-covered America while he was trying to find a route to Asia.' I lean in and kiss her forehead.

'You're not a mistake. You're a marvel. A miracle.'

She breathes in jerkily. 'I'm sorry, I don't usually cry.'

I feel a gut-wrenching sadness at the unsaid part of that sentence because I know she is telling the truth, and I know why she doesn't cry—there would be no point. On a shallower note, I am stupidly pleased that she let herself cry in front of me.

'You have nothing to apologize for.'

Her eyes find mine. The lashes are still wet, and her irises look smudged. 'You don't regret me coming to Milan with you?'

'No, I absolutely don't regret coming with you to Milan as your back-up singer.'

She bites into a smile. 'Don't do that—don't make me laugh.'

'But I like making you laugh.' I touch the corners of her mouth. 'I like watching you smile.'

'There hasn't been much to smile about over the last few days.'

'I disagree. You went into the ring for Wade and Wal-ters. You did something pivotal, and you should be proud of yourself. I'm proud of you.'

Her eyes hold mine a second and then she reaches out and touches my jaw, her fingertips grazing the shadow of stubble. 'You know, you're nice. Nicer than you let on. Nicer than I thought.'

For a second we both stare at one another. Her be-musedly, as if I have shapeshifted from beast to prince. Me guiltily, because my thoughts are not nice. They are raw and inappropriate.

'I should probably get out of this dress.'

We are so close, she feels my body stiffen. I feel hers do the same. There is another quiver of silence that makes me think of bare skin and her eyes rolling back in her head…and then I come to my senses.

Or, more accurately, I block my senses and say gruffly, 'Good idea. Let me get my laptop, and then I'll knock us up some food.'

'You're cooking?' she asks as we walk onto the terrace.

'It's been quite a full-on week. I thought we could both do with a quiet night in without having to talk to anyone else, so I gave the staff the night off. I was thinking of doing fresh pasta. You can help me. I'll try not to mansplain.'

'Yes, chef.' She bites into her lip, and I slip a leash onto the heat building inside me as we walk into the villa. 'But, that'll be the second time you've cooked for me. I can't do that to you.'

We walk into the sitting room. I put down my laptop on one of the small tables dotted around the room.

'You can do anything you want to me,' I say without thinking.

There is a stuttering beat of silence. Behind us, the sky is a ravishing swirl of pink, gold and amber, but I barely register it. All my attention is focused on Hennessy's small, still face.

'Anything I want,' she repeats slowly, the words pulsing between us.

I clear my throat—try to clear my throat—but my voice sounds scratchy and rough-edged, as if it is scraping over sandpaper. 'Anything at all.'

The shadows in the room are turning the colour of her eyes. She keeps staring at me and then her gaze sharpens into something so intent that I momentarily lose my bearings. She leans in and kisses me on the mouth, softly, and I feel the tip of her tongue snake over my lips.

'So, I can kiss you like this…'

Her words vibrate through my skin and my breath catches as her scent climbs into my head and I nod against her mouth.

'And I can touch you like this…'

Her hands move over my stomach, pulling at my shirt buttons, and my hands move automatically to her waist.

'No.' She pushes them away. 'I want to undress you.' Her fingers go back to the buttons but now her mouth moves to nuzzle my throat, grazing it with her teeth and I press my hands against my thighs to stop myself from pulling her closer and taking what I want.

My shirt is undone, and she drags it down my arms, lowers her mouth to my chest and kisses me softly, then licks around the nipples until I groan. My heart is raging. Heat is drifting up and over my body. Not being able to touch her is both accelerating my pleasure and causing me pain, actual pain. I don't think I've ever been this hard.

'Can we get naked now?'

Her question sharpens my hunger and everything—my muscles, my skin, my nerve endings; everything in me that beats and breathes—tenses and stretches towards her. And now I reach for her, my fingers pulling clumsily at the straps of her dress. Because I am clumsy with desire. Eager. Greedy. Just like in New York. But that was like a dam breaking. It was fast and febrile, and it worked in the moment, but this time I want to savour her.

But first I want her naked. She wants that too. She is pulling at her dress, pushing it down over her hips, taking her panties with it, and I lose the ability to breathe.

All I can do is stare, because no memory does justice to the reality of Hennessy in the flesh. I dip my head and suck one nipple, swirl my tongue over the soft point until it hardens, and then I lick a path to the other, grazing it with my teeth, feeling her shudder.

She pushes me away, her hands fumbling for my belt, and my breath staggers from my mouth in time to hers as she unzips me. I step out of my trousers, my heartbeat thundering in my ears. We are both naked now, inches apart, with nothing between us but a sliver of air.

'Renzo…' My name in her mouth sends shivers over my skin. Has my name ever sounded that good?

Her pupils are huge. There is feverishness to her, and I try to steady her with my hand, to slow things down, but she curls her arm round my neck and I lift her onto the sofa, scattering the cushions so that I can lie her flat. I stare down at her, my nerve endings twitching as if I am touching an electric current.

'You're beautiful,' I say, and my breath catches as she reaches down and takes my cock in her hand. Her fingers move up the shaft to smooth the straining head, and the roar in my ears gets louder.

I bat her hand away, but she is insistent. There is urgency to her touch, and I try to still my senses because I'm not going to last. But then she pushes her body up to meet mine and I am suddenly close to the summit, grasping at her hip.

'Hennessy!' I grunt her name, choking on the middle consonants, my breath hot and slippery. I clasp the edge of the sofa for balance, and I thrust upwards, nipping her throat, my heartbeat punching against her breasts as I surge inside her; my body stuttering convulsively with the force of a volcanic eruption.

I am barely human. The noises I am making belong to something undomesticated. I want to lick her all over, to give her the same pleasure she is giving me, and I pull back, wincing as the cool air hits my overheated cock. Lifting her legs, I press the flat of my tongue between her thighs.

'Yes, yes...'

But something is happening. She is making almost the same noises as before, yet it isn't the same. There is something performative about it, and there is tension to her limbs. I slow, but she grabs my head and I start to lick but I feel it again—tension—as if she is bracing herself. Only not for pleasure. This feels as if she is bracing for some kind of exposure.

She starts to arch, lunging towards my mouth, moaning. I feel her body stiffen and she gasps, her fingers biting into my shoulder.

I lift my head to where Hennessy is breathing unsteadily. Her pupils are huge and dark, only not with passion but panic. It doesn't make sense, or maybe I just don't want it to be true, but I think she just faked her orgasm.

CHAPTER EIGHT

Hennessy

IT IS HARD to swallow, to breathe. My throat is full of panic, despair and regret. Because I shouldn't have let this happen. I should have known that last time was an anomaly, a one-off miracle, a fire caused by a lightning strike. I was greedy when I should have been satisfied with the memory of that one perfect night in New York.

But I thought I was cured. Of course, I was kidding myself. There is no cure. I can tell myself that I relaxed my guard too early—or not early enough. But the truth is I don't know what it is that lets in that slippery, suffocating panic. All I know is that it creeps in, under my skin, blotting out my heartbeat, stifling my breath…and the weight of it is pressing down on me.

'I need to move,' I say, and I push my hands against his chest, letting my hair fall in front of my face as he shifts his weight. 'I've got a cramp in my leg,' I lie, rubbing my calf.

'I can do that,' he says, and he starts to massage my leg, but the firm press of his fingers makes my lungs seize up. He can never know that I faked it.

His other hand moves against my hip, a caress that I want to reciprocate but can't, because then he will see that I am a fraud. That I am damaged, incomplete, a letdown. And I don't know why that would feel like the worst thing. I only know that it would be. Worse even than him finding out that I have spent most of my life feeling like a stray cat. So, I need to confuse what is happening now.

'It's fine. I just need to stand on it.' I edge backwards to a kneeling position and then get to my feet, still avoiding his gaze. 'And I need to get up anyway.'

'You do?' His gaze is like a tangible thing, and I want to push it away with my hand, but instead I start to pick up my clothes.

'I want to go to bed. My bed.'

I can feel the pounding of my heart. For a moment he doesn't speak but I can sense his confusion, his disbelief. But then this has probably never happened to him before.

'Of course, if that's what you want.'

It isn't.

It is.

It's both. But to explain why would be too complicated, too unbearable.

'I think it would be a good idea.' I pull the dress over my head. 'I'm not saying it wasn't fun—it was—I just think we don't need this complication.'

His gaze moves over me. Is he relieved? Angry? Indifferent? I don't know and I can't let myself care.

'I'll see you in the morning.' Snatching up my clothes, I walk swiftly out of the living room. As soon as I reach the hallway, I practically sprint up the stairs and into my bedroom. I close the door and press my hand against my throat and the ache that is building there.

I thought it was going to be okay. That I was okay.

And it was, at the start. It wasn't a performance. My

hunger was real. The noises I made, the pulse between my thighs, all of it was real. I felt powerful, alive and demanding. But then he changed tempo, slowing things down, changing position, moving on top of me—and all that power and hunger just evaporated.

There is no lock on the door, but it doesn't matter. I won't be sleeping in the bedroom anyway.

Now I am on autopilot. I have a routine, and I snatch Albert from my bag, pick up the top and shorts I sleep in and a pillow from the bed. I have a momentary panic when I can't find my phone, but I will just have to wing it.

I lock the door. My heart is still thumping against the confines of my ribs, but I strip off, ignoring my reflection, and wrap the bath robe around my body, swaddling myself. If only there was someone out there for me. Someone who would *see* me and still hold me close. For a few seconds downstairs, I thought it might be Renzo, that together we might have cracked this paralysis that comes over me. But I can't tell him. I can't tell anyone. What would be the point? He could have any woman in the world. Why would he ever want a woman like me?

I sleep badly, even for me, jerking awake multiple times throughout the night. At some point dawn starts to creep into the room. I get up and switch off the bathroom lights, then I fall into a deep, dreamless sleep.

It has gone ten when I wake. My shoulders tense as I open the door, but the bedroom is empty, and I do my usual trick of pulling back the duvet and thumping the pillows to make a head-shaped indent.

Finally, I go downstairs and breezily greet Paola.

'*Buongiorno.*'

'*Buongiorno,* Signorina Wade. I can bring coffee and

cornetto to the terrace. Signor Valetti asked me to tell you that he will see you for lunch.'

I feel relief and a sting of rejection, which is stupid and irrational, because I pushed him away. But at least it will give me longer to get my game face on.

Breakfast revives me, and I ask Paola if she has seen my phone. She hasn't, but I can't face looking for it right now, not if it means going into the living room and re-playing what happened yesterday. Besides, all I would do is end up scrolling through all the negative stories with the word 'Wade' in the headline.

Instead, I wander round the garden. There are little brick archways and rough-edged paths that remind me of my grandmother's garden in New York, and there's a tree with wide, flat branches that looks like the perfect place to hide from the world—or, more specifically, Renzo.

I pull myself up onto the lowest branch and hunker down against the warm bark. What would have happened if I'd stayed living with her? Would my life have been different? Would I have finished school and gone to uni-versity? Would I have had normal relationships because I wouldn't have been carrying around this unwieldy mess of fear and doubt that makes it so hard for me to let peo-ple get close?

'Hennessy?'

Renzo is frowning up at me through the leaves. My body tenses for a variety of reasons I choose to ignore, but he looks so beautiful with the sunlight gilding his face that I can't help but stare at him.

'What are you doing?'

'I wanted to see if I could still climb trees.'

'Clearly you can, so perhaps you could come down.'

There is an edge to his voice, and I want it to be concern, but it's probably irritation given that every single day he has to clear up a mess made by one or more members of the Wade family. Hopefully he isn't going to bring up yesterday's encounter on the sofa. I climb down slowly, feeling his gaze on my back.

'I thought we could go and grab some lunch. There's a restaurant I like in Praiano. It's only five minutes away in the car.'

He wants to do what…? My relief that we aren't going to discuss last night is forgotten as I gaze up at him in confusion.

'I don't understand. Aren't we trying to stay off-grid? Isn't that why we came here?'

'We came here because I thought you needed some time away from the spotlight.' He hesitates. 'Back in Milan, I know it must have seemed that I was angry with you. But I was angry *for* you. The party was a triumph. I didn't want all your hard work or your sleep to be wrecked by one stupid photo.'

Reaching into his pocket, he pulls out my phone and holds it out. 'I didn't want you torturing yourself. Obviously, that photo of your parents hasn't disappeared entirely, but there's a hurricane brewing off Florida, so they've been relegated to a couple of paragraphs. I thought we might celebrate at a quiet little restaurant I know that just so happens to serve world-class food…'

Cantina Caterina is very small, so small that I think we have mistakenly wandered into someone's front room.

'Don't worry,' Renzo says as we walk to our table. 'The clientele are local people. If you don't grow up in Praiano then you are irrelevant. Plus, I'm pretty sure most of them still use landlines, not smart phones.'

Renzo is clearly relevant. As we walk through the tiny restaurant, the two waitresses trip over themselves to welcome him and the other diners get to their feet and greet him warmly. But as soon as we take our seats everyone returns their attention to their food.

Which is understandable, I think a little later, putting down my cutlery after finishing what has to have been the most delicious home-made ricotta I've ever eaten.

'Is everything to your satisfaction, Signor Valetti?' the waitress asks as she takes away our plates. She glances at me but seems dazzled by Renzo.

'Yes, thank you, Monica.'

'You know her name? You must come here a lot, and tip large—or is there some other reason that she's being so nice to you? Because I'm famous—infamous, some might say—and she's only got eyes for you.'

'And that bothers you?' He sounds amused but there is an intensity to his gaze that makes me feel agitated.

'No,' I say quickly, too quickly. He smiles now, and I'm not just agitated but adrift, because Renzo's smile feels like the sun breaking through the clouds after a storm.

'Okay, maybe it does a little.' I pinch the grissini he is holding to hide my reaction. 'But it's not often my star power gets eclipsed.'

'Your star power could light up the whole of Italy,' he says, snatching back his grissini. 'And the reason the staff here are so attentive to me is because I own the restaurant.'

Of course he does. Because this is his world. The rest of us are just living in it. Leaning back in my seat, I shake my head. 'So, this is your restaurant. And we're staying in another of your properties, and we flew here in your helicopter. Do you ever let anyone else call the shots?'

'Not often. Although there is this one woman…' I feel a blistering rush of dizziness as his eyes lock onto mine. 'When I'm with her I'm more than happy to get down on my knees.'

We stare at one another for what feels like centuries in a silence that is only broken by the return of Monica bringing us our mains.

Calamarata with squid, white wine, chilli and pistachio follows, and for dessert we share a *cremosa al cioccolato* that has such an intense hit of dark chocolate, it makes my hands shake.

'How is this place not more famous?'

Renzo shrugs. 'Emanuele isn't a trophy hunter. He likes to cook for people who love food, not for food critics. I share his view.'

'It's lucky your paths crossed.' My eyes dance over his beautiful, sculpted face. It's lucky for anyone to cross paths with Renzo.

'Luck didn't have anything to do with it.' He hesitates, as if he is weighing something up. 'We went to the same *scuola materna*. My mum was friends with his mum. Our dads played bocce—you know, bowls?—together.' He frowns. 'Why are you looking at me like that?'

Why? Because this is not a side of Renzo I've seen before. When I was younger, he was Antony's dismissive older brother and my unrequited crush. After I got Antony expelled, he acted like judge, jury and would-be executioner. Then there was Vegas.

All different sides of the same man, but he's always been so intense, mythic almost, in his extremes. This is the first time I can imagine him as having any kind of normal life, and frankly I am fascinated.

'So that's why you bought the restaurant here? This

is where you grew up? But Antony never said anything about living in Italy.'

'Because he didn't. I did. We moved to New York when I was six years old.'

'Why did you move?'

'My parents wanted a better life and my father's cousin ran a bakery in New Jersey. When he offered my father a job as a delivery driver, they thought it would be a new start.'

'Like being a pioneer.'

'I suppose so.'

I suck the spoon into my mouth, relishing the smoothness of the chocolate. 'Did you miss Italy?'

'I did. We didn't have much money, but everyone knows everyone here, so you feel like you matter. It was a big adjustment.'

'You did a good job of adjusting.'

'In the end,' he says cryptically. I want to ask him what that means, but before I can ask, Renzo does one of those tiny tilts of his head that has the waitress cantering to his side.

'One double espresso, please. And could we have another *cremosa*?' he says, ignoring my protests. 'Enjoy it. It's the only time I've seen you eat properly.'

The blue of his eyes is like a wave lapping over my skin. This sounds stupid coming from someone whose face is plastered all over the Internet, but I feel seen for the first time.

'Eating is a bit of a challenge,' I admit after a moment. 'I know it sounds crazy, but it's taken me a long time to get used to eating without alcohol.'

'Not crazy at all. Eating is a social activity. For a lot of people, that means having a drink.'

'It's the restaurants too. They're always sneaking Bloody Marys into their brunch menus. It just makes it hard sometimes to stay focused, to stay sober. It doesn't help that most of the people I used to know are not that thoughtful.' I glance at the water glass in his hand. 'I'm guessing you're not drinking on my account.'

He blinks as if he has forgotten we are in the middle of a conversation.

'I'm not going to put temptation in your path.'

Not true, I think, gazing across the table. But then I remember the mess I made of last night, and I blank my mind to how tempting he is.

'Thank you. It's a bit of a bore for you, though. I mean, this is your day off too, and you can't even have a drink to relax. You have been programmed to relax, haven't you?'

His mouth pulls infinitesimally at the corners into a shape that makes me feel as if gravity has failed. 'I do relax. And no time spent with you is boring, Hennessy.'

'But you like boring.'

'When I choose suits or cars. But I enjoy being stimulated.' As he puts down his glass, it catches the side plate, and it must be that I can feel resonating through my body.

'Take it from me, it's overrated. But at least chocolate is still on the menu.' I tap the spoon against my teeth and his blue gaze flicks to my lips and stays there for a beat too long.

Given that we have nothing in common but work and Antony, I expect our conversation to lull at some point into an awkward silence, but it doesn't. We talk about food, films and the history of Italy. Renzo is intelligent and informed but not opinionated or overbearing. He also makes me laugh. I can't remember the last time I properly laughed.

After lunch is over, we drive back along the twisting coastal road and fall silent, but that's fine too, because it is my first experience of a comfortable silence.

Renzo focuses on the road, and I stare at the sea. It's easy to imagine sailors losing their heart to the Tyrrhenian but, despite its coruscating beauty, I find my gaze keeps returning to my left and, more specifically, to Renzo's brooding profile.

In the end. His words echo inside my head. They don't make sense. He is only thirty-four now and he is one of the richest people on the planet. How could he have done anything sooner or better?

'So, random question.' I turn towards him. 'Why didn't you want to go into the family business—the bakery?' I add after a moment when he doesn't reply. 'The hat is a bit of an ask, but I can really see you kneading bread. That's kind of your thing, isn't it—knocking things into shape?'

After our new easiness over lunch, I glance over, expecting to find Renzo fighting a smile, or better still smiling. Instead, he is staring at the road, his face expressionless, and there is a tension to his shoulders that wasn't there before, as if something is weighing heavily.

'It closed. My father's cousin retired, and my father died. And then my mother died six months later.'

My face is stiff, and I know I must look as shocked as I feel. But I didn't even know his parents were dead. Antony and I never talk about our families. I thought he was being sensitive, because he could see how unhappy I was, and I was so grateful it never occurred to me that there might be another, darker reason for his reticence.

'I'm so sorry. That must have been awful. When was that? I mean, how old were you?'

'Eleven. Antony was two. We ended up in care. We

had eight foster homes together. When I left the children's home, Antony was fostered with another family for nearly three years until I became his guardian when I was nineteen.'

'I thought you went to university.'

'I did. As a mature student. Before that, I worked multiple jobs. I wanted Antony to go to a good school. That isn't a dig, by the way, it's just how I felt. I can see now that it wasn't the best place for him, but I needed him to board so that I could get my degree.'

I stare at his profile. In other words, when he said that everything he'd done was for Antony, he was telling the truth. My words echo inside my head, the accusations jarring and shaming and, biting my lip, I meet his gaze. 'I'm so sorry—for what I said before about you not listening.'

'I said plenty myself. Most of which was inaccurate. All of which I regret.'

'I was not unprovoking,' I say carefully.

He laughs, a proper laugh that rumbles across the car and through my body. 'You were. But I enjoyed not being unprovoked.'

The improbability of this conversation occupies my mind for several more twists of the road. That and watching Renzo drive. Like everything else he does, he drives with focus and care, shifting through the gears as we follow the winding road that hugs the curving cliffs.

For a moment I follow his hands as they slide minutely over the steering wheel, remembering the way they moved over my body to such devastating effect. I want to feel his hands on me again but it's not that simple. I've tried. In the past, with my previous two boyfriends, I persevered unsuccessfully, and I can't go there with Renzo. I just have to accept that first time with him was a one-off, sublime, singular conflation of delayed gratification and explosive need. It was sensual, powerful and unbelievably erotic, and I don't want to turn the memory of that into something ugly. Not when he has given me this day of such sweet normality.

'Thank you for dragging me out of the villa. You were right; I would have just sat around brooding. It was kind of you to distract me.'

'Careful, Hennessy. That sounds almost like a compliment.'

It's on the tip of my tongue to make a joke but for some reason I say instead, 'It is a compliment. You are kind. You looked out for me, even though you hate me.'

'I don't hate you.'

'Okay, not hate, just dislike.'

'I don't dislike you.' His voice is suddenly hoarse, and his hands tighten around the wheel.

'I don't dislike you either.'

There is a silence full of something that feels both meaningful and confusing, and I glance away from his profile towards the sea and the most unbearably romantic sunset I have ever seen.

'Oh, look at that…'

Renzo turns to look at the sky, and I look over at him so that I can watch his reaction, and that's when it happens. One moment there is a moped puttering along on the other side of the road, the next a car is overtaking it, sliding inexorably across the white lines and onto our side of the carriageway.

For a few seconds, it feels as if there will be no escape. We must hit the other car. My seatbelt is taut across my chest, and I catch a glimpse of the driver's face: young, male and petrified. Then Renzo is turning the wheel, and we are on the side of the road, just inches from the crash barrier, the car shuddering around us.

It's only then that I realise it's not my seatbelt that is gripping me fast but Renzo's arm. His fingers are splayed around my shoulder, and I can feel the muscles in his arm flexing against my collarbone.

'Sorry.'

'For what?' His voice sounds as if it is scraping across a box grater, and his eyes are moving rapidly over my face and down my body. 'I'm the driver.'

'Yes, but I distracted you.'

Abruptly he lifts his arm, and I feel the absence of his warmth and strength as if my own arm has been amputated.

'You need to stop doing that. Stop taking the blame for things that other people do.' He breathes in sharply. 'Are you okay?

My heart is pounding, and I manage to nod. 'I'm good.'

The rest of the drive is uneventful. Back at the villa, I follow Renzo into the hallway. Paola comes out to greet us and I make my way up to my room. My legs feel shaky—partly from the near miss on the road but also because of what happened before and afterwards: the two of us eating and talking together; Renzo's arm across my body, shielding me, protecting me, that hoarseness to his voice as he said, 'I don't dislike you.'

I press my hand against my shoulder, seeking out the place that still glows with the imprint of his hand when there is a knock behind me, and I turn to find Renzo standing in the doorway. 'I told Paola what happened in the car, and she suggested this tea.' He puts a tray down on the table.

'Thank you.'

His gaze moves to where my fingers are curled over the top of my arm. 'Is it okay?'

'I'm fine. Truly, I am.'

He nods, turns slightly and then stops, hesitating, as if he has forgotten something. Or remembered it. 'Did I scare you?'

'No. I mean, it was a bit scary, but you were great.'

'I wasn't talking about what happened in the car.' Renzo's dark-blue gaze is steady on my face, and there is something in his eyes that shimmers through my body, a softness, that momentarily lulls me into thinking that everything is okay.

And then quite suddenly it isn't.

'I was talking about what happened last night. Downstairs. On the sofa...' His voice is gentle, but it sears me anyway.

My breath shudders through me like a train hitting the buffers. I stare across the room at him, feeling his words crowd out the air as I picture the moment when my body started to lock down.

I try to reach for anger, partly because anger is always distracting, and partly because I am angry with him. This is his fault. Normally I am so careful. But I haven't been policing myself the way I should. Otherwise, I would never have thought that a man as sober and sexually experienced as Renzo Valetti would be fooled by my theatrics.

I can't look at him, but I know he is looking at me, seeing me, and I feel so ugly.

'I thought... I felt...' He frowns. 'You seemed scared for a moment.'

I shake my head, and now my legs are trembling so much I have to sit down. 'It's not your fault. You didn't scare me.'

Renzo

It hurts, watching her sit down jerkily on the bed like that, like a puppet whose strings have been cut. Suddenly she looks exhausted, but then I think she was up in the night. I was up too, walking in the garden, staring up at her windows, replaying that moment in my head when her body stiffened beneath my tongue. I tried to stop, to pull away, but she kept pulling me back, so I went along with it.

And now I can't stop thinking about her body tensing and then her stumbling from the room, fleeing from me like a witness to a crime. I should have gone after her. The only reason I didn't was because it felt predatory, and I was worried she might run. Worried she might do something reckless.

Because of me.

My heart feels heavy and misshapen. I could have stopped her easily. I could have cross-examined her. It wouldn't be the first time I've donned my metaphorical wig and gown and subjected her to an inquisition, because Hennessy represents the turmoil and lack of control that so nearly pulled my brother and I apart after our parents died—the feeling of powerlessness, all the foster families, children's homes and then, most terrifyingly of all, being homeless, penniless and alone at the age of eighteen.

I need to be in control, but Hennessy doesn't just press my buttons, she can strip me naked with a glance. And all I want is to strip her naked too; everything else is just background noise. So, pinning her down, containing her, always felt necessary and justified.

Now, though, it feels closer to pinning a butterfly in a

specimen case. I glance over to where she is sitting on the bed. She looks stunned and scared. So I do what I should have done last night. I walk over to the bed and kneel in front of her, close enough to touch but not touching.

'But someone did?' I am treading carefully. She looks so brittle and, when she nods, I am terrified she will splinter into a thousand pieces.

'Who hurt you?'

'It wasn't like that. He didn't do anything.' The ache in her voice makes me want to uproot trees, raze buildings to the ground. 'But I was on my own, and I woke up and he was there. In my bedroom.' She presses her hand against her mouth and now I touch her, pulling her into my arms, close enough that I can feel her heart punching unevenly against her ribs, my ribs.

I press my lips against her hair and tell her over and over that everything will be okay. On one level it is meaningless babble designed to offer comfort, but I mean every word. At some point, she shudders against my chest, and I reach into my trousers and hand her a handkerchief. She stares at it for a moment and then wipes her face.

'When did this happen?'

'When I was nine.'

My pulse misses a beat. Nine? I was expecting her to say sixteen or something. But nine? In my entire life I've never felt this way. This feeling is new, unknown. All I know is that it is as intense as pain, brighter than fury and so powerful my skin can hardly contain it.

'Charlie took me to some party, and it was really loud. I started being whiny, and he hates that. He told me to go to bed, and Katie—that was his girlfriend—she took me upstairs and put me in her room, and I was so tired I fell asleep.' I feel her body stiffen. 'But then I woke up and there was this man sitting on my bed. Just sitting, staring at me, and then he tucked the bedding around me tightly so I couldn't move.' She breathes out shakily. 'I wanted to scream but my voice wouldn't work.'

I pull her closer.

'And he didn't…?'

'No. Katie came up to check on me and she put the lights on… She went crazy. She was shouting and the man left. And then Charlie was there, and she was calling him all these names, and he kept saying I'd probably just had a bad dream.'

In other words, he gaslit a nine-year-old.

'I don't think about it most of the time but sometimes it just creeps into my head.'

'Like when you have sex.'

She flinches, then nods.

'The first time, I thought I got panicky because it was my first time. But then it happened again, and it kept happening, and I got so anxious. That's when I started to pretend.' I hear her swallow. 'That makes it sound like I've done it with loads of men, but I've only properly slept with three, including you. All the rest, the ones you see me with in photos, just make stuff up and everyone believes them.'

The tendons on my hands pull tight. *Including me.*

'So, you fake it?'

'Always.' She nods. 'Except that one time in New York with you.' There is a flush of colour on her cheeks.

'And Vegas? Was that kiss real?'

She nods again slowly. 'It was. I'd never felt like that with anyone. I was all churned up after seeing Jade, but then I met you, and I felt safe. I knew you'd never let it go too far. Because you're you. You're not like those other men.'

That nameless feeling is swamping me again. 'Those men—and the people that take those photographs and write the stories that go with them, and the people that look at those photos and read those stories—they're all irrelevant.'

She gives me a watery smile. 'Because they don't come from Praiano.'

'Because they don't know you. They don't see past the headlines. But I do. Listen to me, Hennessy—something terrifying happened to you that you couldn't control.' I understand what it feels like to be that vulnerable, that scared, that alone. But this isn't about me. This is about Hennessy, making her feel safe, feel safer.

'What happened last night, what's happened before, that's your body trying to protect you. And you did the right thing last night, going to your room, getting somewhere safe.'

Safe. I have a sudden, vivid memory of that safe room in her apartment. 'That's why you sleep in the panic room, isn't it?' I say gently.

Her eyes widen. 'How do you know about that?'

'The door was ajar. I didn't go in.' I don't want her to feel that her safe space was violated.

'After it happened, I couldn't sleep. I kept waking up every night screaming, and in the end, Charlie got a panic room fitted in the house.'

'And that helps.'

She nods. 'It changed my life. That's why I bought my apartment—because of the panic room. And Sam. He used to work for Charlie.'

I think back to all the places where she's needed to

sleep without her safe space. 'So how did you manage in my apartment? And Milan and here?'

Her eyes find mine. 'I sleep in the bathroom. It's fine, really. I can catch up when I get home. My home, I mean.'

'What about when you stayed over in my room? Did you sleep then?' I thought she had. When I woke in the night, she seemed peaceful, but...

She nods slowly. 'I did, yes. But that was something of an eventful day.'

I reach out and touch her face. 'You make every day an event.'

'Today was pretty quiet.'

I frown. 'I nearly crashed the car.'

'I still had the best time.'

'I did too.' And I don't know what stuns me more— that I am telling the truth or that she is.

We talk some more, then Hennessy starts to yawn, and we lie down and talk a little more, and at some point, we must have fallen asleep, because I wake up eight hours later, still fully clothed.

The bed is empty, but I can hear the shower running and I wonder how she slept. But mostly I wonder how I have managed to misjudge her so badly. My body feels sodden with guilt at having been so narrow and lazy in my thinking. And I am angry—with Charlie for being so negligent and Jade for being absent. With the world for treating her as a character in a telenovela. And with myself for not protecting her.

I picture the near miss in the car and how I threw my arm in front of her. It was too little, too late. Thinking of her waking in that room with a stranger sitting on her bed makes my hands ache.

'Hi.'

Hennessy is standing in the doorway to the bathroom. She is wrapped in an identical bath robe to mine. She looks better in hers.

'Hi. How are you? Did you sleep okay?'

She nods, and I feel a ridiculous sense of satisfaction. 'That's good. You look…'

Beautiful. Sexy. And off-limits.

'Rested.'

'I feel it. I feel… I don't know what I feel. But it feels good.'

For no reason at all, my pulse twitches. 'I'll let you get dressed.'

I get to my feet and make to move past her, but she moves at the same time so that we almost bump into one another. I feel light-headed with her nearness, so light-headed that I don't get it then. I don't even get it when it happens a second time.

I don't get it until she takes my hand, and even then, I hesitate.

'Hennessy…'

Now she lets go of my hand and tugs at the belt of her bath robe, and I watch as it slides down her body. And just like that she is naked.

CHAPTER NINE

Renzo

WE STARE AT one another in silence that pulses through me like a drum roll. My mind is racing, tumbling over itself like a dog getting tangled up in its lead before a walk. I'm incapable of rational thought.

'What is it?' she says hoarsely. 'Don't you want me?'

I laugh then because I am literally made of wanting. Every fibre of my being is shivering with a hunger that shocks me with its intensity.

'Yes, I want you, but I don't want to take advantage of you.' What I want is to smooth out those two pinching lines between her eyebrows and tell her that the men she'd been with were crap in bed. That sex requires trust, and she can trust me.

'What if I want to take advantage of you?'

She looks at me as she speaks, and I don't know which is more intoxicating—the boldness of that statement or her naked body.

'You made it work before. Made me work.'

There is something lost in her voice, a mix of hope and trust that roughens my voice. 'You do work, *tesoro.*' I glance down at her curving breasts and the flare of her hips. She is a work of art.

Her eyes find mine and I can't help myself. I reach out and smooth that crease between her eyebrows, then run my knuckles against her cheekbone.

'I don't want to fake it with you. I want it to be like the first time.'

My blood thuds in my veins. 'I want that too.'

As she nods, I slide my hand through her hair, pull her closer and kiss her softly on the mouth. My whole life I've wanted, needed, to be in control. Particularly with this woman. But now I want to be her servant. I want to do anything, everything, she wants. I want to give her control and it's a different, new kind of pleasure to know that she wants me, trusts me to do that.

'Tell me what you like. Or, if you can't tell me, show me, and we'll take it from there,' I whisper against her throat, and she reaches for my shirt and pulls it up over my head. Her hands move over my stomach and chest as I tease the upper bow of her lip with my tongue.

We kiss back and forth, softly then deeply, and it's like sipping fine wine. Then she tugs at the top button of my trousers and after a short struggle they join my shirt on the floor.

'You do want me,' she says. I stare down at where my erection is pushing up through the waistband of my trunks and I nod, close the distance between our mouths and let her taste my hunger.

'Okay?' I ask as I feel her shiver.

'Cold.' She bites her lip. 'A bit nervous, maybe.'

'We can just kiss. Or we don't even have to do that. We can figure it out…and you can change your mind, Hennessy. Any time.'

'I haven't. Have you?' Her mouth is trembling slightly, maybe from desire, nerves or both, and for a few half-seconds I try to imagine a world where I would change my mind and get dressed and walk away from Hennessy. And then I shake my head slowly, deliberately, so that there can be no confusion.

My breath punches past my 'No,' as she drops to her knees and presses her lips lightly against the length of my cock, and I reach out to steady myself as she takes the head in her mouth. Her hands are moving over my thighs as she draws down my underwear. The touch of her fingertips, combined with the warmth of her mouth and the sounds she makes as she licks me, make me shake inside.

I grunt as she pulls back. I pull her to her feet, and we kiss the same way as before, back and forth, softer then deeper.

'Can we try something else?' There is a rasp to her voice and her breath is hot against my mouth. I kiss her hungrily. 'Tell me. Show me. I want to learn what you like, what you want. I want to learn you…'

She takes a step back, rests her hands on the top of the dressing table and spreads her legs slightly. I drop to my knees, and I kiss her softly between her thighs. Her hand stiffens against my head, and I wait, wait for her fingers to soften, then I lift my chin and anchor my mouth to her slick heat.

She is breathing scratchily, and her body is trembling, vibrating like a telegraph wire. I taste the salt as I lick her. My hands cup her bottom, and I lift her slightly, spreading her legs, flicking my tongue over the hard pebble of her clitoris so that she arches deeper into my mouth.

Her fingers tighten in my hair, and she pulls me to my feet. We kiss again as I let her tug me towards the bed. As we fall back against the mattress, I stroke between her legs, feeling her pulse beat in my hand. Then I lower my hips so that the hard press of my erection is trapped between her stomach and mine. Sucking in a breath, I ease backwards a fraction and slow the pace, because this is where she lost her way last time.

Hennessy

I can see the tension in his face, the concentration, and I want to cry because he is taking so much care. I know that he must have sensed that I was tense when we did this last time. I feel the shadows seeping across the bed. My pulse is growing hazy, and static starts to fill my head.

'I'm losing you.'

His voice cuts through the noise, and I stare up into his dark eyes. He cups my cheek, kisses me softly on the mouth and rolls over, taking me with him so that I straddle his hips.

'I'm here. You're safe,' he says softly. 'And I'm not going anywhere.'

The panic lapping at my senses recedes and I nod slowly. 'I don't know if I can…'

'I know. But we don't have to do everything right now. We can slow right down.'

He reaches up and pinches my nipples gently and I let out a staccato breath. Now he caresses my breasts, his hands lingering on my skin so that it tingles, sparkles almost, and I want him to keep touching me. I need more. I am nothing but need, and I lower my hips so that I can feel how hard he is.

A noise rises low in my throat, a scrape of hunger, and his pupils snap like an electric current is passing through him. He stares at me as if he is transfixed.

'Is this okay? I can stop.'

'Don't stop.' My blood is roaring in my ears. He is smooth and hard like stone, and the feel of him, the hardness and the heat, are everything I want.

'Hennessy...'

My name is a hiss in his mouth, and I need him to be closer. I pull at his shoulders, and he understands immediately, just as if my wish is his command. He pushes off the mattress so that he is sitting upright, and my nipples are grazing his chest. I reach for his shoulders and his hands grip my waist, and I lean into his neck, moaning into his skin. Then he captures my breasts and circles the nipples with his tongue, sucking first one then the other into his warm, wet mouth.

I am trembling all over, blurring at the edges, dizzy, and something charged is flickering inside me. He is so hard and impossibly big, bigger than before, and that I have this power over him is intoxicating. I buck against him jerkily in a spasm that is intense and involuntary because I am no longer in control of my body, my limbs. Heat is rising, melting me from the inside out, liquefying my bones, and I can feel Renzo pulling me closer, clutching me to him as if I am the treasure he called me earlier.

He rolls his hips against mine, his breath raw and urgent in my ear, and I cling to his body as he swells inside me, grinding against him, desperate for him to fill the ache that is stretching me apart.

My shoulder blades meet as my back arches, and everything but Renzo is beyond my vision, my comprehension. For a shattering half-second I cannot breathe, think or do anything but allow myself to be buffeted by shockwaves. The pleasure is like a supernova exploding. It is bright and burning hot, and it's too much and not enough.

The heat of it licks over my body, searing everything in its path, and I am engulfed.

Renzo's hand is tight in my hair, and I feel him go, his fingers gripping me. I pull him closer, clinging to him as his breath rolls over my skin in hot, shuddering waves. Maybe that's why I feel as if I've drowned.

He is flailing too, his other hand grabbing blindly for me as if I am the only thing keeping him afloat.

'Was that…? Did you…?'

For a moment, I can't answer. I am lost in his closeness, and the size of his pupils and the way his hand circles my wrists, as if he is unable to let go of. And I just nod, because I am crying. Because it was, and I did, and I know now that what happened in New York wasn't a one-off. I can stop the shadows and silence the noise. I'm not broken.

'You're crying.'

'I'm sorry… I'm not sad. I just didn't think, I didn't know if…'

'I know.' He kisses my eyes, my cheeks, my throat, and now I cling to him because I don't want to let him go. I never want this moment to end.

His mouth finds mine. 'Are you okay?'

'I'm amazing.'

'You are.' He touches my face and his forehead creases. 'What is it?'

'I meant to say "amazed", but my brain isn't working.' I lean into his shoulder, laughing, and then he laughs against my mouth, and we kiss. I don't know what is more perfect—the lingering buzz of my orgasm or the sound of Renzo's laughter. I just know that I have never been happier. 'I think you got it right the first time.'

There is a note in his voice I've never heard before. He

sounds at ease, relaxed, young. And he is young, younger than the persona he typically projects. Only it's hard to remember that because he is always such a grown-up. Even when he was the age I am now he seemed like an adult in a way that neither of my parents has ever achieved.

His arm tightens around my waist, and he shifts my weight so that I am looking up into his eyes.

'I need a shower. Do you wanna join me?' he says softly. 'Or shall we grab breakfast first? Or just stay in bed.'

'How about we have a shower together? Then we can have breakfast in bed, and you can show me what *you* like, and we can take it from there.'

His irises are so big that I feel as if I am drowning again.

After our shower, and despite what we agreed, when I suggest going downstairs to get some breakfast Renzo pulls me back to bed and we finally have brunch at nearly noon.

After brunch we lounge by the pool. Or rather, I lounge. Renzo swims lengths until I join him in the water, and we end up getting close to playing a bit more show and tell, so we have to leave and go back to the bedroom.

'We might have missed lunch,' I say as we lie in bed, watching the rippling, aquamarine sea. 'Do you think Paola will mind?'

Renzo reaches out and touches my hip and I feel my body rippling to life again. 'I think she'll be too astonished to mind.'

It's strange, because I am the one who was stymied by my body, but Renzo seems looser too; that tautness in his muscles seems ironed out.

'Why will she be astonished?'

'Because I've probably never missed a meal before.'

He frowns. 'My life is pretty regimented. You know—boring.'

He rolls his eyes like a teenager, and I laugh because this is a Renzo I didn't know existed. 'I'm going to have to disagree with you. I'm pretty sure most people think the octopus is an eight-legged sea creature, not a position in the *Kama Sutra*.'

I shiver with pleasure as he reaches out to lift my hair from my breast, covering it instead with the palm of his hand. 'You liked that, didn't you?'

He gently pinches my nipple, and my body instantly starts to feel liquid and hot, boneless.

'I did. But I might need a bit of practice.'

We practise. Then we have a very late lunch, or perhaps an early supper, and afterwards we check our messages but there is nothing from Charlie or Jade. I take a sneaky peak at the headlines but there aren't any updates. In fact, thanks to an A-list couple splitting acrimoniously, the story has been relegated to an inside page for the first time since the news broke.

'Anything to report?'

Renzo's voice pulls me back into the present and I meet his gaze. That he cares is the best drug on the planet, and I am addicted. Bad analogy, but it feels good to know that he is watching over me.

'Just one from Carrie. What about you?' I glance at Renzo and feel my stomach lurch. 'What is it?'

He is holding up his phone, listening intently. 'It's a voicemail from Noah Barker.'

'The Australian media tycoon? What does he want?'

'Apparently, he's ready to talk about selling his business and he wants to set up a meeting.'

'He owns LNC, doesn't he?' The newest American

news network was initially derided as an upstart funded by an Australian interloper, but in the last year it has started to become a serious rival to the more established networks.

Renzo nods. His blue eyes are blazing. 'He suggests meeting in Scotland. Apparently, he's playing in some golf tournament. Which is fortuitous, because I recently bought a castle there.'

Did he? I'm curious to find out more but his face is stiff with concentration, and I know he is checking all the plates spinning inside his head. Because that's what he does. He makes sure nothing comes crashing to the ground.

I feel a slight ache in my chest, but I push it away. This whole set-up—the villa, the soft sunlight filtering through the shutters, the sudden and miraculous synchronicity of my body, my desire and his desire, but most of all Renzo himself—is irresistible. He's irresistible but I know it's temporary, finite. A one-of-a-kind cocktail of proximity, history and holiday vibes.

Clearing my throat, I say lightly, 'Can you fit him in?'

He nods. 'Gerry will have to move a couple of meetings.' His eyes find mine. 'So, what do you think?'

'I think it's some kind of super-power, the way you make admin so sexy.'

'I mean, what do you think about going to Scotland? We could drop in on the way back to New York. If Barker does business like he does phone calls, it'll be a short, sweet meeting, so there'll be plenty of time for me to show you round the estate.'

I am stunned by his invitation. 'I don't want to get in the way.'

His beautiful face creases into a different kind of smile. I am becoming a private collector. 'I own a castle. How could you be in the way? Besides, I'd value your opinion.'

His words, the truth of them, make me glance away. For so long, I've felt as though I haven't earned my place in the world, but now I am. And I know it's stupid, but I wish my grandmother were here to see it. I wish Charlie was too.

I look up to find Renzo staring down at me; his blue eyes travel over my face, seeing everything.

'Try not to worry.' He takes my hand. 'Charlie looks after number one.'

I nod slowly. 'That's one of the things he always says to me—that and "play stupid". "Don't look back" is another. And he seems to have forgotten me, so maybe that's his favourite.'

I try to smile then, but I can tell from the way Renzo's jaw tightens that I'm not doing a very good job.

'Do you want to hear some good news? JVHM have signed up. Apparently, Monsieur Pinault was impressed by our pitch. Your pitch, I should say.'

I don't even try to hide my pleasure at Renzo's words. 'He's a nice man.'

'He's a good businessman,' he qualifies, but there is no bite to his words. 'And you are a good businesswoman.' He taps my phone. 'Are you going to be able to keep off this now?'

'Maybe.' It's been so relaxing, not having that tug of social media. I feel calmer, steady in myself, without the constant chipping away of the Internet. 'Would you mind holding onto it for just a little longer?'

'Not at all, and I'll let you know if anything changes.' He reaches over and puts my phone in the drawer by the bed.

'So, what did Carrie want?'

I shrug, remembering her text. 'Oh, nothing important. She just wanted to remind me that I've got my three-year milestone coming up.'

'Three years! That's not just important, it's incredible. You're incredible. You're amazing.' Renzo's eyes are steady on my face as if he is spellbound. 'What happens—do you get another chip?'

'If I want one.'

'Don't you?' He frowns.

'Kind of.' Catching sight of his face, I shake my head. 'It's complicated. Since I went sober, I try to do one day at a time. But, when I reach a milestone, I suddenly realise how far I've come.'

'Isn't that a good thing?'

'Yes, but it's also a lot of pressure, and I worry I won't be able to handle it. And if I mess up it'll be so much further to fall.'

'That's not going to happen.'

'Won't it?' There is a twist in my throat. 'It wouldn't be the first time I've given up.'

This is news to Renzo, but he doesn't look shocked or appalled. It is more as if he is processing my words and their implication.

'How long did you manage then?'

'Not long. Months, maybe. But I was doing it on my own and it was so hard. Or maybe I was too weak.'

'You're not weak. You're the strongest person I know. Look at everything you've had to deal with. Your father is on the run. The FBI are on your case. And in the middle of all that you've had to take over the running of a huge global business.'

'Co-running,' I say softly.

'Maybe in New York. In Milan, I was just your backing

singer.' He leans in and nips my shoulder. 'Most people in your position would have crumbled or walked away. But you're not hiding like Charlie. You were in Milan doing your job, hosting a party that the world is talking about.'

'But I'm still a person in recovery.'

'Yes, you are. But those other times you didn't have the support you needed. This is different. You have a sponsor.'

'Yes, I have Carrie.'

Renzo's eyes are steady and such a dark blue that I feel as if I am staring into space and that he has the answers to all the universe's questions.

'And you have me,' he says slowly. 'You don't need to be scared any more, Hennessy. I've got this.'

For a moment we just stare at one another and then he reaches to pick up his phone. 'Is there a specific day when you're supposed to get your chip?'

I hear his question, but I can't answer, because I have just realised something incredible, something fundamental, and it robs me of the ability to speak. I can't understand why I didn't see it sooner. But I can't not see it now, because it is filling me with light. I can feel it illuminating every cell of my body.

I love him. I love Renzo.

I've felt so alone, so adrift, my whole life. Everything has always been so tangled and hard, and this last week should have been the perfect storm of chaos, pressure and panic. But Renzo walked into the storm to find me. And he stayed with me while it howled and raged—a solid presence shielding me, keeping me centred, safe.

He did that. He's still doing it now and it is all so astonishing, new and right. I want to tell him what I'm feeling, to shout it from the rooftops and whisper it into his ear, but I don't want to get it wrong. To go in too fast, too strong. Maybe Scotland will be the right time.

With an effort, I gather my thoughts. 'Carrie is suggesting Friday. So, a week from today.'

'Done.' He taps his phone screen. 'I've got it in my diary. We'll go to Scotland and be back in New York for your meeting.'

'It's in your diary?' My brain skips over his words again. 'You're going to come with me?'

'Unless you don't want me to.'

'No, I do. I'd love that. But don't feel like you have to.'

'Of course I have to. You're my co-CEO. I've got a vested interest in your wellbeing.'

Renzo

That's not the only reason I want to be there for her. She has worked so hard this week. And she really cares. About the business, about the staff. She cares about Charlie, although God knows why. He might be her father, but he is unworthy of the title.

Picturing the little girl waking in a strange bedroom to find a man watching her in the darkness, I could break Charlie's neck with my bare hands. No wonder she lost her way. But I can take care of her. It's what I do, and Hennessy deserves to have a little TLC in her life.

My back stiffens. Truthfully, what she deserves is someone who loves her. But I can't do that. I think those years in care when I had to seal myself off froze out any possibility of loving someone. I'm not built for the risks that loving someone takes. And what do I know about relationships? Aside from Antony, everyone in my life has been transient, and even with him I had to send him away to school to give him stability. I'm just not meant to be tethered to anyone.

But I can treat her with respect and consideration and make her smile. Not the smile-for-the-cameras smile that's just for show. I mean, the smile she shares with me. I'll make sure she keeps getting the support she needs. And, in the meantime, we can enjoy a few more days away from the spotlight. Scotland will be perfect for that. And by the time we reach New York, I might be the owner of an American news network.

I call Barker back and agree to the meeting.

'He suggested a round of golf, but I'm more of an ice-hockey man myself. Do you need more sunblock?'

Hennessy is lying beside me on a sun lounger. Her body is already a light uniform gold, but I am judicious about reapplying protection, mainly because it allows me to run my hands over her smooth, warm skin.

'You play ice-hockey? What is it with you and secrets? It's like you have this whole other life. I'm starting to worry that at some point you're going to tell me you have a secret collection of commemorative plates or samurai swords.'

'Sadly not.' I have a secret life, though. A life of loneliness, loss and responsibility that is too painful for me to talk about, even with Antony. Especially with Antony. I wonder if this is another instance of me selfishly pursuing my own agenda.

'That's a relief.' She runs her hand lightly over my chest. 'I don't know much about ice-hockey, but I like the "snowy warrior" vibe. You know, stubble, fur and sweat.'

'I'm not sure what you think happens in ice-hockey, but I don't remember much fur being involved.'

'Pity.'

Beside me, I feel Hennessy tense as somewhere in the house a phone starts to ring.

'*Scusi,* Signor Valetti…'

We both turn toward where Paola is hurrying towards us. I don't even need to look at her face to know there is a problem. Paola is always composed, always calm. She never hurries.

I get to my feet. 'What is it? Has something happened?'

'I'm sorry to interrupt but I thought you should know. It's all over the news. Signor Wade has been found and arrested.'

There is a moment of pure, stunned silence and I feel the shockwaves ripple across the sunlit pool. And then my phone starts to ring.

'Thank you, Paola. I've got it from here.'

Hennessy is staring past me, her gaze following Paola back into the villa. She looks not just shocked but stricken, and I pull her against me, wrapping her in my arms.

'It's okay. It will be okay.'

'I know I should be pleased that he's been found but…' She breathes out shakily.

'But you're worried about what happens next.' My phone starts to ring again. 'It's Gerry. I should take this.'

I take three more calls in quick succession and then I mute my phone and turn to where Hennessy is sitting on the lounger.

'Okay, so he was picked up in Buenos Aires. He's being held at the central police station. I spoke to Agent Carson. They're on their way out there with all the necessary paperwork but I think it will take a couple of days to process everything.'

'Is Charlie okay?'

I nod.

'And what about Jade? Is she there?'

I shake my head. 'Look, I know this is hard, but try not to panic. Carson said she'll get back to me with any updates, and in the meantime, we can talk to Charlie's lawyers. What are you doing?'

She is sliding her feet into her flip-flops. 'I'm going to get dressed. Do you think we can leave before lunch?'

'Leave?'

'For Buenos Aires.'

'We can't go to Buenos Aires. It'll be a circus.'

Her eyes flutter across my face. She is still in shock, I realise, but when I move towards her she steps backwards uncertainly.

'But you said…you said we were going to talk to the lawyers.'

'Yes. In New York, not in Argentina.'

She is staring at me as if I am a stranger, and I feel like a stranger to myself. But that is the problem—I have become a stranger. Because of her. I've let my defences slide. I've let Hennessy take charge of my life.

My phone vibrates in my hand. I lift it automatically and click on the notification. It is a video of Charlie being jostled through a baying crowd of reporters and photographers. I catch a glimpse of the cuffs on his wrists and then he is engulfed again.

I can feel Hennessy's panic swelling into the warm sunlight, and I want to bridge the gap between us, to comfort her, to explain. But I can't, because this isn't who I am or who I want to be. Since Hennessy walked into the Wade and Walters building, I have been pretending to myself that it doesn't matter. I slipped out of my skin and under hers.

But this is the reality. Chaos. Confusion. Consequences that will be impossible to control.

'Look, I know he's selfish and impulsive...'

'He's reckless. And he is about to become a criminal.'

'I thought people were innocent until proven guilty.'

'You know he's guilty. He knows he's guilty, that's why he went on the run. But we are not guilty. And we have just spent a week persuading the world they can trust us, so the last thing we should be doing is cosying up to Charlie.'

'He's my father.'

'I don't care. He is bad news—literally.'

'What if it was Antony? What would you do then?'

My stomach lurches. The idea of my brother being manhandled into a police station is appalling but it is also a reminder of the difference between Hennessy's life and mine.

'Antony is not Charlie. I'm not Charlie. And I never can be. Because I know what it's like to be powerless—to have no voice, no money. I know that if you're not in control things go wrong. I loved my parents, and they loved me and Antony, but they weren't in charge of their lives. They didn't think about health care, so my dad ignored the signs of heart disease and mum didn't bother checking out the lump in her breast.'

It is the first time I've ever admitted that to anyone, and it hurts. I glance down at myself and frown. What kind of man handles a crisis in swimming shorts? Suddenly I feel angry, an anger that is intense and endless, and I direct it at Hennessy, because I have given her power over me that I should never have yielded. Power I never wanted to yield. This is her doing. She has hijacked me, held me hostage, robbed me of the discipline I need to survive and protect what is mine.

'I don't take risks, Hennessy. I do everything in my power to eliminate them from my life—and Charlie is a risk.'

And, by implication, Hennessy is too. She hears the unsaid part of that sentence. I know because she flinches. 'You're right. I don't know what I was thinking. Obviously, I need to go on my own.'

'If you want my advice, I would stay well away.'

'But I didn't want your advice. I wanted your support. I thought that's what you were offering. I thought we were, well, that it was more than...'

She turns away, but not before I see the hurt in her eyes. 'Hennessy...'

'It's fine. I'm not blaming you. It's not like we talked about it, or us, so don't worry about it. I'm going to go and get dressed. But thanks for rescuing me in Milan. For rescuing me, full-stop.'

'Take the jet. I can organise another. And use the car.'

She doesn't reply, just walks towards the villa. There is a moment when I could stop her. Several, in fact. I could grab her arm. I could call her name. I could stride after her and block her path. But I do none of those things. I watch her leave. I can't go with her. This was only ever going to work here, outside of the real world.

I wait for the feeling of relief to rescue me from the open, empty ache beneath my ribs. And I keep waiting. And waiting...until Paola comes to tell me that Hennessy has left.

And then I wait some more.

CHAPTER TEN

Renzo

'WOULD YOU LIKE a coffee, Mr Valetti?'

It is Chrissie, the air steward but I don't bother to look up from my newspaper.

'Not now,' I say tersely. I sense her retreat, and I know she has gone to confer with Caleb, the other steward. I know because for the last twenty-four hours, my staff has been conferring on and off behind my back about my 'mood'.

You are such a hypocrite. I thought it matters how we behave.

That sentence spoken in Hennessy's voice is so pitch perfect that I glance jerkily over my shoulder around the cabin, because just for a moment I thought she was here.

'Is everything okay, Mr Valetti?' Chrissie again, looking nervous, probably because she's expecting to have her head bitten off.

'Everything's fine. Sorry about snapping at you a moment ago.'

'It's not a problem, Mr Valetti. Would you like that coffee now?'

'Yes…actually, no. Do you have any kind of herbal tea?'

She blinks. 'Of course. I'll go and check which flavours we have.'

'It's fine. Just surprise me.'

Smiling uncertainly, she nods and retreats again. She clearly thinks I'm losing my mind. And it feels as if I am. I have all the symptoms. I know because I looked them up on my laptop last night: behavioural changes; mood swings; lack of appetite; problems sleeping; inability to concentrate.

And then there is the ache. I don't know what that is. It's not on the list. But I feel it all the time. It's as if I've been hollowed out, and yet it drags down inside me like a leaden weight. It is cold like lead too.

Hennessy didn't take the jet, or the car. The local taxi took her to the airport in Naples, which was a blessing of sorts. The city is not a favourite with celebrities, so paparazzi are thin on the ground. The flight to Buenos Aires is a gruelling eighteen hours. And the gods must have smiled on her, because she managed to make her way to the police station unnoticed.

The gods are smiling on me too. The initial due diligence on Noah Barker's assets looks promising and the exodus of advertisers from Wade and Walters has stopped.

Why, then, does it feel as though I've been cast out of paradise?

I lean back against the upholstered head rest and glance down at the crossword I am trying and failing to complete: eight letters; an eighteenth-century French, fruit-based spirit designed to intoxicate. I don't need another clue, but if I did, I could write my own: a blonde beauty with brains, violet eyes and a smile that can melt polar ice.

Dropping the newspaper onto the empty seat beside me, I stare out at the pale-blue sky. I feel as if I've swallowed ice. I'm cold all the time. Even the Italian sun couldn't warm me. It's as if I have the flu. And the symptoms get worse whenever I picture Hennessy trying to hold herself together out by the pool at the villa. I hate everything about that memory. I hate that she looks so stricken and the way her shoulders are braced. But most of all I hate that she is alone.

Because she was alone. I was there. But, when it came to it, I didn't stay by her side. I looked after number one. And I had the gall to say I'm not like Charlie.

Reaching into my pocket, I retrieve Hennessy's sobriety chips. I wanted to take the fear from her eyes, the loneliness and the hurt. But that's all I can see when I remember her face: fear, loneliness and hurt. And I put all those things there.

Where is she now? I check my phone. She is not on a private jet, but the paparazzi have caught up with her now. Her every movement is a matter of public record, so I know that she is no longer in Buenos Aires. Could she be back in New York? No, she won't have landed yet.

But there is one question I can't answer by looking at my phone, and it is the only one that matters. How is she? Is she coping? Is she sleeping?

I grit my teeth and go to loosen my tie, then tug it off and toss it on top of the discarded newspaper, because that is three questions. But I have no restraint anymore, even inside my head.

Especially inside my head. My mind is a tangle of snapshots. Memories of Hennessy fronting up to me that first morning in that dress. Tucking her hair behind her ear as she scanned the guest list for the party. Arching *beneath* my body for the first time. Not on top, but beneath.

'I went for chamomile tea, Mr Valetti. I hope that's okay.'

'Thank you, Chrissie.' This time, I meet her gaze.

'My pleasure. Oh, and just to let you know, sir, we are about three hours out from the airfield in St Andrews, so we're right on schedule.'

She beams at me because my staff know how much I value keeping to my schedule. Time-management increases productivity, which in turn increases profit. But keeping to a schedule also demonstrates that I am in control. In the driver's seat. Because I'm never not the boss. I can't surrender control to anyone.

Except Hennessy.

In Milan, I followed her lead. And in Praiano I let her take control in bed. I let her mould and shape my desire. I surrendered to her. I was her willing slave. And now I can't think, sleep or eat. I have a deal in the pipeline that will give me power I could only imagine as a child in care. But none of it matters. There is only one thing that matters.

Eight letters: a blonde beauty with brains, violet eyes and a smile that can melt polar ice.

I glance up at Chrissie. 'About the schedule—could you have a word with John, please? Tell him that there's been a change of plan? I've changed my plans.'

She stares at me as if I have started capering about the cabin in a kilt. But then those words have never been part of my vocabulary. They couldn't be. Not until Hennessy moved into my life. And into my heart.

My heart?

I can't breathe, and I tell myself I'm mistaken, but it doesn't feel like a mistake. It feels as if I am soaring. That I have won the jackpot, scaled a mountain peak, written a symphony. Because that is what it feels like to love someone.

And I love Hennessy Wade.

'A change of plan?'

Chrissie's voice tugs me out of my stupor, and I nod. 'By which I mean a change of course.'

'So, you don't want to go to Scotland.'

I shake my head. 'No. I want—I need—to get back to New York.'

She nods. 'Yes, sir. Is everything okay?'

I am about to tell her that everything is fine. But then I remember what Hennessy said about admitting she was an alcoholic—that saying it out loud was the first step to real change. And I want to change.

'No, it isn't. I messed up—big time. But I'm going to fix it.'

As Chrissie turns and walks towards the cockpit, my head is spinning, but I let it. After all, who doesn't want to ride on a merry-go-round?

Hennessy

The sky above New York is bruised. Not the dark of a fresh bruise, but that mottled yellow, blue and green that happens a couple of days after the original injury. The sky is basically my heart—a giant bruise that aches and aches. I know one day it will stop aching. Well, maybe not stop, but it will dull to something manageable. But then it is only seven days since I left Renzo's villa in Praiano.

There are some plus points in my life. Wade and Walters' share price has gone up even higher than before Charlie went AWOL.

And speaking of Charlie... We are living together. Not at my apartment; that's under siege from paparazzi right now. This belongs to someone Charlie knows through work, which makes me nervous. But the FBI is allowing it, so I suppose it must be legit. Sharing a space again is strange on multiple levels, mainly because in the past it was always Charlie's space, and I was just tolerated.

But things have changed since I flew out to Argentina. After I left Italy, everything went surprisingly smoothly. I got to the police station without anyone hassling me. Charlie was stunned, then delighted, to see me. Jade had fled, but then the fantasy of life with Charlie was always better than the reality. It took forty-eight hours to sort out all the paperwork with the Argentine authorities and then we flew back to New York five days ago for the bail hearing.

My shoulders stiffen and I stare down at my black coffee. That was hairier. There were so many people, all shouting our names; it was like walking on stage at a rock concert. But Agent Carson and Agent Merrick were really good. Somehow, they cleared a path through the swelling tide of reporters, photographers and news teams, and they let me stay with Charlie right up until he was taken into the court room.

It was a closed court. I think the judge didn't want to get caught up in all the media craziness. Which was for-tuitous because, incredibly, Charlie got bail. He hasn't said so, but I know David must have put up the money.

So, this is our home until the trial. And it's a beautiful home. David has been very generous. It's a duplex with views across the city to the Chrysler building. If Renzo looked out of his apartment, our eyes would meet across the skyscrapers.

Renzo… I try not to think about him because his name is a sharp pain, a stiletto blade beneath the ribs. It's been hard staying sober with that pain, but Carrie has been so supportive. I can call her day or night, but I only call her during the day. At night, Renzo is there in the darkness with me. I know it's stupid. Those things he said to me are just symptomatic of his need to take charge. I know that what happened in Praiano stays in Praiano. But if I call Carrie in the night, he will vanish for ever.

'Essie, do you know where my loafers are—the brown ones that Giorgio gave me? I can't seem to find them.'

A transatlantic drawl snaps my thoughts in two and I turn towards Charlie. My father: the fugitive; the headline maker. In some ways he is the same old Charlie: messy; lazy; funny. He is a survivor, impermeable to bad luck and a badly lived life. But he has aged. Being on the run has aged him—scared him, I think. For the first time in his life, he wanted to look back.

Which might be why the dial on our relationship has shifted. It's not perfect but we have pressed the reset button. Or rather, I pressed it, and Charlie has gone along with it. Because it turns out he needs me as much as I need him, maybe more. I'm not a child now. I'm not dependent on his good mood, or his money.

In fact, he is dependent on mine. His assets have been frozen. But my apartment was bought with money from my grandmother's estate. And the salary from Wade and Walters is mine too. And it's not just the money. I've changed. I'm tougher, more confident. I'm proud of who I am. Finally, I like myself.

I turn to face Charlie. 'You left them in the hallway. Which means they're probably still there.' My father is still adjusting to this brave new world of having to pick up his own clothes.

'There's coffee in the pot,' I say. 'And I made some overnight oats last night.'

Charlie shakes his head. 'You know I can't bear all that healthy crap. I could murder a Bloody Mary, though.' He catches sight of my face and says quickly, 'Obviously I'm not going to have one.'

'Obviously. As there is no alcohol in the apartment and your tag will go off if you leave the building.'

'I know, I know. Why are you drinking coffee anyway?' he says hastily, changing the subject. 'I thought you hated the stuff.'

I do. And I don't drink it. The smell reminds me of Renzo. But I'm not going to share that fact with Charlie.

I haven't seen Renzo since I left Praiano. I haven't seen or spoken to anyone, not even Antony. But then I haven't left the apartment, not even to go to the office. I'm not bunking off. I've been given compassionate leave. And I'm glad I agreed. Even the thought of seeing Renzo again feels like a knife in the stomach.

'Things change. People too. How about I make you a Virgin Mary?'

Charlie scans my face. 'How about I make it, but you have one too? Doesn't do to drink alone, even if it's booze-free.'

Taking two glasses from the cupboard, he put first one then the other under the ice dispenser, grinning as it spits out four perfect cubes of ice.

'I'm not a fan of gadgets normally, but this I love.' He is practically purring. 'I must say this place is very well-equipped. I thought it might be a bit spartan for me. I mean, Valetti is such a cold-blooded bastard.'

The glass almost slips from my fingers. My legs are hollow, and my head feels like the bottom of a muddy stream. I don't understand. Did I mishear? Questions jostle and swell inside my head until finally one bursts from my mouth. 'What's this apartment got to do with Renzo Valetti?'

Charlie rubs his hand over his face, a sure sign he is hiding something. I know it, and he knows I know it, and after a few seconds of silence he sighs.

'He owns it.'

'And you didn't think to tell me?' I haven't told Charlie about what happened with Renzo and me, but still.

'He told me not to. He was quite insistent.'

'You've seen him?'

My father shrugs. 'He came to the bail hearing. He put up the bail,' he adds, and he has the grace to look sheepish now.

Renzo was at the bail hearing. I can't get my head around this. Why would he do that? But I know why. He sees a problem and he feels responsible. What was it he said? *You're my co-CEO. I have a vested interest.*

A vested interest. His words scrape against my skin like a grater. I don't know why, but it hurts way more than it did the first time.

'Did he say anything?'

Charlie's expression changes, and for the first time in my life his sang-froid seems to falter. 'He told me that if I was thinking about disappearing again I should remind myself that he's Italian, and that Italy is a piece of land off Sicily where they take revenge very seriously.'

'Was that all? I mean, he didn't say anything else?' About me? I want to ask. About us? About coming with me to my AA meeting?

My father frowns. 'What else should he say?'

I train my eyes on a place behind Charlie's left shoulder. 'Nothing,' I say finally, his words crushing the last, tiny hope that flickered inside me. 'Nothing at all.'

I spend the rest of the morning rereading old copies of *FROW*. They're pre-Renzo, so there is no risk of stumbling over his name, or worse his photo. Then I go and have a shower. I've spent the last few days in my pyjamas. Now I pull on some jeans, a t-shirt and a hoodie and I wrap a scarf around my neck, pulling it up so that it covers the lower half of my face.

'Where are you going?' Charlie sounds plaintive. He has no idea how to occupy himself without entertainment, but he will have to learn. At least for a couple of hours.

'I've got my AA meeting.'

His eyes hover on my face. 'I could come with you. I can go incognito.' He reaches behind the cushion on the sofa, pulls out a baseball cap and shoves it onto his head. 'See?'

I stare down at him, remembering that day when Renzo gave me a similar cap to disguise myself.

'You have a tag, remember? Thanks for offering, but I'll be fine,' I say firmly. 'I won't be long. I'll switch my phone to silent in the meeting, but you can text me.'

Maybe it's because Charlie reminded me of that first day with Renzo, but I think about him as I head downtown. Or maybe it's because Renzo said he'd come to this meeting. But I know he won't. Any guilt he might feel about dropping out will be more than offset by the bail money he's paid, and the apartment we're living in thanks to him.

My group meets in a church hall opposite Central Park, and I do try to go to the meeting. I stand in front of where we meet, and several times I come close to going in, but in the end, I text Carrie and ask her to collect my chip because I can't face it. I tell her I'm going to grab a coffee at Bezzera.

The coffee shop is quiet. It's mid-afternoon, so for once I get a seat at the window counter. As the waiter approaches, I dump my bag on the neighbouring chair.

'Hi there, what would you like to order?' The waiter smiles at me without really seeing me—perfect.

'Just an espresso, please.'

While I wait for my coffee, I watch the people walking their dogs, torn between relief and disappointment. I should have gone, but I couldn't face that moment when I had to accept once and for all that Renzo isn't coming.

'Is anyone sitting here?'

'No, it's fine.'

I reach for my bag, glancing up automatically to see which clown has to sit next to me even though the café is practically empty and my heart stops beating.

Renzo is standing there. In the fading afternoon sunlight, his solidity and architectural beauty is agonizingly familiar, yet already there is a change in him, in us.

'Are you sure?' The stiffness in his voice makes my skin feel as if it is made of ice and he has just trodden on it. For a moment, I am mute, but then I force myself to speak. 'What are you doing here? Aren't you supposed to be in Scotland with Noah Barker?'

'Yes,' he says simply. 'But when we were en route I realised that I'd made a mistake. I had another, more important, meeting in my diary. A meeting with you.'

He remembered. Worse, he sees me as an obligation to be met. A commitment to be honoured. And there it is—the truth laid bare.

'That's right, I forgot, you have a "vested interest" in me. I'm afraid you missed the meeting, but it really doesn't matter. You've done enough already, Renzo. I know you paid Charlie's bail, and that you're paying for the apartment we're living in. I'm very grateful for that, but I don't need your pity.'

'I don't pity you.'

'Okay, sorry, wrong word—you feel responsible. Is that better? Well, guess what? I'm not your responsibility, Renzo. And I don't want to be.'

I expect him to look relieved or angry, but he doesn't look either. I don't know why but that knocks me off-balance, and quite suddenly I am close to tears. 'Can you please just go?'

'No, I can't.'

My hands push his chest. 'This is so like you, having to be in control of everything.' It's like trying to move a mountain made of muscle and I give up in frustration.

'But I'm not in control, Hennessy,' he says quietly. 'I haven't been in control since we kissed in Las Vegas. And the thing is, I don't care.'

I stare at him, mute, dumbfounded. His words make no sense. Then I remember that he doesn't need to make sense to me.

I reach for my bag, but he steps closer, and that's when I register that there are smudges under his eyes and he is wearing a thick, dark coat even though it is a reasonably warm afternoon.

'Why are you stopping me?'

'Because I didn't stop you before. And I should have done. But then, there are lots of other things I should have done. I should have gone with you to Buenos Aires. I should have been by your side to protect you from the paparazzi.'

There is strain in his voice, pain too, and his body is a quivering line of tension.

'But mostly I should have told you that I love you. You see, I don't have a vested interest in you. I'm not interested in you at all. I'm fascinated. Spellbound. Smitten.'

The silence in the café swells around us. Out of the corner of my eye, I see the waiter retreating with my coffee.

'No.' I shake my head. 'That's a lie. You don't love me, Renzo. You can't. I represent everything you hate. I'm chaos and confusion.'

'You're challenging.'

'I have all this baggage. And you hate baggage.'

'I don't like having too much luggage.' He steps forward and takes hold of my wrists. 'But I love your baggage. Because it's *your* baggage and I love everything about you.'

Renzo

'Why are you lying to me?' Hennessy struggles against my wrists, breaks free and pummels my chest but it's nothing compared to the pain I'm feeling inside. My lungs are burning. My heart is flopping heavily, like a bird with an injured wing.

I stare down at Hennessy's small, quivering face. Her hair is tied up with a thick band, and she is wearing a hoodie that obscures every one of her curves, but I don't think she has ever looked more beautiful.

Or more out of reach. Because I have hurt her. I pushed her away. I put myself first. I left her to face the world alone.

'I'm not lying, not now. But I was, back in Praiano. You were right—you said I had all these secrets. A whole other life. And I did. I had a life filled with fear. When Antony and I got put into care, I never felt so helpless and inadequate. And lonely.'

I breathe out shakily, remembering. 'The staff were mostly kind, but they changed all the time, and they were over-worked. We were cared for, but there were limits, barriers. It wasn't like with my parents. Only they were gone, and I think losing them made me scared of letting those barriers down with anyone else.'

She watches me in that way of hers and I can't believe I am baring my soul to her. But then, I realise that it's because I am baring my soul that I need her gaze. I have never surrendered more power than in this moment and yet I feel nothing but relief.

'I was scared of everything. I couldn't stop thinking about all the things that could happen that I couldn't control. And Antony was depending on me. That fear has driven me, haunted me, my whole life. But it's nothing compared to what I felt when you walked out of the villa, and I thought I'd lost you.'

Her hands unclench a fraction. I know because my whole body is attuned to hers. And then she takes my hand, and my heart flips over with hope. This is a new kind of terror because I don't know if I can bear to let go of her again.

'You didn't lose me.'

'No, I didn't. I abandoned you. And I knew I'd made a terrible mistake. All I could think about was seeing you again and how it would be between us. How I wouldn't be able to hold you and kiss you and—'

'You didn't lose me,' she says again. 'You haven't lost me. You can't lose me because I love you.' She pulls me closer and our mouths meet, and it is a thing of undistilled sweetness to have her in my arms.

We kiss feverishly: lips, cheeks, forehead, lips again.

'I'm so sorry,' I murmur against her hair. 'But for someone supposedly so smart and omniscient I can be really dumb.'

'How did you know I was here?'

'I went to the meeting. Here.' I reach into my pocket

and pull out the chip. 'Carrie gave this to me to give to you. She says congratulations, and to tell you that she couldn't be prouder.'

'You went to the meeting?' Her eyes widen comically, and I am intoxicated by how much that means to her.

'I spoke at the meeting. About you—about how you didn't just turn your life around, you changed mine too, and for the better. That you've made me see I can't control everything. And I don't want to. That's why I've been talking to someone, a therapist, about why I felt like I did and how I can change. Because I want to change. I have to change to be the man you deserve.'

We kiss again and keep kissing until finally we break apart. It's then that I notice the young man glancing furtively at us across the café. I frown. 'Do you know him? Because he can't take his eyes off you. Do you think he's a reporter? Maybe I should…'

Hennessy peers over my shoulder. 'No, he's the waiter. Although, he does seem anxious to serve me,' she says as the young man picks up the coffee cup again. She looks at me suspiciously. 'You don't own this place, do you?'

I laugh. 'No. But I can buy it if you want me to.'

'I don't want you to buy me anything. I just want this.' Her hands curve around my neck and she looks into my eyes. 'I want you.'

'I love you,' I say because it's true. And because I love watching Hennessy's face when I say it.

'And I love you too,' she says softly. Then she kisses me, an open-mouthed kiss of passion and possibilities that only exist because of her, and because of us. And I love that most of all.

* * * * *

PROMOTED TO BOSS'S WIFE

MILLIE ADAMS

MILLS & BOON

To Flo, for being the best.

CHAPTER ONE

VERITY CARMICHAEL SCRUNCHED her brows together and gave her boss the grumpiest look she could manage.

"You aren't eating your salad," she said.

"I told you I didn't like salad."

Alexios Economides was one of the most feared and revered men in the tech industry, a dark imposing storm of a man who—at roughly six foot five—towered over everyone around him. His black hair was always swept back from his forehead, glossy like a raven's wing and with no indication he used styling products of any kind. It was as if every strand was held there through the sheer force of his will. His eyes were a deep brown, with one spot of red in the iris on the right one, she'd taken note.

Alex was unfriendly, ill-tempered, stubborn, maniacally controlled and as beautiful and sharp as a piece of cut obsidian. The blessing and many, many curses of Alexios Economides, et cetera et cetera.

Everyone was afraid of him.

Except Verity.

She hadn't been hired to be scared of him. She was his assistant, but more than that. He'd hired her to be his…

Conscience.

His Cricket, which she had pointed out once in reference to a classic cartoon, and he'd taken it on board as a nickname that she pretended to dislike, but secretly loved.

The idea made her smile just slightly as it always did, and then she frowned because she was trying to look grumpy.

"You did tell me you were going to try and eat more vegetables," she said. "So I decided we could have matching lunches today."

"Did I hire you to be my nutritionist?"

"No. You hired me to talk to you and to presumably listen to you also so when you said you wanted to eat more greens, I listened. I acted."

"Sneaky Cricket," he said.

She smiled. "I wasn't being sneaky. Eat your salad."

He seemed to not know what to do with the lettuce he stabbed up onto his fork.

"I wish I had a steak."

"Try wishing on a star, Alex, I hear your dreams might come true."

"What?"

"It's a… Never mind."

She'd worked for Alex for two years now and it was the weirdest, nicest job she'd ever had. Not just because she was thousands of miles away from her parents, her siblings and their assorted drama and living on the shores of the Aegean Sea. Not just.

That contributed to her happiness, though, without a doubt.

She liked this job because it was an interesting challenge. EconomicTech was on the forefront of hardware and software breakthroughs, with new, exciting innovations happening every few months. It was exciting to work in a company that was this dynamic. There was always a buzz in the building—unless Alex was walking through and then it hushed.

Verity could admit that maybe part of what she enjoyed was being the Alex Whisperer. That was what her coworkers called her. And she simply grinned in response.

That was another bonus of this job. She'd turned childhood trauma into a work skill.

She knew how to soothe; she knew how to smooth over every situation. How to sublimate her own feelings and show nothing but calm.

Blissful, cheerful calm.

She demonstrated her cheerful calm now by taking a smiling bite of her salad, which only seemed to aggravate Alex more.

It was odd to think this was her life now. All because one of her friends from college created an app for elite job postings where every employee would be prescreened, and prevetted. If celebrities could have their own dating apps, why couldn't major corporations and the rich and famous have their own job listings? With confidential terms, only visible by candidates who had agreed to keeping details to themselves.

Knowing the app creator was as vetted as it got, so even without a lot of job experience, Verity found herself approved and given access to the kinds of jobs most people could only dream of.

When she'd first seen the job listing, she had thought it odd. He wasn't only looking for an assistant; he was looking for a confidante. Someone to talk to him, not just about work, but about personal things. She'd been a bit nervous at first. Partly because he was an intimidating man (she'd googled him immediately when she'd seen the job listing) and partly because it seemed almost too good to be true.

Relocation to Greece? Great pay? Reasonable hours? Hot billionaire boss?

Even though there was a layer of protection provided by the system she'd used to get hired, she'd been secretly waiting to discover that "conversation" was code for Wear a Sexy Godzilla Costume and Stomp Around the Office to Satisfy My Dinosaur Fetish.

Which she'd said to him once, after she'd been working at the office for six months and he'd said, simply: "Godzilla isn't a dinosaur."

Then they'd debated what the best actual dinosaur was, because somehow that was her job.

He didn't want anything weird or sexual from her. He really *did* just want conversation.

She'd been given a small packet when she was hired that included a list of hard conversation limits, and she'd been happy to respect them initially because of the money and then later because she genuinely cared for Alex. How could she not?

That didn't mean she didn't wonder about him, of course.

She spent five days a week with him. When she wasn't with him, she thought about new topics she could cover with him. In a professional way, of course.

She didn't feel *like that* about him.

Sure, he was the most handsome man she'd ever seen. Probably because he was the most handsome man on the planet, in a purely aesthetic sense. But he was intense, and Verity could do intense from nine to five, but she would never ever ever sign up for intense in her personal life. In her home. In her heart.

No, thank you.

She was far more interested in men who were nice and smiley. In theory, since she'd never actually dated anyone at the very ripe age of twenty-four, which was starting to be bothersome. But Verity was nothing if not a problem solver.

She'd smoothly and cheerfully problem solved her way out of Oregon, away from her family, away from all the toxicity in her childhood home. She'd worked her way through college and gotten herself this job.

There hadn't been time to date.

There was now, though, and she had a lovely, *lovely* coworker named Stavros who was all the things she could want. He was close to her age, he looked lovely in his navy blue and tan suits that weren't anything like as severe as Alex's commitment to all-black everything.

She took another bite of her salad. "I think I'm going to ask Stavros on a date."

Alex's face did something she'd never seen it do before. It flashed between confusion, irritation and something else she couldn't pinpoint. Then it was like she could see him doing a math equation in his head, and get the answer in record time.

"Stavros from the accounting department who has worked for this company for six months?" he asked.

"That would be him," she said, demurely, crunching her lettuce.

"He is your superior, technically."

"We work in totally different departments and HR allows for romantic relationships at this company as long as both parties sign a waiver."

"I am aware."

"I assumed, but you were acting like maybe you didn't realize that."

"Of course I realize it, Cricket, but from a moral standpoint, he is your superior, and it is problematic."

It was so funny to hear those words come out of his mouth because she had a feeling he had no emotion behind any of them. What he had was a computer program he'd uploaded into his head to make sure he knew what was okay, and what wasn't.

Which was maybe mean, because he wasn't an unkind man—not really if you dug down deep and got to know him over salad—but he was…detached.

There was a reason she'd been hired to be his human connection.

He was deeply unpopular in a world that was skeptical of billionaires. Where investors wanted their money placed at ethical companies, and social media made memes out of every lip twitch and eyebrow lift.

And while the internet agreed that Alexios Economides was hot, in all the various forms the internet declared a man hot, from panting emoji to all caps declarations of DADDY beneath photos of him, they also agreed he was an evil, MORALLY GRAY billionaire who had ice in his veins.

The truth was, Alex was very ethical. He donated to a great many causes and he offset his carbon footprint judiciously. But it was the…general vibe of him. His good deeds couldn't transcend the fact that if he were to stand in front of a podium and tell the world that he was Hades incarnate, they'd believe him.

But that did make the lectures on morality ring a little hollow.

"Are you saying I don't have agency?" she asked, licking some dressing off of her thumb.

"Excuse me?"

"I'm a grown woman, and I like him. I want to date him and yes, he's in a more senior position than I am, I guess, in a department I don't work in, but I'm the one who wants to ask him out. Are you saying that my personhood evaporates when it comes into contact with corporate structure?"

"I'm not saying that at all."

"You kind of are. You're telling me that what I want is problematic."

"Men use positions of power to manipulate women."

"Thank you for that, Alex, I didn't know that until a man in a position of power told me." She stared blandly at him and he shifted, a dark, unamused look in his eyes. Which amused *her* greatly.

He cleared his throat and her heart jumped in her chest, just a little bit.

"No one ever dares speak to me that way," he said, taking another angry bite of his salad.

"You hired me to talk to you like a human being and to teach you to talk to other people like a human being, and I have to tell you, you reciting a list of rules, divorced of context and emotion, doesn't really make you human. It makes you seem even more robotic."

She felt guilty as soon as that came out of her mouth because she could only assume that he'd hired an external conscience for social time in part because the commentary on him being AI rather than a human being made him feel bad.

She didn't want to make him feel bad.

Maybe that was a little bit silly, since most of the time Alex didn't care about making other people feel bad. Or rather, to be fair, he didn't *notice* when he did. Theoretically he was trying to learn—that was why she'd been hired. But often she wondered if she was making much of a difference beyond their lunches.

But he was... He wasn't like anyone she had ever known, and she had learned a lot from him. About technology and business, innovation. She...respected him.

She liked him.

Even when he was being ridiculous.

"I have a board meeting on Friday," he said.

He changed the subject so swiftly and abruptly it nearly gave her whiplash.

"About?"

"Attracting new investors ahead of the next product launch."

"I mean, it's a sensationally slick product. An AI assistant that uses less energy, and also learns from resources that actually gave consent is a really big deal. Not to mention it functions incredibly well."

"You really think the average consumer cares about the ethics of it?"

"Yes."

"They don't. They talk about it, they pretend to care and then they all pick their phones up like everyone else and never give a thought to how much energy is harvested to power that little square that lives in their pockets."

"You think all of humanity is hypocritical then?"

"I think at the intersection of convenience and ethics convenience often wins. But where I really do believe the product could succeed is that it is exceptionally convenient still. It's not the salability that concerns me, it's the fact that investors have been scarce in the past year, after that video went viral of me..."

"Breaking that kid's phone after he stuck it in your face?"

"He wasn't a kid, he was your age. And also, I clearly didn't break it well enough, because there's a video of the entire thing. From that point of view."

"Yes. It did not help humanize you." She paused. "Though at least they called you the Terminator after that instead of Data."

It had been an uncharacteristic display of temper, though it had even had that same robotic, measured manner about it. He hadn't yelled or shouted. He'd simply taken the phone and thrown it to the ground while continuing on his way.

"I don't care what anyone thinks of me, but it's becoming a problem with investors. Which infuriates me." He said that with the same measured tone he'd been using the whole time.

She had to hold back a laugh. "I can see that. You're positively simmering with rage."

He had said all of it in the same calm voice. He didn't seem outraged in the least. Except for the burning embers in his dark eyes.

She knew him well enough to know that she needed to be somewhat careful when he got that look.

She had never seen Alex in a full temper, but she knew

that the potential for it existed. And she was nothing if not an expert at avoiding explosions of temper, tamping them down and keeping them from ever occurring.

"At least the video proves that you're not AI," she pointed out. She had a feeling it was not the least bit helpful. And the irritated look that Alex gave her proved that theory.

"That was not a serious rumor," he said.

"It was," she said softly.

"So it's more believable that I was created in a data mine by an advanced learning module than that I'm a rich man who prefers to keep to himself and stay away from social gatherings?"

"Well. I don't want you to get an inflated ego, but the thing is, you are young…sort of, and you're extremely good-looking. Obviously people expect that you would take the money that you've earned and spend it ostentatiously on parties and yachts. With yacht girls. Or yacht boys, if that's what you're into." She looked at him, and tried to see if there was any reaction to either proposed yacht person.

That was the strangest thing about Alex. In a world that made privacy next to impossible—with cell phones and algorithm-based social media taking small moments and putting them on a world stage on the daily, he remained relatively private. Unknowable. Except of course he had been caught being angry at an obnoxious moron, and somehow had been painted as the bad guy. Well, she knew how. He was the billionaire. The power differential was clear, et cetera et cetera. The expectation that somebody who had a public-facing persona—sort of—was a public commodity was one that Verity didn't agree with, but that didn't make it any less real.

"What do you mean *sort of* young?"

"Well, you *are* in your thirties."

He didn't quite scowl, but he was very close.

"I need you to come to the board meeting," he said.

"Of course I'll be there. It's my job."

"Yes," he said, in total and complete confirmation.

There was something so final and intense about it, he might as well have been agreeing that he owned her in some capacity beyond work, because for some reason she felt like he had. Like there was something deeper than a work contract between them, when she knew there wasn't.

"I'm very helpful," Verity said, and she was teasing him, but part of her wanted him to agree. "I bet you feel better for having eaten a salad."

"I will feel better if I have a steak to follow it up."

"You're ridiculous. You don't need that much red meat midday."

He lifted a dark brow, and leaned back in his chair, which gave her full view of his rather muscular, perfectly hard torso. The crisp white shirt underneath his black jacket did not hide the structure of the musculature there; rather it turned into a sort of tease that appealed to her more than she wished it did.

She wrinkled her nose. "Are you trying to make a point?" she asked.

"Do you take a point by my posture? If so, then I suppose it is made."

"If you're trying to make the point that you having no body fat and well-defined muscles means that you don't need to watch what you eat, then you are woefully behind in regards to your education on health and nutrition."

"Which is another indication that I'm not AI."

"Why is that?"

"I would've been programmed with the latest data."

"More likely you would have eight fingers on one hand, but sure."

That actually did make him smile. It was never a full smile with teeth and crinkling eyes, nothing half so demonstrative with Alex. No. And so she took these rare, small flexes of the corners of his mouth as priceless gems. Because they were. And she had to remind herself yet again that their connection was boss and employee. That he wasn't really her friend. They never did anything outside of work, after all. They would be an improbable match in that regard.

She tried to imagine it. She thought of the things that she used to do at home with her friends. Imagined going through a drive-through coffee stand with Alex, and then going to the mall. It almost made her laugh out loud, but she held it back, because if she laughed, then she would have to explain herself to him.

"You are going to ask Stavros on a date," he said.

And yet again, his abrupt subject changes, which clearly came from some shift in his brain, invisible, sharp and beyond the understanding of everyone else, like all of his innovations, just about made her head spin.

"Yes."

"When?"

"I don't know. But I'm going to."

"You are going to wait and see if he's interested in you first?"

Verity scrunched her face. "No. Because I think that's outdated. I like him, so why play games?"

"I agree with you. It's only that I'm given to understand that games are an essential part of romance."

"Do you...often play games when it comes to romance?" She was skirting around the edges of off-limits topics. Well, actually this wasn't in the list of things they couldn't talk about; it had just always felt like she shouldn't talk about relationships with her boss. Also, it had never come up, since she'd never been in one, or even attempted to be until now.

Something flickered in his dark eyes, another near-imperceptible lift of his brow. "No. I don't. I don't have time for games. If I want sex I can have sex without romance."

Her face went very hot, and she wanted to go back and have never heard that word exit his mouth. She wanted to lecture him about boundaries. But this was the problem. They had personal conversations, she had brought up the subject of dating and she had asked him about his personal romantic life. The truth was, she worked for him, but two years of lunches put them in a space that was not entirely professional. No matter how much they should remain so.

"Spoken like an AI," she muttered, picking up her salad bowl and reaching out for his. He handed it to her without a second thought. Because yes, during lunch hour she was his...something. But after that she was an assistant. Of course genius hands like his did not wash dishes.

"Thank you for the salad," he said.

It was so shocking that it stopped her in her tracks.

She felt something like pleasure bloom at the center of her chest. "You're welcome," she said.

"Verity," he said, before she walked out, his use of her first name rather than the more common Cricket as shocking as the thanks.

"Yes?"

"The board meeting is in London. I've added some money to your expense account for new clothing, so why don't you spend the rest of the day preparing."

And while she should have spent the rest of the day planning how she might approach asking Stavros on a date, instead, as she browsed through the high-end shopping boutiques in Kolonaki, she heard Alex's *thank you* echoing in her head.

CHAPTER TWO

ALEX WATCHED HIS little personal assistant, who could never hide her abject fascination with his private plane no matter how hard she tried. She was always meandering around, opening drawers on furniture, looking inside the well-stocked bar, even though she barely ever drank anything stronger than a Shirley Temple.

She was a fascinating puzzle, was Verity. It was why he had hired her in spite of her lack of experience.

He had brought her in for an interview—a rare thing for him to interview an employee personally, but it was for the position of personal assistant, and more. Because he was beginning to recognize that his lack of human connection, his lack of personability, was becoming a liability.

Such a ridiculous thing.

He had power and money now. And yet still, he had to cater to the whims of others, especially ridiculous when those whims seemed to be created out of the air.

Created out of a false idea of who he was.

He wouldn't say he was a good man, acting out of the goodness of his heart, but he didn't do harm.

His life was his work. Which had made finding success possible in his early years. He had worked his way up in a small, inconsequential tech company where he had found a mentor in the owner. Eventually, he had taken over the business, then it had begun expanding, and he had renamed it. Had made it his own. And had turned it into something else entirely. A leading force in the tech industry, a global success.

Five years ago the company had become publicly traded, and then suddenly, the will of other people had been interjected into his success.

This was where conflict began.

Because it was no longer enough that he was brilliant, or that his product was superior. Small actions could affect the price of his stock, the willingness of investors could be swayed and shifted by public opinion, as everyone fought hard to play the cutthroat game of being beyond reproach in the eyes of a public hungry for that dopamine hit of moral superiority.

Which was why good deeds became public domain, charity was a public performance and attending galas, parties, places where a person could be seen being the sort of person others might be able to admire, was essential. And something that Alex had never personally seen the point of. Now he had to.

Or he could let it crumble. Could let his empire reduce itself, could go back to being a force in business, rather than the force. But relinquishing his grip on the gains he'd made simply wasn't something he was willing to do. And that was where Verity had initially come into the equation. He wanted to begin making moves to take his company to the next level. It had been suggested to him by one of his board members that he might try... practicing. That connection bit.

It wasn't that he didn't believe in it. It was just he had never had it. And therefore didn't especially understand.

He had been with child protective services from near the moment he was born. He didn't even know the circumstances around it. Why his mother had given him up, or why he had been taken away. Which thing it even was.

He had never—not from birth to the age of eighteen—been with a family for longer than six months. And where at first connection had merely felt foreign, it had become something he had guarded himself against. Because the end would always come. Because no one was attached to him, and so there was no point building an attachment to anyone else.

He'd honed so many skills that were valuable to him over the course of that childhood. Difficult though it was, it had made him into a successful man.

How horrendously ironic that the circumstances of that childhood should cause him to trip at the finish line.

No. He had not tripped; he had merely faltered. Now he had Verity, who everyone in the company loved. Verity, who made him eat salad and was currently poking around his plane like a nosy little mole looking for a hidey-hole.

"Sit down, Cricket," he said. "You're making me dizzy."

"I'll never get over how amazing this is. It's really more the house than it is a plane."

"No," he said. "It is a plane."

"You know what I mean. I think my apartment is smaller than this."

"Why?"

She looked at him, humor glittering in her eyes. She

found him funny, which was a strange experience. He didn't think anyone else found him particularly amusing. "Have you looked at the prices for apartments in Athens these days? It's a bit prohibitive."

"I pay you very well."

She nodded. "You do. And I like to have money left over for savings, and to do things. I go to the beach almost every weekend."

"Do you?"

He had never thought about what Verity did in her spare time. Or where she lived. The idea of her doing things when she wasn't in his office was somewhat disconcerting, and he couldn't say why.

Of course, when she had mentioned asking Stavros on a date he had been forced to think of her in another context altogether, and he hadn't liked that either. She was...well, she was Verity. He didn't take much notice of other people. Their clothing, their likes, their dislikes, their moods. He'd hired her to teach him to engage with those things, to talk to him, and he found that he was highly tuned into all those things about her now.

She was going to sit and eat a meal with Stavros? Just as she did with him?

He found that uncomfortable.

"Yes," she said.

She turned from the bar, her gray plaid skirt swirling around with her, revealing a peek at her thighs. He didn't really want to look at his assistant's thighs, and generally speaking, if he didn't want to do something, he didn't. And yet.

She was a fascinating woman, though he would never say that out loud. He wasn't sure he had ever been fascinated by another person before. But she was just so different. From an entirely different world, a different life. While they didn't speak in depth about their families, or the lack of his, she had told him once that she had spent her entire childhood in the same house.

The idea had nestled in the middle of his brain, and centered itself on many afternoons when his mind had begun to wander.

What would it be like to grow up with that sort of stability? To not spend all of your life moving from house to house, between different neighborhoods in a city, or sometimes even hours away. All of your belongings wrapped up in black plastic, your lone pair of shoes on your feet, growing tight and worn, until someone finally noticed but you might need a new pair.

He had a room in his house dedicated to shoes now. He could wear a different pair every day. The moment his feet felt even the slightest discomfort, he would change the shoes.

It was his favorite luxury. That and knowing that he was in charge of where he slept every night. He had multiple homes, and if he wanted to move between them he could, and often he did feel a strange sort of burning sensation in his chest when he spent too many nights in a row in one place.

He had an apartment at the top floor of the office building, and the house up in the hills on the outside of the city. A place by the beach. He could offer to let Verity use it. He supposed.

Those were just his houses within proximity to the company's headquarters.

There were others.

It felt powerful to own so many pieces of the world, when he had owned nothing for so long.

And yet here he was, jumping through hoops he didn't care to even acknowledge.

Thus was the cost of success.

There was a point where one could become success- ful enough that they had to consider nothing and no one else, but now he had begun to arrive at a different part of the curve, where if he wished to continue to progress he had to care.

Verity sat on the love seat opposite him, a keen sort of expression on her face. "What is the meeting about?"

"The product launch."

"I understand that," she said. "But I mean what is the focus of this specific meeting? Why have they called it now, and what are you concerned about?"

"I didn't say that I was concerned," he said.

"No, you didn't."

He stared at her. "And?"

"I can tell you're concerned," she said.

How strange.

"My popularity is in question, as you know."

"Yes, I do know. But what are the real-world conse- quences to that?"

"A disappointing launch. And if we do not remain number one in the quarter during the launch period, then we will have ceded ground, and I refuse."

"Right." She leaned back, her blond curls fanning around her as she rested her head against the back of the love seat. Her hair was one of the first things he had noticed about her. It was wild, and she never tamed it. Even if it was up in a bun, she let tendrils fly free. There was something about that which captured his focus in a way he could not articulate.

It was, he thought then, something to do with the fact that it was so quintessentially Verity.

"But the question I have," she continued, "is what is enough? How many times do you need to be number one? Because success on this level surely can't continue forever. Everybody reaches a peak."

"That might be true when an entity is smaller than mine."

Her lips twitched. "An entity?"

He narrowed his gaze. "You know what I mean. Total domination is possible. And I want to."

"Why?"

How did he explain? How did he explain that in a world he had not asked to be born into, a world that had passed him around like a bad penny that no one wanted, he needed to make an undeniable, unquestionable place for himself? One that would endure after he died.

This launch was the one that would do it, and that made it more important than anything else he'd ever done. He had a chance to set a precedent with new technology, one that would carry on after he did.

He did not have a family. He never would, most likely.

The idea of love and marriage, of hearth and home, when he had never experienced it…

It was a blank space in his mind. He could not have conjured up an image of himself in it any more easily than he could fly.

Yes, he had seen it. Windows into it while watching TV, or worst of all, when he had been with good families in his years in foster care and he had sat down at dinner tables with parents who cared about their children, knowing that he would never be one of those children. Knowing that it wasn't a place that he would stay.

He would never hunger for something he could not have, not again.

This, this total dominion over his market, that he could achieve, and so he would.

He did not have to explain it to Verity, he decided.

She didn't need to understand. She simply needed to collect her paycheck.

He nearly said it to her, but didn't, because he needed her to look as sweet and rosy in the board meeting as she did right now.

"Because," he said. "Because I am an ambitious man, and ambition only partly realized is nothing more than frustration."

"We don't want you to be frustrated."

She sat perched on the edge of the couch now, and he couldn't help but be amused by her London attire, gray wool and a check pattern which he had to admit was charming.

She was charming.

She had an effortlessness about her. A way of making others feel at ease. He didn't like to admit that she did the same thing to him that she did to everyone else. That she seemed to have some sort of magical ability to appease him, like he was a beast who needed soothing.

But she did.

He'd known she was the one he'd hire the moment she walked into his office, and it was like the tension bled from his muscles.

Verity was all things good. He had never thought that about another person before.

Least of all Stavros, who was quite competent in his position, or he wouldn't be working at the company, but he certainly didn't seem good enough for her.

He didn't say that either. Instead, he busied himself with work for the rest of the flight and when they touched down in London, he resumed watching Verity's reaction to everything.

"I would love to come back here on a holiday," she said wistfully as a town car swept them through the city streets, moving quickly to deliver them to the meeting.

"Then you will," he said.

He would give her a bonus. Whatever she needed.

That was another thing he had learned in the formation of this company. If you paid people well enough, they would always stay. His personality didn't seem to matter overmuch as long as they were well compensated.

He could pay people to stay with him.

That thought sat uncomfortably in the center of his chest.

He chose not to analyze it.

When they got out of the car, Verity paused near the entrance to a coffee shop, one that was next to the office building.

"What are you doing?" he asked.

"I think we should stop and get a box of sweets."

He was about to protest, or ask her why, but she was charging ahead, her phone held aloft in front of her, and he could see the digital version of the company's credit card gleaming on her screen.

She immediately charmed every employee in the place, and bought a box full of sweet treats—little cakes and scones and biscuits, which of course Verity called cookies. This did not seem to annoy the employees providing the baked goods; rather they seemed to find her effortlessly charming.

One of the workers behind the counter smiled at him, and he smiled back. The other person's smile faded, and Alex wished that he had a mirror to check his expression because he had been certain that he was being friendly.

Verity was now holding a pink box filled with sweets, and he held the door open for her as she rounded out of the shop, blond curls bouncing against her back.

"And what is this?"

"I'm going to put everybody in a good mood from the beginning. A little bit of cake never hurts, and neither does the gesture."

They walked into the building, where he was recognized on sight, and so they didn't have to stop at registration. Rather they simply stepped into the elevator. "But we don't even know if they're hungry."

"Of course not. But you don't have to be hungry to eat cake."

That was true.

"It's like any gift," she said. "It's the thought that counts."

They made the rest of the elevator ride in silence, and when the door swept open, Verity took the lead, and he watched her walk in the wrong direction, that pink box clutched tightly in her hands.

"Verity," he said. "This way."

She stopped and turned, and he tilted his head the

other direction. Her cheeks went pink, and she scampered back toward him, and he took the lead, as it should be, the two of them headed into the meeting.

"Good morning," he said as he stepped in.

"Good morning," Verity said, the emphasis on the word somehow different, her voice wrapping around each syllable and making it seem warm. "I've brought some goodies to open things up. I'll get everything laid out while Alex... Mr. Economides...begins the introduction."

She set the box down in the center of the table and then left, presumably off to gather plates. Then Verity returned, and while he was speaking, she passed out plates and napkins. And took orders for coffee.

She turned the entire place into a café, and he found it irritating and distracting. Though none of the board members seemed to.

In fact, he had never spoken to such a charmed audience. It wasn't simply that they were interested in what he had to say, though they were, but they seemed...softer. More receptive.

Maybe it was cake.

Maybe it was Verity.

She went off to fetch a second round of coffee, at which one of the board members tapped him on the forearm. "She is delightful."

She was. She was delightful in a way he never could be. Never would be. In a way that seemed effortless.

She was relatable, to everyone somehow. She grounded the entire room. She was like a fairy, though he didn't believe in such things, and had never particularly been fond of childish stories. But there was something magic about her.

The mere fact of her being near him seemed to make everyone react differently to him, as well. The assumption being, of course, that such a sweet, caring woman would never associate with a man who was monstrous.

He could see it, and the way these people who he had met with many times before reacted to him now.

And that was just with her here as his assistant. How could he do this?

How could he bring what Verity offered him here out into the public eye?

Oh. He had an idea. More than an idea—it would happen. All he needed to do was set the wheels in motion. And it would be easy enough. It could coincide with the product launch. It was perfect.

He had hired Verity to be his personal assistant, and he had finally figured out what he needed her for most of all.

CHAPTER THREE

THE TRIP TO London had been all too brief, but Verity decided to turn her attention to Stavros, and her date goal.

She *did* think, a little bit, about the way that Alex had praised her after the meeting. He had told her what a good job she had done, and something had lit up inside of her.

Pleasing him was one of the nicest feelings she could think of. And it wasn't because he was more important than anyone else—it was only that he was so taciturn and difficult to read that when she knew he was happy with her it felt like something came alive inside of her.

She was used to walking on eggshells. She had grown up that way. In a house filled with volatile adults, who held everybody at the mercy of their moods. Her siblings had then learned how to weaponize those moods. Aim them at each other, and Verity had done everything she could to stay away from it. To stay away from them.

It wasn't like that with Alex. Yes, he had a mercurial nature. She could understand why people were afraid of him. But, she knew how to keep things running smoothly, and so she never took the brunt of his temper.

She didn't spend her time trying to avoid his ill will, and as a result, she was able to enjoy the feeling of earning his approval.

She collected those compliments; she thought of them as shiny rocks that she carried around in her pockets. Glimmering pieces of evidence that he was happy with her.

But, she wasn't going to think about Alex right now. Because she had chosen her outfit today specifically to ask Stavros on a date. She didn't usually dress sexy. Not that this was particularly sexy; it was just maybe a little bit bolder than her typical office fare. A purple dress that came a couple of inches above her knees, figure hugging and very flattering if she said so herself.

Her hair was especially wild today, but she had made her peace with her curls a long time ago. Once she'd stopped fighting them and learned to love them she had been much happier. And she had saved a lot of money on product.

Alex had texted her to say that he was coming in late today, which was all fine; she would see him at lunchtime. And then she could talk to him about how she had managed to get a date with Stavros.

She moved quickly down the hall, toward Stavros's office, her heart thundering in her chest. It was echoing just slightly in her ears. She had never done anything like this before. She imagined him, all sunny and pleased to see her, and that made her feel…

Not as good as pleasing Alex, but she wasn't going to dwell on that.

She paused at the door, and knocked.

"Come in."

She pushed the door open, and grinned when she saw him sitting there, just as she had imagined him. Dressed in his navy blue suit looking boyish and charming.

"Verity," he said.

His smile faded slightly, and Verity was confused.

"That's me. I wanted to talk to you."

"Really?"

"Yes. I… I was wondering if you…if you wanted to have dinner sometime. Maybe this weekend."

"Are you joking?"

"No. I'm not joking." Well, of all the responses that she might have received to her dinner invitation, that wasn't one that she had imagined.

"I just saw this."

He turned his computer screen so that it was facing her, and Verity looked at it as shock infiltrated her system. It was a photograph; that was the first thing that she noticed on the screen. A photograph of a London street, her in her little plaid suit, and Alex in all black as always, looking down at her as though he was giving an indulgent smile to a child.

And she couldn't even enjoy the fact that Alex had been caught on camera smiling at her, because her eye went to the headline next.

Tech Mogul Alexios Economides to Wed Personal Assistant!

She blinked.

"Is it true?" Stavros asked.

She didn't know what to say. She didn't know if Alex had seen this. She didn't know where the rumor had come from. She should just say no. It didn't matter what Alex thought, because this wasn't true, so there was no reason to let Stavros think that it was. The man that she wanted to go on a date with. Who she had just asked out on a date.

But if she said no, and… What if there was a reason? And it compromised her job? What if it made Alex angry, or it undermined something? As she stood there, trying to reason this truth quickly as possible, trying to figure out a way to extricate herself from the situation as peacefully as possible, she came to the conclusion that this must be some sort of mistake, but there was going to have to be a delicate extraction from the mistake.

Because it was public. *Grandly* public. This wasn't a gossip rag. This was being featured in a major journalistic publication.

And sure, they had gotten it wrong. Because of course it was possible for news sources to get things wrong. But she just needed to… She needed to talk to Alex. She took her phone out of her pocket and she started to text him.

"Is it true?" Stavros asked. She had totally blanked his existence for a moment. She looked up at him, and guilt gnawed at her. She realized that he looked hurt. Maybe he did like her. She had to fix this. She just needed to…

"Please excuse me for a moment. I'm really sorry. This is… I just need to… Have to make a call."

She abandoned her text message, and opted to call Alex instead. He did not answer. She rang again, and again. He still didn't answer. What was going on?

She opened up social media, and she was shocked to see that his name was trending, along with hers.

She clicked on her name with a sense of growing hesitation.

Verity Carmichael.

There were so many posts.

Verity Carmichael is twenty-four and from Bend, Oregon. Get to know Alexios Economides's future bride!

Snag Verity Carmichael's look! Details here.

Is Verity Carmichael hiding a secret?

Inside the workplace relationship turned romance of Verity Carmichael and Alexios Economides!

How could there be an inside look at something that didn't even exist? She felt nauseous.

Somehow, she was afraid that it was her fault. She could see him storming into the office looking angry. She could feel her control on everything around her beginning to dissolve, beginning to slip away. Already, Stavros was mad at her, and maybe she shouldn't be worried about that right now, but she was. It made her feel queasy. Shaky.

This job meant a lot to her. Pleasing Alex meant a lot to her, and she was going to go ahead and admit that now as she stumbled toward his office. She sat there, a sheen of sweat beginning to form on her forehead.

Where was he?

She called two more times, and he didn't answer the phone. She knew that he had said that he was going to be in late, but it was strange that he wasn't answering the phone. Him being late did not mean that he wasn't working. Alex was almost always working.

And anyway, she was his…mistaken fiancée, so he should be in communication with her. Maybe he hadn't seen any of it yet.

She was going to have to break the news to him.

That made her palms get sweaty.

And then she looked up, through the glass walls that made up his office, and she could see him striding toward her. Could feel him, as if his energy transcended the barriers around her.

She stood up, and walked to the door. She had it opened as soon as he approached it. She started to speak, but words wouldn't come out of her mouth. Coherent sentences wouldn't form.

"I…" She winced. "Somehow, the media got ahold of the mistaken information that you and I are engaged, and it *very much* messed up my attempt at getting a date."

He looked at her, his expression smooth. He didn't look surprised. He didn't look upset.

That tilted her entire world on its axis. She had been afraid of him being angry, but she hadn't imagined him being…placid. Mostly because Alex was never placid. And he seemed suspiciously so right then.

"Oh?"

"It must be a mistake," she said.

"Must it?" He was serene, unruffled. It was…baffling.

"Yes, because we are *not* engaged."

"Indeed not. And I did not intend for the press release to go out so quickly."

She blinked three times. "I'm sorry?"

"Yes. I gave the information to the media."

Oh, so it wasn't baffling. He had gone behind her back and done the most insane thing possible that she would never have guessed in the entire world because *who would ever do such a thing?*

Your eccentric boss who pays you to eat lunch with him.

"You…you gave the information to the media. But we are not… We aren't… I told you that I was going to ask Stavros out."

She didn't know why she was coming back to that, except everything felt absurd at the moment, and returning to that one, grounding thing seemed as sane as anything else.

"Yes, I do remember you telling me that." She sputtered as he continued speaking. "And that is an unfortunate casualty of this turn of events. But I was thinking about it after the board meeting a few days ago, and I decided that the best, most beneficial thing for my image would be if you and I were to be married."

"That's…. Who in the world would think that was a logical thing to do? And what is this? 1950?"

"Do you think that culture isn't traditional anymore? Trust me, Cricket, they are. While the youths posture about their progressive ideals, they still very much gather information about someone's mortality and likeability from their romantic partnerships. And everyone loves you."

"I don't… You don't…"

She didn't even know what to say. She couldn't form sentences. She was standing at the center of his office flustered and speaking in half-realized, choppy sentences like a fool.

"This makes sense, Verity. I have an image problem and I need to fix it. This will work."

"And you didn't…you didn't ask *me*?"

She felt anger rising up inside of her, such an uncommon feeling, and one that she hated. She didn't do anger; she didn't do out-of-control. She was someone who kept her emotions in check at all times. This panic that was taking over her like a ravenous wolf was entirely unwelcome, and the howling anger that accompanied it was even worse.

She tried to calm herself down. Tried to draw a deep breath. This was still Alex, and she still knew him. This was not something that she had expected from him, and indeed nothing that she had ever expected to deal with ever, but she was going to listen to him. Listen to his rational explanation. He was her boss, so she really did need to listen.

And, whatever he said, she needed to try and find a peaceful outcome to it. If she blew everything up she would lose her job; she wouldn't be able to stay in Greece because she wouldn't be able to afford it. Everybody knew that she was Alex's assistant, and now they thought she was his fiancée. So whether she liked it or not, she was in a pickle.

She needed to calm down, be a little bit mindful and figure out what the right thing to do was rather than responding in an emotional state.

Because she wasn't either of her parents, and she didn't fly off the handle at a moment's provocation.

"No. I confess I didn't think to speak to you about it. It is such a logical step."

"It's a logical step," she repeated.

"Yes. Everyone at the board meeting absolutely loved you. You humanize me. That's what I hired you for."

"You hired me to be your *assistant*, and teach you how to have…casual conversations."

"Yes. To humanize me. I realized that it would be much more effective to use you in that capacity in a public sphere."

"But you… You realize that this is my life. You are hijacking my life. This isn't nine-to-five, this isn't office work, you're talking about pretending to be engaged to me."

"Oh no, I'm not."

"Then I'm even more confused."

"I'm talking about *marrying* you."

She clenched her teeth together and had to breathe very deeply because if she didn't she was going to fall over. Or leap across the room and strangle him with his tie. "You must be joking."

He looked down, and then looked at her, like he was staring straight into her soul. "What do you want, Verity? I have spent two years having lunch with you, and I know who you like in this office, what foods you like to eat, your favorite recipes to cook at home. I know where you like to shop around Athens, and I know that you're from Oregon. I know what movies you like, and TV shows. We have talked about every casual, small thing under the sun. What I don't know is what you want to do with your life."

She didn't know why, but the question and the direct nature of his gaze made her teeth chatter. Made it hard for her to breathe, hard for her to think.

"I… I want to be independent. And to have enough money to support myself, but also enough time to enjoy where I live. I want to date. And make new friends, and go out and have fun. I want what most people in their twenties want."

"That's shallow," he said, waving a hand dismissively. "That's what everyone wants."

"I want to have enough that I never have to go back to

where I came from," she said, feeling raw and exposed by those words. Feeling goaded into saying them.

"And that is what I want. And it is also what I offer you. If you do this, if you marry me, for at least six months, and it has the desired effect, after which we will discuss the length and terms even more explicitly, then you and I will both achieve our goals. I will send you on your way with a very healthy hazard pay package."

She took one breath. Then another. And what he said began to sink in.

"What do you mean you'll send me on my way?"

"If this wedding and marriage are supposed to look authentic, then it would be very unusual for us to continue working together afterward."

Her head was spinning. He was proposing that they engage in a fake marriage, and that it would be the end of her relationship with him. Of course she had never imagined that this job would last forever. It had always been a weird job. From the moment that she had first agreed to it, it had seemed too good to be true, and definitely not something that would continue. In fact, she was somewhat surprised that she had been doing it for two years.

That he had continued to want to have lunch with her every weekday during that time.

But she was being torn in half by this. This thing he was proposing that she was still having trouble wrapping her head around. He wanted to marry her. And then he wanted her to go away.

But he was also offering her…

Independence.

"I don't want to get married," she said.

He hadn't asked, and she supposed it didn't really matter for the purposes of what he was talking about.

"I thought you liked Stavros?" he asked.

"I do. But I want to go out with him. And maybe…" The back of her throat felt prickly. "You know, I want the same things that you do when you go out with someone. I don't want forever."

Her cheeks heated. "No. I don't romanticize marriage."

How could she? Her house had been a war zone. She supposed she could be grateful that neither of her parents had abused each other or their children with their fists. But she had learned that psychological warfare could be just as damaging in many ways. It had taken her so long to rebuild any sense of value and herself.

The enormous weight she'd carried every day trying to keep the peace had left her exhausted. She'd put all her own emotions on the back burner to appease them. She had learned that she didn't matter, that everyone else mattered more.

In some ways, she felt like she had truly emerged from her cocoon after college. Those four years she had still felt like it might all be taken away from her at any moment. Like maybe she wasn't good enough or smart enough. Wouldn't be able to finish, wouldn't be able to amount to anything. She had also vowed to herself that she would rather be on the streets than ever go back home.

But because of that anxiety that had dogged her during her college years, she hadn't really had fun. She had been hoping to have some fun. And now Alex was asking her to pretend to be his wife.

Except…

She pressed her fingertips to her temples. "Wait a minute. There's a plot hole here. You think that I can marry you, and then we'll get divorced, and it won't just undo everything that we did with this relationship?"

She still wasn't entirely convinced that them getting married would do what he thought. Though, she could see what he was thinking. It would make him look like a man with an interior life, a man who loved someone, and had someone who loved him in return.

She didn't like the way that thought made her feel. It opened up a strange, yawning ache inside of her that she wished would go away.

And yet, even as she shoved that thought to the side, the feeling remained.

"I don't think that it will undo everything. Particularly not if we make it clear it ended amicably."

"It will just look like I signed an NDA."

"You will be doing just that."

"I already did," she pointed out.

"Yes. So you did. But I will have you sign another one. Because I will make it legally clear that I need you to keep my confidence personally as well as professionally."

Her heart was beating quickly again, and she tried to calm herself. There was no way she was actually considering this.

"You knew that I was going to ask Stavros out," she said.

"Yes. And now I know he isn't the love of your life. Nor did you intend him to be."

Drat.

"But I like him. I wanted to…"

"You will not sleep with other men during the duration of our marriage."

You will not sleep with other men.

Those words scraped along her skin, down her spine; they froze her. Did he mean that she would...?

She stared at him.

Alex was a decade older than her, a billionaire. Hard, intense, everything that she had spent her life actively avoiding.

And here she was, embroiled with him in a way that she would never have been able to explain to younger Verity, who would not believe that she had gotten herself into this situation.

"Yes?" he asked.

Her brain was still frozen. She shook her head, and tried to catch her breath. "You don't mean...?"

"It will be a marriage in name only. We will make the terms of it very clear. You will perform the planning of the wedding. It will be available for public consumption. We will telegraph every part of this to a hungry public, and they will fall in love with you."

He looked at her, his dark eyes burning with conviction. She felt very much like she suddenly understood how it was to be Snow White, offered a poisoned apple. This was a poisoned apple, and she knew it. She still felt drawn to it. Still felt like she wanted it.

Like she might die if she didn't have it.

"You are special, Verity Carmichael. And the whole world will see it. What you did in that board meeting you will do writ large."

A small, angry part of her, wounded and curled up at the center of her chest, was so tempted. Her full name was out there in the media. Her family would see it. They would know that she had left home, and she had made something of herself. That the only reason she had ever seemed small or insignificant was because they had clipped her wings, and once she had some freedom, to heal, to find herself, she had found a way to fly.

If she married Alex, she would be married to one of the most famous, one of the wealthiest men in the world. She could help fix his company. It frightened her, how much that mattered. This idea that she could be responsible for fixing this. That she could be that important. She was the peacekeeper of her house, and she knew that it had been a toxic thing for her to have to do, but part of her still felt desperation where that was concerned. Still felt a deep, unending need to prove her worth. To make something better.

To show everyone that she wasn't the one who was broken.

And yes, it was going to cost her that date with Stavros, but Alex was right. She didn't hold out hope for love, not in the way most people thought of it. Yes, it would be nice. But the idea of living in some suburban fantasy, husband, wife, children, it made her feel almost nauseous. She had felt trapped in her childhood home, and she would be damned if she was ever trapped again. But this was different. This was different.

"I need to know your terms. Specifically."

He nodded. "I have had a document drawn up."

He reached into his jacket pocket, and took out a folded stack of papers. He thrust the sheaf into her hand, and she only looked at them. "I doubt it would be too much work for you to tell me what's in them. Considering that you're demanding I marry you, for real, put my life on hold and have this as part of my story forever, till the end of time."

He shrugged a shoulder. "It will be a marriage in name only. Of course I would never coerce you into intimacy. This is a business deal. Like I said, we will stay married for six months. With the option to extend the marriage by six more months if there is something critical occurring once the six months lapse. You will receive an allowance that is three times your current pay through the duration of the marriage. And then you will receive a lump sum upon the ending of the marriage. Which we will say ended amicably, in a united front. We will have a story that we both tell with matching details. Forever. No one is to ever know that the marriage wasn't real. Not your family, and if you do decide to marry at a later date, you may not tell him either."

Well, she wouldn't decide to get married later. And she didn't have close friends right now that she would be lying to, and she wasn't going to invite her parents to the wedding. Later, when she did make the friends that she hoped to make, when she was traveling the world, which this would allow her to do, she might be sorry that she wouldn't be able to tell them the truth.

But wasn't that a small price to pay?

"I… How much is the lump sum?"

He tapped the paper.

She opened it slowly, and her heart leaped when she saw the amount written there. It was unfathomable. Millions of dollars. Enough to make her independently wealthy for the rest of her life. She could do…whatever she wanted. The only limit would be what she could imagine.

For a woman who had always struggled with the concept of her own self-worth, that was a strange door to open up.

Money was a great reason to not follow your dreams.

But if she had all this money, she could. Which meant that she needed to figure out exactly what those dreams were.

But she would have the time to do that. She would have the time to make herself into a new person. One who wasn't so affected by her parents.

It almost felt like anything was possible. Anything would be possible.

She also knew that she could put up with anything. For a little while. Six months, maybe a year, with somebody that she already knew she liked spending time with. He wasn't asking for anything sexual. He wasn't asking her to give much of anything.

"What am I supposed to do when we are…married?"

"You will support me the way that you do now."

So she would still have her job. Which actually made her feel relieved. Because at least something would be normal.

"Then…" The truth was, she couldn't justify saying no to this. It would be criminally insane to turn him down. "Then I accept. Yes, Alex. I will marry you."

CHAPTER FOUR

HE HAD KNOWN that she would see his way of thinking.
He felt immensely triumphant. She had come around to
his way of thinking easily enough, and he had expected
slightly more of a fight than she had given, if he were
honest. But then, it was a good idea, and what he was
offering her was generous. So what was there to argue
about?

He decided that the wedding would be in one month's
time, and when he sent that missive to Verity, she crashed
through his office door not five minutes later.

"Yes, Cricket?"

If she had been a cat, he was quite certain that her fur
would've stood up on end. "A *month*?"

"Yes. I don't see any point in dragging this out."

"You expect me to plan a wedding in a month?"

"I'm a billionaire, Cricket. If you need resources, you
can buy them."

"I'm aware of that, but you know venues and…"

"We have to capitalize on the momentum of all of this.
Have you seen the sheer volume of stories coming out
just in the last couple of days?"

She stomped over to his desk. "Of course I have.
They're impossible to ignore. Everyone is obsessed with

you being in love. This is the most PR you've ever gotten, good or bad. It's…overwhelming."

"Perhaps for you. But I've never cared what people said about me."

She blinked, then huffed. "Then why are you doing all of this?"

"I don't care what other people think about me, but the board does. Investors do. That's my problem. This is all strictly business, and none of it's personal to me."

"Has anything ever been personal to you?" He had the feeling that it was a loaded question, but he didn't really know why it would be. He didn't know why she would care.

"I enjoy our lunches," he said, because he had the feeling that was what she was getting at.

"But not so much that you think of me as a whole person. Because you wouldn't just announce the engagement between yourself and someone who was equal to you without checking with them."

"Why do you think that?"

"Because that's not what people do."

"That's what I do," he said. "And I'm the same no matter who I'm dealing with."

She was silent for a moment. Then she sat down in the chair just in front of his desk, a blond curl falling down at her face, and he felt the urge to brush it away, though he didn't do it. Because he didn't cross that boundary with her. Ever. Of course, it would be a necessity, to an extent. When they were seen out in public together, they would have to touch.

The very idea of it made a strange, unwanted sort of heat unwind itself in his stomach, made him feel like he was at the mercy of something. And he didn't do helpless. Not these days.

So he pushed it down. Ignored it. Pushed forward.

"That isn't really true," Verity said softly. "You have always been nicer to me. I suppose that's why I thought maybe you would treat me differently than you do the other people around you."

"How do you think I treat the people around me?"

"Like pawns on a chessboard. Like conveniences or inconveniences, but not really like people, and I thought that there was something more to you, Alex, I really did. After two years of taking lunch with you every day, of talking to you about the weather and TV, and…life. I thought that we were friends."

The word sat uncomfortably in his chest, like a brick, and he couldn't grasp why that would be. He had never thought of Verity as a friend, but then, he had never thought of anybody as a friend. But maybe she was right. The way that they had interacted was perhaps something like friendship. And yet, he was still… He still felt as if there was a wall between himself and her. As there was with him and everyone.

A necessity as a child who was never allowed to have attachments, and a matter of course as a man who had never learned any other way.

"I don't have friends," he said.

He regretted it the moment the words left his mouth, because she looked wounded. Like he had slapped her, rather than simply speaking a simple four-word truth.

"It isn't personal," he said. "I don't know how to have friends. I don't have family. I never have. I assume you know I was raised in foster care—that much is public knowledge on the open internet."

She nodded slowly. "Yes. I do know that. But I'm not allowed to ask you about it, it's in my folder."

"Then I will tell you," he said. "I never stayed in one home longer than six months. I have never understood the attachment that people have to one another. Because there has never been anything remotely permanent in my life, nor has there ever been an expectation of it. I never knew my parents. I never will. I don't know why my mother gave me up, I don't know why my father wasn't involved. There is a great, dark void there, and it's one I stopped looking into a long time ago. I'm not sad about it. But it is what made me. That's why we were having lunch together."

"I thought I was sort of…coaching you or…?"

"It was just to get some idea of what it might be like. Of why people do it. How to look like I do it. Whatever I needed to do to bolster the sales of the company."

"So none of it was actually for you? None of it has been to try and…fix…?"

"I'm not going to be *fixed*. Handily, I'm not broken. You cannot miss what you've never had, little Cricket. I don't miss my mother because I didn't know her. I don't miss my father because I've never had one. I created this company and it has been my life. It is what gives me purpose. It's why I wake up in the morning. It is, I suppose, the one connection that I have truly on this entire planet, and I will do whatever I must to make it all that it can be."

She looked stunned. He had never told anyone all of this before, because why would he? It wasn't anyone else's business, and he didn't like the pity that he could see in her eyes. He didn't need pity. He was successful. He was a man who had overcome. A man who had transcended his circumstances, and he didn't need pity from anyone.

And here was this little thing looking at him as if he was a wounded animal. She didn't speak, though. That made him even angrier, because she always had something to say, and the fact that she was being careful spoke to the depth of how much she felt sorry for him.

No one was connected to him enough to feel sorry for him. He didn't want it. And it was unearned.

"Don't look at me like that," he said. "I am still your boss."

"My fiancé," she said softly.

"Employed to be my fiancée," he said. "And so I'm still your boss."

"And not my friend."

"I'm sorry if that hurts you. It's got nothing to do with you."

"Of course not. Why would it? There's nothing personal about any of this, is there?" She stared at the wall behind him, her expression as angry as he'd ever seen it. "Why did you choose me?"

There were reasons. But it was hard to take the shape of those reasons, those feelings, and put them into words. He knew them, but he didn't know how to lay them out to her. And so, he didn't. "You were the first person I interviewed."

The unspoken truth was that he was impatient, overly efficient, at the cost of anything else.

His words made her shrink.

But maybe that wasn't a bad thing. He needed to establish the boundaries here. Because while he was pleased that she had agreed to his plan, he could see that this might become difficult for her. Marriage meant nothing to him. It was as theoretical as all other connections, those mystical bonds he couldn't access, and didn't want to anyway.

She claimed she didn't plan on getting married but she was twenty-four years old, and the truth was, he didn't believe her. She didn't think she wanted to get married, but most people around him seemed to want it, seemed to fall for it in the end, as feelings of loneliness and inadequacy, and swiftly passing time overtook them.

She might think she felt that way now, but he doubted she would feel that way always.

"Well, I suppose that answers that question." Something in her demeanor shifted, there was a sort of distance that came over her and she straightened her shoulders. "If we only have thirty days then we need to begin making appointments. I feel like you and I need to be seen together. There needs to be ample media fodder, because if we're going to do this then we need to do it right. I'm going to need a ring, a dress and various other bridal accessories. We need a venue, flowers, music. Food. A guest list."

"Normally I would put you in charge of several of those things, but you're correct. We need to do the forward-facing work as much as possible. I will have someone in administration handle the venue, music, food and the guest list."

"Acceptable. I will find the best places for you and I

to shop for some of these other things together. And I will present you with a modified schedule."

"A modified schedule?"

She nodded. "Yes. This is your priority now. It has to be. That's simply the only way this is going to work."

"I find that to be extremely heavy-handed of you."

She stood up, and she shot him a narrow glance. "*Do* you? What's good for the Cricket is good for the devil, ponder that."

And then she swept out of his office without a backward glance, and he would never admit it to her, but he did ponder that.

CHAPTER FIVE

VERITY HAD BEEN concerned that she overplayed her hand in Alex's office the other day, but he had acted like he wasn't offended by her during all of their following interactions.

She hated to admit that he had hurt her feelings. She didn't want to unpack any of that. She didn't want to examine it too closely. He was her boss. Her boss that she had agreed to enter into a sham marriage with, so there was a lot there.

And when he had looked at her with those dark, fathomless eyes and said that he had chosen her simply because she was the first person he had interviewed? It had been like a dagger to the heart.

So had what he'd said about his experience in foster care.

No one had kept him for longer than six months? For his entire life?

She was forced to imagine him as a little pinball, being bounced around the system with nowhere to rest. And then she supposed at eighteen he had been out on his own without a support system. There was no way that wouldn't have shaped who he was. It made her understand him to an extent. And made her worry a little bit that he was right. That he wasn't ever going to be able to have human connection the way that other people did.

She had read about things like that. That children needed to form bonds with caregivers before the age of two or they were damaged irreparably.

That just didn't seem fair, though. He hadn't had control over any of that.

It mitigated some of the anger she felt toward him. But just some of it.

It was weird, not having the specter of her Stavros crush standing between her and Alex. She didn't want to ponder why that was different either.

Stavros.

She scrunched her face. She was supposed to be meeting Alex in twenty minutes to go to a jewelry store, and it just occurred to her that she had never followed up with Stavros the previous week. She did feel like she owed him an explanation. But now she was going to have to come up with a lie.

She let out a heavy breath, and slipped down the hallway, finding his office door slightly ajar. She wrapped her fingers around the edge of the door, and pushed it open slowly. "Hi," she said.

He looked up from his desk, and for some reason, she just didn't get the same thrill when his eyes met hers. Eyes that were black like a void. She probably should have found a new therapist when she moved to Greece. It was a little bit too late to worry about that, she supposed.

"I didn't expect to see you," he said.

"I'm sorry. I feel like I owe you an apology. There was obviously a bit of a misunderstanding between us. I haven't been in Greece all that long… You know, comparatively. And I really enjoy talking to you. And I thought that maybe we could be friends. But I realize that the way that I asked you to spend time outside of work might have been misinterpreted, and it had some very strange timing."

He frowned. "I see."

"I'm sorry. I imagine women generally don't just want to be friends with you."

He laughed, and leaned back in his chair. "That makes me sound like a jerk," he said.

"Well. No. It doesn't. It's just…" She felt like a jerk. Because she was the one who was lying to the man. Gaslighting him, really. But she was trying to do it in a nice way. "I can see in hindsight how it looked. And of course Alex was very protective of the nature of our relationship because he is my boss, and he actually takes all the appropriateness of all that very seriously."

"Does he? Because it seems to me like you were in a pretty easy position for him to take advantage of you, speaking of the fact that you are only newly in this country and you do work for him. Plus, you're quite a bit younger than he is."

"I do have agency," she said, using the exact same line of attack against Stavros as she had on Alex.

"I didn't mean to say you didn't. Only that there is definitely an appearance of impropriety," Stavros said.

"Well, there wasn't. But that is why we were so careful. We both understand how it looks. Anyway, I just wanted to clarify, because I feel like I looked really flaky, and maybe even not very nice, and I didn't want to hurt your feelings and…" Suddenly, Stavros was looking behind her, and he went a shade or two paler.

She turned, and there he was. Dark eyes like a void. Radiating dark flame.

"Verity. We were meant to meet."

Verity snatched her phone out of her bag, and looked at the time on the screen. "Not for ten more minutes."

"I expect to be able to find you in your office."

"I don't live in my office, Alex."

A muscle in his jaw jumped, and she could see that he was legitimately angry. She needed to get this out of Stavros's office before something blew up. She didn't know what, and she didn't know why, but she knew that something was in danger of exploding.

"Thank you," she said to Stavros. Which was maybe the wrong thing to say? But she was in a hurry. "I'll… see you later." Then when she reached out and grabbed hold of Alex's arm without thinking, and began to drag him away from the room, she was completely engulfed by him. His hardness, his heat, the overwhelming sensation of what it was to touch him.

She lost the ability to think, the ability to speak. He smelled like Cyprus. Like the sea. She wanted to lean in and smell him, sniff his jacket, right where it fell against his bicep. She wanted to move her hand up from where she gripped him at the crook of his elbow and touch that bicep.

Oh dear. She was drowning. In her embarrassment at having all of this happen in front of Stavros, in her anger at Alex for being… Alex, and in this new hell of knowing that touching him turned her into a creature made entirely of sensation and need.

And this is why not having the illusion of Stavros is a problem…

She wanted to strangle that sage inner voice.

"What was that?" she asked, letting go of his arm and turning toward him as soon as they were out of view of Stavros's office.

"Not here," he said.

He took hold of her again, and practically frog-marched her to the elevator, and as soon as they were closed inside, he released his hold on her. "I don't need you causing gossip by speaking to another man that you formerly had feelings for."

"That I formerly had feelings for? How do you know I don't currently have feelings for him? This is not real," she said, gesturing wildly between them.

"I didn't mean in reality," he said. "I mean it was terribly obvious to anyone who looked at you that you had a crush on him."

"Oh, I know. Which is why I was in there trying to come up with a different story for him, because he is very confused as to why I asked him on a date, only to have a headline about our engagement come out that very same day."

"Right," said Alex, clearly having only just thought of this for the first time. Because of course that would mean thinking outside of himself more than he was accustomed to doing.

"Yes, right. He is in fact the reason I knew that we were engaged, because you didn't tell me. So I had to explain…all of that, or we were going to have a loose end. And then you came in there like…like that, which only made things look weird."

"Aren't men often jealous when their fiancées speak to other men?"

"Insecure men, maybe."

He said nothing, and a muscle jumped in his jaw. He was actually upset. He was unhappy that she had been in there talking to Stavros. He couldn't be jealous, it was... He was possessive. In the way he might be of a paperweight that he really liked. Because they weren't friends, but there was a strange sort of...something. He tried to deny it, he tried to play it off, but it was there. He might not understand connections between people, but she did. She was very sensitive to them, and she maybe understood them a little bit better than she even wanted to. Because the kind of life she'd had growing up had forced her to be so very aware of the inner workings of people around her at all times.

It wasn't her that was wrong about the two of them. It was definitely him. But she did understand now that it wasn't...it wasn't quite a typical sort of connection. Because he didn't understand those sorts of things.

The elevator arrived at its destination, and they walked out the doors in unison. Then they stood there, side by side in the lobby of the building. "Hold my hand," he said, looking at her, his dark eyes presenting something like a challenge.

She took a deep breath, and curled her fingers around his. She was shocked by how rough his hands were. He was a man with a desk job; she didn't expect to find calluses there. His hand was so big. It overtook hers entirely. Just as he would if he were to...take her into his arms, press her against the wall...

She needed to stop thinking like this.

He was beautiful, and she had known that from the first day she had met him, but it had been easy to put him in his own category. She had made a lot of decisions about what she wanted her life to look like when she had left home. And one of the first decisions she made was regarding romantic relationships.

She didn't want someone volatile. She had felt like it was important to make those decisions before she had ever jumped into the dating pool because she knew that romance could make people silly. Alex had not been a viable candidate for romance of any kind, not just because of his age, or because he was her boss, but because he exhibited the kinds of characteristics she wanted to stay away from.

Friendship was fine. Even though they weren't friends. Her being his employee was fine, because she actually was so good at managing intensity that it was second nature to deal with him. But...

There was a very good reason that any attraction she felt had needed to be squashed instantly.

She didn't want anything to do with...that feeling that he created at the center of her chest. It was like there was a tuning fork just there at the center of her rib cage, and looking at him struck it, sending a note radiating throughout her entire being. It had been that way from the first moment she set eyes on him, and it had been her cue to find something else to distract her. Someone else.

And now she was holding his hand.

Grappling with the intense honesty unraveling inside of her. Because she hadn't thought all of this through. It was her natural instinct. Her survival mechanism kicking in. She hadn't thought: *Do not ever look at this man, look at this one instead who will never create complicated emotions inside of you, but will feel easy and fun.*

No, really don't look at your boss, because he could wreck you.

It had been as natural as a gazelle turning and running from a predator in the grass.

But now that her skin was touching his she was forced to engage with the truth.

This was dangerous. She had walked straight into the lion's den.

Or maybe more appropriately she had taken herself right down into the underworld, into Hades's lair.

It was difficult to feel any sympathy for Persephone when she caused her own problems.

"Are we taking a car?"

She shook her head. "No. The jewelry store's just several blocks up that way, and I thought it would be good if we walked. Because you know..." She cleared her throat and started to walk. He was behind her a step for only a moment, and then took the lead, which she thought was absurd, because he didn't even really know where they were going.

"I'm the one who knows where it is," she pointed out.

"You said this way. I'll find it."

For some reason that felt poignant to her. She should be mad at him. Instead, it made her think about his childhood. About how he hadn't had anyone to guide him all that time. Of course he'd had to be decisive. Of course he'd had to take the lead even when he didn't know where he was going.

And look where it had gotten him.

Why are you feeling sympathy for him when you should punch him?

The paradox of Alexios Economides. The rest of the

world might look at him and see an emotionless man with all the power and money in the world who didn't deserve any sort of compassion or sympathy or leeway. She saw something else, and she hated that she did.

Because had she done enough human projects in her life? She knew the outcome of it too. Nothing she had ever said or done had changed the way that her parents acted. And her siblings had followed right along with them. They had no self-awareness; they had no desire to be better, to be different. It was like everybody was born into the same toxic sludge and decided to keep rolling around in it. It could never be her.

It could just never be her.

But she didn't see toxic sludge when she looked at Alex, unfortunately. And part of her did want to change him.

She was relieved when they came upon the jewelry store, because it gave her an excuse to talk, and not think anymore. And definitely not focus on the way it felt for her hand to be in his.

When they walked into the glorious store, they were greeted by a short woman with a blunt bob and bangs, and glasses that took up over a third of her face.

"Good afternoon Mr. Economides, and bride," she said. "When I received the notification that you wished to come in and have a look at the jewelry selection today I immediately cleared the schedule."

Alex regarded the woman coolly. "How lovely. Though, it was my bride, Verity Carmichael, who made the arrangements for today."

There was a subtle scolding in the words, as though he was making it clear that she was to be addressed as an equal to him. The problem was, it was performative. Funny, because she had never really seen Alex perform. Normally, he was exactly who he appeared to be.

She didn't think she liked this.

Because there was always a little bit of distance between the two of them. There was distance between Alex and everyone. But this was different. This required translation. She wasn't used to having to do that with Alex.

"Apologies," the woman said. "Of course. My name is Laura Braxton, and I'm the manager of the gallery. Whatever you're looking for, we have it here."

She looked at Alex. "I… I don't know what I want," she said. That much was honest.

"I know exactly what you should have," Alex said.

"Oh?"

He nodded. "I would like to see a selection of pink diamonds. Yellow gold for the setting."

Perhaps Alex had never been engaged before but she wondered how many women he had bought jewelry for. But then, as he had said only recently, he didn't need romance to get sex. She had certainly never seen him buying jewelry for anyone before, and yet he seemed utterly at ease and confident in this setting.

Though, that was just him.

He seemed to take for granted that he belonged wherever he was.

The trick she had never mastered. She always wanted to make herself small. Make herself disappear so that she wouldn't be visible, so that she wouldn't cause any problems. And wouldn't have any anger directed at her.

She had learned not to do that, but it still wasn't second nature to stand like he did, with straight posture and broad shoulders, like he was the master of all he surveyed.

Ironic, because it seemed like the world was asking him to show a little bit more humility. Normally, she would enjoy that on a poetic level, because so many times in life men were given passes that women simply weren't, but in this instance, she found it annoying.

Because Alex wasn't the standard rich boogeyman that needed to be taken down. He had been through… hell. He had clawed his way up into his position. He hadn't been handed something by a dying relative, given chances simply because of who he was related to. She thought that should matter. That people should see who he actually was. Instead, they wanted him to sublimate his trauma and perform for them in the way they saw fit.

Honestly, she would be really annoyed about it if he hadn't just co-opted her entire life.

It only took a moment for a tray of pink diamonds to appear.

Verity had never given much thought to what sort of ring she would like.

Mainly because she had never thought about getting engaged. Of course, if she wanted a ring she could buy one for herself, but nothing this beautiful.

How had he been *right*? That was what she couldn't understand. Because these were the most beautiful rings she had ever seen in her life. Gleaming pink surrounded by that glorious gold. There was one at the center, pear shaped surrounded by darker pink gems in the shape of seeds.

"You found one you like," he said, his eyes trained on her, not on the jewels. She felt like she was pinned to the spot. Felt like he was looking into her, and it wasn't the first time she had felt that with him.

She didn't know how he could maintain that he was entirely unable to connect with people, that he didn't know a way to make them…like him, when it was so clear to her that if he took a moment he could see exactly what another person was thinking. He was insightful. Not just with machines.

Maybe it was just it was a skill he had never valued before, so it wasn't one he overly identified with.

One he didn't care about.

"Maybe," she said.

She was very aware that they were supposed to seem like a normal couple. That she needed to appear to be flirting with him, or something. But she was as much a novice at that as he claimed to be. The only man she had ever tried to flirt with was Stavros, and that hadn't gone well at all. Of course, that was Alex's fault.

He reached his hand out, and he plucked the exact one she had been looking at from the center of the tray. "This one would suit you," he said.

She didn't want to betray how beautiful she thought it was. That he had chosen the one she had set her sights on unerringly. But she didn't know how to hide it either. This was such a strange moment, outside of his office, unguarded without the strictures of their work environment.

In the office, they had a set pattern for how to be. But out here, they had held hands. And now he was standing there holding a ring out to her. She could only think to do one thing in response. She extended her left hand, and tried to ignore that her fingers were trembling. She knew that he would be able to see it. She knew that she couldn't hide this.

He said nothing, though; he merely extended his own hand, and took hold of hers. Then with his other slipped the ring onto her finger. It fit perfectly, like she was some sort of corporate Cinderella who was most definitely going to turn into a pumpkin at midnight—or at least six months from now.

But it was perfect. Beautiful beyond measure, and when she looked up into his eyes her breath was pulled straight from her lungs. She couldn't move. It was something like being prey in the sights of a predator, and yet it felt all the more dangerous. There was a sickly sweet feeling in the back of her throat, and her limbs felt languid. There was a deep response at the center of her thighs that she could feel yawn through her entire being. These were feelings she had never experienced when she had looked at Stavros. She had felt something pleasant when she interacted with him. Butterflies.

This was nothing like that. It wasn't the fluttery feeling you got with a grade-school crush.

This was decidedly adult, and was something she hadn't been looking for. But it had come and found her all the same. Perhaps that was why she felt hunted. And he was still touching her, his hands hot and rough, still looking at her, those eyes fathomlessly deep and utterly unreadable. If he was feeling what she did, she would never know. His was the black unknown of the darkest sea.

"Yes," he said. "This will be perfect."

She took a breath, desperate to gain her footing back. To gain some of her own back. He might be her boss, he might be older, he might be more experienced in life, in the world, but they had sat across from each other eating lunch for two years, and she would be damned if she let him make her feel small.

"I need to look at rings for him as well." She smiled at the attendant.

"Of course."

"Gold," she said. "Yellow gold. I would prefer something with symbolism."

"It will only be one moment."

He didn't say anything, but he was watchful in that way of his. That way that let her know she might well be in danger. That was just fine with her.

She would take the danger. She would take the challenge.

A tray was presented only a few moments later. Rings of gold, many woven together in a knot pattern. But her eye was caught by a simple design, a gold band with a geometric pattern that she recognized as being quintessentially Greek.

"What is that?"

"Oh," the woman said, picking up one of the gleaming rings and holding it out toward her. "This is Meandros. The interlocking pattern is unbroken and is a symbol of infinity."

She was suddenly filled with spite. And took the ring out of the woman's hand, and held it in her palm. "I think that will be perfect. Unbroken. Eternity. With the one thing you value most." She lifted her eyes and met his gaze. Of course anyone watching would think that she meant her. What she meant was his company. This would be her wedding gift to him. She would pay for it herself out of her outrageous earnings. Because the one thing he would have left would be his company. She needed to remember that. That this had nothing to do with her. That there was nothing romantic about it.

Of course he had managed to choose a ring that was perfect for her. Because he knew her. Perhaps that was why it had been so easy for him to manipulate her into doing this.

You were hardly manipulated.

She wanted to snuff her inner voice out like a misbehaving candle. She hadn't asked for a fair and balanced reporting of the situation. She wanted to feel sorry for herself. Standing there wearing a diamond ring with astronomical value.

"If that is what you think suits us best, my Cricket," he said.

"I think so. But unfortunately you can't wear it until the wedding."

"Unfortunately," he said.

He selected a matching band to go with her ring, and those jewels were packed up and sent back to his home, while she wore the outrageous engagement ring on her hand.

From there they went to the bridal store, where he sat in a room by himself while she tried on gorgeous bespoke gowns made of the most glorious fabric she had ever beheld. Buttery smooth and light. This wasn't a real wedding, but she didn't plan on ever getting married. So she let herself get lost in the fantasy. There was no other man she ever meant to do this with.

She put on a strapless gown with a sweetheart neckline with a glorious chiffon overlay that made her look like she was floating when she walked. The trouble was it was far too easy to imagine walking toward Alex like it was something romantic. She felt dizzy after the whole day. Everything was Alex, everything.

That moment in the ring shop.

She had tried to gain her own footing back. But...

This was all beginning to get to her.

When she was out of the gown and back in her street clothes, Alex came back and pointed at a vivid pink dress on a mannequin. "And what is that?"

"A special occasion dress." The attendant looked at him. "Would you like me to get that down for her to try on?"

"Yes. She can wear it to dinner."

Verity didn't have time to argue before she was bundled back into the dressing room, and practically stitched into the dress. It had a flowing skirt, and the top gave away almost every secret she possessed.

The attendant gave her a pair of hot pink Barbie heels to put on with it, and when she stumbled out of the dressing room like a frightened, sexed-up baby deer, she was sure that she must look ridiculous. She didn't look at the mirror. Rather she looked at Alex's face. And she saw...

Exactly what she had hoped to see when she had played games with his wedding band. He was the one who was dumbfounded. Except she realized, it wasn't about a ring, or about her knowing him. It was her boobs. Which was actually not all that satisfying.

Liar.

Okay. Maybe it was a little bit satisfying to know that she had affected him in some way.

"Perfect," he said.

She was hungry for more. For something. For it to not feel like there was a wall between the two of them. She wondered if she was asking for just a bit too much. But the way that he had looked at her had hooked on to something inside of her, was forcing her to reckon with some hard truths.

If she didn't have Stavros to distract her then she had to admit that she found her boss more compelling than any other man she had ever met. Her boss, who was absolutely, unequivocally the last man she should ever be interested in.

Not only because he was her boss, but because he was everything she had ever told herself she needed to avoid. He could hurt her.

She had been hurt enough.

So she locked down any of the feelings that were trying to claw their way to the surface, and she met his gaze. "Perfect for?"

"Dinner. We are dining in the city tonight."

CHAPTER SIX

THE AMOUNT OF money he paid for the garments that she bought, shoes, undergarments, the dresses, was enough to make her eyes bleed, and when they arrived at the restaurant in question, she was still reeling.

The restaurant was beautiful, with climbing vines all down the side. Those same climbing vines continued onto the rooftop, a canopy of green raining down over the diners. A glorious balcony with vine-covered walls, and a view of the Parthenon stretching out before them.

All heads turned to look at them when they walked through the dining area, and she had to wonder if it was because of just how chesty her dress was. Though, then she rationalized that Alex was very famous. And of course it had to do with the fascination of him, and definitely not her rather average rack. The truth was, it was only unusual to her that she was showing this much skin. It wasn't notable to anyone else.

Except maybe Alex.

But then, he also knew her. So he knew that this wasn't typical for her.

Maybe she should've pushed back when he suggested the dress, but part of her felt lovely in it. So it was convenient to hand over the decision to wear it to Alex, rather than having to own it herself.

Was she that big of a coward? She asked herself that as they were seated in the most glorious spot on the rooftop, the warm breeze fluttering through her hair, the view of all that ancient glory giving her goose bumps.

It wasn't because of Alex.

"This is what you wanted?" he asked.

"We definitely have left an impression all over the city today," she said. She had considered, for a split second, acting like she didn't know what he was talking about, but there was no point. He was only thinking of the game. And all of the conflicted feelings that she'd had over the last few hours were only hers.

She needed to remember that. That no matter how tempted she was to think there was some sort of personal connection between the two of them, there wasn't. No matter how much she liked to scratch at him and mention her agency, he did have power over her.

Yes, she was getting something in this bargain, but she was only agreeing to it because it opened up avenues for her. If she were independently wealthy, then she wouldn't. So that was evidence all on its own of who had the power here.

The evening was so lovely, the setting sun turning the sky muted orange tinged with blue as darkness consumed what remained of the day.

Had it only been a day? It had been the longest day on record.

"I would like a glass of wine," she said.

"It shall be done."

He lifted a hand, and the server appeared immediately. "Yes, sir?"

"My fiancée will have a glass of whatever you recommend. I will have something red. We will take a sample of the menu."

"Of course, sir."

"A sample?" she asked when the waiter vanished.

"I thought you might like to try everything they have to offer. This is one of the most sought-after reservations in all of Athens."

"And you just managed to get it at the last minute?"

"Yes."

"Did someone else lose their table so that you can have it?"

He lifted a shoulder, so unconcerned. "If so, that was the restaurant's decision, and not mine."

"But you have to realize that someone had to rearrange their entire… The restaurant had to rearrange things for you, or someone had to rearrange their dinner plans for you. You don't shuffle around in empty space, commanding whatever you like without affecting people. Just because you aren't connected to others, doesn't mean you don't impact them."

Okay, she didn't really care so much about the situation with the restaurant. Maybe she was just venting her feelings about being caught up in all of this.

"I'm aware of that. I'm not… I understand how the world works, Verity, and I understand the way that people's relationships work."

"Do you?"

"I do not owe you this explanation," he said, his voice hard. "But I will give it."

"Gee, thanks, Alex."

"You are marrying me, so perhaps you need to know."

"I'd like to," she said, getting exasperated.

"But it is like… I will use Christmas as an example. It never meant anything to me. And no matter how much someone tells me it's magical, or that it makes them feel a certain feeling, I can never have it. What they are talking about is nostalgia. I will never have nostalgia associated with the holiday. It is nothing but bad memories for me, if anything. Mostly, it didn't signify. You cannot take understanding and turn it into feeling. That is how family is for me. It's how friendship is for me. I can understand the purpose of it, I can understand how it functions, and why other people want it. But I don't."

It made such horrible sense that she almost felt guilty for talking to him the way that she had. For being angry.

Because the deeper she got into this part of him, the more she understood that he had not escaped his upbringing unscathed.

No. He was everything he was because of that upbringing. Successful, yes, but also disconnected.

"Romance is the same," he said. "I understand what it means to other people. But it will never mean that for me."

"You have no issue with sex," she said, her entire face burning as soon as the words left her mouth.

Right then, the waiter reappeared with their wine and a selection of appetizers. Which looked lovely, but she had just made herself feel slightly ill.

Alex took his wine in hand and leaned back in his chair, regarding her coolly. "To me it is a drive like anything else. I eat and enjoy good food, but I don't long for family dinners. That makes sense?"

Sadly. Very sadly it did.

She was honestly annoyed that he was so good at making this understandable.

"You're angry with me," he said, reaching out and putting a small selection of appetizers onto her plate. "I think you're angry with me because you have an argument."

"This is the problem. You know me. And for me, knowing someone means…feeling something. Whether it's distaste or…friendship. You know me, and you don't feel any of that. You just have the benefit of being able to look inside my head without paying the cost of caring. That doesn't seem fair."

"Consider this," he said, his dark eyes nearly glowing in the faltering light. "I have no choice. There is an entire world within this world that I can see, I can understand, but I cannot enter. All the money in the world won't fix that."

There was no pity in his voice; there was no sadness. It was blunt and matter-of-fact. And she found it desperately sad. Was that just something he had to accept? That circumstances in his childhood had robbed him of something he could never get back?

But then she thought about her own, and the things she had accepted she wouldn't have. That she didn't want a husband and children because being in a family unit had been such a terrible thing for her. She didn't let herself feel wistful about it. Because the institution of family wasn't something that made her feel…warm or happy. Maybe it was the same for him.

Everything was so disconnected from what it was supposed to be, so you couldn't long for it the way that other people did.

She thought about saying that to him, but instead she took a bite of a small cracker in front of her and moaned with delight as the freshness of the fish and radishes on top hit her palate. Maybe it was just better to exist in the moment. Maybe this was the problem. She was so focused on trying to rationalize this moment, fix something, feel better, when maybe she just needed to live in it.

She was hardly being tortured, after all.

She took a sip of her wine, and surrendered. There was no further action to be taken in the conversation unless she was going to start tearing strips of her own skin off and revealing all the issues she had underneath. And that would be silly, because they weren't friends. Because he was her boss. She might as well just stay Verity as he knew her. Because the Verity he knew was always together, always well-adjusted and fine. There had been a little bit less of that over the past week given the whole... everything, but she didn't need to go showing him her soft white underbelly.

"This is beautiful," she said.

He looked at her, his eyes meeting hers, then drifting to her mouth, down to her breasts, which made her nipples go tight, and her stomach feel fluttery. Then back up in her eyes. He was so gorgeous. And dangerous. They had just had a conversation about why he was especially dangerous. He was her boss, he knew her, he didn't feel anything for her.

Unfortunately, her particular brand of trauma hadn't made her disconnect from people. In fact, she wanted connection, just something that looked different from what she'd had growing up. The idea that she could have someone in her life who wanted her around, who appreciated what she did...

She took another long sip of her wine. Oh. Alex was that relationship. He wanted her around, even if it was in a professional capacity. He liked the things that she did, and he was quick to praise her.

It was easy for her to assume that she kept the peace with him, and managed him so well because of her ability to read impending dark moods, and her motivation to avoid them. But it was more than that. It wasn't enough for her to avoid his ire; the past two years she had been existing on his praise.

She had all these thoughts about friendships she might make. About dates she might go on, but she hadn't done that, had she? Because Alex was fulfilling this role in her life that meant so much to her. Because she was actually consumed by her relationship with him.

Thankfully, a lovely course of pasta came out on the heels of that realization, and she was able to take another sip of wine and finish the glass, and chase the thought away.

Music began to play, live guitars, and some of the couples around them got up and started dancing beneath the string lights on the roof.

If she weren't here with a man who had a brick in his chest where his heart should be, it might've been romantic. Of course, it would've been dangerous. Emotionally. They were both the problem.

She could see that very clearly. She had been allowing her boss to fulfill something in her emotionally that a boss shouldn't be fulfilling, and she was now angry at him for not reciprocating.

She was also angry at him for the whole convenient marriage thing, which in fairness to her was absolutely stepping over a line, but still.

"Dance with me," he said, his eyes burning into hers, the statement emphatic, and in no way a request.

Her heart jumped in her chest because it had not gotten the memo that this wasn't romantic.

They were supposed to be performing. She couldn't say no.

So when he extended his hand, she took it. And when he lifted her from her seat and onto her feet she felt like she was flying. He wrapped his arm around her waist and swept her to the dance floor, and any protests or sharp comments she wanted to make were swallowed up by the feeling swelling in her chest. Overwhelming. Brilliant. Beautiful. Horrible.

He pulled her in to his chest, one hand clasping hers, the other wrapped firmly around her waist. She put her hand on his shoulder; she was reasonably sure that was what you were supposed to do when you were dancing. She had never really done it before. If doing it alone in your bedroom didn't count, that was.

He took the lead, strong and steady, and took the guesswork out of everything. His confident steps made her own move easily. Helped her find her rhythm.

The music wrapped itself around them like an intimate veil, and it was as if they were the only two people on the roof. Her heart was pounding, and it wasn't from physical exertion. His body was hot against hers, and she realized she had never been so close to another person before.

It was easier, for some reason, to admit that she had fallen into the trap of getting emotional validation from him, than to admit that she was attracted to him. That she had been attracted to him from the first moment they had met, and that Stavros was a bad decoy for the better, more reasonable aspect of herself that would have screeched an alarm about Alex if she hadn't distracted it.

It had been him. From the beginning. And she was so dedicated to her self protection that she had done her best to hide it from her higher self so that her lower self could have what he wanted.

And now he was holding her. Carrying her across the dance floor like she wasn't a burden. Like he had been born to do it.

If he was so dangerous then why did she fit in his arms like this?

Why did her body feel both relaxed and on edge because of his touch? Why did she feel cherished and safe and electrified all at once?

You don't have a trademark on delusion, Verity. Your feelings aren't facts.

That was true.

But she wasn't like Alex. She had feelings. She just squished them down. Manipulated them. Hid them. Didn't let herself happen. And in effect, it was like she was still letting her parents keep her from having nice things. Or was it protection? It was a question she was having a difficult time answering. Especially while she was in Alex's arms.

There were other people around them, but she didn't have a sense for them. She didn't care about them. This wasn't a performance anymore, not for her. This was her, sorting out her own feelings with fear and trembling. This was her, indulging herself while punishing herself, and examining the punishment.

She sensed something dangerous in Alex, and she had from the beginning. She knew what it was. He would never have feelings for her. It wasn't a great mystery. But she didn't want a forever sort of love anyway, so what did it matter? Except she knew it did, because it hurt her that he didn't consider them friends, so she couldn't even imagine the cost if she were to sleep with him and then…

Her heart started to beat erratically. This was the closest she had come to admitting that she wanted him like that. She looked up at him, her eyes landing first on the sharp cut of his jaw, the curve of his lips, that blade-straight nose. His black lashes, and his dark, fathomless eyes.

She knew why people were afraid of him. Hell, she was afraid of him. For very good reason. She really did need to find a new therapist, because there was something happening here. All this fear, and yet she was drawn to the fearsome thing. Wanted to reach out and touch it, tame it, make it her own.

And she knew she couldn't do that.

He would dominate. He would force submission. Because that was who he was; she wasn't going to be the one…

And anyway, he didn't want her.

She thought of the way that he had looked when she had come out of the dressing room in the pink dress. And then, the way that he had looked at her breasts at the table. Maybe he did. But it was in a base way. It had nothing to do with who she was as a person. It had nothing to do with her.

Do you need it to be?

She didn't know how to answer that question. One posed by herself, to herself. What kind of sad idiot didn't know herself to this degree?

She knew all her warning signs, all her triggers. But that was different than actually knowing what she wanted and why. It was different than being honest about what she was feeling. She was good at building fences and observing the boundaries. She was not good at re-evaluating those boundaries around existing feelings.

She was good at making rules and following them.

Alex had nothing to do with her rules.

He never had. If she had an ounce of real self-preservation inside of her, or even self-awareness, she probably wouldn't have continued working for him, much less said yes to all of this. But right now it felt like a tangle. Wanting to continue to please him and wanting to keep herself safe. But also wanting to continue to be near him.

He moved his hand, and it drifted down her back making her shiver. This was dangerous. So very dangerous.

The worst part was, she was sure she was feeling alone. Just like the sense of friendship, just like—

Her thoughts were interrupted when he swept her around the corner on the dance floor, and backed her up against a vine-covered wall, his dark eyes burning. Her breath caught, her heart slamming hard against her breastbone.

He pressed her hand to the wall, his fingers still laced between hers, and he touched the engagement ring there, a look of something like reverence on his face. She had never seen him look like this before. There was fire in his eyes, something like the expression she had found there when he had seen her in the dress just an hour ago, but also something more.

Something confused, hunted, ravenous.

It mirrored the feelings that were inside of her, finally.

Finally it wasn't only her. Who felt like a victim of this thing, who felt like she was at its mercy.

Was he feeling all of this conflicting attraction? This need to embrace it and turn away all at once? This desperate desire to know what it would be like to touch, to taste?

She felt overwhelmed by it, swamped with it, like it might drown her.

He was a man with experience, and she was nothing more than his virgin secretary. That was the tragic fact of it all. She was a stereotype. Ripe for the picking, even. If she tried to explain it to someone, they would scoff. They would say she was being taken advantage of. They would say she was a fool. But they didn't know what it felt like. And they couldn't.

She knew. And judging by the look in his eyes so did he.

They had stopped. The music kept on playing, and people around the corner were probably still dancing, but they had stopped. Almost like they had frozen time itself. There was nothing but this growing, throbbing need between them. It was so real. It was so…all-encompassing. And then, on the breeze, with her breath, it was over. He moved away from her, pulled her from the wall and swept her back to the dance floor, with no explanation, no commentary, nothing.

She took a breath, a gasp, really, and only then did she realize she hadn't been breathing at all.

"Alex…"

"It looks as if the meat course has been served. Would you like another drink?"

He took her hand and led her back to the table, and her head was swimming.

Maybe this was a gift. Maybe it was a reprieve. A chance to make a better choice, instead of giving into... whatever that was. She wanted to say something. She wanted to push.

But something stopped her. Held her back. The same old things.

The fear of what would happen if she pushed at the wrong time.

She was tired of herself. Tired of how much she didn't know. And she was resentful. Of him. For unmasking so much inside of her that was still so broken. It was so easy for her to look at him and have thoughts about his trauma. About his coping mechanisms, and his protections and layers, but looking at her own was just...

She just wanted to be fine.

That was why she had come to Greece. To be fine. To start living.

Maybe when all this was over she finally could. Maybe it wasn't enough to run away from her family. She needed to run away from Alex too.

And once this was done, she would have the means to do it.

Until then...

She would just plan the wedding. Look at it as another part of the job.

They weren't friends.

And whatever she had seen in his eyes before, she would ignore it.

Because God knew he would.

CHAPTER SEVEN

THE WEDDING CAME upon them quite quickly, and Alex did not think Verity was as appreciative of all he was doing for her as she ought to be. Not only was this a spectacular affair, not only was her name being plastered across the headlines in only glowing terms, but he had done a Herculean job of reining in his attraction to her.

He paused in his room, looking at himself in the mirror, clothed in the tuxedo he would be wearing to the wedding in less than an hour.

Verity was beautiful. He had been conscious of that from the moment he'd hired her. The way he was affected by her beauty had been different. At least initially. There was something young and fresh about her that he had responded to that first day. Something that made him want to protect her. Her beauty—he had told himself—had been something like a lovely figurine he wanted to collect.

Being with her outside of the office—confronting the idea that she might go on a date with someone else—had been taking that figurine and making her flesh and blood. And then it was difficult to avoid the truth that they could only ever see her that way as long as no one else was touching her. As long as he wasn't touching her.

When they had danced at the rooftop bar, he had been so close to taking her in his arms and claiming her. But it wouldn't have stopped at a kiss. He knew that. All too well.

So he had not kissed her. He had turned away from the moment, as he must. All of their outings had since then been confined to holding hands. And she seemed... subdued. Not quite herself.

Almost as if she was angry at him, and yet she never showed such an emotion.

Not his cricket. She seemed as placid and smooth as ever, like the surface of a lake, and the harder he stared, the more he could only see himself looking back. Perversely, it made him more attracted to her. It made him want to create a reaction in her.

He did not.

He was her boss. And while he felt no guilt over using her for this particular endeavor, he was aware of the complexity of it. She had very little choice in the matter. Taking advantage of her physically on top of it would be reprehensible.

He cared about that. He always had. Perhaps because so much of his life had been determined by the whims and failures of other people. He hadn't lied to her when he'd said that he understood the way that human connection worked. He understood all too well. When other people had control over you they could make your life as wonderful or miserable as they wanted to make it. When you had nothing, it gave every meal, every night's rest, every breath a greater weight. And often, you had to observe the rules of a game in order to ensure you would continue to have those things.

It was one reason getting as far away as he could from that state was so important to him. But he would never, ever intentionally put someone else in that position. And in some ways, he had with Verity. He had changed the rules of the job. And the outcome was that he would give her financial freedom, but he had flexed his power over her in a way that he was not proud of.

He wasn't redirecting either.

The wedding was today, and it was going ahead.

The one thing he couldn't do was cross that physical line.

Not and live with himself.

He opted to walk to the ruin where they would be getting married. It was a long walk, but he was in need of some time to clear his head. To gain control over his desires. He was on the cusp of getting what he wanted professionally; why images of Verity should dominate his thoughts was beyond him.

When he arrived at the outskirts of the venue, he looked up and stopped. There she was, sitting in the window on the third floor, her long blond hair blowing in the wind. She was wearing a robe of some kind, and was staring out pensively. She was like a medieval maiden, the sort that knights wrote poetry about. Untouchable and glorious.

His chest felt sore. His heart was beating faster. An old feeling swept through him on the wind. This feeling of wanting without being able to have. It wasn't nostalgia. Not in the way people spoke about it. Not like Christmas as a child. He resented it. Hated it. He was never supposed to want what he couldn't have again. And here he was, standing three floors below his assistant with his heart nearly beating out of his chest.

She wished that when she saw him it didn't make her heart almost explode. But if she could have her way where Alex was concerned, she would be in an entirely different situation right now.

She had opted to have no one help her get ready today. She was putting it off, sitting at the edge of the window and looking down at the glorious view. And that was when he had appeared, like this was some kind of fairy tale and she could let down her hair and he could climb up and… Rescue her? From what? Himself? That was unlikely.

She pretended she didn't see him, or at least she didn't acknowledge his presence before standing up and turning away. She took her robe off and stared at herself in the full-length mirror. The underwear that had been chosen for her to go with the wedding dress was… beautiful and definitely designed for someone to see them. A strapless corset made of white lace and a white lace thong that barely covered anything at all.

Of course, no one would be seeing these.

She told herself that didn't make her ache with regret. She told herself that she could run away if she wanted to. That she didn't have to go through with this. And then she told herself it really wasn't that big of a deal. It was just a ceremony. She wouldn't even know anyone here. It would be media and potential investors, and all of Alex's colleagues. Hers too, of course, but they weren't really hers. In the sense that of course their real loyalty was to the man who wrote their paychecks, and not to her.

But that should make everything easier. This was all part of a life she would leave behind. She had thought things would go differently. She had thought this would be the place where she would settle in, make space for herself. But it wasn't going to be. And that was fine. She didn't care about marriage.

She told herself that repeatedly as she put her dress on. As she scrunched and then fluffed her curls, as she put her minimal makeup on and picked up the glorious bouquet of pale pink roses that were sitting there waiting for her.

She didn't have any bridesmaids. Just as Alex didn't have any groomsmen. Did anything speak more profoundly about the two of them than that? She took a breath, and looked at her reflection one last time before she turned away and began to walk for the door. The place they were getting married at was glorious. And if she was ever going to plan a wedding, it probably would have looked like this.

She giggled. To no one, and really nothing, but it was silly to think she would have ever been able to have a wedding like this without Alex.

Was she already getting used to the things that came with being attached to a billionaire?

Financially, her family had always been comfortable enough. Not wealthy, but they'd had stability externally. A nice enough house on a nice enough street. It was only inside that things had been rotten. Still, a fabulous wedding at a glorious Grecian ruin would have been beyond them.

But if it was just a fantasy, and she could have whatever she could dream of, she would have dreamed of this. The facility she'd gotten ready in was essentially a castle, the winding staircase leading down to a courtyard that had once been a library. Now it was half-crumbled walls and pillars, which had been decked in roses and lights, a grand arbor standing between two of the most intact pillars.

And she could see as she peered through the windows on her way down the spiraling staircase, that that courtyard was now filled with guests sitting in the golden chairs that had been set out in the vast space. She was making false vows in front of strangers. And maybe the Greek gods. But they would enjoy the farce, honestly. So she didn't need to worry about that either. Surely Zeus could appreciate marital shenanigans.

She swallowed hard. This was the best decision. It was.

When she arrived down at the base of the staircase the doors parted for her, and the sun shone upon her. Like a sign from above. So she pressed forward, out into the gloriously beautiful day, and toward her husband.

Music played by a string quartet filtered around her, the same song they had danced to at the rooftop bar, but surely that was a coincidence. Her heart began to beat faster. She could see him now, standing there at the head of the altar looking resplendent in that black tuxedo. Her glimpse of him out the window from that distance hadn't given her the full story of all that glory.

She was drawn to him, and this no longer felt fake.

A smile spread across her face, and she wished that she could stop it. She couldn't. And then, just as she got to the end of the aisle, she turned, and saw her mother.

Next to her was Verity's father. Her brother was next to him, and right beside her brother was her sister.

And suddenly everything stopped. Her heart, the world, that strange sensation of joy that had made her feel like everything was going to be okay. And suddenly, it felt like there were eggshells beneath her feet, like every step risked breaking something essential.

She didn't want to look at them. She kept on looking at Alex. She knew that she looked affected. There was nothing she could do about it. She couldn't speak. And when they joined hands at the altar, his were like fire.

Or perhaps her own had turned to ice.

CHAPTER EIGHT

HE COULD SEE the exact moment when her entire countenance changed. She had seen her family sitting in the front row of the wedding, and it was like all the life had been drained from her.

He had thought it would be a given that her family would come to the wedding. When he had turned over the task of who to invite to one of the administrators in the office, he had told her to include people who might be connected to Verity. She had been like a robot throughout the entire ceremony, and then had gone into hiding for about fifteen minutes before finally appearing at the reception.

She had a sparkling smile on her face, but there was something odd about it. Something frozen and stuck, not her usual applied neutrality, but a sort of manic false joy that made him feel ill at ease.

The guests, however, did not seem aware of the situation.

When she joined him at their banquet table, he leaned in toward her. "Is something wrong?"

"Of course not," she said. "Nothing is wrong."

He could see that half her focus was devoted to watching her family. They didn't approach the table, nor did they socialize with other guests. But he supposed they were very much out of place at the event. Nearly everyone was a business contact of his, and the primary language being spoken around the room was Greek so it was not entirely strange that her family might be keeping to themselves.

"You're welcome to mingle," he said.

She laughed. "Am I? Well, that's fantastic. I wasn't certain what the rules were."

"Rules?"

"Yes. Rules. Of course there are rules." She lowered her voice. "This is your game, not mine, and I'm not a real bride."

"Be careful," he said, warning her because it was very important they didn't disrupt the facade, but part of him found that wasn't even his primary concern. She was acting strangely, but he couldn't pinpoint why, and he found that disconcerting.

"Yes. Of course. I don't think you have any idea how careful I'll be for the whole rest of the evening."

Dinner was served, and she spent the entire meal eating while staring blandly ahead with the same sort of serene smile on her face. As soon as she was finished, she stood up and made her way over to her family's table. Her posture was straight, her smile only growing brighter. She laughed too loudly at everything her brother said, and every time her father asked for something she moved quickly to see it done.

He had a steady stream of well-wishers moving to speak to him, but he finally excused himself and made his way over to Verity's family. "Pleased to meet you," he said. "I'm Alex."

"It's very nice to meet you," said Verity's mother. "I'm Dorothy. It's shocking, really, that Verity has found herself in such a grand position."

"Is it?" he asked.

"Well, she was such a terribly average child. When she took off to Greece it was a surprise."

The smile on Verity's face looked like it might shatter. "It surprised me too. But opportunity was calling. And apparently Alex. Everything worked out exactly like it was supposed to. Amazing."

"You could always thank your old man for paying for your college," her dad said. It was not spoken with familial warmth, and Alex didn't need to be an expert on family to recognize that.

"Of course I'm grateful," Verity said. "I am exceedingly thankful for everything you've done for me. All of you. Without you I wouldn't be here. Of course. Marrying Alex. Which is my dream come true."

The doors opened, and revealed a cake on a rolling cart being brought over to the banquet table.

"Excuse us," Verity said. "It's time to cut the cake."

She cut the cake with the same sort of manic energy she was doing everything else. After that it was time for them to dance, and where there had been an erotic edge to their touching the last time he'd held her in his arms, it didn't exist now. She was practically vibrating with unrest. After the dance, she went back to her family, where she spent the rest of the evening. It was like watching a vaudevillian show. She was performing with so much effort that he could feel the force of it from across the room.

He knew that anyone else would just think she was smiling, happy even. But this wasn't Verity. He knew her. He could feel her.

And he also knew enough to know this wasn't a terribly normal family dynamic, but he couldn't read exactly what it was either. It took him an hour to realize she was counting the amount of drinks her mother and father were having, and attempting to slow the amount of alcohol being served to them.

He wondered if the issue was she was afraid they would recognize that this wasn't a real relationship. That they weren't a real couple. Nobody knew Alex, but of course her family knew her.

Nothing happened. Not a single outburst or moment of unpleasantness. And soon, the wedding was over, and it was time for the two of them to go up to the honeymoon suite. It was a room large enough for him to take his space and her to have hers. As soon as they walked out of the ballroom, cheers echoing behind them, and entered the foyer of the castle, at the foot of the stairs, she pulled away from him.

"What is it?"

"How dare you?" She spoke in a voice that wasn't familiar to him. It was vibrating with rage, low and trembling.

"How dare I what?"

"You invited my family to the wedding, and you didn't ask me. You didn't tell me. I wasn't prepared."

"I'm sorry. If you are afraid that they might identify that this wasn't—"

"You think I'm worried about the fake wedding?" She laughed. "I'm not worried about that. And believe me, they would never be able to identify whether this was real or not. They would have to have the slightest bit of insight into me, and I guarantee you they don't."

They reached the top of the stairs, and she stormed ahead, pushing open the door to the bridal suite, and slamming the door in his face. He caught it with his hand and pushed it open. "Tell me what the problem is."

"The problem is that you don't know me. At all. And not only that, you haven't even taken the slightest bit of effort to get to know me. If you had, then you would know that my mother, father, brother and sister being here is quite literally my worst nightmare." She shook her head. "It doesn't matter how much I try, does it? I was so afraid to be angry at you. I'm so afraid to be angry at anyone. I spent the entire night performing to try and make them happy. I left this behind, I wasn't supposed to have to do it again. I wasn't ready to. There were digs every few minutes. About how this is above me, and now I'm above them, about what I owed them. And I just have to take it on the chin. I have to pretend that I don't hear it." She took a deep breath, and tried to steady herself.

Then she continued. "You don't have a family, so you don't understand what a nightmare they can be."

"You didn't tell me you had an issue with your family," he said, surprised that her mention of his lack sparked his temper the way that it did. "It seemed like an entirely reasonable thing to make sure they were invited."

"If they're around then I can guarantee I will spend the entire time trying to keep my feelings from getting hurt, while I try to keep them from making a scene. If my parents end up drinking, then they will end up screaming at each other. Or a waiter. Or someone who happens to look at them wrong. Though, usually it's me. Because my brother and sister learned how to fight back, and I spent all of my time trying to fix everything. That makes me the referee. It makes me everything that I don't want to be. And this is why I have to live in a different country. This is why I…"

She stood there, breathing hard, her breasts rising and falling with the motion. And suddenly, she threw her head back and let out a feral scream. "This is why I'm scared to have any feeling that isn't…conciliatory." She shook her head. "This is why I didn't have your head for getting me involved in this…this farce. I can't believe you did this. I can't believe you railroaded me into it. You used the promise of financial freedom to lure me here. And for what? So you can have more. More and more. I don't matter to you at all. You could've asked any random woman who passed you on the street to pretend to be your wife and it would've worked just as well."

"That isn't true," he said. "Everyone loves you."

He knew immediately that was the wrong thing to say. Even if he didn't know why. Because her face turned red.

"Yes. Everyone loves me. Because I have a lifetime of practice at making everyone else happy. I have a lifetime of managing all that. And I turned around and I did it with you. I do it with everyone at the company. I do it all the time. And I can't… I don't even know who I am. I'm afraid of the stupidest things. Scared to make a mistake. Scared to make people angry. I'm always walking on my tiptoes. I'm tired of it. I can't do this anymore."

Her breathing got faster and faster. "I can't… I can't breathe." She reached around behind herself and she unzipped the wedding dress, tearing at it, shoving it down to the floor, leaving her standing there in nothing but white lace undergarments that left little to the imagination.

It was a rare thing for Alex to be surprised. But this had caught him entirely off guard, and he had no idea what he was supposed to do now. Another rarity.

"What has it gotten me?" she asked, standing there

in half-naked fury, her blond hair a wild ride around her shoulders, her breasts rising and falling with each outraged breath. "Absolutely nothing. Saddled with this ridiculous situation, and I don't matter. Not to anyone. My parents came to seek spectacle, undoubtedly they came to see if they could get any money from you. Or maybe they just wanted to make this difficult for me. Maybe they don't even know that they make things difficult for me. Maybe they've never thought about my perspective even one time." She laughed. "I think that's it. I think they never thought even one time about how they made me feel. Exactly like you."

She shook her head. "You never think about how I feel."

Anger galvanized him now. He growled, and moved toward her. "That's not true. I didn't coerce you into this. You agreed."

"You released a statement before you ever spoke to me."

"What have I asked of you?"

"You asked me to marry you. You forced me to."

"I offered you good money to marry me, and if you didn't want the money, you could've said no."

"Everyone wants the money. And now you see why I wanted it. It's to never have to go back to that. Ever."

"There's a lot of space between that and the sort of riches that I've given you. Don't turn me into the enemy because you're angry at your father."

"Oh I'm plenty angry at him, and I know well that I am. But I'm angry at you too."

"You have given me no credit for all that I've done for you. For the way that I protected you."

"Protected me? Protecting me would have been to ask the basic question of whether or not I had moved halfway across the world to get away from my parents, rather than just making assumptions."

"Yes, I have protected you."

"How?" She took a step toward him, all fire and glory. "By bringing my worst nightmare to me on my fake wedding day?"

It was his turn to move toward her, and he had been paying attention to where they were in the room, but it brought her back up against one of the ornately carved wooden posts on the stately canopy bed at the center of the room.

"Yes," he ground out. "I have protected you. I did my level best to keep this as professional as possible."

"You married me."

"You know what I mean," he said, all restraint flooding out of him. She had no idea. He was not the sort of man who wanted something and didn't get it. No. That had been his entire childhood, and as an adult he didn't do that. With her, he had made an exception. With her, he had observed best practices. He had been a good man where she had been concerned, and she was acting like he was the very monster from the Black Lagoon for bringing her parents to see her.

"No. I don't."

He lifted his hand, and reached out and touched her face. Dragging his finger slowly along her cheekbone, down to her jaw. That silenced her. She drew a sharp breath, her eyes going glossy. "You don't know?"

"No," she whispered.

"Then I will have to show you."

And then he lowered his head and claimed her mouth with his own.

CHAPTER NINE

HER THOUGHTS WERE a whirlwind wrapped in a sensual haze. She couldn't make sense of anything. A moment ago she had been yelling at Alex, and now he was kissing her.

Even more confusing, a moment ago she had stripped her dress off with him in the room.

Like she hadn't thought this would be the end result.

Well, she hadn't been thinking at all. She'd been feeling. She had been ready to come out of her skin, and was tired, so desperately tired of having to make everything palatable. Having to make herself palatable. Her feelings were confused and sharp and she wanted him to feel them. She didn't want to hide them.

So she kissed him back. Deep and long, pouring every ounce of her anger, of her hurt, of the impossible to define, spiky feelings that she couldn't even put names to, that attached themselves to her heart like barbs, hellish and painful, and impossible to dig out.

Kissing him seemed to make her feel better. Or if not better, seemed to make her feel something else. Something more. Something good mixed in with all of the bad. It was intense; she hadn't been wrong. She had known that this was the sort of connection that could consume her. The sort of attraction that could crash over her like

a tsunami and claim her. She was jumping into it now.
Without thought, without reserve.

He thought he had been protecting her by not kissing
her? It was probably the best thing he had done in the
last month. She would tell him that, when she decided
to come up for air. But for now, she was reveling in this.

The heat of his mouth, the expert slide of his tongue
against hers, the way that his large hands moved over her
body, the way that he gripped her hips, and pulled her
toward him so that she could feel the burgeoning length
of his arousal. She might be a virgin, but she knew how
it all worked. She wasn't afraid.

Because she had to face down her biggest fear. She
hadn't even realized that this specific thing was her biggest fear, but if she had really sat down and thought about
it she would have said that having her family at her actual
wedding would have been her worst nightmare. And she
would've also said that it would only happen in her nightmares, because there was no way she would ever get married, and no way she would invite her family if she did.

But here she was, married to this man. And her family had been there.

She hadn't died, but she had felt damn near close to it.

What could scare her after this?

Certainly not his kiss, which was expert and drug-
ging. Glorious and all-consuming. Certainly not his kiss,
her first, the greatest. She was so glad she had gone on
a date with Stavros, because would she have given him
this? Would she have surrendered her lips to him, her
body, when it was so clear that this belonged to Alex?

That it had from the moment she had first met him.

What Verity was good at, very good at, was not just

smoothing things over for everyone else, but for herself. She was so good at avoiding difficult feelings, and the truth about herself. But not now.

She was just admitting it, even if it **was** internal.

She wanted Alex.

She had from the very first moment she had laid eyes on him. She had wanted to be near him. Every moment that she could be. She had wanted him like this. Even if she couldn't allow herself to so much as fantasize about it in the dead of night. But it was so easy now. It felt so right now. Because on some level she had always known.

He pulled away from her, and she leaned back against the bedpost, breathing hard. Her lips felt hot and swollen; her breasts felt heavy. That place between her legs was wet and throbbing, and needy. She wanted him to touch her. When she had thought about her first time, she had imagined that it would be awkward. That she wouldn't know what she wanted, that she would feel hesitant. That wasn't true. Not at all. She knew exactly what she wanted. And she wasn't ashamed.

"Take your clothes off," she said, clutching the post for emotional and physical support as she watched him.

"Will that satisfy your anger?"

"It depends on how much I like what I see."

"I'm not concerned," he said, reaching for the knot on his tie.

Just then she felt like she was existing in two different spaces and times. Like she was watching him in his position at his desk, eating his usual lunch, then angrily eating a salad, and then she was back here. Watching him loosen the knot on his tie, watching him deftly unbutton his shirt. Same man. It was a very difficult process.

It was getting harder and harder to breathe. Especially as he revealed more and more of his toned, glorious chest. Covered in dark hair, and sculpted like a work of classical art. Oh goodness. He was getting naked.

She had asked him to.

No, she had demanded it.

She wasn't afraid. She was just a little bit in awe that it was happening. But that wasn't the same as being afraid.

He stripped off his shirt, his jacket, let it all fall to the floor. She was speechless, her mouth dry. He had muscles in places she didn't even know men had muscles. Definition all down that ridged abdomen, and glorious cuts that created an arrow leading her eye down to the waistband of his pants. His hands went to the buckle of his belt, and he began to undo it slowly, his methodical movements maddening.

She had a feeling he knew it. She kept holding onto the bed.

Because if she didn't she might fall to pieces. Because if she didn't she might melt into a puddle. Because if she didn't, maybe she would just fall over, like an imbalanced quail that couldn't stand on its own two feet.

She refused to be a tilting bird. She would not tip over. She didn't trust herself, though, so she gripped even more tightly to the carved wood, her nails scraping against the surface.

She watched with rapt attention as he removed the rest of his clothes, and she did feel lightheaded at the first glimpse she got of a fully naked man in the flesh.

And what a naked man he was.

She had seen quite a lot of naked male statues about Greece in the last few years, and as their masculinity could be easily hidden by fig leaves, it had never seemed like much to write home about, if Verity would write home about anything. Alex would not be able to be concealed by a single fig leaf. Not even close.

And there were the virginal nerves. The ones that she had thought she had perhaps dodged. Right on time. But thankfully, the bedpost held her upright, and so she didn't falter or collapse.

"I have done as you commanded, Cricket. Is there a reward for me?"

"I…am thinking about it."

She was racking her brain trying to come up with what might be an equivalent reward.

"I think perhaps it is your turn to remove your clothing."

She blinked. "That isn't an equivalent trade."

"Why?"

"Because you are… You look like that."

"I can practically see all there is to see of you now, Cricket. I'm confident that what you have to reveal is better."

This was even better than getting a compliment at work. She was tempted to try and get more. Oh, she was so very tempted. With shaking knees, she released her hold on the bedpost, reached behind her back and began to undo the clips on the corset. Then, on a swift and drawn breath she let it drop to the ground, revealing the upper half of her body.

He made a short, masculine sound of approval in the back of his throat that sent her heartbeat into overdrive. And it was the approval she needed to take the rest of her clothing off.

"Yes," he said. "That's right. You're a beautiful girl. Do you know how beautiful you are? I have never seen such glory."

This time, when her knees went weak it was with pleasure. She could see that he was telling the truth. The way that he was looking at her didn't lie. He was aroused, yes, but it was more than that. He approved of her. He was looking at her and finding her to be enough. To be perfect.

She would give him anything he wanted. Right then, she really thought she would.

She would live under his desk in his office, rest her head on his thigh while he worked, be on hand to fetch things for him, whatever, as long as he would look at her like that.

"Such a good girl," he said, those words the final arrow in any resistance that might have remained.

She was his. He had seen into her, and she had been afraid of that. The way that he knew her, the way that he understood her, almost better than she understood herself, without giving any of himself. But right now it didn't matter.

Couldn't this just be about her? Her getting everything she wanted? Her having her every fantasy realized?

He thought she was beautiful.

And after today, after having to manage her family like that, didn't she deserve something nice?

He might have delivered her worst nightmare to her doorstep, but now he was giving her the deepest, dearest fantasy she'd never quite known she had. It was terrifying. It made her quake inside and out.

Would she have slept with someone a lot earlier if she

had realized? If she had realized what it would make her feel for a man to praise her like this?

No. The answer echoed inside of her, whispered through her with total certainty. Because just anyone's praise wouldn't mean anything. It had to be Alex. Because he was so exacting, so difficult.

She wanted to please him. She wanted to please him because doing so meant something. Healed something inside of her. So she would let herself have it.

Tonight, she would let herself have it, and damn the consequences.

"Sit on the bed," he commanded. And she wanted to do what she was told. She didn't feel like he was taking something from her by taking command. She felt like he was giving her the opportunity to give him everything he wanted, to let her please him, and she wanted that more than anything. That was pleasing herself, and maybe she would never be able to untangle that and make it make sense to somebody else, but she didn't need it to.

It made sense to her.

Or maybe it didn't. Maybe it just felt good. That was enough. For now, that was enough.

"Lay down, and spread your legs, let me get a good look at you."

Her exacting boss was exactly like she should have imagined he would be in bed. She hadn't let herself, because she had been too afraid, because she had been too deep in denial, but of course this was how he was.

He was a man who knew exactly what he wanted, and gave explicit instruction on how he might get it.

And she was the woman who did his bidding. So she did now.

She parted her thighs, and ignored a rush of heat that flooded her cheeks.

"I never thought that I would get married, much less have a wedding night. But you are certainly making a case for why I was foolish in neglecting such a pleasure. Of course, no other woman would do, not like this."

Her thighs began to tremble. His words were amping up her pleasure in a way she had never imagined possible. When he touched her, all was lost. She would be lost. She wasn't afraid of it; she was anticipating it. She needed it.

"Touch yourself," he said. "Show me what you like."

She sucked in a sharp breath, nerves overtaking her now. She wanted to do it right. She wanted to arouse him. She wanted—

"You cannot do it wrong," he said. "Nothing that you do could ever be wrong. Not here."

She bit her lip and nodded slowly, brought one hand up to cup her breast, moved her own thumb over her tightened nipple, her hips arching up off the bed as pleasure arrowed through her. He was watching her with rapt attention, and she kept her eyes on his as she moved her other hand down between her legs and pushed her fingers through her slick folds. White-hot pleasure lanced through her as she stroked herself beneath his intent gaze.

Her hips canted up off the bed in time with her movements, her breathing shortening, coming faster, harder.

"Stop," he said.

She froze.

"You're not allowed to make yourself come. Only I get to do that. And now I have seen just how. You are beautiful when you pleasure yourself. Now let's see how beautiful you are when I pleasure you."

He moved to the bed, his wide shoulders between her thighs as he forced them farther apart, gazing intently at that most intimate part of her. Then he lowered his head and licked her, long and slow.

She gasped, desire nearly pulling her apart. He moved his thumb to where his lips had just been, and stroked her where she was most sensitive, rolling pleasure moving through her like a wave. And then his mouth was on her again as he pushed a finger inside of her making her entirely incoherent.

He pleasured her like that until she was begging. Until she had no more control over herself.

He moved up her body, pressing his forehead to hers, his mouth just a whisper away. She could smell her own arousal on his lips, the realization making her shiver. "Beautiful," he whispered. "Perfection."

"I take the pill," she said. She was on it for her cycle, but she figured she might as well use it for its intended purpose.

She trusted him. She knew him well enough to know that he was fastidious in all things, and that if there was any doubt they couldn't do this safely, he wouldn't.

But he took her words as she meant them, pressing himself inside of her on one smooth thrust. She cried out, the shock at the invasion almost making her fly off the mattress.

"Cricket?" he asked, his voice rough.

"I'm okay," she said. "It just surprised me. Please. I… I wanted to be good for you. I want you to like it. I need you to—"

He silenced her with a kiss, deep and long. Then he smoothed her hair out of her face. "You are perfect. Of course I like this. You fit me perfectly. I only wish I had known so that I hadn't hurt you."

But the pain didn't matter. She had pleased him. That made it all fade away. Made the pleasure rise up inside of her. Made everything turn to glittering gold and glory.

"I'm just fine."

She kissed him, softly, and then he growled and began to move within her, building the pleasure back up inside of her with each decisive stroke.

She clung to him, arching her hips in time with the movement.

This was terrifying. She'd had every good reason to be afraid of this. Because it was intense. Because it was all-consuming. But right now, it was hers. And nothing could take this moment from her. He whispered words of affirmation in her ear, the kind that could never be repeated in polite company, her pleasure building inside of her like a tide, and when it finally flooded through her, she dug her fingernails into his shoulders and called out his name.

"Alex," she whimpered.

All the years, all the lunches, all their time flashed back through her eyes until she came back to this moment. In bed with him, her husband.

He had given her this most beautiful night. This most brilliant gift.

And she realized, with a crushing weight, that while this had changed so much for her, it would have changed absolutely nothing for him.

CHAPTER TEN

ALEX DIDN'T SLEEP. He sat beside the bed, wearing only his tuxedo pants, watching Verity sleep fitfully.

When she shifted and the covers lowered, exposing her breasts, he covered her back up, and when the sun rose he called downstairs to have breakfast brought to them.

He opened up the curtains, and allowed a shaft of light to bathe Verity where she still slept. It had the desired effect. She began to stir, then sat up, rubbing at the sleep in her eyes.

"Breakfast," he said.

He set the tray on the foot of the bed, and she pulled the blankets up to her chin, snuggling deeper into the mattress and closing her eyes purposefully.

"You should eat," he said. "And have coffee."

She opened her eyes and fixed him with the same sort of grumpy look she had given him the day she'd fed him salad. Except this one felt a lot more genuinely outraged.

"I don't need you to tell me what to do," she said.

"Is this how you're going to play this?"

"I'm not playing anything," she said, rolling onto her back and flinging her arm over her eyes. "I don't feel well."

"Are you ill, or are you upset?"

"Does it matter?"

"Yes, it does matter. Because if you feel ill I will have someone fetch you medicine. If you're upset, then I fear you're stuck with me and I'm not well versed in how to handle emotions."

"I thought you understood the workings of humanity and human relationships, you're just above them."

"I'm not above them. I'm outside them. Two different things. I owe you an apology, Verity."

She looked at him then. "For what?"

"That's not…"

"I need to know what you're actually sorry for. I need to know if you have any actual idea what you did. I don't want you to apologize just because you think it's going to make me more…pliant."

"No. That's not why I'm apologizing. I used you badly. I didn't realize how badly until… I didn't know you were a virgin."

"Oh my God," Verity said, sitting up and letting her blankets fall down around her waist. "That's what you're apologizing for? Because you've attached some kind of meaning to…to that? That is the most basic, asinine, male thing you have ever done."

"No," he said, realizing that he was messing this up, and realizing he cared, which was honestly the extraordinary part. He often made people angry, uncomfortable and annoyed. He did not often feel so desperate to fix it. "It's only that it speaks to… I don't know you. Obviously. I spent two years having lunch with you, and I don't know you, and that is a flaw in my system, but you didn't ask to be a victim of that. All of the things you said to me last night are true. I manipulated you into this. I didn't even realize that I did."

"Great. A marriage license and one virginity later and now you have regrets."

"I want to fix this."

"I don't think Scotch tape works on hymens."

"What happened to my biddable assistant?"

"She is now your tired wife who expended all her appeasement energy yesterday on her parents."

"Are you going to be difficult or are you going to have a conversation with me?"

"I've already had the conversation. I was desperately vulnerable and honest with you last night. And you think that you can…express a moment of regret and offer me— well, you really can offer me coffee—and that will make it go away?"

"No. I don't know. I don't know what I can do to fix this. I don't know what I can do…"

"Give me some coffee," she said.

"Okay," he said, reaching for the carafe and pouring a generous mug of hot liquid, handing it to her.

She snatched it away and hoarded it against her chest like a small dragon keeping watch on a precious jewel.

She had told him about herself last night, as she had yelled at him. It was up to him to do more with that, not to ask her to give more, he supposed. Or maybe it was up to him to give something.

"I was five years old when I realized my life wasn't normal." He looked at his hands, then out the window. "When I realized that most children lived in one house, with the same caregivers. Even if it was a grandmother, a single mom, they had stability. Someone who loved them.

That kids who were passed around like objects were the strange ones." He felt something catching his chest. "I know many kids in my position spend a lot of time asking themselves why their parents didn't want them. I know little enough about my parents that I'm not sure if they wanted me or not. They could've lost custody because of addiction. Perhaps they did want me. They are a void in my mind. There's nothing there, not enough to grasp onto. Not enough to question. Mainly, I wonder why no one else wanted me. I went into the system when I was an infant. I had the highest chances of being adopted because of that. So many children are taken away from their parents when they're older. People don't want older children. They don't want the trauma that comes with them. They want babies. But nobody wanted me."

He felt very much like he had taken a knife and peeled a layer off of his skin. Exposed something, not just to her, but to himself. "Part of what I did with your parents came from a place of arrogance, I admit. But when you told me that you had lived in one house your entire life, one house growing up, I also admit that I imagined it must've been happy. You are soft, and it seems as if connecting with people is easy for you. I never asked you about your experiences growing up, because I thought that I knew. I thought someone like you must have a good family."

He looked back at her then, and saw that his words had done something to soften her.

"I never thought of that. How…normal it must've seemed to you to move from one place to the next. And what that must've felt like when you realized it wasn't. It must've been confusing."

He nodded. "Yes."

"I can also understand that for you it must feel...ungrateful. Ungrateful of me to have a family, to have a house like that and to have a complicated relationship with those things."

"No," he said. "You forget I lived with a lot of families. Even though they weren't mine, even though I wasn't really a part of them, I have a very clear sense for how every family is different. Some of those families I stayed with were warm and wonderful, and leaving them hurt. Some of them had beautiful dinners every night, and they sat and spoke to each other about their days, and even asked me about mine. Some families are all silent resentment, or everyone in the house bending over backward to placate the member of the family who has a temper. It sounds as if you lived in a house where you were the one who contorted yourself around everyone else."

She sighed. "Yes. I didn't realize how much I did it until I was thirteen. I had a friend over and she said that I acted so different around my family. Strange. Like a robot. She's not wrong. In order to deal with them I learned to sand all the difficult edges off my own feelings and make everything about theirs."

"Were your parents violent with you?"

"No. It's all shouting or... You heard what my mom said. About me being average. That's just normal conversation for her. But if you get her angry...every poisonous thought she's ever had about you will come out of her mouth. And as much as I try to tell myself that it's just her, that it has nothing to do with me, it stings. She's a bitter, unhappy woman. My father is a small, angry man who constantly needs everyone to tell him how important he is. My siblings learned how to trade on that economy. And I just wanted nothing to do with it. I just wanted everything to be as smooth as possible. I just wanted to get through my childhood, and get out on my own."

"You did."

"I did. I went to college, I went to Greece."

"You went to college, but you never dated anyone."

She shook her head. "No. I am nothing if not very protective of myself. That's why I got so angry with you last night. I ran away from this. From all of these hard feelings."

"I didn't know."

"I know. Because I'm protective of myself." She laughed. "Somehow, I protected myself right into this situation." She took a deep breath. "But I did get angry at you. I can't decide if I'm proud of myself for that or not. I can't decide if that makes me like my parents, or if... I finally let myself have all the anger that I wasn't allowed to have in that house full of people who made everything about them."

"There's nothing wrong with being angry," he said. "If there is then my entire life is a problem." He laughed. "Maybe it is. But I would think that as long as you don't use your anger to hurt other people there's nothing inherently wrong with it. Anyway, I deserve it."

"I can't argue with that."

Silence lapsed between them.

She reached over and picked up a croissant from the tray, and he felt that was a victory of a kind.

"Are you entirely angry with me?"

She wrinkled her nose. "What do you mean by that?"

"I mean, you woke up extremely angry. Is that the

only…?" Their eyes caught and held, and he felt desire tightening in his gut. This was such a novel experience, to have slept with a woman he knew so well.

She might argue that he didn't know her, or hadn't before last night, but in the context of his life, he knew her better than he knew most anyone.

So there wasn't just desire, but a strange, fierce feeling of tenderness which was entirely foreign to him.

"Are you wanting to know if I enjoyed what we did last night?"

"I need to know."

"You couldn't tell?"

"Physically, I can tell that you did, but this morning you're upset. I want to know if you regret it."

She looked down. "No. It was a gift to myself. Because I wanted you. Because I have wanted you."

Satisfaction gripped him low and hard.

She narrowed her eyes. "Don't look so pleased with yourself."

"Do I look pleased with myself?"

"You do. I'm still kind of mad at you."

"But you wanted me."

She looked away. And he wanted…he wanted something he didn't have a name for. He wanted to feel connected to her again. As he had last night. When they had made love.

He moved to the edge of the bed, and pressed his knee down on the mattress, then he leaned in and cupped her cheek with his hand. She didn't move away from him. So he leaned in and kissed her softly on the lips.

She whimpered, and went pliant against him. "Alex," she breathed.

"Very good," he whispered. And then she arched against him.

He knew that she liked this. That she craved his praise, but the truth was, he wanted to give it to her. Nothing and no one had ever been his. And she could be. His perfect, beautiful wife. She could belong to him.

The idea of that was intoxicating. She could be his perfect one, adored and kept safe by him. He wanted to give her everything she wanted, to lavish her with jewels and designer dresses, to give her food and beautiful shelter and trips to anywhere in the world she wanted to go.

He had never had anyone to take care of him; it was true. But he had also never had anyone to take care of, and the idea of Verity being his in this way was…

Now that he had taken hold of the idea he couldn't let it go.

He wanted her. Needed her. Craved her like a drug in his system.

He had never wanted another person like this. Sex for him had always been a practicality, as he had said to Verity. Something like being hungry and making sure that he could be satiated.

But there had never been an emotional component, and now there was this, and he was drowning in it. The depth of it. The possibility of it.

He stripped the blankets away from her, took her coffee out of her hand and set the cup on the nightstand.

Then he stripped himself naked and kissed her lips, her neck, down the gorgeous swell of her breasts, down her stomach, to the curls between her legs.

She was addicting. Incredible. He could never get enough of this; he was certain of it. It had altered him fundamentally on some level inside of him he hadn't known existed. And he wanted more. He craved more.

He licked her until she was screaming, until she cried out his name. Then he kissed her inner thigh, pulled away from her and grabbed her chin, tilting her face up toward him. "I want you to do the same for me."

She lowered her eyes, her lashes fanning out over her cheeks. Demure, beautiful. "I don't know how."

"I don't need you to have skill. I simply need you to be who you are. I want you, I don't want generic pleasure. You, your mouth, your body, that's what I want. You will be perfect, because you are perfect for me."

He watched as color suffused her cheeks, as pleasure overtook her. She loved when he praised her, emotionally, but also he could see that it aroused her. That it satisfied her on so many essential planes. It made him want to give her more. Always.

He stroked her cheek, then released his hold on her. She adjusted their positions so that she was hovering over him, her lips pressed against his shaft.

He groaned, letting his head fall back as she swallowed him down, as she began to pleasure him with all her inexpert ministrations. He loved it. Loved that he could feel that she was learning on him, that she was finding her way with him. She was his.

He hadn't known that connection could make sex better. That this deep yearning need to hang onto a partner and care for her in every way, pleasure her, wrap her in blankets, give her good food, would be the ultimate in satisfaction. But it was.

His Verity. His Cricket.

His.

She pleasured him until he reached the summit, and he pulled her away from him, because he couldn't let it end like this.

"Did I not please you?"

"Yes," he said, pressing his thumb to her lips. "You did. You were perfect. But too good. I don't want to finish like that. Someday I will. And you will swallow all of me, won't you?"

Her cheeks went bright red. "Of course I will."

"Yes. I know you will, because you're so good for me. But now, I need to be inside of you. I need you all around me. Do you understand?"

She nodded, lying back on the bed and arching upward, an invitation that he wasn't going to refuse. "You're so tight and wet," he growled, moving into position. "So perfect for me. And only mine. Do know how much that pleases me?"

She nodded. "Yes. I think I waited for you."

As soon as those words left her mouth, he lost all of his control. He thrust inside of her, the warm welcome of her body pushing him to the edge. His teeth were gritted together, and he fought for any control he might find.

In the end, he could find none, so he surrendered. To her, to this. To the inevitability of it.

He was never going to let her go.

Never.

She was his. His.

His good girl. His wife. His everything.

There was no one else. There was nothing else.

He had found a link, he had found a connection; in this, in this moment, in this feeling, he knew what it was to be joined to another person. To truly have another person he couldn't imagine living without, breathing without.

Too soon, his pleasure overtook him. Too soon, he lost control. "Come for me, beautiful girl," he said.

He was desperate for her to return pleasure, and she did, arching against him and riding out her release, pushing him toward his own.

He clung to the feeling. To the certainty. But it rolled away along with his pleasure, and when it was over, he was just Alex again. And she was Verity. He had lost the connection.

The feeling that had overtaken him.

He sat up, breathing hard, his skin slicked and sweat. He felt like he was coming down from a high, and it was brutal.

He was still trying to find his breath when the words tumbled from his mouth. "It will be impossible to resist you."

"You sound angry about that," she said, shrinking away from him.

He regretted the way he'd spoken but he was still reeling, still dizzy. Still grappling with the way things had changed.

"What will become of us over the next six months?"

Her face went stony. "Right. Because it's still…it's still all about that, isn't it? Your business."

"My goal hasn't changed," he said.

And yet he knew it wasn't that simple.

His goal hadn't changed, but he had. What he wanted, the way he saw the future. He had felt something he hadn't known was possible when he was with her and he didn't want to give it up. Not ever.

"No, of course it hasn't," she said.

"My goal hasn't changed, but my vision of this marriage has. You didn't want to get married, I understand that. But you can be angry with me, you discovered that last night. I won't force you to change the shape of yourself to keep peace. And I… Verity, what if you and I could have a family? What if we could be one?"

"I don't understand," she said.

Maybe it didn't make sense and he couldn't tell, because he didn't know how to do this. Because he wasn't as accomplished with human connection as he was at anything else.

"This marriage. What if we made it real?"

CHAPTER ELEVEN

WHEN VERITY HAD woken up this morning, she'd had to force herself to be angry. She had felt like her pride necessitated that she find a little bit of outrage and aim it at him, rather than letting him see that she was physically sated and ready to crawl in his lap and purr like a kitten.

So she had brought up the indignity of it all. Had tapped into the anger that had brought her into his bed in the first place last night. But he had met it with vulnerability, and that was something she didn't have a defense against.

Then he'd kissed her, and all of her anger had dissolved into a lavender haze. His touch, the things he said to her, the things he demanded of her, it was like he had reached into her and taken the golden threads of her deepest fantasies and spun them into a glorious reality.

He seemed to know her body better than she did.

And now *this*.

He was asking her for a real marriage, when they were both still breathing hard from the pleasure they'd found together. When she was still dizzy with her need for him.

"A real marriage?"

"Yes. It was a business arrangement before we slept together."

She wanted to get huffy about that. She wanted to minimize the meaning of what had happened between them the night before. Just like she had tried to do when he had brought up her virginity. She didn't want to be vulnerable about it; she didn't want to lend any credence to the idea that…that it had mattered that he was the first one.

But the truth was, it did.

And the truth was, it had changed everything to sleep with him.

Even if she didn't want to admit it. In fact, it didn't matter if she admitted it or not; he could clearly see it. Even Alex could see it.

He had told her things about himself. Not just the facts of his upbringing, but the way it made him feel. The image of him as a little boy in a classroom with other five-year-olds, realizing that they all went home to the same mom and dad every night, while his circumstances changed with the whims of the system, was truly heart-breaking. She couldn't hold her outrage as tightly as she wanted to with that picture in her mind.

But a real marriage…

She tried to drum up some of the horror she usually felt when she thought of marriage. A family. Of quiet suburban desperation.

But, Alex was not suburban. He could no more live on a cul-de-sac than he could fly to the moon. Actually, he was way more likely to fly to the moon. He was a billionaire after all, and space travel was accessible to him. Normality? Not so much.

So right there and then, she didn't need to worry about that. The image of life with him was… Well, it was dif-

ferent. Different than the generic imaginings she'd had
of married life, whenever she had taken the time to think
of them.

And maybe some of it was that she'd already lived
through the wedding. Her family was there, and there
hadn't even been a large explosion, even though she had
felt like she was tearing herself into pieces to prevent it
from happening.

So one of the worst parts of marriage had already
been dealt with.

Are you insane?

Maybe. Maybe not. What was the alternative? The alternative was the two of them separating in six months
like this had never happened. Her going on to live that
independent life she had always thought she wanted.

Flashes of last night, of what had just happened, made
her heart beat faster, made her body feel weak. She was
just going to walk away from him when all this was done
and never feel…this again?

"Six months," she said.

"What?"

"We make the decision in six months. Just like we
were going to do, as far as how well the marriage was
working externally. Only we'll be evaluating how well
it's working…internally." She blinked, and noticed how
scratchy her eyes felt. "I don't really know myself," she
said. "It comes back to that protection thing. And I'm
willing to entertain the idea of my life looking differently
than I thought it would. But you're not wildly in love with
me. That's not why you're suggesting we stay together."

"You're not wildly in love with me either."

Her comment and his returned volley were like arrows, whizzing by, but not hitting the target. Dangerous, somehow, even without contact. Certainly not an arrow she was willing to jump in front of, not now.

"No. But that isn't what we're talking about, is it? You hired me because you wanted a taste of the state that you don't know how to have. You wanted a sample of friendship. And I gave it to you. Now you want to see what it would be like to have a family. I know what it's like to have a family, and for me, it isn't happy or warm. Between us, maybe the potential is there. But that's all we are talking about. We are talking about making plans, laying out our terms, we're not talking about jumping headlong into an affair."

"You can say that after what happened last night?"

"Is that why you're asking me to stay married to you? You want more sex? What if I would have sex with you no matter what?"

She already knew that she would. She already knew that she didn't possess the self-control to stay away from him. Even if it would be smarter. Even if it would be the more prudent thing to do.

"I would still want more."

"Why?"

It was almost like she had reached out and grabbed him by the throat. He looked stricken. He looked like he didn't know the answer, and she realized right then that she had never seen Alex looking uncertain. Perhaps he had been at different times, but not so she could tell.

"Because when I think about what's on the other side of this, I no longer find pure satisfaction in the idea of simply achieving greater financial success. I… I tricked myself into thinking that's what I was looking for. It's not what I'm looking for. There is something missing from me. Something missing from my life, from my future. I cannot buy it, Verity, and you have no idea how much that...how much that burns. Because I never wanted to be helpless, not again. You make me feel more connected with a part of myself that I have never...that I have never touched before. Perhaps we are *friends*."

Friends.

Now, after he'd been inside of her, they were friends.

He had done it. Stuck the knife right between her ribs. Gotten her right where she was vulnerable.

The truth was, if he had tried to profess wild and sudden love for her she never would've believed him. She would've laughed at him; she would have said that he was manipulating her.

Friendship, though, and the chance to suit his soul, that was appealing in a way that she couldn't quite articulate. It appealed to the loneliness in her. Maybe that was why this made sense to them both. They were both essentially quite lonely—wasn't that obvious? She had taken a job that included surrendering her lunch hour to her boss. You only did that when you had no one else to take the hour with. So maybe this wasn't about love.

Maybe it was just chemistry mixed with the deep desire for both of them to not feel quite so alone. She had dedicated her life to protecting herself. But that protection had only built a wall around her that had left her isolated. Maybe this was a chance to knock that down.

"Six months," she said. "We can see how we both feel about it then."

"And you will live with me as my wife until then?"

"Yes. Though I think we need to define that."

"Forsaking all others. Giving yourself to me."

"Yes," she said. "You have to do the same."

"Easily done."

Whatever past affairs he'd had they were virtually invisible. If he was a playboy, he certainly didn't flaunt it, and so it was easy enough to believe him now. She would ask him about that someday. What his first time was like. How he treated sex, and lovers and all of that. She needed to ask him so many things. Because they didn't really know each other.

They sort of did. There was a veneer of knowledge that was a very good veneer, but it was a veneer nonetheless. It didn't go deep.

They had started to talk about real things just recently. They were going to have to keep doing that.

"All the rules that we had when we…when we worked together, they can't be the rules anymore. Every topic has to be open for conversation. Otherwise we can't get to know each other."

He stared past her. "That seems reasonable."

"You don't like it, though."

"I don't like my past. But I have shared more of it with you than I ever have with anyone, and I will answer any questions that you have."

But he wouldn't freely share. Maybe it wasn't fair to expect him to simply…start talking about things that he had always kept guarded. She couldn't demand everything from him at once. Just like she couldn't demand everything from herself at once. She was going to have to spend the next six months not just getting to know him, but really getting to know herself.

They were both going to have to be vulnerable.

Some secret, romantic part of her had longed for this. That felt very dangerous. The urge to romanticize this. That she had met him, and this was inevitable, whatever both of them had planned about their lives. That they would be swept into something bigger than themselves, bigger than everything.

No. She had to be honest. As Alex had. He might understand this, he might even want it, but it wouldn't be the deep love connection that other people looked for in marriage. And maybe that would make it safer. They could have boundaries, and discussions; it would be like working together. Everyone would have clear roles, and they would talk about things, and it would be…

She imagined holding a baby. The image was visceral and raw, and something that she had never let herself think about before.

When she had decided she didn't want family, she had included children in that.

But what if they could have a baby?

Part him, and part her.

A beautiful connection that maybe Alex would feel.

What if he didn't?

She would. She had two whole parents who didn't care that much about her. If her baby had one that loved her with everything, she would be doing much better than Verity. And Alex would try. She knew that much.

For a moment she had an image of Alex standing on the other side of a glass divider, looking in at herself and that baby. That was tragic. She hoped that wouldn't be their future. But all she knew was self-protection, avoiding things like this, avoiding wanting too much to keep herself safe. She couldn't plan all this out.

She couldn't see every possible outcome.

But maybe she could hope. Maybe that wouldn't be so bad.

"Is your family still here?"

"Wow. I don't know, because I didn't plan any of this. And you know I didn't look at my phone even one time between last night and now."

"Yes. My apologies. Also find out their whereabouts and send them on their way. Then you and I shall go on our honeymoon."

"Honeymoon? Where?"

"Wherever you would like to go, Verity. Because this marriage was once about me, my company and what you would get when it ended. But now it's about us. And so I want you to be happy. I want you to want to be with me."

She had the briefest notion that this was all too good to be true. But she and Alex had already lived lives that seemed a little bit too tragic to not be exaggerated. So why couldn't they have this instead?

This was a big step, a frightening one.

But the alternative was to go back.

And somehow, after everything, she knew that was impossible.

So she had to keep going forward.

Maybe this would be the key to finding herself.

Maybe she could fix him.

CHAPTER TWELVE

SHE HAD AGREED. All he knew was triumph. From the moment she said yes, to the moment his plane touched down on the private Caribbean island where they would be spending their honeymoon.

He had bought it some years earlier, but had never been, and it felt like the perfect place to try and become something different.

And she responded to the beauty of the location just as he hoped. As they disembarked from the plane, and she looked around at the smooth, crystal blue water, the white sand and bright pink flowers dotting the bushes, her face lit up with joy.

The over-water villa had been stocked in preparation for their stay and as they walked out on the gangway that took them to their accommodation, it wasn't the view that captivated him most. It was her.

The opportunity to give this to her. To watch her face as she took in each detail around them.

As she smiled when the breeze blew through her hair, the way her mouth dropped when he opened up the front door to the villa, and revealed an expansive living area with a vaulted ceiling. There was a small kitchen area with glossy black countertops and a bowl of fruit placed at the center.

And she was enraptured by all of it. "This is the most beautiful place I've ever seen," she said, taking a turn around the room, and then moving into the bedroom, before coming back out. "And this is the biggest bed I've ever seen."

Her cheeks turned instantly pink.

"Good for our purposes," he said.

He went into the kitchen area and opened up the fridge, where he found wrapped trays with precut fruit, a bottle of champagne and a tray of meat and cheese.

He began to get all of it out, taking down glasses and pouring a measure in his and hers.

"Why don't you go out to the deck. There should be appropriate clothing for you in the bedroom."

She looked at him with intrigue, then vanished back into the bedroom. He took his time preparing the trays, walking out to the expansive deck area and going to the loungers just outside the bedroom. He set the trays of food and champagne flutes on a table between two of the loungers, and then Verity appeared, wearing…

Nothing.

He thought his heart might beat itself through his chest.

"There are some beautiful things in there," she said. "But I did sort of think that since it's a private island…"

"I very much like the way you think."

She smiled at him and sat down in the lounger.

This, he knew, was a tease, because she was going to drink her champagne and have her snack. And he wanted her to be happy.

He was hard, though, and it made it difficult to focus on the food.

"This is really beautiful."

"I know," he said, never taking his eyes off her.

"Have you ever done anything like this before? I mean, with anyone else."

"No," he said. He looked at her. "Do you actually want to hear about past lovers?"

"No and yes. I'm curious how much of this is…a routine for you."

"None of it," he said, honestly. "I told you, I can have sex without romance. I do it all the time."

"How much is all the time?"

"Don't ask questions you don't want the answer to, Cricket."

"Ah. I am Cricket again."

"Does that bother you?"

"No. I like it. Because it's something that only you call me. But I also like it when you call me by my name. Because you never did, so when you started it felt like something. Special. Maybe that's why I'm asking you these questions. This feels special. I want to believe that it is."

"You're the only woman I've ever married. I wasn't protecting myself, not the way that you were. I wasn't afraid of accidentally getting attached to somebody that I didn't want to be attached to, or getting hurt by someone. I never have been. The first time I had sex was one of the most truly disappointing experiences of my life."

"Why?" She sat up, naked and holding a champagne flute, and it distracted him from the disturbing feelings that were rising up inside of him.

"I thought… I thought I might feel something. You're supposed to. The first time, it's supposed to mean something. It's supposed to matter. I didn't feel anything. If anything I felt more alone then than I ever had before. Like I was lying next to a stranger, and also like I was one." He tried to smile. "I suppose that's how it is when you sleep with a stranger. It feels like exactly what it is."

"How old were you?"

"Twenty-one. I didn't ever sleep with a woman until I had somewhere nice to take her. So not until I had some money. So that I could take her to a nice hotel. I dressed it up as something that looked like romance, and I thought perhaps I would feel it. I didn't. That was the day I knew that I was truly broken. I said goodbye to her, and I can't even remember her face now, all these years later. I couldn't remember her face very soon after, if I'm honest."

She got off the lounger, and moved onto his, scooting right next to him, then wrapped her arms around him, the gesture so unusual, so foreign to him, that he almost didn't know what she was doing. Hugging him. She was giving him a hug.

"That's very sad," she whispered. "And I'm sorry."

"Are you hugging me?"

"Yes. Because someone should."

Someone should. Was that true? Did he deserve those things, those simple gestures, connections, when he didn't know how to give them back? Or maybe what she meant was that he should've had them in the beginning, because then maybe he wouldn't be the way he was now. That he could see.

"To answer your question," he said, because he didn't know how to continue the conversation about hugging, "no. I have never brought anyone to a place like this. I've never spent time with a lover before. I've never had a relationship. And I suspect that's what this is."

"Is it?" She turned her head, rubbing her nose against his neck.

"I suspect."

"You're so funny, Alex."

"Not on purpose."

"I know."

They sat like that for a long time. It was an incredible thing, to want her, but to also be able to sit with her. In silence or otherwise.

"I think," she whispered finally, "you might be protecting yourself more than you know."

"In what way?"

"Never trying to have relationships."

"Why would I try something I felt I would inevitably fail?"

"You're trying with me."

It was true. He was. Except... She understood. She understood that he might not be able to...give what most men could.

"You know, though," he said, suddenly desperate to hear her say it. "You know who I am. You know how I am. You know that I might not be able to give you something that feels like...what every other relationship feels like."

"I don't know what any other relationship feels like. So I guess that's a good thing, isn't it? I don't know what it feels like to be with someone else. And I never wanted to be, not before you. When I said that I didn't know myself, what I meant was...admitting to myself that you were the one I wanted was a shock."

"What?"

"I never wanted Stavros. He was safe. I made rules

for myself. Before I went off to school, I told myself I would never get involved with a man who would make me lose my head. I never wanted anyone who was intense, someone that I felt like I needed to manage them, or… You know how my family is. So I told myself that if I was going to date, it was going to be someone that I could manage. Then I took a job working for you, and you were definitely not someone that I could manage. Stavros being in the same building was convenient. He's handsome, he's not demanding. He smiles all the time. I could distract myself looking at him, and fill that surface need to be distracted by someone. So that I didn't have to admit I wanted you."

"You wanted me?"

"Yes. From the very beginning. That's also why it took me two years to ask Stavros out. I didn't really want to go out with him. I didn't really want him. I had gotten to the point where I thought maybe I was going to just have to do it, and maybe I would have. But somehow I doubt it. Being with you… I didn't even have to think about it. I didn't have to question it. It was right. It was what I wanted. That's why I'm here. It's easy for me to say that you railroaded me into this. Comfortable, even." She smiled. "But I'm not really being tortured, am I?"

"You might feel differently after several days in my company."

She laughed. "Maybe. Maybe. I'm trying to figure out all the things I've been ignoring. All the things I've been pushing down. You definitely taught me something about myself when we…"

"You like it when I praise you."

"Yes. I guess it doesn't take a psychologist to figure out why. I spent a long time feeling like I wasn't enough. Not good enough, not smart enough, not anything enough. That's one reason I enjoyed working for you so much. Because you are such a pain. You are so exacting, all the things that other people don't like about you I—" She stopped talking. "Sorry. I guess I shouldn't say it like that."

"It doesn't hurt my feelings that people don't like me. I've never tried to make them like me."

And there he wondered if she had spoken some wisdom to him a few moments ago.

He had never tried to make anyone like him. He had never tried to have a relationship. What if that was a version of self-protection?

No. He had wanted to feel something. There were times in his life when he'd wanted it desperately. But the feelings had never been there. It would be a convenient fantasy to tell himself that it had been self-protection all along. It would make him feel better, in some ways. But it would give both of them false hope.

"And then you had to. For work."

"Yes. I have always seen my company as my legacy. I always thought that I would never have children, and so it would have to be what remained of me. Do you understand?"

She nodded slowly. "And what do you think of children now? Hypothetically. If we were to stay married."

The idea fascinated and terrified him. Made him feel like he was on the edge of a cliff, and also on the edge of a brilliant discovery. A child. His child. A great and terrible experiment, he thought. Maybe the only chance he would ever have to love someone or something instantly and in an all-consuming way, but if he couldn't...

"Don't try to figure out if you'll be good at it. Just... Do you want a child?"

He nodded slowly. "Yes. I do."

"Me too. I didn't think I did, but thinking about it now it makes me realize that I do. But I want to build a family on my own terms. Can you imagine that? The power in finally taking control. You can have a family, and it doesn't depend on choices other people made. I can have a family, one that's as good as I make it. Choosing to avoid this, it was always giving our power away. I realize that now."

When she said it like that it made sense. It was giving their power away. And neither of them would do that, not anymore.

"Finish your champagne. I need you."

"Oh. I'm finished."

Then he swept her into his arms and carried her to that big bed, and showed her exactly why they needed all that room.

CHAPTER THIRTEEN

AFTER TWO WEEKS on the island, Verity had forgotten who she was away from it. It was a blissful respite from reality that she had never really imagined taking before. And it was amazing. All they had done for two weeks was eat, make love, swim in the ocean and make love again. Sometimes she cooked food for him; sometimes he did it for her. They dined on the beach, on the deck outside of their bedroom, in bed.

If their lives could be like this, always, then everything would be okay. She was certain of that.

It was just too bad that away from here they had lives. Though, they got along so well in their professional lives. Maybe she could keep on being his assistant, even though she was his wife.

But this was only two weeks into the six months. She wasn't supposed to be making decisions about the future this early. Of course, they had talked about the future. About children.

Part of her wanted to throw caution to the wind and her birth control pills into the trash and tell him she wanted everything right now.

But she had a feeling that her desperation was more of her instinct to protect herself. To make this permanent.

Because at this point, she was terrified of what it would look like if she lost him.

She was also struck by the difference between managing someone, and doing things for them because she wanted to. She had thought that a relationship would be labor. Work.

She and Alex did things for each other, and it made her happy. Cooking for him delighted her, because he enjoyed it. And she had never really gotten to take care of another person before. There was something lovely about it. Something deeply satisfying.

One night over dinner she realized that she didn't know one of the most basic things about him.

"When is your birthday?"

"Why?" he asked, looking deeply suspicious of her.

"Because I want to know what your astrological sign is so I can do our chart."

"You must be joking."

"I think you're a Taurus. But I am joking."

"I don't know what that means, but… I don't know exactly."

"What do you mean you don't know exactly?"

"I don't have a birth certificate from when I was actually born. I had one that the state filled out, but they can only approximate my age. I have never celebrated it on a specific day. It's in April. At least, that is their best guess."

"A Taurus. Most likely." She said that, and tried to smile, but mostly what he had just said hurt. It hurt badly, because he didn't even know this most…basic thing about himself. She wished that she didn't know who his parents were, because she wanted to go and fight them. She wanted to go and fight a state that had made him feel useless, made him feel like his failure to be adopted was his fault.

She wanted to bake him a birthday cake and celebrate him and give him everything that he had ever been denied.

"It's never meant anything to me. My understanding is that those things only matter when you have someone to celebrate with."

"I don't know. I like my birthday just fine, even with the family that I have."

"I've never celebrated."

She decided that wasn't acceptable. She called their supply source and arranged for some gifts to be brought to the island, along with decorations and supplies for a recipe she'd been wanting to try for a while.

And then there was the cake. She was the most excited about the cake. Of course, with their situation on the island it wasn't exactly like she could surprise him. And anyway, she wasn't sure surprising Alex was the best thing to do with him. What she surprised him with, were the supplies.

"What is all this?" he asked as he helped arrange everything in the kitchen.

"I've decided that you're going to have a birthday party. I'm going to bake you a cake."

"It's not my birthday."

"I don't care. You've missed too many celebrations. And I'm going to celebrate you, dammit."

He looked at her like she was something strange and foreign, and maybe even wondrous. She couldn't deny that it made her feel a shimmering, pleasurable sensation.

She wanted him to say that he was happy with her. That the idea was wonderful. He didn't say that, but he didn't tell her not to do it. He hung out on the periphery of the kitchen area like an animal that had been banished, prowling like he was waiting for something.

"What are you cooking?" he asked over the invisible line that he had drawn for himself.

"Homemade pasta and scallops."

His eyes went sharp, and she recognized that he was pleased with that answer. Even though he didn't say, she was warmed.

He went back to pacing.

When she started hanging streamers around the room, his expression shifted to one of total shock.

"What?" she asked. "You can't have a party without streamers."

"I... I didn't know that."

"Well, now you do. It's festive."

There was something strange about the way he behaved after that. It reminded her the most of the way he was during work. That wall in place, like he was trying to observe some sort of custom very carefully. It was definitely not how he'd been acting during their time here. But she was determined to persist even though he was being weird.

Of course he was, if she really thought about it. He wasn't used to anything like this. He had said so himself.

The Happy Birthday that she wrote on the cake was a little bit lopsided, but she was pleased with it all the same. It was chocolate, and it would taste good, so it didn't really matter if it was pretty.

She put a candle in the center, ready for her to light once they were done with dinner.

"Go sit down outside, and I'll serve you."

He did what she said, but his movements were robotic.

And when she served him, he didn't get any warmer. She sat across from him, hoping to draw him out. He was stilted, but not unkind.

"I didn't even make you eat salad," she said, and that coaxed a small smile from him.

When they finished with dinner she went into the kitchen, lit the candle on the cake and brought it out to him. She sang, even if badly, and set the cake down in front of him. "And now you blow out the candle and make a wish."

He blew the candle out, and looked up at her with haunted, hollow eyes. And then he stood up, and walked over to the railing of the deck, resting his forearms against the top of it, staring out sightlessly at the dark water.

"Alex," she said. "What's wrong?"

"It doesn't mean anything to me," he said, his voice rough. "I don't...care about this."

The first thing she felt was pity. An enormous heaping of self-pity, actually, not pity for him. She had worked so hard on this, and he didn't care. It meant nothing to him that she had put all this effort in, that she had thought of him, that she had wanted to give him something that he had never had before. It meant absolutely nothing.

And then, just as suddenly as that welled up inside of her, it went away. Because of course that wasn't what he was saying. He wasn't saying that it didn't matter that she had done this; it was the party itself. It was his first birthday party, and he didn't know what to feel.

Because he didn't understand this. He had already explained how Christmas was for him. That he couldn't feel this thing he was certain he was supposed to because he had no nostalgia attached to it. Even worse, she suspected he had a host of pain associated with these things. Whether he wanted to admit it or not. Whether he even knew it or not. He had missed a lifetime of this.

And this was his deepest fear. She hadn't even thought of that. Hadn't considered it.

"Maybe it doesn't this time," she said. "But it can. This is just the first one. But next year, you'll remember this."

His face was half in shadows, his eyes black. "Why would I ever want to remember this? This reminder of everything that I'm not. Everything that I can't be."

"Then…" She felt like she was bleeding from the inside. She felt like she had caused him pain when that was the last thing she wanted to do. And all she wanted to do was fix it. She just wanted to fix it. "Then let's make this the memory."

She kissed him. With everything she had. Kissed him with everything she had tried to put into the birthday party. Kissed him with all the desire inside of her. To be good for him. To be perfect for him.

To gain his praise, but now more than that. To make him feel. She wanted it. So much. So badly. To be the one who could change this. Who could change him.

He wrapped his arms around her, and kissed her back, his desperation matching hers. "I need you," she whispered. "I want you." She wanted to find the words. To find something to make him feel even half for her what she did for him. He knew exactly what to say to her. She didn't have the words for him.

"I need you," she said. Because it was true. Because it was the only thing she could think of.

He didn't carry her inside. Rather he picked her up and carried her over to the lounger, stripping her of her party dress and growling when she was naked beneath the moonlight. This wasn't that sweet gesture she was trying to offer him. This was something else. Something intense. Something feral. But this was what he needed, and she was going to give it to him.

Even if it cost her.

Intense. She had always sought to avoid intensity. She had wanted to go through life without connections that cost her.

That was her mistake.

This was so much better than being protected.

This was so much better than being safe.

She wanted him. Everything that he was. Everything. Even the broken things, the frightening things. The things that could wound her. After all, the way he was hurt him. Why wouldn't it hurt her sometimes? And the way she was... She had hurt herself with it. She had spent all this time denying herself. Hiding.

She wasn't afraid, not anymore. Maybe Alex would end up hurting her.

But he was worth it. He was so infinitely worth it.

That was the difference. The difference between him and her parents. The difference between everything that they could be, and everything that her family had been.

She chose Alex. And that was different in and of itself.

But more than that, he gave to her too. He had, over the years that she had known him, and he had while they had been here on the island. He took care of her. He gave her the words that she needed. Maybe he was best at all of it when they were in bed, but that was just the way he found it easiest.

He gave her something that made her feel good. He cared about making her feel good. This wasn't a one-way street. This was caring. Whether he knew it or not. She wanted him to understand that. This was connection. Maybe it was the only place he could feel it. Maybe. But then she would be here for him this way.

"I'm yours," she whispered. "You don't have to do anything to try and keep me. I'm already here. I married you. You're my husband. I'm yours."

He shivered beneath her touch, and she maneuvered herself that she was straddling him on the lounger, unbuttoned his shirt as she felt him growing hard between her thighs. She kissed him. "I belong to you."

He reached up and gripped the back of her hair, pulling hard. The noise that he made was savage, and she kissed him, swallowing the end of it, claiming it for herself.

He wanted that. He wanted her. He wanted that connection that he didn't think he could feel. He wanted some external marker. Some form of proof. Her word. Her promise. She would give it to him. Because she cared for him. She cared for him so much.

She…

She pushed that thought away. She kissed him. Deeper, harder. Making a physical vow out of what she had already spoken.

Naked in the moonlight, she straddled him as she undid the closure on his pants and freed him so that she could position herself over him, take him inside, moving up and down slowly, luxuriating in the feel of him inside of her. The feel of this connection. "You don't feel nothing with me," she whispered.

She wasn't even sure if he could understand her. She wasn't sure if she was coherent.

But she knew that much was true. She wasn't some stranger that he lost his virginity to; she wasn't a birth-day party.

He felt something for her. And he felt connected to her now. In this moment, they were something. In this moment, they were real.

She pushed them both to the brink, until he was shaking, sweating. Until a horrible, hollow-eyed look was gone, and it was replaced with need. Desire.

He was hers. She was his. This was true. Undeniably.

Even if he had a hard time admitting it. Even if right now he couldn't understand it.

He gripped her hips and took the control from her, thrusting up inside of her, his strength, the ruthlessness of each thrust driving her closer to the edge.

And when they fell, they fell together, even connected in this. In pleasure.

She lay down over him, her hair spread out over his chest like a blanket.

"You felt something then," she said.

He wrapped his arm around her, but said nothing.

Still. She knew that it was true.

She had to believe that it was true.

CHAPTER FOURTEEN

ALEX DIDN'T APPRECIATE work intruding on their honeymoon. The reports that he was getting back were all positive; everyone who had an opinion on such things was fascinated by his marriage. Some thought it was a PR move, but many thought it was a romance novel come to life. A workplace romance between the beautiful and warm heroine and the hard remote hero. But one thing was becoming abundantly clear: his time away from work was beginning to be a bit too much, and he and Verity were needed back in the real world.

He found himself reluctant to leave, which was a strange feeling. Normally, his drive to work was the strongest drive he possessed.

But he found he wanted to stay here.

All the more reason to go, he supposed.

He took a breath, and walked through the kitchen area, deliberately not thinking about the failed birthday party from a week ago, through his shared bedroom with Verity, where she was not, and then outside. He looked down, and saw her in the clear water, swimming like a mermaid with her blond hair streaming behind her.

"Wife," he said, the word catching in his throat. "I need to speak to you."

She swam over to where he was, looking up at him, her smile in pitch. "I'm afraid we have go back."

"Oh," she said, looking disappointed. He hated that he had disappointed her. He hated that he had made her frown.

He had never cared how he made another person feel before. It was the strangest thing. Sometimes watching Verity was like watching a piece of himself out in the world. He could not explain it. Like she had taken something essential from him, stolen it and repurposed it. He wasn't even certain if he wanted it back.

"We must. While the headlines about our marriage have been positive, ahead of the product launch we need to be seen."

"Of course," she said.

"And so, we will be," he said.

A few hours later they were on the private plane headed back to Athens. "You said you wanted to go to London," he said.

"Well, yes, I would like that."

"Then we shall go. As part of all of this."

She tilted her head to the side. "Oh right. Just for show."

"We just had an entire honeymoon that had nothing to do with the outside world."

"I know. But it's hard to forget that this is actually why we got married in the first place." She sighed. "Actually, it was really easy to forget. For a while. And now…reality is kind of lurching up to bite us in the face."

"Is that how you feel?"

She lifted her hand and made a claw with it. "Yes."

"Reality doesn't have to be a bad thing."

"In my experience, it is."

"Ah yes. Because in reality, it is not a fairy-tale wedding, it is a secret ambush by your family."

"Well. Yes. Not trying to be rude or whiny about that or anything, but that was a little bit rough."

"I had thought that we were past that."

"We are. Intermittently. Sometimes, I get a little bit mad about it, though."

"Well, I will tell you what I have planned. We must be seen tonight going back to our home in Athens."

She blinked. "I didn't move out of my apartment yet."

"Yes, you have. I took care of everything while we were on the island."

Her eyes nearly bugged out of her head. "You have had all my things moved?"

"Yes," he said. "It was a mere detail that needed to be seen to."

"Right. My entire life was a mere detail."

"That little apartment was not your entire life."

"I guess not." She looked irritated.

"Are you going to sulk, or are you going to tell me why you're being difficult?"

"What we had was really special. And now we're going back to life. We're going back to work. It can work, I know it can. But I'm worried."

"Verity, I cannot promise you that I'll be a perfect husband in the way that the world would define it. But I'm not leaving everything that we were behind on that island."

He didn't know what else to say.

She seemed mollified by that. She looked almost happy.

"Well, I guess I can live with that."

"I would hope so."

"What is your plan then?"

"My plan is for us to be seen returning home tonight. Tomorrow we will fly out to London, we will stay in my town house there. Then we will go to dinner. I will take you off to Paris afterward, where we will swan romantically around the museums."

"Right. For everyone else."

"Also for us. Will you not enjoy it?"

"I will," she said. "I will. I'm determined to."

Though she didn't sound pleased in any fashion. "Good," he said.

When the plane touched down in Athens, he could feel her tension rising.

It was a short trip from the airfield back to his house, and he watched her face closely as they walked inside the ornate living quarters. Classical architecture mixed with modern design. If she was impressed, that wasn't what she was conveying. Rather she seemed perplexed.

"What is the matter?"

"I feel like a commoner going to live in a palace, I guess. I feel like… Okay, I don't actually care about that. I don't know how to live with another person. All of my things are here. With your things. We are going to share a bedroom. A life. It was different when we were in a neutral place, but this is your house. Your house, and here I am in it. And what do I even…? What you might even do to take up even a corner of a place like this? I worked really hard to become myself and I…"

"You're afraid of losing yourself," he said.

Because of course she was. She had shrunk herself, made herself small and insignificant in order to please her family. And now she was staring down watching herself melt into his world.

"I do not wish for you to become someone else. I don't need you to. I am strong enough to stand on my own feet, Verity, and I would think you would know that. Little Cricket, I want you to be my conscience. I want you to tell me what you need. And I want you to make your presence known. I always have. I did not hire you to sit there sight unseen. But you know that."

"But you don't feel attachment for anything. Or anyone. So what's to keep me rooted to this place? What's to keep you from replacing me? Or worse, me trying to reshape myself into something easier?"

He couldn't really argue with the thesis of that question. And yet, he didn't know for sure if he could say that he wasn't attached to her. For a moment, he let that thought sit there, marinate, grow in weight.

"It is not so simple. I want you with me. I know that much."

She softened. "Okay. Then I'll stay with you." She let out a long, hard sigh. "I'm sorry. You've been nothing but wonderful to me, all through our honeymoon together. You have never acted like you were a cruel man, and I've known you now for two years. But it's amazing how much weight parental issues carry. I know you didn't have them, but it's not…it's not different, not really."

"I know," he said. "I… I carry the issues of my childhood obviously. They have made me into who I am. And who I cannot be. For you or for anyone. But I have decided to vow myself to you. To make a family with you. Do you understand that's not something I would ever do lightly?"

"Yes," she whispered. "I understand that."

"Good. I'm glad that you do."

"It's so funny, because a few weeks ago it seemed reasonable to perform this for everybody. And now it feels a little bit too private."

"We will not show them everything."

"Of course."

Then, he picked her up off the floor, and swept her up the stairs, because he couldn't bear the weight of her uncertainty or sadness for another moment. He wasn't sure if that conversation had solved anything. Had made her feel any better. He wasn't entirely sure that he had gotten down to the heart of what was bothering her. But he cared about her. And he wanted her to be happy. Or perhaps he only cared about himself and he wanted his home to be happy. Either way, he knew that talking wasn't the answer right now.

And when he laid her down in their bed, they didn't talk anymore.

And he felt everything he could not put into words.

The next morning they were off to London, and Verity was poring over the photographs of them entering their house in Greece.

"People really are…interested in us."

She had had a near breakdown last night, and she felt a little bit embarrassed by it now. Because it had been a full panic with very little articulation behind it. She supposed she should feel proud that she had been able to have it, and not worry so much about what he would do or think.

She had wanted him to say that he…that he cared about her. She had wanted something stronger than what she had gotten.

But if she wasn't willing to say…

She couldn't quite find it in her to put words to her feelings yet. And if she couldn't do that, then how could she expect him to do it? It wouldn't be fair.

She took a sharp breath, and looked at the photos. Looked at the two of them. She could see her bad mood, but it didn't seem like anyone else could.

She felt so exposed. They had been thrown from the gorgeous Caribbean and into a fishbowl. But that was the idea. This whole relationship was supposed to be for show. Acting upset about it now was pointless. Silly.

Childish, even.

Yes. It was childish.

She swallowed hard, trying to ignore the tenderness in the center of her chest. And trying to drum up some excitement for London.

"Yes, of course people are interested in us," he said. "Because I've never been attached to anyone before."

"I guess that's the thing. I should say that people are interested in you. They're only interested in me as an accessory."

"It is important. If you were a sort of corporate-looking woman, you wouldn't be right for the part."

The word *part* graded.

"Yes. Of course. It was a good casting decision. Going with kind of a bohemian hippie chick."

"I wouldn't call you that."

"Because you haven't really seen me in my own clothes."

He tilted his head, looked at her as if she had gone mad. "Of course I have. I've seen you at work every day for the last two years."

"Those are my work clothes."

"But then I saw you on our honeymoon."

"Mostly naked, and otherwise in clothes that were furnished by you. Or rather, your people."

"What do you normally wear?"

"Lots of bracelets, flowing skirts."

"I saw your family. They were aggressively…"

"Mid-level department store?"

"Well. Yes."

"When I was younger, I wanted to find some way to be an individual. To be me. Little things that were authentic, especially because I was always shoving pieces of myself down to make everybody else happy."

"I want to see them. I want to see that part of yourself."

His eyes glowed with the truth of that, and she felt so warmed by it. Renewed.

"Then, you will."

It was always nice when she found ways to talk to him. She could info dump on him, sure, the same way that he did her when they had gone over their pasts, but it was exciting to discover these kinds of things. These little things that they didn't know about each other yet, even though they have been so intimate with each other.

Even though she was finding new ways to touch him every day, there were still so many things to discover.

And every time he did, he seemed happy. He seemed to care. No one else in her life ever had.

When the plane touched down in London, the first thing they did was go to his town house. She realized that this was the opportunity she had missed when they had gone to Athens. She was busy feeling afraid. Because she had gone ahead and let herself get worried about what it meant for the two of them to be in the public eye. But here she was, in a house that had been put together especially for Alex. That meant that she could get to know him in a different way.

It was wild to her to think that she had married this man and she hadn't really been to his house.

She walked straight through the entryway, down the hall and into the kitchen. She went over to the stove and opened a cupboard just above it.

"What are you doing?"

"Looking for coffee. Tea. Little things about you. I haven't really snooped around one of your houses."

"We just stayed in my over-water villa."

"Well yes. But also no. Because you said yourself you hadn't even been there. You bought it sight unseen. It wasn't really yours."

"I rarely spend any time here."

"What do you like?"

"Coffee. Not tea."

"Okay. What else?"

"We have a dinner reservation, and you should get dressed."

"When is it?"

"Soon."

She fixed him with an irritated scowl. "Okay. Do I have enough time to go out and buy something for myself?"

"I... Why?"

"You said you wanted to see *me*. My taste. Who I am outside the office, who I was before I came here. I want you to know me."

"We don't have time tonight. And, also, this is for the cameras, it isn't for us."

She felt a little bit like she had had her hand slapped. Like she had found her limit. She knew that it was a silly thing to be upset about, but she felt herself deflate. "Oh."

"Why are you looking at me like that?"

"You said you wanted to see my clothes. You said you wanted to see *me*. You don't, really. Do you?"

"I do. But tonight we are performing for the cameras. I will wear a suit and tie, regardless of what I might wear if we were on an island together."

"Right. Sorry. It's a silly thing. I'm being oversensitive. I feel like I've been oversensitive since we got back."

"Well. I didn't want to say anything."

She made a tsk-tsking sound, and went up the palatial staircase without asking him where his bedroom was. She had a feeling she could guess the whereabouts easily enough. He followed her, though.

"If you know you're oversensitive then why are you being oversensitive?"

She turned around, her head practically swiveled all the way around, in fact. He was standing in the doorway, looking maddeningly male, and she had the sudden blessed insight as to why she hadn't pursued relationships ever, in her whole life. Because this was the exact thing women complained about.

"I can't stop myself from having feelings. Moreover, very importantly, I won't. I have feelings, Alex. Having to leave the island like that, it was abrupt. I'm adjusting. I told you that this feels really personal."

"And I told you that I can't quite understand that."

"I'm sorry that you can't. But it's not going to make me feel any different. What the two of us have is intimate for me. I've never slept with anyone else. I've never…

Alex, the relationship that I have with you is not like any other relationship I've ever had. I want to protect it. And I wanted to be mine. I want…to make you birthday cakes and be your wife. I don't want to perform it. It just reminds me that you didn't choose me. Not really. I'm part of the scheme."

"That's where you're wrong. I did choose you. I told you. Everyone likes you. There is something in you that draws people to you, and I don't even have a fraction of that. I'm brilliant," he said.

"And very modest," she pointed out.

"Honest," he said. "I'm brilliant at certain things. But I can't do the things that you do. The way that you make people feel is… You warm them up from the inside out, Verity. You even do it to me. You asked me…you asked me why I hired you. And I lied to you."

She froze. "You did?"

"Yes. I said that you were the first applicant. That wasn't true. I had interviewed several people at that point. Men, women. People closer to my own age. People with similar interests in technology. No one was you. There was something about you when you walked in, and I just knew that I couldn't let you walk back out. I knew that I had to have you. Every day. I knew that I needed you sitting across from me. I knew that you were the person that was going to teach me what I needed to know. And it couldn't have been just anyone. That's why I wanted you to marry me. Because I knew that you would affect everyone the way that you do me. Because no one affects me. Nothing. Which means the board is going to love you—and they do. The public is going to love you."

It was very nearly the sweetest thing anyone had ever said to her. It was maybe the sweetest thing he'd ever said. But it wasn't altogether that sweet.

She had touched something in him, and he had immediately figured out how to make it useful.

She was awash in a strange sort of sentimentality, and also a fair amount of pain. Because it was just the most Alex. She meant something to him, and so he had figured out a way to make it relevant to his business.

Maybe she should just be happy that she meant something to him.

"Sorry. I will let you get dressed."

"Yes. Thank you."

She went to the closet, and fished out the most flowy dress she could find. Amazing how he had brought a whole wardrobe here too. She frowned as she touched the dress. These were the things that he saw her in. Because he knew her at the office. She fought off an intense wave of sadness. Fought off the terrible impression that in some ways, she was just still his assistant; it was just now it was for better or worse until death, rather than until HR separated them.

She had the jarring realization as soon as she finished getting dressed that this wasn't even permanent.

She really had lost all sense of everything on that island. She had lost all sense of self-preservation—that was for sure. She was in the deep end. She was also acting like he had all the control. When in fact, she could choose to walk away just as easily as he could choose to boot her back out into obscurity.

That should be cheering. It wasn't.

She took a deep breath, and walked out the door, coming face-to-face with him. And right then, she realized something. "I'm sorry," she said.

"You're sorry?"

"Yes. I'm acting… I'm being… It's fine. The way I'm being is actually fine, because my feelings are actually fine. But I realize that I feel insecure about how well we know each other, and how well we don't. I don't know my parents. Not as human beings. I know them as these terrible people that inflicted so much damage on to me, but I have no idea how they turned into those people. And I had to build up so many walls to keep myself safe, that I think I'm just very aware of…walls."

"I do not wish to hurt you, but I'm…me. And that means the wall is somewhat inevitable. Especially right now. Because this is the business aspect of this arrangement. But I gave you the honeymoon."

She wished that he didn't make it sound so much like a forfeit.

"True. You did."

She decided to let it go, because now they had to go out. And she did feel a moment of radiant sun when he held her hand, and led her into the restaurant. She didn't know why she felt so raw about them being on display. But she had to try and sort it out instead of just taking it out on him. No, she didn't want to get into a situation where she suppressed her feelings, but at this point, she was just whining at him.

You're being a coward, is what you're doing.

She shut that thought aside.

And she had a lovely dinner with her husband, and didn't let herself worry for the whole rest of the night.

CHAPTER FIFTEEN

THE HEADLINES WERE FANTASTIC, but his wife was prickly. And he didn't quite know what to do with her. So when they went to Paris the next day, he made a few calls. Yes, they would have to do some things that put them in front of the public, but he wanted...he wanted to give her something. Something he had never given to anyone before. Not that it was difficult. He had never given anything to anyone before. That was one of the astonishing things about Verity. Taking care of her was something glorious.

When they were in bed, he had an easy time praising her. Telling her how special she was, but he could see that it wasn't quite enough for her.

He could see that she was craving something more, and he wanted to find a way to give her that.

He wanted to give her everything. It was just he didn't know where everything extended inside of him. Where it began. Where it ended.

"I want to go shopping," he said.

She looked up at him from their lunch table, right at the base of the Eiffel Tower. "You want me to...go shopping? For something that will look good in photographs?"

"Something that looks good to you. You have no budget. I have a few things to arrange, and then I will have you meet me back at our hotel."

"Very heavy-handed."

"Perhaps. But you're a good girl," he said. "And you will do as I say."

She flushed with pleasure, and he thought perhaps that he had done well.

Taking care of business was actual torture, when in fact he wanted to be with her. She kept sending him photographs from dressing rooms, and he didn't quite know what to do with it. She was asking his opinion, and he found himself more interested in the cut of flowy skirts than he had ever been before in his life.

He had thought that he would prefer the outfits that showed more skin, that were tighter, the sorts of things that she often wore to the office, or the shockingly pink dress that she had worn to dinner that night in Athens. He found that he could easily make a fantasy out of swirling, flowing fabric.

And all that wild blond hair.

He was on a video call, and it was his head of production that caught him being distracted. "Mr. Economides?"

"Sorry," he said. "My wife is texting me."

It was perhaps the most normal sentence he'd ever said in his life.

It made him feel something. The beginning of something warm, right there at the center of his chest. He put his hand there, and he tried to ignore the burning pain that accompanied it.

He tried to get his focus back on the meeting.

He was meeting her soon. He was quite literally counting down the minutes.

When at last he was free of his obligations, he raced to the front of the hotel, where she stood wearing a glorious, emerald green dress with a drop waist and glimmering gems all over it. She was wearing a large cuff on her wrist, and it made him think of how he wanted to grab her, hold her down, hold her to him. It was shockingly erotic, as was every detail. Including the long teardrop earrings that nearly kissed her shoulders. It was different to what he had seen her in before, except it did remind him just slightly of the wedding gown that she had selected. Something ethereal about it. Magical.

That same, painful feeling began to splinter at the center of his chest.

He swallowed hard. "Let's go."

He swept her into the back of the limousine that took them across the city to the Musée d'Orsay. He had rented it out for the night, only for the two of them.

"Isn't this closed?" she asked as they approached the ornate building.

"Yes. For everyone who isn't us. But tonight, you and I get to have a private tour."

A flush of pleasure overtook her face.

"Just us?"

"Yes."

"Not for show?"

"No," he said. "I just want to see your face."

It was true. He wanted to give her something. In this museum, which contained so many of the beautiful works of art in the world, that seemed like a small thing. Something lovely that he could make for the two of them. They walked inside, beneath the glorious arched roof. The garden of sculptures greeted them.

It was lit still, but there were not even security guards. He had paid handsomely for the privilege. And for all of the security cameras to be turned off.

Tonight, this place might as well be their own private bedroom.

It was their own world.

"Do you like museums?" she asked, circling the first sculpture with an expression of wonder on her face.

"I never have. Do you like it, though?"

"I do," she said. "How did you know that I would?"

"You're one of those rare people who finds the beauty in so many things. You've talked to me often about how you used to walk through the art museum at your university. You always go to the beach on your day off, even though it's a long drive, and it eats into your precious free time. You like the beauty of things. This outfit that you chose tonight…it reflects that. You're a sensual creature, and you love things that are beautiful just for the sake of it. And so a museum is the perfect place for you, I would think."

"Tell me again," she said. "Tell me again why you hired me."

"Because I couldn't let you go," he said.

There was a real, raw emotion behind those words, even if he couldn't quite untangle what it was.

He paused for a moment, and stopped with her in front of a sculpture of a young woman sitting down, a harp beside her. It was so real, like she might grab hold of the instrument and begin playing at any moment. But she was just marble. Like him. The notion was so funny, he nearly laughed.

He looked real. Sometimes, he even thought he might be. When he was with her. When he could feel her heart beating next to his. But it was just her.

It had been, from the beginning.

He had wanted to cling to it, wanted to grab onto it, not let it go. From the first.

It would be so easy to confuse it with his own humanity.

"You know," he said. "I used to tell myself that I was only the right visit away from having a real set of parents. And every time a couple would come and see me and leave without me, never call back, never seek me out again, I would tell myself that perhaps I had gotten close that time. Perhaps, I had been on the cusp of having a family, and it had been cruelly snatched away from me. And then one day, I was perhaps nine, I realized that I was never close. They came on a visit to see a child. That visit didn't mean they thought anything about me in particular. It only meant they wanted a boy of my age. Nothing was taken from me, because nothing was ever mine. Because it was all forms and paperwork and things like that. It was nothing real. It was never me. I let go of all of it. Of even the wish for a family."

"Were you ever angry?"

"Yes. But I realize, you don't do anything to be born into a family. You simply are. You don't ask to be created. God knows I didn't. But here I am. Here you are. You didn't ask for your parents, any more than I asked to not have any. I imagine there are a great many children who are terrible. Who hate their parents, despise them, and aren't grateful for a single moment they spend with them. It's a lottery of birth, isn't it? I didn't deserve my life any more than you deserved yours. So yes. I used to be very, very angry about that. But there's no point to it. No purpose. It's just easier for there to be nothing," he said.

"You did feel," she said. "You used to be attached."

"What? There was never anything there."

"There was, though. A woman gave birth to you. She carried you in her womb for nine months. Just because you didn't know her didn't mean that connection didn't exist."

"I don't even know if she ever held me."

His words were far too loud in the silence of the museum.

"She did, though. Even if it wasn't in her arms."

"So did your mother," he said.

"I can't deny that. And you know, you don't have to be grateful to her. I'm not grateful to my mother. It's still a loss, though. That potential. It's a connection. And I think maybe it's even worse because it is, even if it was severed the moment she gave birth to you."

"No," he said. "Don't mistake me. If any part of me ever felt connection, it was gone a long time ago."

"It still does. Or you would've been happy enough to let me walk back out of your life the day that I walked in."

Her words were like a knife slipped beneath his skin. "Verity…"

"Let's walk," she said, taking his hand and moving him into another display room. The works of Monet were hung with only dark walls and spare lighting to highlight them. One painting in particular caught his eye. It was meant to be Parliament, but it was obscured. The shape of it was clear, but it was like there was a fog all around it. And yet again, he couldn't help but think of himself.

Only the shape of a man, obscured by too much to ever really be clear.

Perhaps this was why he didn't like museums.

There were too many opportunities to look at himself. And if he wanted to gaze into a mirror he could've stayed back at the hotel.

They entered the display room for van Gogh, and Verity exhaled a reverent breath. They might have stepped into a church.

The approached the *Starry Night* painting, her features softening, a small smile on her lips. "It's so beautiful in person, I had no idea."

He looked at it, at the strokes and color, the bright and the dark. He didn't feel whatever Verity did. When he looked at her, though, he felt…

She closed her eyes.

"What are you doing?" he asked.

"Wishing," she said, looking up at him. "If you wish on a star, your dreams could come true."

She'd said that once, in his office more than a month ago. "I never do that."

"You try it."

"I have everything already." Those words felt hollow, though, until she touched him, leaning against his arm, and right then he had the sense they could be true.

He said nothing, and the two of them continued to walk through the museum, back around into the hall filled with sculpture.

He looked at her standing there. "You could be one of these works of art," he said. "Aphrodite."

Her cheeks went flushed. "I think you're flattering me."

He grabbed her chin. "When have I ever given you the impression that I care to flatter anyone? I don't. I never have." It was the deepest truth he had. She was beautiful. She belonged here. She belonged...with someone who really cared about her. She was precious and perfect and lovely. And it was like a wall stood between them, and he did not know how to scale it. A fog, a great mist. Or perhaps he was simply made of marble. That was the truth of it. It was easy to say she belonged in the museum because of her beauty, but he was the one frozen.

He could be locked away in here for the rest of time and stay the same.

He felt a clawing desperation, to make these thoughts go away. To feel something. Anything. The way he could only feel when he touched her.

"Beautiful," he said again. He leaned in and kissed her neck, and she shivered. "We are the only ones here," he said.

"I know," she whispered.

"There are no cameras. There are no guards."

"We can't," she said, a fierce spark in her eyes.

"We can."

He was beginning to realize something. And he didn't want to have the realization. What he wanted to have was her. At least one last time. "Let me," he whispered.

He reached around to the back of her dress, and unzipped it slowly, letting it fall around her. And she truly did become one of the glorious pieces of art, standing there with her blond hair wild around her shoulders, her breasts full and glorious, her waist nipped in, her hips round. That pale thatch of curls between her legs a glorious temptation.

This was the closest he would ever come. To feeling real. Because of her.

This was what he had known from the moment he had met her. That there was a power that she held to reach him. But he didn't have the power to take hold of her. He could keep her. Physically.

But he would never be able to...

He didn't want to think. For the first time in his life, he wanted to feel. Only.

He moved toward her, and kissed her on the lips. "Oh, Verity."

He lifted her up, and laid her down on one of the white stone benches, and she let her head fall back as she looked up. She did look just like one of those statues. Except she was real.

Except she was there. He could touch her. He could taste her. He could have her.

They were flesh and blood. For now.

It didn't matter he saw himself obscured in all of these art pieces. It didn't matter if outside of these walls he was nothing more than cold marble. Right now, with her, he was a life. Breathing.

Right now he could have her.

Right now.

He began to undress, leaving his clothes scattered on the floor along with hers. She looked up at him, a smile curving her lips. "You look like you're cut from stone."

He grabbed her hand and put it up against his stomach. Moved it up toward his chest.

"Oh, but no you're not," she whispered. She closed her eyes. "I can feel your heartbeat. So fast."

"Only for you," he said.

He had never been conscious of his heartbeat before. Only with her.

He kissed her, all the better to drown out his thoughts. But he could still hear his own heart raging in his ears.

Kissed her neck, down to her breasts.

And he poured all of his desire out onto her. He told her how beautiful she was. Because he never got tired of praising her.

In this, he understood what it was to have someone. For the first time.

Oh God, to have someone and to want to keep her forever.

No one had ever wanted him in that way. No one had ever held onto him. But maybe it was because they couldn't.

And maybe if you couldn't, the kindest thing to do was to let the person go.

Verity had been trapped. In a house full of people who cared for themselves and not for her. Here she was, free and beautiful and his, but what would the cost be to her? She had been unhappy from the moment they had gotten here. She didn't like having to perform. Obviously reminded her of living with her parents. Would he ever be able to be any different?

He had never wanted something for someone else more than he wanted something for himself, but he was feeling the deepest desire for it now. For her. To be happy. Even if it meant being away from him.

His first impulse had been to hold her forever. To hire her, to keep her with him.

It had been like that from the beginning. She had never only been an employee to him. Not even for a moment.

No. She had been special, from the very beginning. And he was…broken. He could hide it because of all the money he had made. Because of all the success that he had.

He had told her with such confidence he wasn't broken, but where was the evidence of that?

His bank account? What did it matter? It meant nothing. Anyone could have money. Anyone could lose it. Anyone could be born into a family or make a child. But connection. Love. That was the one thing that wasn't guaranteed to everyone. The one thing you couldn't create or manipulate or buy.

He had none of it. If it was possible, his money would have been sufficient.

But it wasn't. It wasn't.

And neither was he.

But he was too weak to let her go before he took her again. Surrounded by all this beauty.

He claimed her, he said goodbye to her, he kissed her, and he fought against the crumbling feeling at the center of his chest. Because there was no point. There was no point. He had to keep the wall because it served him. He didn't know how to let go of the wall because it kept him safe. And somewhere in there all of his thoughts became confused, because if he had to hang onto the wall then was it inevitable? Or could he knock it down, could he…?

No. No.

She arched against him, and he gave himself over to her as he felt her take her pleasure. He took his own. Clung to her until the last bit of pleasure had been wrung from him.

She sat up and touched his face. He closed his eyes.

"Let us get dressed," he said.

She looked concerned, and he knew why. He was already putting distance between the two of them.

She dressed, and the two of them walked out of the museum, where their car was waiting.

"That was…that was quite literally the wildest thing I have ever done, or considered doing. That was—"

"I can't talk about this," he said.

She frowned. "That was… It was good, right?"

She was talking about sex. And something was falling to pieces inside of him. Anger rose up inside of him, and he knew it wasn't fair. None of this was fair.

He texted instructions to the driver, who began to pull away from the curb.

"Where we going?"

"The airport."

"Why?"

"You're going back to Athens."

"I am?"

"Yes, Verity. You're going back to Athens. Because this… We cannot continue this. I'm sorry. I manipulated you into this, and I have been using you. I can't do it anymore. This is…this is a broken man's equivalent of trying to be a real boy, and I am not accomplishing it. I'm just hurting you."

"I don't understand. We just had the most beautiful evening. We just had… we just had sex on a bench in a museum. And now you're telling me that you're sending me away?"

"You've been unhappy since we came back from our honeymoon."

She froze for a moment, looking straight ahead. "I

haven't been unhappy since we got back from the honeymoon. I've been freaking out. Because… It was so easy when we were in that little cocoon. And suddenly we came back here, and I realized that my feelings were different. It was easy to tell myself it was the honeymoon, but we came back to reality and they came with me. I'm sorry. I should've told you. I love you, Alex."

The words hit him with the force of a slap.

"You don't love me," he said. Those words, those words that had never been said to him before, being spoken so easily in the silence of a car moving through the prison streets, seemed grotesque. They seemed like a farce; they had to be. Because it could not be so easy. It couldn't be.

For someone to love him, after all these years. No one ever had.

No one ever had.

"I do. I love you and—"

"You loved Stavros two months ago."

"I didn't. I already explained that to you. He was a distraction. Because the minute that I walked into your office I was drawn to you. Why do you think I took the job? Why do you think I threw myself into being the best assistant to you? Why do you think I said yes when you told me that I was going to marry you?"

"I manipulated you. I manipulated the entire situation. I made it so you couldn't say no, and you made it very clear that I did that."

"As I'm fond of saying to you when I'm trying to be a brat, I do have agency. And yes, I also like to avoid unpleasant situations, and I definitely didn't speak up for myself when I should have or could have. But I would've chosen to marry you either way. You deserved to be scolded for the way that you went about it, but I would have… I would have. Because…because I love you. I made all these rules for myself. Not to get involved with an intense man. Not to want a man that could hurt me. And I knew you were that man. From the moment I met you I knew you were that man. But that wasn't about there being something wrong with you. It was about there being fear in me."

"This isn't what I wanted."

"Then what did you want? You said you wanted to try this. What did you think it would be? What did you think marriage would look like? Did you honestly want me to never have any feelings for you? Did you think that was the key to happiness?"

"No. I didn't think. I just wanted to keep you trapped. I wanted to keep you mine. You're right, though. It has nothing to do with you." The lie tripped off his tongue, because he knew that it would keep him safe. Because he knew that it was exactly what he needed to push her away.

To keep the walls safe inside of him.

"What I wanted was for you to be that perfect version of yourself that you are when you're pleasing everybody. What I wanted was your trauma, Verity, because it helps cover mine. That has nothing to do with you. It isn't right for me to keep you with me."

He could tell that he had done it. That he had taken a verbal knife and stabbed it straight through her heart.

She took a deep breath. "Okay. I'm not going to debase myself for the privilege of more rejection. But I'm also not going to make this easy for you. Because if that's true, then you're everything you said. You're a liar, you're cold, you're heartless. But I don't think you are. I think what you are is a coward. Do you know how I know that? Because you said you didn't feel anything when I made you that dinner, when I made you a birthday cake, but I think you did. The way that you prowled around the kitchen like a hungry dog looking for scraps. You want it so much and it scares you. You're afraid to admit it. All of the stories that you've told me of the boy that you were don't make me think of a man with no feelings. No. You're just still that terrified boy. Waiting for someone to love you, and now that it's happening you don't know what to do. Even worse, I think you love me. I think it scares you."

"No," he said. "Because I don't know how to love, and I never have."

"I just think you don't know what it is. This terrible, awful, clawing feeling inside of you, that's love. It's uncomfortable. It pushes you, it challenges you. Love does not ask you to sit comfortably, it asks you to do things. To sacrifice. It isn't a warm, fuzzy feeling that makes you feel a sense of euphoria. It can be that, it has been that. When we're together and you tell me that I please you, it is that. When I can be perfect for you and you can be perfect for me, and we are naked, but that's the honeymoon. Then we have to bring it into the real world, and that's when it's hard. We have to confront the things about ourselves that aren't whole. And that's hard. You're going to have to change. That's hard. But that doesn't mean that it's wrong. It doesn't mean we aren't supposed to have this.

"I learned this from loving you. I know you can feel

something," she said. "You're just going to have to risk your feelings. I think you have them. I think you have more than most people, not less. You just need to be brave enough to let yourself have them." She reached forward and knocked on the divider between them and the driver.

The divider went down. "Stop the car," she said.

"Verity? What are you doing?"

"I'm getting out. I'm not going back to Athens. I'm not going back to work with you, I'm not... Whatever you think is happening—"

"You aren't getting out here in the middle of the city."

"Yes, I will. I can. I don't care if you're mad at me." She took a deep breath. "I don't care if you're mad at me," she repeated. "You deserve to be uncomfortable. You'll have to figure out why. And I'm not going to make it easier for you. I'm going to make you do the hard work. Because I deserve that. Don't you understand? This, this thing we have, it's real. We didn't just take care of ourselves, we took care of each other. And it could be the most wonderful... It could be everything. If you would just let it."

She pushed open the car door and got out, stumbling onto the street. He unbuckled and followed her. "You've lost it," he said.

"Who cares?" she shouted back, walking away from him.

"And you're making a scene."

"I don't care about that either. You can keep your money. You can keep everything. I always had a choice. And now I'm choosing myself. My self-respect, if nothing else. And I'm choosing to value what I feel. I'm not going to squish it down, squeeze it, contort it into something to make you feel better. I'm not. I have my own money saved up. And I can get another job. I walked away from a situation that didn't fit me before, and I made it out the other side. I'm going to keep doing it. I really wish… I really wish you would let yourself be happy someday, Alex. Even if it isn't with me." She turned away, and kept walking. Then she paused. "Just make sure you eat a salad every once in a while, please." She lifted her hand and wiped a tear away from her cheek, and kept on walking.

He wanted to go after her. But something stopped him.

The very thing that had told him to send her home in the first place.

It stopped him now; all he did was stand there.

Yes. He was a billionaire. With all this power.

Left frozen by a woman.

By that woman.

And he did not think he would ever be the same.

CHAPTER SIXTEEN

By the time she checked into the small hotel—which was a serious downgrade from where she had been with Alex, Verity felt crumpled and reduced.

The whole day had been an emotional roller coaster, and the end of it had been…everything she was afraid of, really.

Everything.

It was why she had been holding it back. That declaration of love. Because what good had it done to say it?

She wiped at the tears that kept on tracking down her cheeks. "Alex, you idiot."

He had taken her on the most romantic date. He had made love to her, and it was glorious like always. He had made her believe in something impossible, beautiful and glorious. And then he had gone into hiding again.

She supposed yelling at him had been character development for her. She hadn't felt the need to placate him either. How funny. His anger didn't scare her. Her own didn't either, not now.

However, it felt like a hollow victory. Maybe she wouldn't really feel like she had changed until she yelled at her parents like that. She thought about it. She thought about calling them and screaming at them, years' worth of pent-up rage. But the idea didn't… It didn't fill her with any kind of satisfaction.

Mostly because it wasn't what she wanted. She didn't get mad at Alex to satisfy something in herself. She had done it because she was desperate to reach him. There had been a purpose to it. There was no purpose talking to her parents. They wouldn't change. They hadn't. But she had. She would continue to change. She would keep on doing it, even without Alex. Even though…

Her life would be less without him. She had loved him from the first moment she had met him. Someday, maybe she would celebrate the risk she had taken. That she had taken steps to actually get to know herself rather than just protect herself. He had taught her a lot. About her own bravery. About her desires. About what mattered to her, and what wasn't negotiable in the end. So maybe she should just be happy. Someday. Not now. Now she would be miserable. She would eat pastries, and lament. She would sit in her feelings and feel them. Because she wasn't hiding from anyone. Not him, not herself.

They had both spent their whole lives being so afraid of discomfort. So afraid that it would never end. She had put on a happy face and tried to make everything around her nicer, more comfortable. He pretended he didn't feel. And she could see now that a lifetime of that created a bland life that contained no authenticity.

They had touched it with each other.

But she was ready to drown in it. He wasn't.

He had hired her to be his conscience. So she had to stand firm even now. Because letting him continue to lie to himself, letting herself live a lie, that would be against everything that was right.

She lay back on the bed, and tried to sleep. But the bed was too empty without him. So instead, she went to the window and looked out at the city below.

The city of love.

Well. She had risked everything for love here. Had incredible sex in a museum. It was an exceedingly Parisian thing to do.

As she sat staring at the Eiffel Tower lit up in the distance, and crying over her broken heart, she figured that was very Parisian of her too.

In the end, he had gone back to his hotel room in Paris, and hadn't come out for two days. He finally got a call from the board president telling him he needed to get back out there.

"I have no desire to. Not now. My wife and I are separating."

"You can't separate from your wife now," the man said, practically spluttering with outrage.

"Well, it's a shame, because I am. She has left me."

"You have to get her back. You have to pay for her to come back."

"It will fix nothing."

"It will fix the optics for the company. Your relationship with Verity Carmichael is the single best thing that has ever happened to you."

Those words echoed inside of him. Because he agreed. He agreed on every level.

Verity had been the single greatest thing that had ever happened to him, and in the end, he had to send her away. Because just looking at her…

He felt sick with regret. With helplessness.

It reminded him of being a boy. Passed around from home to home. Gawked at by potential parents but never taken home. He had always vowed he would never feel this way again. And she had made him. She had done this to him. She…

She had fundamentally changed something inside of him. He had lost control of himself. He had thought all of his life that he didn't have the ability to connect to another person, and she had shown him what that could be like. Just for a moment. And she was acting like he chose…like he chose to stay alone?

He had never chosen this. Not ever.

For the first time in your life someone reached out to you, someone said they wanted to be with you, and what did you do?

He growled.

"Mr. Economides," the president said, his voice placating. It brought Alex back to the moment.

"What is happening between myself and Verity has nothing to do with business. It is my life," he said.

His *life*. She was his life. The business was no longer his life. He didn't care what happened with the product launch. It would be successful even if he went out into the street and stole an ice cream cone from a child. It might not be as successful, it might not be as popular, but it didn't functionally matter. Not truly. Yes, he could do more. The company could be bigger. It always could be. It could be more essential. That had been his plan, it had been his legacy, and what was it now? It was hollow. It felt like nothing. It meant nothing.

Verity…

She was everything. She meant everything.

You could wish on that star...

The way she looked at him, with all that hope. But if it were that simple, if he could just wish on a star and have everything be fixed, then he would. He would.

She said that even if it was hard it was worth it…

But there was hard, and there was impossible. And he couldn't…

He thought about the birthday party again. About the way she had seen it. The way that she described him.

He thought about Christmas. Christmas didn't mean anything.

He had an image of a tree, and a house that wasn't his, children opening presents. None for him. For the real family members. A family that he would never be a part of. On the outside looking in.

Christmas didn't mean anything.

Except it did. It had been taken away from him. He had hoped that someone would adopt him and every time they came to see him, he had something taken from him. His hope. With each passing day. He had only been a small boy. He had asked for none of it. None of it. He had only been a boy. He had not been born with a mother who cared for him, but he had been born with hope.

And slowly, very slowly, the world had taken it from him. So he'd had to stop hoping. He had to stop caring. He had to stop believing that he might find someone to care for him. He had given the control over to himself. He had turned it into a choice.

He had built up a wall inside of him so thick and tall and strong that he was the one keeping others out. Instead of the other way around.

He thought of Verity, decorating that ridiculous cake.

Her scrawl of Happy Birthday written across the top. No one had ever baked him a birthday cake before. No one had ever told him they loved him.

The president of the board of directors was still talking; he couldn't hear him. He hung up the phone. It rang instantly. He didn't answer it. He didn't care.

Because it was like everything inside of him was falling to pieces. That wall cracking down the middle. "It matters," he said. "It matters."

He saw her. Looking at him across the desk, eating her salad and laughing at him. Talking to him about her day, every detail, great and small. Her, naked in the overwater villa. The way she had been hurt after the encounter with her parents. Her cooking for him, laughing with him. And finally, the museum.

Verity, naked beneath him. He had been certain the sex with her was some sort of strange magic, conjuring up a feeling that only existed then.

But it was the only place where he lost himself just enough to feel it.

It was the truth. Everything else was a lie.

He had to find her. He had to find her and give her everything.

He closed his eyes, a feeling so big it nearly knocked him over expanding in his chest.

Hope.

CHAPTER SEVENTEEN

VERITY DECIDED THAT she had to stop moping, and go eat at a café or something. Which was how she found herself wandering down the sidewalk feeling sad at 11:00 a.m. in Paris.

"Verity." She stopped, and straightened, goose bumps rising up on her arms. "Cricket."

She turned around, and there was Alex. Well, a version of Alex anyway. This man was not smooth or fathomless. His eyes were not dark voids.

He was on fire.

He ran to her, like he wasn't in public, like there weren't people standing there staring at him. This man could never be confused for a robot. Could never be mistaken for AI. But then, she never had. She had always known.

Yes. She had always known.

"Alex," she said.

"You were right," he said, his voice fractured.

He cupped her face with his hands and leaned down and kissed her. "My beautiful Cricket, you were right. You knew. All this time. That I could feel something. That I was hiding. I…am so incredibly wounded by the things that happened to me. I don't want that to be true.

I want to believe that I'm stronger than that. But I can outrun it. With money, with power. I wanted to believe that I could make a name for myself with this business and have it be the only thing that truly mattered." He took a shuddering breath, his voice shattered. "Money doesn't fix this. And neither does protecting yourself. It only puts a wall in front of all that pain. But it doesn't make it go away. You...you made me knock it down. Because I would rather be in pain. I would rather bleed out on the street and have you for those last moments of my life than live forever safe without you," he whispered. "I did care about Christmas. I did care about my birthday. I wanted those people to adopt me. I wanted my life to be better. I wanted someone to love me. It took thirty-four years. Finally you did. I didn't know what to do with it."

"Of course," she said, holding him close, tears falling already. "Of course."

"I tried to pretend that I was the one in control. That I was the one who didn't care."

"It was never a problem with you, Alex. It was always a flaw in the world, and I know it's hard to believe that. But you always mattered. Always. It isn't your success that makes that true. It's you."

He lowered his head. "When we were in the museum I panicked. I saw myself in the statue, hard and cold. In that painting, foggy and misty and unreachable. And I couldn't bring myself to wish on a star. Because wishing is hope. And I cut myself off from it so long ago. But I need it. I need it or I might as well not even be here. I didn't realize how important it was. I didn't realize what I was missing. Until you walked into my life, and by some miracle, you reached over the wall. You infiltrated. Reached parts of me that no one and nothing ever has. I couldn't even reach."

She touched his face, tilted it upward so his gaze met hers. "You did the same for me. Alex, you did. You really showed me who I am, and what I want. And you made me feel strong enough to ask for it. Demand it, even, even though it hurt."

"I'm so sorry," he said. "My perfect girl. I will never hurt you like that again. I want us to be together. I told the president of the board that I didn't care about the product launch. I don't. I'll tell the whole story, the real story to the whole world."

"You don't have to do that," she said. "I don't need you to prove anything. You're here. And that's proof enough."

"I love you," he said. "I've never said those words to another person. To anything. I love you, Verity."

She closed her eyes, and let them wash over her. "I know," she said. "I'm really glad you said it. But I know, because even if you didn't know it, you were showing me that you loved me. Until you freaked out."

"I'm sorry."

"It had to happen. Just like I had to yell at you after the wedding. Sometimes I think…you have to feel these things. You can't push them down. Not forever. We're going to have to feel difficult things sometimes. But we have each other."

"Yes," he said. "And we…we are a family."

"Yes, Alex," she said, tears filling her eyes. "We are."

He took her hand, and looked down at her. "Where were you headed?"

"To get some lunch."

"I have missed having lunch with you," he said.

"Me too. Salad?"

He threw his head back and laughed, and pulled her into his arms and kissed her. "On second thought. Why don't we skip to dessert."

EPILOGUE

ONE THING ALEX learned over the next decade was that love was an infinitely renewable resource. The love he had for Verity increased by the day, and when she got pregnant with their first child, he felt that love grow. Expand. Change shape as he appreciated new things about her.

When she gave birth to their first child, it was like discovering love all over again.

And the same was true with their second, and their third.

Back at the over-water villa for their anniversary, he had to admit that it was different now. Not so much a grotto of sex and privacy. His children's screams filled the air as they splashed each other in the waves beneath the full moon, the sky scattered with stars.

He gave thanks for the additional rooms they'd had built on a few years back.

"Not exactly a private island anymore," Verity said, sitting beside him, mirroring his thoughts.

"No. It's a family island." He turned to her and smiled. "I think that's better. I've had enough isolation."

"I agree." She grabbed his arm and rested her head

on his shoulder. "Look. The stars are out. You could make a wish."

"Little Cricket," he said, kissing her on the head. "Don't you know I already have everything I could ever want?"

* * * * *

If you just couldn't get enough of
Promoted to Boss's Wife,
then be sure to check out
these other passion-fuelled stories
by Millie Adams!

Italian's Christmas Acquisition
Billionaire's Bride Bargain
His Highness's Diamond Decree
After-Hours Heir
Dragos's Broken Vows

Available now!

MILLS & BOON®

Coming next month

ENEMY IN HIS BOARDROOM
Emmy Grayson

'Leave and I'll sue you and your firm for breach of contract.'

Her fury washes over me, hot and potent. It hits my skin, slips beneath. The air sharpens, not just with anger, but with the one thing I swore I would never let myself feel for this woman again.

Desire.

We stare each other down, wills clashing, breaths mingling. Her lips are parted, her breathing growing more ragged with each passing second.

I should let her walk out. Put as much distance between us as possible and never contact her again. No woman has ever tested my control, let alone made me want to throw the rules I live by out the window. She's dangerous.

But letting her walk away would be failing. And AuraGeothermal needs her expertise.

'Make your choice, Miss North.'

Despite the blush of embarrassment in her cheeks, she tilts her chin up. Damn it if I don't respect her for standing her ground.

'You've already made it for me, Mr. Valdasson.'

Continue reading

ENEMY IN HIS BOARDROOM
Emmy Grayson

Available next month
millsandboon.co.uk

COMING SOON!

We really hope you enjoyed reading this book.
If you're looking for more romance
be sure to head to the shops when
new books are available on

Thursday 20th November

To see which titles are coming soon, please visit
millsandboon.co.uk/nextmonth

MILLS & BOON

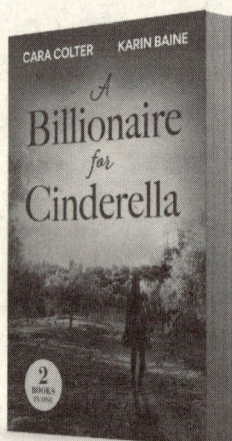

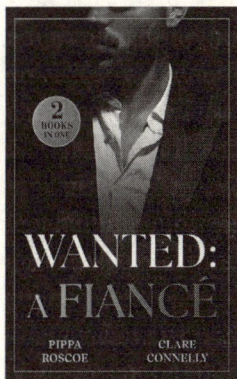

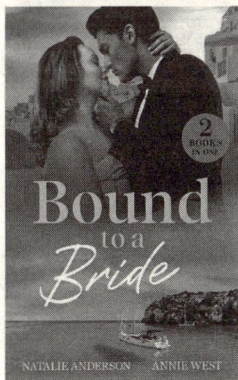

afterglow BOOKS

Afterglow Books is a trend-led, trope-filled list of books with diverse, authentic and relatable characters, a wide array of voices and representations, plus real world trials and tribulations. Featuring all the tropes you could possibly want (think small-town settings, fake relationships, grumpy vs sunshine, enemies to lovers) and all with a generous dose of spice in every story.

♪ @millsandboonuk
⊙ @millsandboonuk
afterglowbooks.co.uk
#AfterglowBooks

For all the latest book news, exclusive content and giveaways scan the QR code below to sign up to the Afterglow newsletter:

SCAN ME

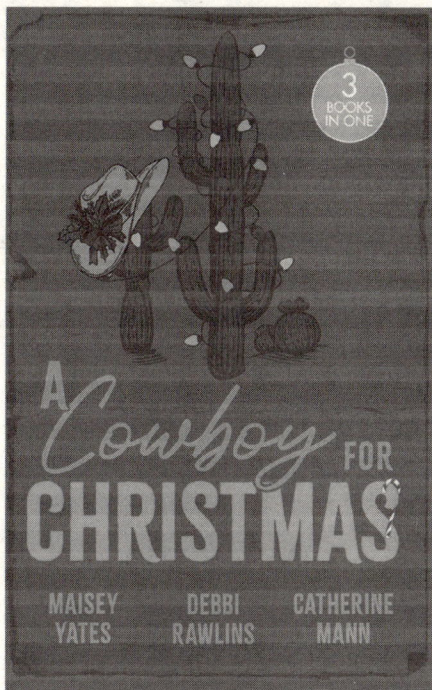

LET'S TALK

Romance

For exclusive extracts, competitions and special offers, find us online:

f MillsandBoon

X @MillsandBoon

⊙ @MillsandBoonUK

♪ @MillsandBoonUK

Get in touch on 01413 063 232